SARA
CRAVEN

Duet

DEVIL AND THE DEEP SEA

DEVIL AND THE DEEP SEA

BY
SARA CRAVEN

MILLS & BOON LIMITED
Eton House, 18-24 Paradise Road
Richmond, Surrey TW9 1SR

First published in Great Britain in 1988
by Mills & Boon Limited

© Sara Craven 1988

Australian copyright 1988
Philippine copyright 1988
Reprinted 1988
This edition 1993

ISBN 0 263 78411 8

Set in Plantin 11 on 11 pt.
19-9308-47272

Made and printed in Great Britain

CHAPTER ONE

THE breeze from the sea whipped a strand of pale fair hair across Samma Briant's cheek, and she flicked it back impatiently as she bent over her drawing-board.

The waterfront at Cristoforo was crowded, as it always was when a cruise ship was in. Tourists were eagerly exploring the bars and souvenir shops along the quayside, and stopping to look at the stalls which sold locally made jewellery, carvings and paintings of island scenes. And a lot of them lingered where Samma sat on an upturned crate, amused and fascinated by her talent for capturing an instant likeness on paper, and willing to pay the modest fee she charged for her portraits.

She didn't consider herself to be an artist. She possessed a knack, no more, for fixing on some facial characteristic of each subject, and subtly exploiting it. But she enjoyed her work, and on days like this it was even reasonably lucrative.

She had a small crowd around her already, and her day would have been just about perfect, except for one large, mauve, chrome-glittering cloud on her horizon—*Sea Anemone,* surely the most vulgar motor yacht in the Caribbean, currently moored a few hundred yards away in Porto Cristo's marina. Because *Sea Anemone's* presence at Cristoforo meant that her owner, the equally large and garish Mr Hugo Baxter, would be at the hotel tonight, playing poker with Samma's stepfather, Clyde Lawson.

One glimpse of that monstrous mauve hulk lying at

anchor had been enough to start Samma's stomach churning uneasily. It was only six weeks since Hugo Baxter's last visit. She'd thought they were safe for at least another month or two. Yet, here he was again closing in for the kill, she thought bitterly, as she signed the portrait she'd just finished with a small flourish, and handed it over to her delighted sitter with a brief, professional smile.

The fact was they couldn't afford another visit from Hugo Baxter. Samma had no idea what her stepfather's exact financial position was—he would never discuss it with her—but she suspected it might be desperately precarious.

When Clyde had met and married her mother during a visit to Britain, he had been a moderately affluent businessman, owning a small but prosperous hotel, and a restaurant on the small Caribbean island of Cristoforo. The island was just beginning to take off as a cruise ship stopping-point, and the future should have been rosy—except for Clyde's predilection for gambling. While Samma's mother had been alive, he'd kept his proclivities more or less under control, but since her death two years earlier things had gone from bad to worse. The restaurant had had to be sold to pay his debts, and the hotel hadn't had the redecoration and refurbishment it needed, either.

Clyde seemed to win so seldom, Samma thought broodingly, and when Hugo Baxter was in the game his losses worsened to a frightening extent.

She motioned her next customer to the folding chair in front of her, and began to sketch in the preliminary shape of her head and shoulders with rapid, confident strokes.

Clyde's only remaining asset was the hotel. And if we lose that, she thought despondently, I'm never going to get off this island.

Probably the woman she was sketching would have thrown up her hands in horror at the thought of anyone wanting to leave Cristoforo. 'Isn't this paradise?' was the usual tourist cry.

Well, it was and it wasn't, Samma thought cynically. During the years when she'd spent her school holidays here, she'd taken the romantic view, too. She'd been in the middle of her A-level course when her mother had collapsed and died from a heart attack. She'd flown to Cristoforo for the funeral, only to discover when it was over that the trust which was paying her school fees had ceased with her mother's death, and that Clyde had no intention of paying out for her to complete her education.

'It's time you started working to keep yourself,' he told her aggressively. 'Besides, I need you here to take your mother's place.'

Sick at heart, confused by her grief for her mother, Samma had agreed to stay. But it had been a serious mistake. When Clyde had spoken of her working for her keep, he meant just that, she'd found. She received no wage for her work at the hotel. The only money she earned was through her sketches, and although she saved as much as she could towards her airfare back to the United Kingdom, it was a wretchedly slow process.

But even if she'd been reasonably affluent, she would still have been disenchanted with Cristoforo. It was a small island, socially and culturally limited, with a hideously high cost of living. And, when the holiday season ended, it was dull.

And working at the hotel, and more particularly in the small nightclub Clyde had opened in the grounds, Samma had been shocked when she'd experienced the

leering attentions of many of the male guests. Coming
from the comparative shelter of boarding-school, almost
overnight she'd discovered that to most of the male
visitors to the island she was an object, rather than a
person, and she'd been revolted by the blatant sexism of
their attitude to her. She'd soon learned to hide herself
in a shell of aloof reserve which chilled the ardour of the
most determined predator. But she was aware that, by
doing so, she was also cutting herself off from the chance
of perhaps forming a real and lasting relationship.
However, this was a risk she had to take, although she
was forced to admit she'd never been even mildly
attracted by any of the men who stayed at the hotel, or
hung round the bar at the Black Grotto club.

One day, she thought, one day, when she got back to
England and found herself a decent job, and a life of her
own, she would meet someone she could be happy with.
Until then, she'd stay insulated in her cocoon of
indifference.

Except when Hugo Baxter was around, she reminded
herself uneasily. He seemed impervious to any rebuff,
seeking her out, taking any opportunity to touch her,
Samma's skin crawled at the thought. One thing was
certain, she was keeping well away from the Black
Grotto tonight.

She handed over her completed portrait, and glanced
at her watch. It was nearly noon, and people were
drifting away in search of lunch and shade. Time for a
break, Samma thought, getting to her feet and stretching
vigorously. As she lifted her arms above her head, she
was suddenly aware she was being watched, and she
looked round.

Startled, her eyes met another gaze, dark, faintly
amused and totally male in its assessment of the thrust of
her rounded breasts against her brief cotton top,

Samma realised in the embarrassed moment before she looked away with icy disdain.

But she was left with a disturbing impression of height and strength, and sun-bronzed skin revealed by a brief pair of cut-off denims. As well as an absurd feeling of self-consciousness, she thought resentfully.

She should be used to being looked at. In a community where most people were dark-haired and dark-skinned, her pale skin and blonde hair, as straight and shining as rain water, naturally attracted attention, and usually she could cope with this.

But there had been something so provocatively and deliberately—masculine about this stranger's regard that it had flicked her on the raw.

And her antennae told her that he was still looking. She picked up her sketch-block, and began drawing at random—the neighbouring stall, where Mindy, its owner, was selling a view of the marina to a tourist couple who were trying and failing to beat him down over the price. But her fingers, inexplicably, were all thumbs, fudging the lines, and she tore the sheet off, crumpling it irritably.

She stole a sideways glance under her lashes, making an assessment of her own. He was leaning on the rail of one of the sleekest and glossiest of the many craft in the marina, and looking totally out of place, she decided critically, although she supposed he was good-looking, in a disreputable way—that was, if you liked over-long and untidy black hair, and a great beak of a nose which looked as if it had been broken at least once in its career.

He was the image, she thought contemptuously, of some old-time pirate chief, surveying the captive maiden from his quarter-deck. He only needed a cutlass and a parrot—and she would give them to him!

Her mouth curving, she drew the preliminary outline, emphasising the stranger's nose almost to the point of caricature, adding extra rakishness with earrings, and a bandanna swathed round that shock of dark hair. She transformed his expression of faint amusement into an evil leer, gave the parrot on his shoulder a squint, then pinned the sketch up on the display board behind her with a flourish.

He would never see it, of course. The boat's owner had clearly left him on watch, and probably with good reason. Only a thief bent on suicide would want to tangle with a physique that tough, and shoulders that broad.

She had a quick, retentive eye for detail, but it annoyed her just the same to find how deeply his image had impressed itself on her consciousness. One eyeball-to-eyeball confrontation and a quick sideways glance, and she'd been able to draw him at once, whereas she normally allowed herself a much more searching scrutiny before she began. Yet this sketch had worked, even if it was a shade vindictive.

And, in its way, it turned out to be a good advertisement. People strolling past stopped to laugh, and stayed to be drawn themselves. They seemed to like the element of cartoon she'd incorporated, although Mindy, loping across with a slice of water melon for her, raised his brows when he saw it, and murmured, 'Friend of yours, gal?'

'Figment of my imagination,' she retorted cheerfully.

Another swift glance had revealed, to her relief, that the rail of the boat was now deserted. Doubtless he'd remembered the owner didn't pay him for standing about, eyeing up the local talent, she thought, scooping a handful of hair back from her face with a slim, suntanned hand.

She was putting the finishing touches to the portrait of a pretty redhead with amazing dimples, undoubtedly on honeymoon with the young man who watched her so adoringly, when a shadow fell across her pad.

Samma glanced up in irritation, the words 'Excuse me' freezing unspoken on her lips.

Close to, he was even more formidable. Distance had cloaked the determination of that chin, and the firm, uncompromising lines of his mouth. There was a distinct glitter, too, in those midnight-dark eyes which Samma found distinctly unnerving.

It annoyed her, too, that he was standing over her like this, putting her at a disadvantage. He was the kind of man she'd have preferred to face on equal terms—although to do so she'd probably have to stand on her crate, she thought, her mouth quirking involuntarily.

But there was no answering softness in the face of the man towering over her. He was looking past her at the display board, where the pirate drawing fluttered in the breeze.

He said, 'I have come to share the joke.' His voice was low and resonant, with the faintest trace of an accent.

'Is there one?' Samma, aware that her fingers were trembling, concentrated hard on the elaborate combination of her initials which she used as a signature, before passing over the new sketch.

'It seems so.' His voice cut coldly across the excited thanks of the young couple, as they paid and departed. 'They say it is always instructive to see oneself through the eyes of another. I am not sure I agree.'

The pirate sketch was outrageous, over the top,

totally out of order, and Samma knew that now, but she wasn't going to apologise. He'd damned well asked for it, staring at her like that. Mentally undressing her, she added for good measure.

She smiled lightly, and got to her feet, hoping he'd step back and give her room, but he didn't.

'An interesting philosophical point,' she said. 'Forgive me if I don't hang around to debate it with you. It's time I took a break.'

'Ideal.' The brief smile which touched his lips didn't reach his eyes. 'I was about to offer you lunch, *mademoiselle*.'

So, he was French. Samma could see Mindy listening avidly. She said, 'Thank you, but I'm not hungry.'

She used the tone of cool, bored finality which worked so well with the would-be Romeos at the hotel, but its only effect on this aggravating man was to widen his smile.

'A drink, then?'

'Thanks, but no thanks.' Samma was angrily aware she was being baited.

'Then a tour of *Allegra*. You seemed very interested in her earlier.'

'Then my interest has waned—sharply,' Samma snapped. 'And maybe you should learn to take "no" for an answer.'

He shrugged. His skin was like teak, she noticed irrelevantly, darkened even further by the shadowing of hair on the muscular chest, forearms, and long, sinewy legs.

'Is that what a pirate would do? I think not.'

Before she could guess his intention, or make any more to thwart him, he reached for her, his hands clamping on her waist, hoisting her into the air, and over his shoulder like a sack of potatoes. For a moment she was stunned, dangling there, staring down at the dusty stones of the quay; then, as he began to move, she came to furious life, struggling, kicking, pummelling the strong, smooth back with her fists.

But it was like punching reinforced concrete, and he didn't even flinch. To make matters worse, she could hear laughter and even a smattering of applause from the watchers on the quay as he walked off with her.

Mindy was her friend, but he wasn't lifting a finger to help her, and if he imagined for one moment she relished this kind of treatment then she would be happy to disillusion him, she thought, almost incandescent with rage and humiliation.

She saw the slats of the gangplank beneath her. She expected that he would put her down when they reached the deck, but she was wrong. With alarming effortlessness, he negotiated a companionway, and entered a big, sunny saloon. Then, at last, he lowered her to her feet.

Breathless and giddy, she confronted him. 'You bastard!' Her voice shook. 'How dare you treat me like that?'

He shrugged again. He wasn't smiling any more. 'You chose to hold me up to ridicule. You can hardly complain if I make you look a little foolish also.'

'Well, you've achieved your objective,' Samma said grimly. 'And now I'm leaving.'

'But I prefer that you stay.' His voice was soft, but it held a note which told her that he meant it. That, if she tried to leave, she would be prevented.

'I don't know what you hope to gain by this behaviour.' With an effort, she kept her voice steady.

'Nothing too devastating, *chérie*,' he drawled.

'Merely a companion to share some food and wine with me in the middle of the day.'

Samma lifted her brows. 'Do you always have to resort to strong-arm tactics when you need company? You must be desperate.'

He laughed, showing very white teeth. 'You think so?'

No, not for a moment she didn't. This man would only have to click his fingers and women would come running, but she was on the ropes in this bout, and she would say or do anything to escape.

The saloon was enormous, and luxuriously furnished, but somehow he made it seem cramped.

He was too tall, too dominating, the kind of man she would go out of her way to avoid, and she'd been mad to provoke him with the pirate sketch.

But there wasn't anything too major to worry about, she tried to assure herself. After all, his employer could return at any time, or so she supposed. And, if the going really got tough, she could always scream for Mindy.

She gave him a straight look. 'Fine—you've had your joke. Now, I'd like to get on with my life—quietly, and without hassle.'

'Later,' he said. 'Nothing happens on these islands around noon, or hadn't you noticed?'

'I should do,' Samma said tartly. 'I've lived here for long enough.'

'You are a permanent resident?' His tone held a trace of surprise. 'But you certainly weren't born here. I thought you were one of the new generation of island-hoppers, drifting from one location to the next like a butterfly—using your—talent—to buy your living.'

There was something in his voice which told

Samma he wasn't referring to her artistic gifts, such as they were, and in spite of herself she felt a hot blush burn her face.

'Well, you thought wrong,' she said grittily. 'And now we've cleared up that little misunderstanding, perhaps you'll let me go. My friends will be wondering where I am.'

He laughed out loud at that. 'Oh, I think they know—don't you?'

Samma almost ground her teeth. Why had she got involved in this kind of verbal sparring? she asked herself despairingly. Why hadn't she adopted her usual ploy of blank eyes and assumed deafness? Why had she let him get to her like this?

She said quietly, 'Look, you've made your point. Is there any need to go on—punishing me like this?'

'Punishment?' His mouth curled, drawing her unwilling attention to the sensual line of his lower lip. 'Is that how you regard the offer of a meal. The food on *Allegra* isn't that bad.'

'You know what I mean.' Her eyes met his directly.

'Yes, I know,' he acknowledged sardonically, 'So—what do you suppose you deserve for your impudence in drawing me as you did?'

'I draw what I see,' Samma flashed. 'And everything that you've said or done since has only convinced me how right I was.'

'Is that a fact?' His voice slowed to a drawl. 'So, you really think I'm a pirate.' He shrugged. 'Then it seems I need have no compunction.'

He moved towards her, purposefully, but without haste and Samma backed away, until the pressure of the long, cushioned seat which ran the length of the saloon prevented any further retreat.

'Keep away from me.' To her fury, she sounded

breathless and very young, her words more an appeal than a command.

'Make me,' he invited silkily. There was a disturbing glint in the dark eyes as he moved closer. With one hand, he pushed her gently down on the cushion, then sat beside her.

Samma's mouth was suddenly dry. For the first time she had to question her actual physical ability to scream if the situation demanded it. She wanted to look away from him, but she couldn't. It was as if she was mesmerised—like a rabbit with a snake, she thought hysterically. She tried to steady her breathing, to mentally reject the effect his proximity was having on her. She could feel prickles of sweat breaking out all over her body, allied to a strange trembling in her lower limbs, and she tensed, bewildered by the unfamiliarity of her own reactions.

His gaze travelled slowly and relentlessly down her body, and she shivered as if it was his hands which were touching her. Since her return to Cristoforo, she'd never worn a bra, considering her firm young breasts made such a restriction unnecessary. Now, as they seemed to swell and grow heavy against the thin fabric of her top, she began to wish she was encased in whalebone from head to foot—armour-plated, even.

She saw him smile, as if he'd guessed exactly what she was thinking. His eyes continued their downward journey, resting appraisingly on the curve of her hips, and the slender length of her thighs, revealed by her brief white shorts.

She had never, she thought dazedly, been made so thoroughly aware that she was female.

He said softly, 'There are many ways of taming a woman—and I am tempted. But for an impertinent child—this is altogether more appropriate.'

Before she knew what was happening, Samma found herself face downwards over his knee, suffering the unbearable indignity of half a dozen hard and practised slaps on her rear. The first was enough to drag a startled gasp from her, and she sank her teeth into her lower lip, pride forbidding her to make another sound.

Then, with appalling briskness, he set her upright again, his amused glance taking in her flushed face and watery eyes.

When she could speak, she said chokingly, 'You swine—you bloody sadist . . . '

He tutted reprovingly. 'Your language, *mademoiselle*, is as ill-advised as your sense of humour. I have taught you one lesson,' he added coldly. 'Please do not make it necessary for me to administer another.'

'I'll find out who owns this boat,' she promised huskily. 'And when I do—I'll have you fired. I'm sure your boss would be delighted to know you take advantage of his absence by—by abusing girls in his saloon.'

He stared at her for a moment, then began to laugh. 'Considering the provocation, I think he would say you had got off lightly.' He paused. 'Had you been adult, then retribution might have taken a very different form. Perhaps you should think yourself fortunate.' He gave her a swiftly measuring look. 'And perhaps, too, you should leave—before I change my mind.'

'Don't worry,' Samma said thickly. 'I'm going.'

Uncaring of the few remaining rags of dignity left to her, she half ran, half stumbled to the door, only to hear as she scrambled up the companionway to freedom, fighting angry tears, his laughter following her.

CHAPTER TWO

IF SAMMA thought her day could not possibly get any worse, she was wrong.

She'd grabbed her drawing materials and fled back to the hotel, evading the good-humouredly ribald teasing from Mindy and the others. And she was half-way home when she realised she'd still left that damned drawing pinned to the board. But wild horses wouldn't have dragged her back there to retrieve it. Mindy would throw it away with the rest of her unsold sketches at the end of the day.

And she would have to keep away from the waterfront until she could be sure that *Allegra* had sailed, even though it would mean a reduction in her small income.

Clyde was waiting for her. 'So there you are,' he said in the grumbling tone which had become the norm in the past year. 'That blasted Nina won't be in tonight, so you'll have to take her place.'

Samma was still quivering with reaction. Flatly, she said, 'No.'

His sunburned face went a deeper shade of brick-red. 'What do you mean—no?'

'Exactly what I say.' She glared back at him. 'I hate being in the club, and I won't sit with the customers and encourage them to buy expensive drinks they can't afford. It's degrading.'

'When I want your moral judgements, I'll ask for them,' Clyde snapped. 'You don't pick and choose what you do round here, and tonight you're standing

in for Nina in the Grotto. It's no big deal,' he added
disgustedly. 'Just sit with the punters, and be nice to
them. No one's suggesting you sleep with them.'

Samma's delicate mouth curled. 'Meaning Nina
doesn't?'

'That's no concern of yours,' Clyde blustered. 'Now,
be a good girl,' he went on, a wheedling note entering
his voice. 'And do something about your hair,' he added,
giving its shining length a disparaging glance. 'Nina's
left one of her cocktail dresses in the dressing-room, so
you can wear that. You're near enough the same size.'

'It's not a question of size,' Samma said with irony.
'It's taste—something Nina's not conspicuous for.'

Clyde shrugged. 'Well, at least she doesn't look as if
she's just stepped out of a kindergarten,' he countered
brutally. 'Maybe you should ask her for a few lessons.
Anyway, I haven't time to argue the toss with you. I
have a busy evening ahead of me.'

She said evenly, 'Playing poker, I suppose.
Clyde—couldn't you give the game a miss for once?'

'No, I couldn't,' he said sullenly. 'Baxter's here again,
and he's loaded. All I need is one good win. His luck
can't last for ever.'

'Can't it? Does it ever occur to you that he wins too
often and too much for it to be purely luck?'

'You don't know what you're talking about,' he
dismissed crossly. 'Now, get on with some work, please.
And chivvy up those girls who work on the bedrooms.
Number Thirty-three claims his bed was made up with a
torn sheet.'

Samma sighed. 'A lot of the linen's threadbare. We
need to replace it,' she began, but Clyde was already
disappearing, as he invariably did when she tried to
discuss anything about expenditure with him.

She sighed again, as she went into the hotel office

at the back of the reception desk. In spite of her intentions, it seemed she had to put in an appearance at the club that night. And it occurred to her too that Clyde, who knew how much she hated being there, had never pressured her quite so much before. In the past, he'd been prepared, albeit sulkily, to accept her excuses. Now, it seemed, they had entered on a new phase in their uneasy working relationship, and Samma wasn't sure how to deal with it. But it was beginning to seem even more imperative that she should get away from Cristoforo, and fast.

But without money, how can I? she thought despairingly. And I can't even do my portraits for the next few days because of that damned Frenchman.

She bit her lip. Meeting an—animal like him was another incentive for her to get back to civilisation without delay.

She might have behaved badly—she was prepared to admit that, but his reaction had been unforgivable. Clearly he was the kind of man who was unable to overlook any slight to his self-esteem, which made him both macho and humourless, she thought—faults which far outweighed the overwhelming physical attraction which she'd been unable to deny, or even resist.

In the same way, she was unable to escape a lingering curiosity about him. He looked tough, and eminently capable, the typical roughneck who made a precarious living, crewing on charter hire boats for fair-weather sailors. But his voice had been educated, she thought frowning, so that didn't add up.

Perhaps, like herself, he was trying to scrape together the fare back to Europe, she decided with a mental shrug. In the event, speculation was useless. She would never see him again. Fortunately, the

did you expect?'

'Now that is something we could more profitably discuss over a drink.' His hand grasped her elbow, urging her away from the bar and towards a vacant table at the edge of the small dance-floor. 'But my expectations did not include this—metamorphosis,' he added, a note of unholy amusement in his voice. 'Are you sure, *mademoiselle,* you have no younger sister?'

She was sorely tempted to tell him she had, but her previous experience at his hands warned her it might be unwise to play any more games.

She said coolly, 'I don't know why or how you found your way here, but if you've come to score points, maybe I should warn you it'll cost you a week's wages, plus an arm and a leg. I should get back to the waterfront. You'll find the bars cheaper there.'

'Yes, I heard this was a clip-joint,' he said, unruffled. 'But it makes no difference. I came because poker is a favourite relaxation of mine, and I am told there is a game here tonight.'

There is.' Samma raised her eyebrows. 'But I think you'll find the other players take it rather more seriously than that.'

'They may need to.' A faint smile twisted round the corners of the firm mouth. 'So—how do you fit into this set-up?'

'My stepfather owns the hotel, and the club,' she said reluctantly. 'I help out when necessary.'

'I see.' His glance rested briefly and intimately on the flimsy sequin flowers which cupped her breasts, and Samma choked back a little gasp, thankful the club's dim lighting masked the colour rising hotly in her face.

She said tautly, 'I doubt it. Anyway, I don't have to explain myself to you, so perhaps you'll go now and leave me in peace.'

His sardonic gaze took in the crowded, smoke-filled room, where a buzz of laughing, chattering voices vied for supremacy with the band.

'This is your idea of peace, *chérie*? ' he drawled. 'I had a different impression of you this morning.'

'I remember it well,' Samma flashed. 'I still have the bruises.'

'I think you exaggerate. Besides,' he glanced towards the bar, where Hugo Baxter still glowered in their direction, 'you surely do not wish to be left to the mercies of that wolf?'

'You're so much better?' She sent him a muted glare. 'But you really don't have to bother about me. I can take care of myself. And he's not a wolf,' she added, reverting in her mind's eye to the portrait she'd planned. 'He's a pig, all pink and smooth, with a snout, and nasty little eyes half buried in fat.'

His brows rose mockingly. 'You take a scurrilous view of the rest of humanity, *mignonne.* I hope this time your picture remains in your imagination only. Mr Baxter would be even less amused than I was if he knew how you saw him.'

'So, you know who he is.' Samma remembered that brief confrontation at the bar.

'Who does not?' He lifted a shoulder. 'Both he—and his boat—tend to be unforgettable.'

Samma recalled just in time that this man was an enemy, and managed to stifle a giggle.

'Then perhaps you should know he's also a member of this poker school you're so keen to join,' she said tartly. 'And he can afford to lose a great deal more than a deckhand's wages.'

'So I believe.' He smiled faintly. 'But your concern is unnecessary.'

'I'm not concerned in the slightest,' Samma denied instantly. 'It wouldn't matter to me if you lost every cent you possessed, but you could turn out to be a sore loser,' she added, with a dubious look at the dark, tough face, and the raw strength of his shoulders.

He said softly, 'It is true I prefer to win,' and once again Samma was aware of that swift, appraising glance. She saw with relief that a waiter was approaching.

'Good evening, sir. What may I get you?' The cover charge was already noted on his pad as he waited deferentially.

'A straight Jack Daniels,' the Frenchman said, looking enquiringly at Samma. But the waiter interposed smoothly.

'And a champagne cocktail for the lady, sir?'

Her companion shrugged again, his mouth twisting derisively. 'If that is the usual practice—then by all means.'

Samma would have preferred fruit juice, but she knew protest was useless. She sat in smouldering silence until the drinks arrived, waiting vengefully for him to pick up the bill. But his face was expressionless as he glanced at the total, and it was Samma who found herself gaping, as he produced a bulging bill-fold, and peeled off the necessary amount, adding, she noticed, a tip for the waiter.

God, it was galling to find that he had all that money to waste on alcohol and gambling, when she was struggling to raise the price of an airfare to the United Kingdom! She tasted her cocktail, repressing a slight shudder. She knew that, if this man had been one of her island friends, she would have swallowed her pride, and asked for a loan.

Oh, why do friends have to be poor, and enemies

rich? she wondered bitterly.

'Well, why don't you ask me?' he said, and she bit
back a startled gasp, wondering whether he included
thought-reading among his other unpleasant attri-
butes.

'Ask what?' She took another sip of her drink.

'How I make my money,' he drawled. 'Your face,
ma belle, is most revealing. You're wondering how a
humble deckhand could posibly have amassed so
much money—or, if your earliest assessment is
correct, and it is—pirate's loot.'

'Nothing about you, *monsieur*, would surprise me.
But it isn't very wise to flaunt quite so openly the fact
that you're loaded. Aren't you afraid of being ripped
off?'

He said coolly, 'No.' And she had to believe him. If
this man chose to keep a gold ingot as a pet, she
couldn't see anyone trying to take it away from him.

He went on, 'But when I see something I want, I'm
prepared to pay the full price for it.' Across the table
his eyes met hers, then with cool deliberation he
counted off some more money and pushed the bills
across to her.

It was only to be expected, working where she was,
dressed as she was, and she knew it, but she was
burning all over, rage and humiliation rendering her
speechless.

When she could speak, she said thickly, 'I am—not
for sale.'

'And I am not in the market.' He leaned forward.
'Didn't you hear me say, *chérie*, that I'm here to play
poker? No, this is payment for the sketch you did of
me. I presume it is enough. Your artist friend on the
quay told me your usual charges, and where I would
find you.'

More than ever, she wished she'd ripped that
particular sketch to pieces. 'I don't want your money.'

'Then you're no businesswoman.' His voice gentled
slightly. 'Forget how much you loathe me, and take
the money. You cannot afford such gestures, and you
know it.'

Samma bit her lip savagely, wondering exactly how
much Mindy had told him.

'I make a perfectly good living,' she said defiantly.
She gestured around her. 'As you see, business is
booming.'

'I see a great many things,' he said slowly. 'And I
hear even more. So this is your life, Mademoiselle
Samantha Briant, and you are content with it? To
sketch in the sunlight by day, and at night lure the
unwary to their doom in a net of smiles and blonde
hair?'

No, she thought. It's not like that at all.

Aloud, she said, 'If that's how you want to put
it—yes.'

'Did you never have any other ambitions?'

She was startled into candour. 'I wanted originally
to teach—art, I suppose. But I haven't any
qualifications.'

'You could acquire some.'

Samma's lips parted impulsively, then closed again.
She'd been, she thought with concern, on the very
brink of confessing her financial plight to this man.

She shrugged. 'Why should I—when I'm having
such a wonderful time?' She pushed back her chair,
and got to her feet. 'And you've acquired an instant
portrait—not exclusive rights to my company. I'm
neglecting the other customers.'

As she made to move away, his hand captured her
wrist, not hurting her, but at the same time making it
impossible for her to free herself. The dark eyes were

unsmiling as they studied her. 'And what would a
man have to pay for such rights, my little siren?'

She tried to free herself, and failed. 'More than you
could afford,' she said bitingly, and he laughed.

'You estimate yourself highly, *mignonne*. I am not
speaking of a lifetime's devotion, you understand, but
perhaps a year out of your life. What price would you
place on that?'

Something inside Samma snapped. Her free hand
closed round the stem of her glass, and threw the
remains of her cocktail straight at his darkly mocking
face.

She could hear the sudden stillness all around them
as her deed was registered at the adjoining tables, then
the subdued, amused hum of interest which followed.
And, out of the corner of her eye, she saw Clyde
bearing down on her, bursting with righteous
indignation.

'Have you taken leave of your senses?' he stormed at
her, before turning deferentially to the Frenchman
who was removing the worst of the moisture with an
immaculate linen handkerchief.

'I can't apologise enough,' he went on. 'Naturally,
we'll be happy to arrange any cleaning of your clothes
which is necessary, Mr—er . . .?' He paused.

'Delacroix,' the Frenchman said. 'Roche Delacroix.'

Clyde's mouth dropped open. 'From Grand Cay?'
he asked weakly, and at the affirmative nod he gave
Samma an accusing glance. 'You'd better get out of
here, my girl. You've done enough damage for one
evening.'

'Don't be too hard on your *belle fille, monsieur,*'
Roche Delacroix said. 'She has been—provoked, I
confess.'

'I don't need you to fight my battles for me,' Samma

flared hardily. 'And nothing would prevail on me to stay in this place another moment.'

Her legs were shaking under her, but she managed to walk to the door, ignoring the murmured comments and speculative looks following her, then she dashed for the comparative refuge of the dressing-room.

Margot, one of the other hostesses, was in there, sharing a cigarette with Cicero the barman. They looked up in surprise as Samma came bursting in.

'What's the matter, honey?' Cicero asked teasingly. 'Devil chasing your tail?'

Samma sank down on the nearest chair. She said, 'I've done an awful thing. I—I threw a drink over a customer.'

'That old Baxter man?' Margot laughed. 'I wish I'd seen it.'

Samma gulped. 'No, it was a stranger—or nearly. I—I had a run in with him this morning, as a matter of fact.'

'That's not like you.' Margot gave her a sympathetic look. 'What do they call this man?'

Samma frowned. 'He said his name was Roche Delacroix and that he came from Grand Cay.'

There was an odd silence, and she looked up to see them both staring at her. 'Why—what is it?'

'I said the devil was chasing you,' Cicero muttered. 'It's one of those Devil Delacroixes from Lucifer's own island.'

'You—know him?' Samma asked rather dazedly.

'Not in person, honey, but everyone round here knows the Delacroix name. Why, his ancestor was the greatest pirate who ever sailed these waters. Every time he left Grand Cay, a fleet of merchant ships went to the bottom, and he didn't care whether they were

English or Spanish, or even French like himself. He'd
had to leave France because he'd quarrelled with the
King, which was a mighty bad thing to do in those
days, and he figured the whole world was his enemy.
So they called him *Le Diable,* yessir.' Cicero laughed
softly. 'And they called his hideout Lucifer's Cay.'

'Did they, indeed?' Samma said grimly. 'Well, I
hope they caught him and hanged him from his own
yardarm.'

'Not on your life,' said Cicero. 'He turned
respectable, got a free pardon, and took up sugar
planting. But they say every now and then the
breeding throws up another Devil—a chip off the old
block, like that old pirate.'

He paused. 'This Mr Roche Delacroix now, why,
they reckon he's made more money than old Devil
Delacroix himself. He owns the casino, right there on
Grand Cay, and he has a boat-chartering business as
well. He's one rich guy, all right.'

'And he's here in this club right now?' Margot
asked huskily, her full lips curving in a smile. 'This I
have to see. Maybe when he's dried off, he'd like some
company.'

'Perhaps—but I think he's more interested in
playing poker.' Samma forced a smile. 'Maybe I
should have found someone else to pour a drink over.'

'You sure should,' Cicero agreed sombrely. 'Why,
honey, you don't ever want to cross anyone from
Lucifer's Cay—specially someone by the name of
Delacroix. That was one bad mistake.'

Margot rose, pretty and sinuous as a cat. 'Then I'll
have to try and make up for it,' she said, her lips
curving in an anticipatory smile. 'Wish me luck,
now.'

She drifted out, and Cicero followed a moment or

two later, leaving Samma alone.

She tore off Nina's dress and bundled it back on a hanger. Never, ever again would she work at the Black Grotto in any capacity, although Clyde was unlikely even to ask her again, after tonight's performance, she reminded herself wryly.

She dragged on her T-shirt and jeans, and walked back through the grounds towards the small bungalow she shared with Clyde.

She felt restless—on edge, and it was all the fault of that foul man. In just a few hours, he'd turned the quiet backwater of her life into some kind of raging torrent, she thought resentfully.

And nothing Cicero had told her had done anything to put her mind at ease. It was no wonder Roche Delacroix had been annoyed at her sketch, she thought restively. He probably considered she knew who he was, and was taking a petty swipe at his family history.

Well, let him think what he wanted. He would be leaving soon and, anyway, his opinions were of no concern to her. Indeed, she didn't know why she was wasting a second thought on the creature.

But, at this rate, she wasn't going to sleep tonight. Some hard physical exercise was what she needed to calm her down, and tire her out. She turned down the path which led to the hotel's small swimming pool. She rarely got the chance to use the pool during the day, but that wasn't too much of a hardship when she could come down here at night, and have it all to herself. And there was the added bonus that she didn't have to bother with a costume.

She collected a towel from one of the changing cabins, stripped and plunged into the water. But, as she struck out with her swift, practised crawl, she couldn't seem to capture her usual sense of wellbeing.

Oh, it wasn't fair, she thought with a kind of desperate impatience. Of all the men who'd passed through Cristoforo, there had never been one who'd come even close to touching her emotions. Yet, in the space of a few minutes, Roche Delacroix, of all people, had given her a swift, disturbing insight into what it might mean to be a woman—even though he'd treated her for most of the time like a child, she thought stormily, as she turned for another length.

And then—paradoxically—had come that cynical —that abominable offer.

'*A year out of your life.*' His words seemed to beat a tattoo in her brain. How dared he? she raged inwardly. Oh, how dared he? And it was no comfort to tell herself that he'd simply been amusing himself at her expense. After all, a man like that could have no real interest in an inexperienced nineteen-year-old. Margot, or even the absent Nina, would be far more his type.

But soon *Allegra* would be gone, she tried to console herself, and she would never have to see Roche Delacroix or think about him again.

She hauled herself out of the water, and began to blot the moisture from her arms and body, then paused suddenly, a strange prickle of awareness alerting her nerve-endings as if—as if someone was watching her.

She stopped towelling her hair, and glanced over her shoulder, searching for a betraying movement in the shadows, listening for some sound. But there was nothing.

She was being over-imaginative, she told herself, but she still felt disturbed, and she resolved to give nude swimming a miss for a while. If one of the waiters from the club, say, was taking a short-cut through the garden, there was no need to give him a field day.

She pulled her clothes on to her still-damp body, and set off back towards the bungalow, her head high, looking neither to right or left.

Probably there was no one there at all. But everything was off-key tonight because of Roche Delacroix, and she would be eternally grateful when he turned his back on Cristoforo for ever.

Because, to her shame, she knew she would always be left wondering just what that—that year out of her life might have been like—with him.

CHAPTER THREE

SAMMA was woken from a light, unsatisfactory sleep by a crash, and a muffled curse. She sat up, glancing at the illuminated dial of the clock beside her bed, whistling faintly when she saw the time. The poker game had gone on for longer than usual.

She lay for a few moments, listening to the sounds of movement from the kitchen, then reached resignedly for her robe.

Clyde was sitting at the table, staring into space, a bottle and glass in front of him. The eyes he turned on her were glazed and bloodshot.

He muttered, 'Oh, there you are,' as if he'd been waiting for her to join him.

She said, 'I'll make some black coffee.'

'No, sit down. I've got to talk to you.'

She said, 'If it's about what happened earlier—I'm sorry . . .'

'Oh, that.' He made a vague, dismissive gesture. 'No, it's something else.'

He was a terrible colour, she thought uneasily.

He said, 'Tonight—I lost tonight, Samma.'

The fact that she'd been expecting such news made it no easier to hear, she discovered.

She said steadily, 'How much?'

'A lot. More than a lot. Money I didn't have.' He paused, and added like a death knell, 'Everything.'

Samma closed her eyes for a moment. 'The hotel?'

'That, too. It was the last game, Samma. I had the chance to win back all that I'd lost and more. You

34

never saw anything like it. There were only the two of us left in, and he kept raising me. I had a running flush, king high. Almost the best hand you can get.'

She said in a small, wintry voice, 'Almost, but not quite it seems.'

Clyde looked like a collapsed balloon. She was afraid he was going to burst into tears. 'He had—a running flush in spades, beginning with the ace.'

There was a long silence, then Samma roused herself from the numbness which had descended on her.

She said, 'You and Hugo Baxter have been playing poker together for a long time. Surely he'll be prepared to give you time—come to some arrangement over the property . . .'

'Baxter?' he said hoarsely. 'I'm not talking about Baxter. It was the Frenchman, Delacroix.'

This time, the silence was electric. Samma's hand crept to her mouth.

She felt icy cold. 'What—what are we going to do?'

'Baxter will help us,' he said rapidly. 'He promised me he would. He—he doesn't want to see us go under. He's going to see Delacroix with me tomorrow to—work something out. He's being—very generous.'

There was something about the way he said it—the way he didn't meet her gaze.

She said, 'Why is he being so—generous? What have you promised in return. Me?'

He looked self-righteous. 'What do you take me for?'

'Shall we try pimp?' Samma said, and Clyde came out of his chair, roaring like a bull, his fists clenched. He met her calm, cold stare and subsided again.

'We—we mustn't quarrel,' he muttered. 'We have to stick by each other. Baxter—likes you, you know that. And he's lonely. It wouldn't hurt to be nice to him, that's all he wants. Why, you could probably get him to marry you . . .'

'Which would make everything all right, of course,' she said bitterly. 'Forget it, Clyde, the idea makes me sick to my stomach.'

'Samma, don't be hasty. What choice do we have? Unless Baxter supports me in some deal with Delacroix, we'll be bankrupt—not even a roof over our heads.'

She rose to her feet. 'This is your mess, Clyde,' she said. 'Don't expect me to get you out of it.'

Back in her own room, she leaned against the closed door and began to tremble like a leaf. In spite of her defiant words, she had never felt so frightened, so helpless in her life. She seemed incapable of rational thought. She wanted to cry. She wanted to be sick. She wanted to lie down on the floor, and drum with her heels, and scream at the top of her voice.

All she seemed to see in front of her was Hugo Baxter's sweating moon face, his gaze a trail of slime as it slid over her body.

No, she thought, pressing a convulsive fist against her lips. Oh God, no!

Clyde said there was no other choice, but there had to be. Had to . . .

'A year out of your life.' The words seemed to reverberate mockingly in her brain. *'A year out of your life.'*

She wrapped her arms round her body, shivering. No, that was unthinkable, too. She shouldn't even be allowing such an idea to enter her mind.

And yet, what could she do—caught, as she was, between the devil and the deep sea once again? But surely that didn't mean she had to sell herself to the devil?

She lay on the bed, staring into the darkness, her tired mind turning over the alternatives. She was blushing all over, as she realised exactly what she was contemplating.

But wasn't she being rather melodramatic about the whole thing? She didn't have to meekly submit to the fate being designed for her. She was no stranger, after all, to keeping men at arm's length. Surely, she could manage to hold him off at least until they reached *Allegra's* first port of call when, with luck, she could simply slip ashore and vanish, she thought feverishly. Her savings were meagre, but they would tide her over until she could find work, and save for her flight home.

She couldn't let herself think too deeply about the inevitable problems. The important thing was to escape from Cristoforo—nothing mattered more than that—before she found herself trapped into a situation with Hugo Baxter that she could not evade. Because it was clear she couldn't count on Clyde to assist her.

She began to plan. She would take the bare minimum from her scanty wardrobe—just what she could pack into her bicycle basket. And she'd leave a note for Clyde saying she was having a day on the beach to think. With luck, she would be long gone before he realised she was not coming back.

When it was daylight, she went over to the hotel, and carried out her usual early morning duties, warning the staff not to expect Clyde until later in the day. Then she collected a few belongings together, wrapped them in a towel to back up her beach story, and cycled down the quay.

Apart from the fishermen preparing to embark,

there were few people about. Samma bit her lip as she approached *Allegra's* gangplank. She wished she could have said goodbye to Mindy and the rest of her friends, but at the same time she was glad they weren't around to witness what she was doing.

'Can I help you, *ma'mselle?'* At the top of the gangway, her path was blocked very definitely by a tall coloured man, with shoulders like a American quarter-back.

She squared her shoulders, and said, with a coolness she was far from feeling, 'Would you tell Monsieur Delacroix that Samantha Briant would like to speak with him.'

The man gave her a narrow-eyed look. 'Mist' Roche ain't seeing anyone right now, *ma'mselle.* You come back in an hour or two.'

In an hour or two, her courage might have deserted her, she thought. She said with equal firmness, 'Please tell him I'm here, and I have some money for him.'

It was partly true. The small roll of bills representing her savings reposed in the pocket of her faded yellow sundress.

The man gave her another sceptical glance, and vanished. After a few minutes, he returned.

'Come with me, please.'

The companionway and the passage to the saloon were only too familiar, but she was led further along to another door, standing slightly ajar. The man tapped lightly on the woodwork, said, 'Your visitor, boss,' and disappeared back the way he'd come, leaving Samma nervously on her own.

She pushed open the door, and walked in. It was a stateroom, the first glance told her, and furnished more luxuriously than any bedroom she'd ever been in on dry land.

And in the sole berth—as wide as any double bed—was Roche Delacroix, propped up against pillows, a scatter of papers across the sheet which barely covered the lower half of his body, a tray of coffee and fruit on the fitment beside him.

Samma took a step backwards. She said nervously, 'I'm sorry—I didn't realise. I'll wait outside until you're dressed.'

'Then you will wait for some considerable time.' He didn't even look at her. His attention was fixed frowningly on the document he was scanning. 'Sit down.'

Samma perched resentfully on the edge of a thickly padded armchair. Its silky upholstery matched the other drapes in the room, she noticed. She wasn't passionately interested in interior decoration, but anything was better than having to look at him.

She thought working in the hotel would have inured her by now to encountering people in various stages of nudity, but none of their guests had ever exuded Roche Delacroix's brand of raw masculinity. Or perhaps it was the contrast between his deeply bronzed skin, and the white of the bed linen which made him look so flagrantly—undressed.

The aroma of the coffee reached her beguilingly and, in spite of herself, her small straight nose twitched, her stomach reminding her that she'd eaten and drunk nothing yet that day.

Nor, it appeared, was she to be offered anything—not even a slice of the mango he was eating with such open enjoyment.

'So—Mademoiselle Briant,' he said at last, a note of faint derision in his voice. 'Why am I honoured by this early visit? Have you come to pay your stepfather's poker debts? I am surprised he could raise such a sum so quickly.'

'Not—not exactly.' A combination of thirst and nerves had turned her mouth as dry as a desert.

His brows lifted. 'What then?'

She couldn't prevaricate, and she knew it. She said, 'I know you're leaving Cristoforo today. I came to ask you to—take me with you.'

They were the hardest words she'd ever had to utter, and they were greeted by complete silence.

He sat up, disposing his pillows more comfortably, and Samma averted her gaze in a hurry. When she glanced back, he was rearranging the sheet over his hips with cynical ostentation.

'Why should I?' he asked baldly.

'I need a passage out of here, and I need it today.' She swallowed. 'I could—pay something. Or I could work.'

'I already have a perfectly adequate crew. And I don't want your money.' His even glance didn't leave her face. 'So—what else can you offer?'

She'd been praying he would be magnanimous—let her down lightly, but she realised now it was a forlorn hope.

She gripped her hands together, hoping to disguise the fact they were trembling.

'Last night—you asked me for a year out of my life.'

'I have not forgotten,' he said. 'And you reacted like an outraged nun.' The bare, shoulders lifted in a negligent shrug. 'But that, of course, is your prerogative.'

'But, it's also a woman's prerogative to—change her mind.'

When she dared look at him again, he was pouring himself some more coffee, his face inscrutable.

At last he said, 'I assume there has been some crisis in your life which has made you favour my offer. May

I know what it is?'

She said in a small voice, 'I think you already know. My stepfather lost everything he possesses to you last night.'

'He did, indeed,' he agreed. 'Have you come to offer yourself in lieu of payment, *chérie?* If so, I am bound to tell you that you rate your rather immature charms altogether too highly.'

This was worse than she could have imagined. She said, 'He's going to pay you—everything. But he's going to borrow—from Hugo Baxter.'

'A large loan,' he said meditatively. 'And the collateral, presumably, is yourself?'

She nodded wordlessly.

'Now I understand,' he said softly. 'It becomes a choice, in fact—my bed or that of Hugo Baxter. The lesser of two evils.'

Put like that, it sounded awful, but it also happened to be the truth, she thought, gritting her teeth. 'Yes.'

'Naturally, I am flattered that your choice should have fallen on me,' the smooth voice went on relentlessly. 'But perhaps you are not the only one to have had—second thoughts. The prospect of being—doused in alcohol for the next twelve months is not an appealing one.'

'I'm sorry about that.' Her hands were clenched so tightly, the knuckles were turning white. She said raggedly, 'Please—please take me out of here. I'm—desperate.' Her voice broke. 'I'll do anything you ask—anything . . .'

'*Vraiment?*' He replaced his cup on the tray, and deftly shuffled his papers together. 'Then let us test your resolve, *mignonne*. Close the door.'

In slight bewilderment, she obeyed. Then, as she turned back, realisation dawned, and she stopped dead, staring at him in a kind of fascinated horror.

He took one of the pillows from behind him, and tossed it down at his side, moving slightly at the same time to make room for her. His arm curved across the top of the pillow in invitation and command.

'Now ?' She uttered the word as a croak.

His dark eyes glittered at her. 'What better way to begin the day?' He patted the space beside him. *'Viens, ma belle.'* He added, almost as an afterthought, 'You may leave your clothes on that chair.'

Shock held her prisoner. She couldn't deny that she'd invited this, but she hadn't expected this kind of demand so soon. Had counted, in fact, on being allowed a little leeway. Time to adjust, she thought. Time to escape . . .

'You are keeping me waiting,' his even voice reminded her.

She took a few leaden steps forward, reached the chair, and paused. She could refuse, she supposed, or beg for a breathing space. And probably find herself summarily back on the quayside with her belongings, she realised, moistening her dry lips with the tip of her tongue, as she eased her slender feet out of her espadrilles.

Her heart was beating rapidly, violently, like a drum sending out an alarm signal, a warning tattoo. She had never in her life taken off her clothes in front of a man, and she didn't know how to begin. What was he expecting? she wondered wildly. Some kind of striptease—all smiles and tantalisation? Because she couldn't—couldn't . . .

She put up a hand and tugged at the ribbon which confined her hair at the nape of her neck, jerking it loose.

He was propped on one elbow, watching her in

silence, his face enigmatic, but she had the feeling he wasn't overly impressed with her performance so far.

She supposed she couldn't blame him. He'd spelt it out for her, after all. 'My bed or that of Hugo Baxter,' he'd said. 'The lesser of two evils.' Well, she'd made her decision, and now, it seemed, she had to suffer the consequences.

She bent her head, letting her hair swing forwards to curtain her flushed face while she tried to concentrate her fumbling fingers on the buttons which fastened the front of her dress.

The sharp, imperative knock on the stateroom door was as shocking as a whiplash laid across her overburdened senses, and she jumped.

'Radio message for you, boss. Maître Giraud—and I reckon it's urgent.'

Roche Delacroix swore under his breath, and made to throw back the sheet, pausing when he encountered Samma's stricken look. He paused, his mouth twisting cynically. 'You'll find a robe in that closet, chérie. Get it for me.'

She hurried to obey, holding the garment out to him almost at arm's length.

He laughed. 'Now turn your back, my little Puritan.'

Heart hammering unevenly, she heard the sounds of movement, the rustle of silk as he put on the robe. But when his hands descended on her shoulders, turning her to face him again, a little cry escaped her.

'How nervous you are.' The laughter was still there in his voice. 'Like a little cat who has never known kindness.' He picked up her hand, and pressed a swift, sensuous kiss into its soft palm. 'I am desolated our time together has been interrupted, ma belle, but it is only a pleasure postponed, after all.'

He strode across the cabin, and left, closing the door

behind him.

Samma's legs gave way, and she sank down on to the chair. She lifted her hand, and stared at it stupidly, as if she expected to see the mark of his lips, burning there like a brand.

He'd only kissed her hand, she told herself weakly. There was nothing in that to set her trembling, every sense, every nerve-ending tingling in some mysterious way. What would she do if—when he really kissed her? When he . . .

Her mind blanked out. She couldn't let herself think about that. She would cope with it when she had to.

And she would soon have to, a sly inner voice reminded her. 'A pleasure postponed,' he'd said.

For the first time in her life, Samma found herself cursing her own inexperience. She wished she had some real idea of what Roche Delacroix was going to expect from her—when he returned. Would he make allowances for her ignorance—or would impatience make him brutal?

She bit her lip. Oh, God, what right had anyone as sexually untutored as she was to throw herself at a man of the world like Roche Delacroix?

I can't stay here, she thought, panicking. I can't! I'll have to leave—go back on shore—find some other way out. I must have been mad.

She retrieved her espadrilles and ribbon and, picking up her bundle, went to the door. The handle turned easily enough, but the door itself didn't budge.

She twisted the handle the other way, pushing at the solid wood panels, but it made no difference. He'd locked her in, she thought wildly.

She might have come here of her own free will, but she was staying as a prisoner. And when her jailer came back—what then?

When the door eventually opened half an hour later, Samma was as taut as a bowstring.

'How dare you lock me in?' she stormed.

Roche Delacroix's expression was preoccupied, and he looked at her with faint surprise. 'I did not,' he said. 'The door sticks sometimes, that is all. I'll have it corrected when we reach Grand Cay.'

That's all? Samma thought, wincing. Because of a sticking door, and her own horrendous stupidity, she was still trapped on *Allegra* with this—this pirate.

She said. 'I've been thinking it over, and I've decided I'd prefer to forego this cruise, after all.' She picked up her bundle. 'I'd like to go ashore, please.'

'You are just hungry,' he said calmly. 'Jerome is waiting to take you to the saloon for some ham and eggs.'

The words alone made her stomach swoon, but Samma didn't relax her stance for an instant. 'I refuse to eat a mouthful of food on this boat!'

'You are such a poor sailor?' He sounded almost solicitous, but the gleam in the dark eyes told a different story. 'But we have not yet left harbour.'

'I'm a perfectly good sailor,' she said between her teeth. 'What I'm trying to convey is that I'd rather choke than eat any food of yours.'

He shrugged. 'As you please, but you will be very hungry by the time we reach our destination. Besides, I thought you would prefer to occupy yourself with breakfast while I dressed,' he added, loosening the belt of his robe. 'However, if you would rather watch me . . .'

Samma fled. Jerome was waiting outside, so there was no chance to make a dash for it, as he escorted her to the saloon.

'I'll be just within call, *ma'mselle*, if you need anything.' The words were polite, but she was being warned that he was keeping an eye on her, she thought miserably as she sank down on to the long, padded seat, and looked at the table which had been set up. There was a tantalising aroma emanating from a covered dish on a hot-plate.

She groaned silently, feeling her mouth fill with saliva. Oh, God, but she was ravenous! She'd meant every word she'd said, but surely no one would notice if she took just one—tiny piece of ham? Using her fingers, she pulled off a crisp brown morsel. It was done to a turn, of course, succulent and flavoursome, and Samma was lost.

Ten minutes later, every scrap on the platter had gone, and she was on her second cup of coffee.

'I am glad you decided to relent. I have a very sensitive chef,' a sardonic voice said from the doorway, and Roche Delacroix joined her.

The thick, black hair was slightly damp, and the sharp scent of some expensive cologne hung in the air as he came to sit beside her. He'd dressed, if that was the word, in the most disreputable pair of jeans in the history of the world. Not only were they torn, and stained with oil, but they also fitted him like a second skin, drawing attention Samma would rather not have spared to his lean hips and long legs.

She said breathlessly, 'I haven't relented at all, really. I still want to go ashore.'

He shook his head. 'That is impossible. The bargain between us is made. The next year of your life belongs to me, and it starts here on *Allegra*. You knew that when you came to me—offered yourself.'

'I—I wasn't thinking clearly,' she said huskily. She

took a deep breath. 'Monsieur Delacroix, it was terribly wrong of me to rush on board—and throw myself at you like this, and I'm deeply ashamed, believe me. But I have to tell you—it—it wouldn't work out between us—really.' She was beginning to flounder. 'I'd just be a—terrible disappointment to you—in every way.'

'Don't you mean—in bed?' She heard the grin in his voice. 'You know this from bitter experience, perhaps?'

'No.' That ridiculous blush was burning her up again!

'As I thought.' He studied her for a moment, his expression unreadable. 'So—Samantha, *ma belle,* have you made some resolve to stay a virgin all your life?'

'No—I—I mean I don't know . . .' She was stammering, and it was no wonder when his hands were on her shoulders, impelling her towards him, and every cell in her body seemed to have taken on quivering, independent life.

His eyes were darkness itself, deep obsidian wells in which she could be lost for ever. Then he kissed her, and her innocence ended. As simply as that.

It would have been easier if he'd behaved like the brute she'd feared, because she could have fought that. But he was terrifyingly gentle, awesomely persuasive, just brushing his lips across hers at first, then exploring the softly trembling contours with the tip of his tongue, coaxing her lips apart.

And when he'd achieved his objective, and gained access to the moist, inner sweetness she could not deny him, he was still unhurried, totally in control, his tongue barely flickering against hers.

His mouth pressed more insistently, became more demanding. He took her hands and placed them round his neck, pulling her against him, so that her breasts were crushed achingly against the heated muscular hardness of his bare chest.

His arms tightened round her, and his kiss deepened beyond all imagination, draining her dizzily, enforcing a submission which instinct told her was only a foreshadowing of the ultimate surrender he would ask of her.

She was breathless. She was going to faint, but if he stopped kissing her then she would die. She was burning, fevered beyond control.

With shocking suddenness he lifted his head, then put her away from him, surveying her with almost clinical detachment.

He said coolly, 'I suspect you could be a willing pupil, *ma belle*. What a pity I have neither the time, nor the patience, to be your teacher.' He reached out, and almost austerely tucked an errant strand of hair behind her ear, before straightening the straps of her dress. He said mockingly, 'Pull yourself together, *ma belle*. We have guests.'

The saloon door opened, and Clyde came in, followed by Hugo Baxter.

CHAPTER FOUR

'SAMMA?' Clyde's voice was aggressive with suspicion. 'What the hell are you doing here?'

She couldn't find her voice. Physically and emotionally, she was still reeling.

'Mademoiselle Briant is here at my invitation,' Roche Delacroix said blandly. 'She has, after all, a vested interest in our negotiations.'

Clyde stared at him. 'The hotel belongs to me, not her.'

'I was not referring to the hotel.' Roche Delacroix's eyes drifted over Hugo Baxter, inappropriately garbed for his size in Bermuda shorts and a loud tropical shirt. He gave Clyde a faint smile. 'I am sure we understand each other. Sit down, *messieurs.*' He clicked his fingers. 'Jerome,' he snapped, indicating briefly that the table should be cleared.

It was done with the speed of light. Even in those appalling jeans, Roche Delacroix was every inch the autocrat, accustomed to having his commands obeyed instantly. She couldn't understand why she hadn't recognised that when she first saw him.

'I shall be sailing soon, so there is no need for these transactions to take long,' Roche Delacroix said. 'The terms I have decided on are quite simple. Your hotel, *monsieur,* belongs to me, and I am not prepared to sell it. Instead, I shall retain you to run it for me, as my manager, and at a token salary.' He paused. 'From what I was able to see last night, some renovation is necessary. This will be carried out. I intend, you see,

49

that the hotel should make a profit. By ensuring, as manager, that it does so, you will begin to pay off the money you owe me.' He gave Clyde a long, level look. 'When the debt has been satisfied, you will be free to leave, if you will wish. But not until then. And do not imagine you can cheat me. I imagine you know the attorney Philip Marquis on Alliance Street? *Eh bien,* he is to act as my agent in this matter. That is all.'

'It's not even the beginning,' Clyde said thickly, banging the table with his fist. 'I'm not acting as your unpaid servant. I can pay you off here and now, friend, and Mr Baxter here is prepared to make you a good offer for the hotel.'

Roche Delacroix shrugged. 'I am not open to offers. Monsieur Baxter's intervention is unnecessary. Nor is it certain you will be able to count on his generosity.'

'He can count on me for anything he likes,' Hugo Baxter declared, darting a look at Samma.

Roche Delacroix smiled. 'Even when I tell you that Mademoiselle Briant is coming with me?' he asked softly.

Hugo Baxter uttered an obscenity. He turned on Clyde. 'What's he talking about? You swore she'd stay here—that you'd talked her round. What the hell are you trying to pull?'

Clyde's face was grey. He stared at Samma. 'Is this—true?'

'Yes,' she said with a little sigh. There was no retreat now. Roche took her hand, and carried it swiftly and gracefully to his lips.

'You dirty little slag,' Hugo Baxter said hoarsely. 'Always too pure and high and mighty to give me a second look. But you'll go off with a man you only met last night. I always knew under that touch-me-not air you were a whore, like all the rest of them!'

The words made her cringe, but she was in no position to deny them, she thought wretchedly.

Roche said icily, 'Any more filth from your lips, *monsieur*, and you will go to be cleansed in the harbour.' His face was granite-hard as he looked at Baxter. 'Don't judge everyone by your own standards, you animal. Samantha is to be my employee, not my mistress. She is coming to Grand Cay to take charge of my young daughter.'

It was as if a bombshell had hit them, and Samma felt her own jaw dropping as well. Was he serious? she wondered dazedly. Did he really have a daughter? Until that moment, she'd had no idea he was even married. And, if he'd intended all along for her to be some kind of governess, why had he let her think—let her think . . .? She bent her head and stared at the floor, furiously aware that he was watching her, his mouth twisting in amusement.

'You can, of course, reject my offer completely,' Roche went on calmly, addressing Clyde. 'In which case, you no longer have a roof over your head, or any form of livelihood. I do not advise you to take up gambling as a profession,' he added dispassionately. 'You are neither lucky, nor always wise in your choice of opponents.' He sent a dry look towards Hugo Baxter.

Baxter began to bluster. 'What is that supposed to mean?'

'Only, *monsieur*, that if some ill wind should bring you to Grand Cay, do not trouble yourself to visit my casino. You will not be admitted.' He looked at his watch, then glanced back at Clyde. 'Your decision, *monsieur*. I have no more time to waste on you.'

There was a long fraught silence, then Clyde said heavily, 'I agree—I suppose.'

'Very wise.' Roche rose to his feet. 'I will not detain either of you any longer. Jerome is waiting to escort you off my boat. In a few days' time, Philip Marquis will call on you with the requisite papers for your signature. I advise you not to cause him any problems. *Mes adieux.*'

Allegra sailed an hour later. Samma sat slumped on the seat in the cabin, staring into space, barely aware of the powerful engine which was carrying her away to Lucifer's Cay.

'Don't you want to say farewell to Cristoforo?' Roche had come back into the saloon so noiselessly, she hadn't been conscious of his approach.

She started nervously, and swallowed. 'No. I—I never want to see it again.'

'Then you don't have to.' He walked to one of the lockers, and she heard the chink of a bottle against glass. He returned with a measure of amber liquid in a tumbler, which he handed to her. 'Drink this,' he directed briefly. 'You look as if you need it, and then I'll tell you fully what I want from you.'

She swallowed some of the cognac. It felt like fire in her throat, but it put heart into her. 'Won't your wife have something to say about you hiring a total stranger as a governess without consulting her?'

'My wife has been dead for over a year.'

Biting her lip, Samma began to say something awkwardly, and he held up a silencing hand. 'There is no need to express regret. Marie-Christine and I did not enjoy a day's happiness together, and parted immediately after the honeymoon, so don't pity me as a grieving widower. For seven years we lived completely separate lives, then she arrived unexpectedly on Grand Cay, bringing *la petite* Solange with her.'

'She wanted a reconciliation?'

His mouth curled. 'She wanted richer pickings than the maintenance payments her lawyers had exacted from me. She had not prospered during our separation. So—she moved into Belmanoir, my family home, and I occupied a suite at the casino, and life went on much as before, except that now there was Solange.'

'You hadn't seen her—had access to her?'

'I never sought it. I had put my so-called marriage behind me as a hideous mistake, best forgotten. But when I saw the child, I realised she needed a father.'

'You're very cold-blooded about it,' Samma said indignantly.

'You think so?' His brows rose consideringly. 'But then, I married Marie-Christine in an excess of hot-blooded passion, and that taught me a valuable lesson.' He paused. 'But I have tried to do my best for Solange. I have hired other companions for her, but unfortunately few of them have remained for any length of time.'

'Why not?'

He shrugged. 'For a number of reasons. Solange is not an easy child, and Belmanoir itself is remote, cut off from the social life of St Laurent, the capital.' He paused. 'And some of these ladies had a regrettable tendency to believe that—I was the one in need of companionship.'

Samma took another hurried sip of brandy.

'Unlike you, *chérie,*' he went on, mockingly. 'Who came to me only with a pistol at your head.'

She said stiltedly, 'Why didn't you tell me—what you really wanted?'

'Because you made me angry.' The dark eyes met hers implacably. 'You were so ready to believe I was just another womaniser with an eye for a pretty blonde. So—I decided to let you suffer a little.' He smiled. 'And you did suffer, didn't you, *ma belle?*'

She stared at him for a long moment, then said, 'You mean that, when you told me to—undress, you were just punishing me again?'

'The slapping I administered seemed to have had little effect,' he said coolly. 'I thought I would try other tactics.'

She went on looking at him. 'But you didn't know that radio message was going to come through just then. You couldn't have done. So—if there'd been no message—when would the—punishment have stopped precisely?'

'It would not have stopped.' His dark gaze touched her mouth, lingered there in reminiscence. 'Nor would you have wished it to,' he added almost casually.

In the silence that followed, Samma could hear the beating of her heart like thunder in her own ears. She tried to think of something equally blasé to reply and failed completely.

Roche watched her mental struggles with amusement. 'Also, *chérie,* I needed to gauge just how desperate you were in your resolve to leave Cristoforo. Because I must tell you now, I did not speak the whole truth to your *beau-père* and that other one. An employee is no longer sufficient for my purpose. You are coming to Grand Cay as my wife.'

There was another stunned silence. Samma said breathlessly. 'You want me to—marry you? But I couldn't . . .'

'I regret you have no choice in the matter,' he cut incisively across her stumbling words. 'You are not the only one to have reached a crisis in your affairs. Marie-Christine's parents are making a belated but sustained effort to gain the custody of Solange. Not out of affection, you understand, but because they would enjoy the allowance the court would exact on her behalf. This is not going to happen.'

'But surely they have no grounds for such a thing?'

'I am prepared to take no risks with Solange's future,' he said quietly. 'The Augustins have compiled a dossier on my shortcomings as a father for a young girl. It complains of my frequent absences from home on business, the fact that much of my income is derived from the casino, and also that Solange lacks a stable female influence in her life. All these charges have some foundation.'

'And you think if you can produce a wife—any wife, they'll just—go away?'

'No, that would be naïve. But a large part of their case would instantly cease to exist.' The dark eyes bored into hers. 'You promised me a year of your life. This is the form it will take.' His mouth curled slightly. 'To use an expression which may be familiar to you, Samantha, you have made your bed, and now you must lie on it. I do not, however, insist that you lie upon it with me.'

She said shakily, 'I don't understand any of this.'

'Next year, Solange will be old enough to go away to school, to the most respectable convent I can find for her. And then you will also be free to live your life in any way you wish—anywhere you wish. I am offering you a business arrangement, no more. You will not be a wife to me in any real sense at all, if that is the assurance you need.' He added, flatly, 'Nervous virgins are not to my taste.'

'So—we just—pretend?' The memory of that slow,

sensuous kiss was still burning a hole in her brain.

'There will naturally have to be a ceremony. Fortunately, our local laws impose no unnecessary hold-ups. If you agree, my attorney can make the necessary arrangements before we even arrive on Grand Cay.

Just like that, Samma thought, hysteria bubbling inside her. All cut and dried.

'And you think your—in-laws will be satisfied with this—charade?'

'They will not be satisfied in the least,' he said coldly. 'They are, like their daughter, selfish, greedy and deceitful. And they imagine that, knowing this, I would allow Solange to go to them? *Pauvre petite,* it is not her fault . . .'

He stopped abruptly, and she gave him a questioning look. 'What isn't her fault?'

'That my relationship with her mother was a disaster,' he said curtly, but Samma was left with the odd feeling this was not what he'd originally started to say.

'And when the year is up, you'll let me go?' She was still trying to make sense of it all. 'Isn't Solange still rather young to be sent away to school like that?'

His brows snapped together. 'I need you to play the part of my wife, *mademoiselle,* not advise me on my child's upbringing. You are, after all, scarcely more than a child yourself. When your year with us is over, you will still be young enough to train for some profession—teaching perhaps, as you once intended. Naturally, I will pay for this training, and in addition you will receive the usual alimony.' He paused. 'A new life for your old one, Samantha. Is a year really so much to ask?'

'I don't know.' Her hands twisted together. 'It's all

been such a shock. I must have time . . .'

'There is no time. Tomorrow we will arrive on Grand Cay, and I expect our marriage to take place at once.' He leaned back, studying her through half closed eyes. 'What is the matter? Are my terms not reasonable enough?' His mouth curled. 'And is it not a relief to find you have nothing to fear from my unbridled lusts, after all?'

She looked back at him coolly. 'Because Solange will be there to act as chaperon?'

'No,' he said, briefly. 'Because I have a mistress already. Is that enough for you?'

It seemed more than enough, Samma thought, swallowing the rest of her cognac. She said, 'If there's a lady in your life, why don't you get her to marry you?'

His smile was cynical now. 'Because I have no more taste for marriage than you have, *ma belle*. And my—lady might not be so ready to vanish when the year is over as you are. Does that answer you? And in return will you give your answer? Do you agree to my terms—yes, or no?'

There was a silence, then she said huskily, 'Yes, but not because I'm impressed by what you're offering. I just feel sorry for your little girl.' She put down her glass, and rose to her feet. 'And now I'd like to be alone for a while.'

'Jerome has prepared a stateroom for you.' As she began to move away, he detained her, a hand on her arm. 'May I ask if that ungainly bundle on the floor represents your total wardrobe?'

'I only brought what I could carry,' she said defensively.

'Hm.' His eyes rested with disfavour on the shabby folds of the yellow sundress. 'Then you will need clothes for your new role. Shall we call it a trousseau?'

'I'd prefer not to,' she said, with a slight catch in her voice.

'As you wish,' he said indifferently. 'However, I shall buy the clothes for you, and you will wear them. It is understood?' He tapped her cheek with a careless finger. 'Now, run away to your solitude.'

She wished she could run—preferably into the next universe, or anywhere which would take her away from him.

And this was only the beginning, she thought as she walked to the door. Ahead of her was a year—a whole year.

Oh, God, she thought. What have I promised? What have I done?

The road to Belmanoir was straight and dusty, flanked by the ripe gold of canefields. Ahead of her, Samma could see dark green forest clustering round the foot of one solitary, central peak, pointing towards the sky in admonition or warning.

But in my case, she thought wryly, the warning has come too late.

She still could not believe the events of the past forty-eight hours. She felt as if she had been caught up in some hurricane, which had left her battered, stripped of everything, including her own identity.

She gave a swift downwards glance at the slender white skirt, topped by the overblouse in a stinging shade of violet. It was not a colour she would ever have chosen for herself, but she had to grudgingly admit that it deepened her eyes to indigo. And it had been selected, like everything else in the new hide cases currently reposing in the boot of this air-conditioned limousine, by the man seated beside her in the driving seat.

Well, almost everything else, Samma thought, remembering with chagrin how he'd made her model the clothes for him. At least he'd left her in peace and privacy to choose her lingerie and swimwear.

Her eyes caught the alien golden gleam of her wedding ring, and she covered it clumsily with her other hand, biting her lip as she did so. It was less than an hour since Roche Delacroix had placed the ring on her finger, in a brief ceremony which had consisted of joint and formal legal declarations, and their signatures on a piece of paper.

Not a word, she thought, about loving or honouring. And, if that was supposed to make her feel better about the whole thing, then, in some odd way, it had been a dismal failure.

Easily made, this contract, she realised. And easily broken when its usefulness had passed.

But the ordeals of the day were not over yet. The next item on schedule was her meeting with her new stepdaughter. And this afternoon she had to face a preliminary hearing before a Judge Lefèvre of the custody battle for Solange between Roche and the Augustins. She wasn't sure which she was dreading most.

She stole a covert look at her new husband. He was wearing a beautifully cut lightweight suit in pale grey, and the black hair had been tamed to comparative respectability, but in spite of these conventional trappings he still looked as tough and uncompromising as any pirate ancestor could have done.

She wondered if he was thinking about the wedding —and that his second venture into marriage was even less promising than the first had been—but his dark face gave nothing away. He was lucky to have his driving to concentrate on, she thought, although they hadn't encountered so much as a donkey and cart since leaving St Laurent, the capital. Roche had been right when he'd warned her that Belmanoir was remote.

'You are very quiet.' His voice cut across her thoughts, making her jump.

'I think I'm nervous.' She paused. 'Suppose Solange doesn't like me?'

'You are being defeatist.' His brows drew together. 'Why should she not like you?'

'Because I'm the stranger you're putting in her mother's place.'

'Marie-Christine had no place in my life,' he said harshly. 'I thought you understood that. And it is your task to win Solange's confidence—make her enjoy your company. You have one great advantage over your predecessors, after all.' His mouth twisted in faint derision. 'You cannot simply hand in your notice when the going gets tough.'

Samma swallowed. Lucky me, she thought.

She said quietly, 'You can enforce obedience, but not affection. And I want Solange to be fond of me—genuinely.'

'In a year?' The reminder was faintly brutal. 'Don't hope for too much, Samantha.'

She bent her head. 'I don't expect very much at all.'

At dinner on *Allegra* the previous evening, she'd tried to ask him a little about life at Belmanoir, and Solange in particular, but his replies had been almost terse. For a man so determined to retain the custody of his child, he seemed to know very little about her, she thought unhappily. For Solange's sake, she hoped he wasn't being a dog in the manger about her.

The car turned suddenly under a high stone gateway on to a drive flanked by tall hibiscus hedges.

Samma peered ahead of her through the windscreen,
aware that her heart was beating hard and fast. She was
on Lucifer's Cay, after all, and somewhere beyond the
bright normality of the flowers was the house which *Le
Diable* had built for himself and his dynasty.

She didn't know what she'd been expecting—a
Gothic ruin, perhaps, with a skull and crossbones
fluttering from the battlements. But it wasn't like that
at all—just a rambling white mansion with a pillared
portico, and an elegant wrought-iron balcony
encircling the upper storey.

And, at the top of the steps leading to the front
entrance, someone was waiting. A girl, Samma saw,
no more than in her twenties, with an exquisite *café au
lait* skin, and black hair coiled into a sleek chignon at
the nape of her neck. The neat dark dress she was
wearing did nothing to disguise ripe breasts and
rounded hips, as she walked with a graceful, swaying
motion down the wide, shallow flight of steps towards
them.

'Roche.' Her voice was like sunwarmed honey. '*Sois
le bienvenu.* It is good to have you at home again.' She
turned her smile on Samma. 'And welcome to you
also, *madame.*'

Samma felt something clench inside her, as Roche
bent to kiss the girl lightly on both cheeks, murmuring something in his own language as he did so.

'Samantha?' He turned to her. 'Allow me to present
Elvire Casson, my—housekeeper.'

His slight hesitation wasn't lost on her for a
moment. Samma smiled politely, and shook hands,
her mind working furiously.

'I have a mistress,' he'd said. Why hadn't he also
mentioned that Samma would have to share a roof
with her at Belmanoir? Or did he think she was so

young and naïve that she wouldn't think to put two and two together and come up with the right answer? To which the answer was—probably.

'Where is Solange?' Roche was looking around him, frowning.

It was Elvire's turn to hesitate. 'She reacted badly to your news,' she said at last. 'She refused to go to school this morning, because she claimed to have a fever. I took a pitcher of juice to her room, and she was gone.'

His firm mouth tautened in annoyance. 'To Les Arbres, *sans doute.*'

'*Mais oui.* Madame Duvalle telephoned to say she was there, so I asked for her to be returned.'

Like an overdue library book, Samma thought, bristling, as they walked up the steps into the house.

'We have arranged a small celebration to greet your bride,' Elvire announced. 'The staff are naturally eager to greet her.'

Samma wondered if she was merely imagining that faintly derisive note in the older girl's voice.

She said quietly, 'I'd prefer to go straight to my room, if you don't mind.'

'Just as you wish, *madame.* I will have Hippolyte bring up your cases.'

Samma found herself mounting the broad sweep of the staircase, with Roche's hand cupped round her arm, which wasn't what she'd intended at all. He didn't have to play the part of the devoted husband in front of Elvire Casson, she thought, fuming. She, of all people, would be bound to know the reality of the situation. She wrenched herself free when they reached the gallery, avoiding the ironic look he sent her.

'The master suite occupies this entire wing of the

house,' he said after a pause. He pointed to a door.
'That is Solange's room.' He stopped in front of the
adjoining door, and flung it open. 'And this is yours.'

It was a beautiful room. Even seething with angry
resentment as she was, Samma could appreciate that.
The carpet was old rose, and the walls were ivory, and
these colours were repeated in the drapes which hung
at the open windows, and festooned the wide Empire-
style bed.

'It's—lovely,' she said stiltedly. 'Thank you.'

One wall was panelled, concealing a comprehensive
range of closets, and a further door led into a small but
luxuriously equipped bathroom. On the far side of the
room was yet another door, and Samma pointed to it.

'What's that?'

Roche opened it, and she peered in. It was another
bedroom even vaster that the one in which they now
stood, its focal point being a magnificent four-poster
bed standing on a dais. The canopy and coverlet were
green and gold, and Samma found herself thinking,
absurdly, that sleeping in that bed would be like lying
in some jungle clearing, with the sun dappling
through tropical leaves.

The master suite, Roche had said. And it didn't
need the casual litter of masculine toiletries on the big
antique dressing-chest to tell her that this was the
master's bedroom.

She stepped backwards hurriedly, aware that she
was flushing slightly, and that he knew it.

'Satisfied, *ma belle?*' There was open mockery in his
voice.

'Not really.' Samma bit her lip. 'There doesn't seem
to be a key. I'd like one—and on my side of the door,
please.'

He was silent for a moment. 'That door has never been locked,' he said. 'I doubt if a key for it even exists.'

She said rather breathlessly, 'Then I'd like one made. I think our—contract entitles me to some privacy.'

'That is something we will discuss later.' He closed the door. 'Now, tidy yourself and come downstairs and meet the staff.'

'Is that—strictly necessary——?'

Roche frowned. 'Of course. In normal circumstances, a Delacroix wedding would be a major event on Grand Cay. Having cheated them of that, the least we can do is drink some champagne with them.'

'I—I'm not really in a celebratory mood.'

'Then pretend.' His smile was brief, and unamused. 'That, too, *chérie*, is part of your contract.'

She watched him stride to the door, and disappear.

She took a deep, unsteady breath as she looked around her. She supposed she should have expected a room that communicated with his, but she hadn't. Belmanoir was turning out to be full of surprises, she thought with irony. And Elvire wasn't the least of them.

She bit her lip. He probably thought a door that locked was an unnecessary refinement, because he knew how little time he'd be spending in that room. He could hardly make love to his mistress in that pagan green and gold bed with his wife within earshot, even if they all knew that the marriage existed only on paper.

She would sleep here in splendid isolation, as no doubt Marie-Christine had done before her.

She was roused from her reverie by the sound of a car approaching up the drive. She went over to the window and stepped out on to the balcony, peering cautiously over the balustrade.

The car, an elderly saloon, had stopped in front of the house, and a woman with chestnut hair climbed out of the driver's seat, and went round to the passenger side. After what could only be a low-voiced argument, the car door opened, and a child emerged, slowly and sullenly.

She was small for her age, Samma thought, and not a particularly attractive little girl, with skinny arms and legs, and dark hair scraped back into two tight and unbecoming braids. And her pugnacious scowl didn't help, either.

Samma watched the pair of them disappear into the house, and drew back with a sigh. It was clear she could expect no welcome from Solange. In fact, she was probably going to have her work cut out, but at least that would prevent her thinking about what Roche and his mistress were doing, each time her back was turned.

She flexed her shoulders wearily. Not that it was any of her business, anyway. To his credit, Roche had made no pretence about that. He had been as frank as he thought necessary about the situation.

As she walked slowly back into the bedroom, there was an impatient rap on the door, and Roche strode in.

'Why do you stay up here?' he demanded. 'Solange has returned, and the household is waiting to welcome you. Elvire has even provided a wedding cake.'

'Then let her eat it herself.' Samma found she was hovering on the edge of a dangerous combination of tears and temper.

His mouth tightened. 'What is that supposed to mean?' he asked with dangerous softness.

Samma studied the potential confrontation, and decided to back down.

'Not a thing,' she said. 'I'm rather tired, and all this pretence is a strain.'

'I have seen very little pretence as yet,' he said coldly. 'At the moment, all I recognise is the insolent brat I met on the quay at Cristoforo.'

'Then maybe you should remember I'm an artist, not an actress,' she flung back at him defiantly.

'In fact, you are my wife,' he said flatly. 'And you will not boycott our wedding reception, whatever your personal inclination.' He held out a hand to her. 'Now, come down and play your part as you agreed, and let there be no more senseless argument.'

'Very well,' Samma said angrily. 'But I don't guarantee the performance.'

He was angry, too, as he said grimly, 'Then perhaps there should be a rehearsal,' and reached for her.

This time, there was no gentleness in him at all. His mouth possessed hers harshly, and without grace. Her body was crushed mercilessly against his. She couldn't breathe. She could barely think.

Some instinct warned that to struggle, to fight, would only make things infinitely worse, so she stayed mute and passive in the punishing circle of his arms until the violent ruthless kiss came to an end at last.

She was very pale, her mouth trembling and swollen from his passion, as she looked up into his dark, relentless face.

'You—you really are a pirate, aren't you?' she managed. 'I bet the original Devil Delacroix couldn't teach you a thing.'

'Then learn not to annoy me,' he returned brusquely. 'I give you five minutes in which to join me in the *salon.*' He paused. 'And you would be wise, *mignonne,* not to make me fetch you a second time. I am sure that everyone has already drawn their own—romantic conclusions about the reason for our delayed appearance.' He flicked a deliberate glance towards the bed. 'Next time, I might justify their suspicions.'

The door slammed behind him. Samma sank down on the dressing-stool, her legs giving way under her. She stared at herself in the mirror with wide, bruised eyes.

She thought, He couldn't—he wouldn't . . . Not when he promised . . .

And paused, shivering. For what did a promise mean to a man who demonstrated quite clearly that he made his own rules?

And was, she realised, as she laid a finger on the tender, blurred contour of her mouth, prepared to enforce them.

CHAPTER FIVE

SHE had expected to find the *salon* full of people but, in fact, Roche was alone there with Solange and her companion.

Samma hesitated in the doorway, aware of the overt hostility in the child's face as her presence was registered.

'Come in, *chérie.*' Roche came swiftly to her side, drawing her forwards into the room. 'Solange, *ma petite,* here is someone I wish you to meet.'

'Papa.' The child's voice was clear, and simmering with resentment. 'Have you truly married this person?'

Samma saw his face darken, and intervened hastily. 'My name is Samantha, but usually my friends call me Samma.'

'I do not wish to be your friend,' Solange flared. 'I do not want you here. But you will not stay. The Delacroix curse will send you away, like all those other silly women.'

'Solange!' Roche's voice was like the crack of a whip. 'You will stop this nonsense at once, do you hear? And you will apologise . . .'

'I will not. It is not nonsense. She will leave. They all do.' She glared at Samma. 'Go, *madame*, while you are still safe.'

Coming from an angry little girl in broad daylight, it should have been ridiculous, yet Samma felt herself shiver involuntarily.

'You are insolent and unkind, *ma fille,*' Roche said

icily. 'If you are not prepared to welcome Samantha, then you may go to your room—and this time remain there.'

Solange looked as if she was on the verge of protest, then thought better of it, and left the *salon*, shutting the door behind her with more than a suspicion of a slam.

Samma realised she had been holding her breath, and released it slowly.

'You must excuse her, Roche.' The other woman, who had been a silent spectator until then, rose from her chair, and came forward. 'It is natural she should find her first meeting with her *belle-mère* a traumatic one.' She smiled pleasantly at Samma. 'Please make allowances for *la petite, madame.*'

'I've been a stepdaughter myself,' Samma said neutrally. 'I know what the problems are.'

'And I have been neglecting my manners,' Roche said, frowning. 'Samantha, may I present Liliane Duvalle, who is our closest neighbour?'

They shook hands. It occurred to Samma that her new acquaintance was slightly older than she'd originally thought, but she was startlingly attractive with her magnolia skin and slanting brown eyes, coupled with an entirely French air of confidence and chic.

'*La petite* is not the only one to have had a shock,' Madame Duvalle was saying with a humorous grimace. 'You kept your marriage plans a great secret, *mon ami.*'

He drawled, 'I feared the gods might become envious and steal her from me, Liliane.'

She laughed. 'A romantic notion! Allow me to welcome you to Grand Cay, *madame*—also a place of romance.'

'If that is how you regard murder, robbery and rape,' Roche agreed levelly. He turned to Samma. 'Liliane is writing a guide to the island, *ma belle*, which naturally includes the history of the Delacroix family.'

Liliane Duvalle smiled. 'Which your husband would prefer forgotten. But that is impossible, *mon ami*. *Le Diable* and his exploits—the tourists find them fascinating.'

'Solange seems to be equally interested,' Samma remarked. 'Not a very savoury subject for a child of her age, I would have thought.' She paused, then said, trying to sound casual, 'What is this curse she mentioned?'

Roche snorted. 'An old and foolish legend. It is said that *Le Diable* was cursed by one of the prisoners he held to ransom. The surprise is that it was only one of them,' he added cynically. 'But, of course, when any tragedy befalls the Delacroix name, it is said immediately to be the family curse.'

'Well, Solange clearly believes in it,' Samma said, half to herself.

Liliane Duvalle shrugged. 'Perhaps—but it is part of her blood—her heritage. It is natural she should be intrigued.' She smiled at Samma. 'They say, too, Madame Delacroix, that the ghost of *Le Diable* walks at Belmanoir.'

'Then they do not say it to me,' Roche said grimly. 'I have no patience with such idiocies.'

Liliane Duvalle heaved a sigh. 'I withdraw my earlier statement, Roche. You are not at all romantic, after all.' She patted his arm. 'And do not frown, *mon vieux*. Remember, this is your honeymoon—and I am intruding,' she added with a pretty *moue*. 'Forgive me. I only wished to see Solange safely home.'

'We are about to have some champagne,' Roche said. 'Won't you stay and drink our health?'

'Not this time.' She smiled at Samma. 'But perhaps in a week or so, you will give me the pleasure of dining with me. In the meantime . . .' She paused.

'Yes?' Samma prompted.

Liliane looked faintly embarrassed. 'I am so fond of *la petite*. Will it be in order for me to continue my visits here? I would not wish to interfere, *naturellement*.'

'Of course.' Samma forced a smile, aware that the idea didn't fill her with total delight. It wouldn't be easy for her to form a relationship with Solange, if the child was constantly being visited by someone she preferred.

'You are too good.' She turned to Roche. 'You have married an angel, *mon ami*. Now, permit me to leave you alone together, as you must wish.'

Samma turned away hurriedly, aware of the amused irony in Roche's glance, as he escorted their visitor from the room.

When he returned, she said, 'This ghost—is this really why the others wouldn't stay?'

'Understand this, *ma belle*,' he said harshly. 'There are no ghosts at Belmanoir. Your predecessors were victims of their own hysterical imaginings, nothing more.'

'And Solange?'

'That is another matter.' He frowned. 'I dislike this preoccupation with the past. I hope you will be able to divert her thoughts into healthier channels, more suitable for her age.'

Outside in the hall, there was the muffled sound of voices, and excited laughter. Roche reached for her hand, drawing it through his arm. 'Now it begins,' he said, half to himself. He glanced down at her. 'Play your part well, *mignonne*.'

But that, Samma thought, as she pinned on an obedient smile, was easier said than done.

Judge Lefèvre was a small, rotund man with shrewd eyes behind gold-rimmed glasses.

He said briskly, 'Be seated, if you please.'

Samma sank into the chair he indicated, aware that her legs were trembling. The awkwardness of the celebration party at Belmanoir was behind her, but this promised to be the greatest ordeal so far.

She felt such a fraud, she thought passionately. Back at the house, they'd all been so welcoming, so delighted to see her, from Roxanne, the fat and smiling cook, to Hippolyte, the gardener-cum-handyman, not to mention the maids, and the casual workers employed in the house and grounds. Their delight in the fact that 'Mist' Roche' had taken a wife, and their robustly expressed good wishes had been embarrassing in the extreme—especially under Elvire's enigmatic regard.

Samma had found herself wondering if the other staff knew what had been going on between their master and his supposed housekeeper, and disapproved.

Her hands clenched together in her lap as Roche took his seat beside her, and his attorney, Maître Jean-Paul Giraud, sat down on her other side.

The lawyer was much younger than she'd expected, loose-limbed, with a smiling, attractive face. When Roche had introduced them, he had kissed her hand with an exaggerated but heart-warming admiration.

'Madame, when Roche informed me he was to be married in such haste, I admit I wondered, but now that I have seen you I understand everything. He is the most fortunate man in the world.'

As she'd walked into the judge's private office, Samma had been blushing, and she'd heard a faint hiss from the other side of the table.

The Augustins were not a prepossessing couple, both plump, with discontented expressions. Their lawyer, Maître Felix, looked irritated and resigned.

Samma hardly heard the opening statements by both attorneys. She was waiting tensely for the announcement of her marriage. When it came, she was still totally unprepared for the sensation it caused.

'*Married?*' Madame Augustin shrilled. 'What lie is this?'

'It is the truth, *madame.*' Maître Felix studied the marriage certificate, then passed it back to Judge Lefèvre. 'A valid ceremony has taken place. Your son-in-law has legally remarried.'

There was a silence, then the woman shrugged a shoulder. 'What difference does it make? Now that he has a new wife, he will simply neglect *la pauvre petite* all the more.'

'*Au contraire,*' Maître Giraud said. 'Madame Delacroix is anxious to care for Solange—to establish a stable home background for the child.'

Madame Augustin gave an incredulous laugh. 'Look at her! She is scarcely more than a child herself.'

Judge Lefèvre gave a slight cough. 'If you will permit me,' he said austerely. He studied Samma unnervingly for a long moment. 'May I ask, *madame,* if you were acquainted with your *belle-fille* before the marriage took place?'

She said huskily, 'No, I—I met her for the first time today.'

'And did it go well—this meeting?'

Samma met his gaze, and realised that he would detect any attempt at a cosy lie. She said, 'Actually, it was pretty much of a disaster.'

'You see!' exclaimed Madame Augustin, and was hushed by her lawyer.

'So,' Judge Lefèvre said slowly, 'there is little chance of any immediate rapport between you?'

'Within the near future, very little.' Samma was aware of Roche's restive, angry movement. 'But we're talking about a lifetime—the building of trust—of a stable relationship.' She took a deep breath. 'Solange, frankly, doesn't want me in her life, or anyone else for that matter, but I intend to be there for her, just the same. She may never accept me, but that's a chance I'm prepared to take. Maybe I'm too young to be a—a conventional mother to her, but I can be her friend, and that's what I'm offering, now and in the future—to be there for her when—if she wants me.' She bit her lip. 'I've been a stepdaughter myself. I don't expect instant miracles.'

'Words.' Madame Augustin dripped contempt into the thoughtful silence which followed Samma's little speech. 'We can offer *la petite* a secure, familiar home.'

'Familiar?' Jean-Paul Giraud queried. He glanced at his papers. 'I understand there was little contact between yourselves and the late Marie-Christine Delacroix.'

'My poor child.' Madame produced a handkerchief. 'Trapped in her tragic marriage to that—monster. Is it any wonder she lived like a recluse?'

Roche's face looked as if it was carved out of stone.

'Control yourself, *madame*.' The judge gave her a grim look.

'How can I?' The woman gave a hysterical laugh. 'This marriage is a trick—a fabrication by this brute—this womaniser.' She turned the venom of her gaze on Samma. 'You may think you have done well for yourself, Madame Delacroix, but you will live to regret this day, as my poor Marie-Christine did. He used my child, and when he no longer wanted her, he cast her aside.'

Maître Felix took her arm, trying to hush her, but she shook him off. 'He killed my girl—he shut her in that terrible house alone—and drove her to her death with his cruelty and neglect. And he will do the same with this new girl, once he has taken what he wants from her. Wife!' She uttered a snort, then burst into loud, dramatic sobs. 'She will soon find out what it means to be Roche Delacroix's wife. Married to the incarnation of *Le Diable!*'

'Babette——' Monsieur Augustin, his face sweating and ashen, tried to calm her, as the two lawyers exchanged discreetly appalled glances.

Above the tumult, Judge Lefèvre made himself heard. 'There will be silence.'

Amazingly, there was. Then he spoke again slowly, his eyes fixed meditatively on Samma. 'I am not convinced the interests of the child Solange Delacroix would be best served at this juncture by placing her in the custody of her grandparents. Therefore, I shall adjourn this matter, *sine die.*' He removed his glasses, and inclined his head courteously. 'I wish you good fortune, Madame Delacroix.'

And I'm going to need every scrap of it, thought Samma as Roche's hand closed with disconcerting firmness round her own, and he led her from the room.

'You are very pale, *madame.*' Jean-Paul's voice was

sharp with concern. 'May I fetch you something—some coffee, perhaps?'

'Thank you.' Samma found herself in a kind of
waiting-room, furnished with easy chairs, and sank
into one of them gratefully. She accepted the coffee
Jean-Paul brought her, then looked up at Roche. 'I
don't understand. Did we win?'

'You could say so,' Roche acknowledged. 'Judge
Lefèvre has postponed any further hearing
indefinitely. The Augustins will have to think
carefully before taking any further action.'

'And they will have to find a new lawyer to
represent them.' Jean-Paul put in. '*Dieu*, but that
woman is poison!'

'The man is no better, believe me,' Roche told him
grimly. 'What do you imagine their next move will
be?'

Jean-Paul shrugged. 'To return to France. Maître
Felix intends personally to put them on the next plane
out of here.'

'I can only hope they never return,' Roche said with
disgust.

Jean-Paul smiled at Samma. 'Judge Lefèvre
preferred your honesty to their malice, *madame*. My
felicitations.'

She bit her lip. 'I wondered if I'd been a little too
honest.' She caught Roche's ironic look, and flung up
her head defiantly. 'But there have been too many lies,
too much pretence already.'

Jean-Paul kissed her hand. 'Your husband is a
fortunate man,' he told her. 'I am sorry that these
Augustins should have clouded your wedding day.'
He clapped Roche on the shoulder, with a grin. 'But
nothing will be allowed to spoil the night to follow,
eh, *mon vieux?*'

Samma swallowed the rest of her cooling coffee with something of a gulp.

The square outside the town hall was crowded when they emerged. Strolling pedestrians spilled on to the road, jostling for position with cyclists and elderly taxis brightly painted in a variety of bizarre colours.

'Will you wait here while I fetch the car?' Roche asked, and she nodded.

'Have I got time to do some shopping?'

He frowned slightly. 'Did we forget something earlier?'

'No,' she said. 'It's just an idea I've had.'

She found what she was looking for in a toyshop in a quiet side street. It was a doll with long blonde hair, limbs that moved, and clothes which could be removed for laundering, and almost identical to one Samma had possessed herself at Solange's age.

Roche's brows rose sardonically when he saw her purchase. 'I thought you did not believe in instant miracles, *ma belle.*'

'I don't. This is—an olive branch.' She paused. 'I suppose Solange does play with dolls?'

Roche shrugged, starting the car. 'You had better ask Elvire.'

All hell will freeze first, she told herself silently. She said, 'She's your daughter. Don't you know?'

'I thought I had made it clear how little time I have been able to spend with her,' he said coldly. 'That, *ma chère*, is why you are here, after all.'

And there was no comeback to that, she thought despondently. In future, she would remember her place.

And, just in case there was any danger of her forgetting, the first person she met as she walked into the house was Elvire, descending the stairs.

She paused in evident surprise. 'The hearing is over already?'

'*Mais oui*, and it has gone in our favour—for the time being,' Roche said.

'I am so happy for you, and for *la petite*.' She bestowed a polite smile on Samma. 'And for you too, of course, Madame Delacroix.'

Samma said with a faint snap, 'Would you mind not calling me that, please?'

Elvire's brows lifted. 'There is some other form of address you would prefer?'

Samma was tempted to say, Why don't you call me by my given name—as you do my husband? But she knew the answer to that already.

She said, 'I'll try and think of something,' and turned towards the stairs, the box containing the doll tucked under her arm.

Half-way up the flight, Roche caught up with her, gripping her arm with fingers that bruised.

He said quietly, 'You were less than polite to Elvire. May I remind you that she has been the mainstay of this household for some time.'

'There's no need.' Samma wrenched herself free. 'She's exactly the image of what a mainstay should be.'

The dark eyes narrowed. 'What does that mean?'

'Nothing at all.' Samma ran her fingers along the gleaming polish of the banister rail. 'She's—obviously very efficient,' she added lamely. She tried an awkward smile. 'I just expect—housekeepers to be older, handing out hot broth, and homespun advice. That kind of thing.'

He looked at her for a long, edged moment, then turned away with a faint shrug. 'I will see you at dinner.'

'May Solange join us?'

He glanced back, clearly surprised. 'If you can persuade her.' His tone doubted it, and Samma's spine stiffened in determination.

Solange's room was dim and shuttered, but the small mound in the bed wriggled as Samma entered.

She said cheerfully, 'I'm glad you're not asleep,' and threw back the shutters, letting the afternoon sun pour in.

The face which regarded her over the top of the sheet was still mutinous, but also distinctly woebegone.

'What do you want?' was the uncompromising question.

Samma sat down on the edge of the bed. 'To talk. To explain why we should at least try and get along together for your Papa's sake.'

'Why should we?'

Samma shrugged. 'Because men get very bored and cross when their womenfolk are always bickering,' she returned. 'You don't want Papa to get annoyed with us.'

Solange considered this for a moment. She said dubiously, 'When Maman was alive, Papa lived at the casino.'

'Well, we don't want that to happen again.'

There was a long pause, then Solange nodded slowly and reluctantly. She said, 'But I won't call you Maman.'

'I don't expect you to.' Samma kept her voice matter-of-fact, avoiding even the slightest taint of triumph. It was, after all, a very small victory. She put the doll on the bed between them. 'I brought you this.'

'Why?'

Again Samma decided nothing but the truth would do. 'As a bribe,' she said.

Solange stared at her. 'You mean—so that I will behave well?' At Samma's nod, she looked down at the doll, touching the fair hair, and the lace-edged skirts. She said, half to herself, 'I had a doll once, and when we came here, Maman said there was no room in the case.' She gave Samma a fierce look. 'But I make no promises, *madame.*'

'Nor do I—and my name is Samma.' She paused. 'Also, Roxanne tells me it's your favourite, chicken Creole, for dinner tonight.'

Solange's lower lip jutted woefully. 'Papa said I had to stay here.'

'I think you'll find Papa has changed his mind,' Samma told her gently, getting to her feet.

As she reached the door, she heard Solange say, 'But you will not stay here. When the curse begins to work on you, you will be glad to leave.'

Samma forced a smile. 'Perhaps I'm not that easily frightened,' she said lightly, and went back to her own room.

It was a delicious dinner, but it was not the easiest meal Samma had ever sat through. Solange had come downstairs, bringing her doll with her, which was a small step in the right direction.

The little girl was wearing a brown dress with a crocheted collar, which had a distinctly old-fashioned look. Roche should apply some of his acumen about women's clothing to his daughter's appearance, Samma thought. Beginning with those awful braids.

It was clear that Solange was carefully on her best behaviour. In fact, Samma thought ruefully, they were all trying rather too hard. And Elvire's presence, supervising the meal, didn't help.

If I wasn't here, Samma thought, she would probably be sitting in my place, smiling at Roche across the table, letting him refill her glass with wine.

Whereas, because of me, she's now some kind of second-class citizen. I bet she hates my guts. Because she must have hoped that Roche would marry her one day.

But there was no clue to any inner emotional turmoil in the beautiful, serene face as Elvire moved about the table.

Coffee was served in the *salon*. Samma had been too fraught earlier to fully appreciate her surroundings, but now she felt free to wander round the large room, examining the pictures—none of *Le Diable* as far as she could see—as well as the cabinets with their collections of porcelain, antique fans and *étuis*.

It was all very gracious and elegant—and founded on blood and plunder, she thought with a faint sigh as she sank down on one of the soft and massive leather sofas which flanked the hearth.

'May I have some coffee, Papa? May I?' Solange appealed, as Elvire brought in the tray, and Roche smiled faintly.

'Well, perhaps, as this is a special occasion.' His eyes met Samma's almost caressingly, and she looked away, blushing.

Life would be easier to cope with when these first, loaded days were over, and they were no longer forced to behave like conventional newly-weds, she thought uncomfortably. At the reception that morning, she'd had to stand in the circle of his arm, smiling radiantly, even lifting her face for his kiss when the toast to their happiness was drunk, and she'd felt a total hypocrite.

Roche brought her some cognac in a balloon glass. 'For enjoyment rather than medicine this time,' he told her in an undertone.

'Have you seen my doll, Papa?' Solange broke in impatiently. 'See, I can brush its hair, and it has petticoats with real lace.'

'*Très belle,*' Roche agreed gravely, sitting down beside her to admire the toy's manifold perfections.

Watching them covertly, Samma saw Solange glow perceptibly as he talked to her. He was kind, she thought, but aloof. He showed the child little open affection, and Solange seemed to accept this, not climbing on his knee, or throwing her arms around him, as anyone might have expected.

There was a soft cough, and Samma saw that Elvire had rejoined them.

'It is time Solange was in bed.' She held out a hand. 'Come, *p'tite*. I have run your bath.'

'Must I go, Papa?' Solange looked prepared to pout, then thought better of it, putting her hand into Elvire's, her doll securely tucked under her other arm.

Elvire paused. 'Will there be anything else this evening, Roche? If not, I will bid you goodnight.'

Samma stared rigidly at the floor. Who was supposed to be kidding whom? she wondered angrily.

'Thank you, Elvire. There is nothing more we require.' Roche sounded casual. '*Bonne nuit.*'

'*Bonne nuit,* Papa. Sleep well,' Solange piped, and Samma heard Elvire giggle softly as they left the room.

'Another cognac?' Roche asked.

She shook her head. She said, 'Roche—would you mind if I had Solange's hair cut?'

He burst out laughing. 'Hardly a romantic topic for our wedding night, *mignonne,* but, of course, you must do as you think best. Solange is your responsibility now.'

She said stiltedly, 'I suppose so.' She glanced at her

watch. 'I—I think I might have an early night.'

'An excellent idea, *ma belle.*' There was a note of amusement in his smooth voice, and something else—not so easily deciphered and far more disturbing. 'I was about to suggest it myself.'

Her heart began to thud, painfully and unevenly. She stole a nervous glance at him. 'Yes—well . . .' She rose, putting down her empty glass. 'If you'll—excuse me . . .'

Roche said softly, 'Not so fast.' He walked over to her, resting his hands lightly on her shoulders. The dark eyes glinted down at her. 'Are you so eager to run away from me? What refuge are you seeking, I wonder? This is, after all, my house. And you are my wife.'

She tried to pull away, but his grasp tightened. 'But I'm not your wife—not really. This isn't a proper marriage. You—you said that yourself—just an arrangement—you know you did.' She was gabbling, and she knew it.

He said, 'Ah, but that was before I was sure of you.' He lifted the hand which wore his ring. 'Now, you belong to me, *ma belle.*'

She snatched her hand away. She said breathlessly, 'You bought a year—not my whole life. Now, let me go.'

For a moment, she felt as if she was balanced on some kind of a knife-edge, then Roche released her, stepping backwards with a small, ironic bow.

She knew he was watching her as she walked to the door, and she was terrified of making a fool of herself—stumbling over her feet, perhaps, or betraying her inner strain in some other blatant way.

She didn't relax until she was in her bedroom, with the door closed behind her.

She said, aloud, 'I'm safe now.' Then repeated, 'Safe,' and wished, almost desperately, that she could believe it.

CHAPTER SIX

ALL desire for sleep seemed to have left Samma, although the bed had been turned down invitingly, she saw, and one of her new broderie anglaise nightgowns fanned out on the coverlet. And before dinner she'd found all her new clothes unpacked and neatly put away in the closets.

Elvire might only be playing at being Roche's housekeeper, as she herself was pretending to be his wife, but it was impossible to fault the way the other girl carried out her duties, Samma thought grudgingly.

She took a leisurely shower, put on her nightdress, and sat down at the dressing-table to give her hair its nightly brushing, tensing as she wondered if she could hear the sound of movement from the adjoining room.

She picked up her brush, grimacing. She would have to get used to this unaccustomed proximity, or she would end up a nervous wreck. It was his room, after all, and he was entitled to use it—or find more congenial surroundings as the mood took him, she told herself, as she began to tug the brush through her hair.

And stopped, her attention totally arrested by the noiseless opening of the communicating door.

Roche walked into the room. His hair was damp, as if he too had been in the shower, and he was wearing a dark blue silk robe, and nothing else, as far as she could gather.

She dropped her brush with a clatter. 'What are you

doing here? What do you want?'

He said quite gently, 'You are not a child or a fool, *ma belle*. I made my intentions clear downstairs.'

'But you promised you'd leave me alone—you said . . .'

'We seem to have said a great deal in our short acquaintance, and little of it makes any sense at all.' He came to her side, and lifted her bodily off the stool and into his arms in one smooth, co-ordinated movement. His voice was almost rough. 'I spent my first wedding night alone, Samantha. That is not going to happen a second time, whether you wish it or not.'

He carried her into his room without haste, and put her down beside the enormous bed. He looked at her for a long, measuring moment, then slid a finger under the narrow ribbon strap of her demure nightdress. 'Did you buy this today?'

Mutely, she nodded.

He said with a ghost of laughter in his voice, 'Then it would be a pity to tear it. Take it off, *chérie*.'

'No.' Her voice was scarcely more than a breath. 'I—I couldn't—please . . .'

'So modest?' he asked softly. 'Is it only beside swimming pools in the moonlight that you discard your inhibitions along with your clothes, my little nymph?'

'What—what do you mean?' Samma faltered, her heart doing a frantic somersault.

'I think you know.' Roche's eyes never left hers, and his thumb drew small circles on the bare flesh of her shoulder. 'Did you really think you were alone that night on Cristoforo?'

Samma gasped, colour flooding her face, as she remembered that sudden, unnerving conviction that she was being watched as she swam. 'You mean you were—spying on me?' she choked. 'Oh, you're vile . . .'

'You'd have preferred me to declare my presence—join you, perhaps?' His white teeth flashed in a wicked grin. 'I don't think so. I thought it showed considerable delicacy to remain in the background, *ma belle*, and make sure there were no other intruders.'

'You think that justifies you being a—a voyeur?' Samma pushed his caressing hand away. 'You're despicable!'

'But seeing you naked in the moonlight persuaded me to overlook your temper, my little shrew, and take you with me when I left Cristoforo.' He was openly laughing at her, she realised furiously. 'I restrained myself that night—and since—with true chivalry. But now, I want to touch—and kiss, as well as look.' His voice dropped sensuously.

'And what I want, of course, is immaterial,' Samma flung at him bitterly.

'*Au contraire,*' he said ironically. 'But I think you have needs you are not yet even aware of, my innocent wife.' His eyes moved to the hurried rise and fall of her breasts beneath their fragile cotton veiling. 'And it would be cruelty to us both to leave you in ignorance any longer,' he murmured, and held out his arms to her. 'Don't fight me any more, *mignonne.*'

His smile beckoned her, the dark gaze warm and infinitely seductive. Samma was trembling suddenly, but not only from fright. She was being besieged, she realised, by a welter of very different emotions.

She was remembering—unwillingly, vividly—the way he'd kissed her that first time on *Allegra*—wondering how it would be if he kissed her like that again . . .

With something like panic, she pulled herself together. 'You seem to be forgetting something.' Her voice sounded high, and very young. 'Your—your mistress. Won't she be expecting you? She can't feel very happy about the situation as it is . . .'

For a moment he looked almost startled, then his expression relaxed. 'Oh, she will adapt to the change in circumstances,' he drawled. 'In fact, she has no choice.'

Samma felt almost sorry for Elvire, dismissed so casually. But Roche's words reminded her just in time that her own fate would be no different when her year in Grand Cay was over. He would let her go as easily, with as few regrets, she realised, wincing. But, if she was completely his, could she just walk away when he'd finished with her?

She said shakily, 'Well, I do have a choice, and I still say—no. I'm not just a convenient female body for you to—use when it suits you, then discard. I belong to myself. And if you—if you persist in this—I shall fight you—every step of the way,' she ended with a little rush.

'Will you, *chérie?*' His mouth twisted. 'Eh bien, we shall see . . .'

His hands reached for her. But before her lips had even parted, she heard the scream in her head—high, shrill, utterly terrified—going on and on endlessly.

Yet she wasn't making a sound, she realised, and at the same time she saw Roche's face change from half-amused, half-sensual anticipation to shocked concern.

'Mon Dieu,' he whispered. 'Solange!'

Samma was right behind him as he threw open the child's door, and raced in.

Solange was sitting up in bed, her eyes staring, the screams dying to small, sobbing moans when she saw her father.

'Papa, oh, Papa! I saw *Le Diable*. He was here in this room.'

'*P'tite.*' Roche's voice was gentle, as he sat down on the bed beside her. 'That is impossible. You had a dream, that's all. A bad dream. Now, lie down . . .'

'Don't leave me.' The small hands clutched at the lapels of his robe. 'Oh, Papa, please . . .'

Samma saw him hesitate, and intervened. 'I'll stay with her—if she'll let me. After all, I'm responsible for her now.'

'No.' There was a grim weariness in Roche's voice. 'I will remain.'

He rose and fetched a chair from the corner of the room, placing it beside Solange's bed.

His eyes met Samma's. 'Go, *ma belle*;' he said with dangerous softness. 'And say a thanksgiving to whatever god you believe in, because I would not have spared you, believe me.' He added, flatly, 'There must be more of *Le Diable* in me than I thought.'

Samma stared at him wordlessly, then turned and fled back to the fragile security of her room, where she flung herself across the bed, shaking like a leaf.

Because of Solange's nightmare she had been reprieved, it seemed, at least for the time being.

And the shaming truth she had to face was that she didn't know whether to be glad—or sorry.

When Samma awoke slowly and reluctantly the next day, the sunlight was flooding into her room and, sitting in a patch of it, cross-legged on the floor, was Solange, staring at her unblinkingly.

Samma propped herself up on an elbow. 'Good morning,' she said awkwardly. 'Are—are you feeling better today?'

Solange hunched a shoulder. 'I was not ill,' she retorted. She gave Samma a speculative look. 'If you are married to Papa, why don't you sleep in his bed, in there?' She pointed to the adjoining room. 'Lisette Varray says married people sleep in the same bed, so they can cuddle and make babies.'

Samma was crossly aware of that betraying blush again. 'Well—perhaps. But last night, Papa had to look after you.'

'Not all night,' Solange denied with a shake of her head. 'When he thought I was asleep, he went away.'

'Oh.' There was a sudden hollow feeling in the pit of Samma's stomach as she registered this. So he had gone to Elvire after all, she thought. And she had no one but herself to blame, because she'd sent him there. He must have cynically decided she was not worth the fight she had promised him, and settled for what was readily available instead. She swallowed past the swift, painful lump in her throat and said, 'Do you often have bad dreams?'

Solange paused, as if weighing up the question, then she said, 'I was not dreaming. *Le Diable* was there. He came to warn you to leave Belmanoir, *madame.*'

'Oh, really?' Samma asked levelly. 'Then why didn't he come to me in person?'

Solange's expression went suddenly blank, as if this was a point of view which had not previously occurred to her.

Watching her, Samma felt an unworthy suspicion budding and coming to bloom inside her.

'What did he look like?' she asked.

Solange shrugged. 'Like a pirate,' she returned sullenly. She paused. 'And he frowned and shook his fist a lot.'

Samma stifled an unwilling grin. 'I'm not surprised. It must be very boring for him to have to tramp round this house for all these centuries, warning people about the curse.'

'It is not a joke,' Solange flared.

'I quite agree,' Samma nodded. 'And I don't suppose any of your previous companions found it very funny, either,' she added casually, looking Solange straight in the eye.

'Naturally, they were very afraid.' Solange gave a dramatic shudder. 'Who would not be?'

'Who, indeed?' Samma agreed. 'Did you have similar dreams before they left?'

Solange's gaze fell away. 'I think so.'

And I'm sure of it, Samma told herself silently. Aloud, she said, 'This is a lovely room. Did your mother like it, too?'

'She did not sleep here,' Solange said. 'She had a suite at the other end of the house. But all the rooms are pretty. Grandmère Delacroix chose all the new things in the house. She could not walk after her accident, and Papa said it gave her a new interest in life.'

Samma's brows lifted. 'What happened to your grandmother?'

'She fell off her horse,' Solange said calmly. 'It was the curse. And when Maman died, that was the curse, too.'

Samma frowned incredulously. 'Who in the world has been telling you these things?' she demanded.

Solange looked evasive. '*Tout le monde.* Everyone knows it.' She got up. 'I think I will go downstairs. Shall I tell Elvire to bring your breakfast here?'

'No, thank you,' Samma said hastily. The last person in the world she wanted to face, under the present circumstances, was Elvire, no doubt discreetly revelling in the fact that her lover still wanted her, in spite of his marriage. She tore her thoughts away from the unwelcome images beginning to form in her mind. 'Are you going to school today?'

Solange shrugged ungraciously. 'I wanted to, but Elvire said I had to stay here with you, instead.'

Samma bit her lip. Gee, thanks, Elvire, she thought. Trying to sound cheerful, she said, 'Well, you can show me over the rest of the house—and the gardens. Is there a swimming pool?'

'A big one.'

'Can you swim?'

'No.' Solange glared at her. 'And you will not make me.'

'God forbid!' Samma threw up her hands ironically. 'You don't mind if I use the pool, I hope.'

Solange shrugged again. 'It is your pool,' she returned reluctantly. 'Elvire says everything in Belmanoir belongs to you now.'

No, Samma thought with a sudden unbidden pang—not everything.

She bathed, and put on the simple dark blue *maillot* she had chosen in preference to the minimal bikinis on offer in the boutiques, topping it with a loose shift in a swirling jungle print. She collected her sketching things, and sun oil, before making her way downstairs.

She was frankly nervous about encountering Roche, or Elvire, unable to decide how she should react. But the decision was postponed, when she found no one about but one of the maids, who told her cheerfully that 'Mist' Roche' had gone into St Laurent to the casino, just like always.

Business as usual, Samma thought, and something

she would have to get used to. Roche had warned her
he spent little time at home. She stifled the troubling
twinge of regret which assailed her. After all, the last
thing in the world she wanted was Roche's
company—wasn't it?

The pool lay at the rear of the house, masked by
high, flowering hedges. To Samma's surprise,
Solange was there ahead of her, sitting on one of the
cushioned loungers, undressing her doll. Her face
intent, she made a delightful picture. Samma sat down
quietly, and opened her sketching block.

'What are you doing?' Solange demanded
eventually and suspiciously.

'Drawing your portrait.' As Solange came to her
side, Samma demonstrated. 'See, I put a line
here—and a curve here, and some shading—and, *voilà*,
we have Solange.'

'It is like me.' Solange gave an endearing hop of
excitement. 'And yet it is not. The hair is wrong,' she
added, pointing to the feathery bob and softly flicked
fringe which Samma had created.

'Not wrong, just different.' Samma touched one of
the braids. 'Have you never thought of changing your
style?'

'Maman wanted my hair like this. She said it was
suitable.'

Samma trod carefully. 'Well, I'm sure it was—then.
But you're so much more grown-up now. You can't
have pigtails for ever.'

Solange stared down at the sketch, her brows drawn
together, then jumped as a smiling voice called out,
'Bonjour.'

'It is Tante Liliane,' Solange announced, and ran to
the new arrival.

Samma's own feelings were mixed. She had agreed

to this, she told herself, but she hadn't expected Madame Duvalle to put in an appearance quite so soon. She fastened on a polite smile.

'But where is Roche?' Madame Duvalle enquired, as she sank into the chair next to Samma's, under the multi-coloured sunshade. She sent Samma an engaging smile. 'Surely he cannot be neglecting you already?'

Samma bit her lip. 'Neglecting' had too many connotations of Madame Augustin, she thought with distaste.

She said evenly, 'He has businesses to run.'

'And very successfully too,' Liliane said gushingly. 'Grand Cay is becoming quite a mecca for wealthy tourists, and Roche has been the moving force behind much of the island's development.'

'Were you born here?' Samma asked.

'*Hélas*, no. But my husband and I visited here many times. My happy memories brought me back here.' Madame Duvalle gave a faint sigh. 'It was François who inspired my interest in the island's history to begin with.'

Samma wondered whether the older woman was widowed, or simply divorced, but did not feel equal to enquiring.

'And Roche has always been so kind,' Liliane continued. 'He has rented me the former overseer's house at the plantation at a nominal sum.' She smiled. 'He may not agree with my researches, but he allows me every facility to proceed with them.'

'Is the plantation still in operation?' Samma asked, and Liliane shot her a surprised look.

'*Mais oui*, although it is run as a co-operative these days, and not controlled solely by the Delacroix family.' Her laugh tinkled. 'Has Roche not discussed the extent of his business interests with you? But how wicked, in these days of equality!'

'There hasn't really been time,' Samma said evasively.

'A whirlwind romance, *hein*? And just when one thought he would never . . .' Liliane paused, then shrugged, turning her attention to Solange, much to Samma's relief. 'You look a little pale this morning, *mon trésor.*'

'A disturbed night,' Samma put in neutrally.

Liliane compressed her lips. 'Not another nightmare—just when we hoped she had begun to forget.'

'Solange,' Samma said quietly, 'would you go up to the house and ask Elvire to bring us some coffee, *s'il te plaît?*'

Solange hesitated, then took herself off, dragging her feet.

'She is not an easy child to manage. You seem to have made a good beginning,' Liliane commented, leaning back in her chair.

'Maybe,' Samma said non-committally. She hesitated. 'If there's some cause for Solange's nightmares, it might be better if we didn't refer to it in front of her. She seems to listen to far too much round here as it is.'

'But of course you are right.' Liliane looked distressed. '*Mon Dieu*, but I am criminally thoughtless!'

'On the other hand,' Samma went on. 'If there's something I should know . . .' She paused enquiringly.

'You mean Roche has not told you—warned you? *Mais, c'est impossible, ça!*' Liliane looked aghast. 'And yet, can one blame him for wishing to bury the past?

The gossip and rumours were, after all, *formidable.*'

'Gossip?' Samma frowned.

Liliane looked at her sympathetically. 'About Marie-Christine—her death.'

'What about it?'

Liliane shrugged. 'There was an accident. Her car ran off the road, and into a ravine. She was killed instantly.'

'That's awful,' Samma said slowly. 'But why should anyone gossip about it?'

Liliane spread out her hands. 'Because it was said that the verdict was a cover-up—that Marie-Christine had in fact killed herself—crashed the car deliberately. It was known, you see, that the marriage was not a success—that they lived separately. She made emotional scenes—wild claims that the house hated her. That she would die if she had to live here alone.' She paused. 'That was when Elvire came. She was, you may know, a trained nurse, experienced in such cases.'

'No,' Samma said numbly, 'I—I didn't know.' She bit her lip. 'I still don't really understand. Was it just the house . . .?'

Liliane shook her head. 'I do not like to speak of it. I tried, you see, to be Marie-Christine's friend. In many ways I pitied her—loving Roche so much—receiving only coldness and rejection in return.' She sighed. 'It was a tragic situation. No wonder, *la pauvre,* that she turned to alcohol for consolation.'

'I—see.' Samma touched the tip of her tongue to suddenly dry lips. 'Had she been drinking when—when . . .'

'It seems so. This is when the talk began because she was not, *naturellement,* allowed the use of a car, or even to leave Belmanoir alone. Yet somehow she obtained the keys and set off. Also, no one could understand where she got her supplies of vodka. She was strictly forbidden alcohol of any kind, and Mademoiselle Casson watched her constantly. A servant, I believe, was dismissed, although nothing was proved. Yet still she continued to drink—in the end, fatally.' Liliane paused. 'The effect on the child can, of course, be imagined.'

'Of course,' Samma echoed dazedly, then straightened, as she heard the sound of voices approaching. The coffee, it seemed, was arriving.

'Elvire,' Solange pounced at the table, 'Madame has drawn this picture of me. It is good, *hein*?'

'Excellent.' Elvire arranged the coffee things with minute care, having greeted Liliane Duvalle with politeness rather than warmth. 'Madame has many talents, that is clear.' She gave Samma a bland look. 'Will Roche be returning for lunch?'

'I'm not quite sure.' Samma's hands gripped together in her lap, out of sight under the table. She thought savagely—Why didn't you ask him yourself, when he climbed out of your bed this morning?

'And that is not all.' Solange snatched up her doll. 'See, Tante Liliane?'

'But how charming.' Liliane Duvalle studied the doll with interest. 'And how clever of your *belle-mère* to find you a doll that looks like herself. You see the hair—and the colour of the eyes?'

With a sinking heart, Samma saw the animation fade from Solange's expression, as if a new and unpleasant thought had come to her.

'I—suppose,' the little girl said at last, colourlessly, and made no attempt to reclaim her toy. It was obvious that a chance resemblance, which had escaped Samma completely, had spoiled the gift for her.

And put me back at square one, Samma thought, sighing inwardly as she poured the coffee.

Liliane, aware she'd been tactless, hurried into speech. 'So you are also an artist. Do you accept commissions?'

'Not exactly,' Samma said warily.

'You should paint Elvire. She is like the portraits of the ladies in the house, only more beautiful,' Solange put in unexpectedly.

Samma felt a dismayed flush rise in her face, and saw it echoed, to her surprise, in Elvire's own heightened colour.

Elvire said sharply, 'That is nonsense, Solange,' and walked away, back to the house.

So she can actually be embarrassed, Samma thought. Amazing!

But at least she knew now how Roche and his mistress had met. She'd come to Belmanoir to act as watchdog for his alcoholic wife. Samma wondered with a pang if the *affaire* had begun while Marie-Christine was still alive, and whether the knowledge of it had driven her towards the final tragedy. The thought made her shiver.

Conversation over coffee proved desultory, and Samma wasn't sorry when Liliane Duvalle excused herself afterwards, on the grounds that she had work to do.

'My little book, which Roche hates so much,' she said with a little laugh. 'Perhaps you would care to read some time what I have completed so far—learn a little about the past of this family that has become your own.'

'Thank you,' Samma said politely. But she knew she wouldn't be taking Madame Duvalle up on her offer. I'm not a Delacroix, and I never will be, she thought. I'm just an imposter here. Another unwanted wife.

And definitely an unwanted stepmother. Samma was aware of Solange watching her, with a kind of quietly hostile speculation. And she made no attempt to touch her doll, lying half dressed and face-down beside the lounger.

She sighed inwardly. She couldn't blame Solange for being so prickly. She'd had a raw deal out of life, so far. A father who virtually ignored her, and a mother who drank. No wonder she'd lashed out at all well-meaning attempts to provide her with companionship. And, each time she'd succeeded in driving one of her companions away, it must have reinforced her doubts about her own lovableness, Samma thought with a swift ache of her heart. Whatever pranks she'd played must have been some kind of test, which no one had ever passed. Or not until now.

She longed to put her arms round Solange, and reassure her in some way, but she knew it was too soon, that they might never, in the year she'd been allowed, achieve such terms of intimacy. The person best able to help Solange was her father, she thought restlessly, but was he prepared to do it? Or was Solange, perhaps, an all too potent reminder of the wife he'd hated?

Samma shivered. Because suddenly, frighteningly, she understood only too well the desperation which must have driven Marie-Christine when she finally realised Roche would never be hers. Perhaps, to her fuddled mind, life without him would have seemed just another form of eternal darkness.

Oh, God—that's how I could feel—only too easily, she thought. And knew with a pain too deep for words that it was already too late.

CHAPTER SEVEN

SAMMA hauled herself out of the pool, and reached for a towel, blotting the water from her shoulders and arms, and wringing the excess moisture from her hair.

Her swim had refreshed her physically, but not mentally. She was still reeling from the implications of that unheralded, unwanted self-revelation.

She couldn't have fallen in love with Roche Delacroix! Common sense, logic and even decency all legislated against it. She knew so terrifyingly little about him, she thought. The only certainty was that he was quite cynically prepared to exploit her for his own purposes, and made no bones about doing so.

But as a man, and certainly as her husband, he remained an enigma.

She sighed as she walked back to the table. It was proving to be a long and disturbing day, and, as an exercise in togetherness for Solange and herself, it had to be marked down as a dismal failure. The child had barely addressed a remark to her over the delicious fruit-filled salad they had shared for lunch, or afterwards.

Now she was sitting, staring down at her portrait-sketch, her brows drawn together.

'Do you like drawing?' Samma prepared herself for another monosyllabic answer.

'I do not make very good pictures.' Solange hesitated, then pushed the sketching-block towards Samma. 'Draw Papa.'

'I already did,' Samma said wryly. 'And it wasn't a

great success.'

'Well, draw Tante Liliane.'

Well, it was something, Samma thought, as she tried to comply, but even after several attempts Madame Duvalle's likeness failed to transpire. As she scrunched up yet another page, a shadow fell across her.

Roche said, 'Employing your dubious talents, *ma belle?*'

Samma looked up with a startled, indrawn breath, aware her skin was tingling suddenly at his proximity. She said inanely, 'I—I wasn't expecting to see you.'

'*Evidemment,*' he agreed drily, his brows lifting slightly as he regarded her. 'Yet, here I am.'

'Papa!' Solange ran to him. 'Look—Madame has done a picture of me. I look very different, *hein?*'

'Very different indeed, *petite.*' Roche's face softened as he looked down at her. He tweaked one of her braids. 'Perhaps it is time we carried the difference into real life. Go up to the house, and Elvire will take you to the hairdresser in St Laurent.'

'Oh!' Solange digested this. 'And may I have my hair cut to look like this?' She held up the sketch.

He smiled. 'Take your portrait with you, *chérie,* so that you can show the *coiffeuse* exactly what you want.'

Solange needed no further bidding, her thin legs galvanised into a sprint as she made off, shouting excitedly for Elvire.

Samma pushed the sketching-block away, aware that her hands were shaking. It was just shock, she told herself defensively. She'd expected him to be away all day, and yet here he was in the early afternoon, and, judging by the fact that he was wearing only brief swimming trunks, and carrying a towel

slung over one bronzed shoulder, with every intention
of remaining.

She hurried into speech. 'Thank you for
remembering about her hair. You—you didn't waste
any time.'

He gave her a level look. 'You don't think so? Yet at
times, I think I have wasted a great deal.'

She wasn't sure what he meant, but she wasn't
going to hang around and find out, she thought
confusedly. She said, 'Well, if Solange is going to St
Laurent, I may as well go, too.'

'No.' Roche was smiling, but his tone was definite.
'I prefer, *ma femme,* that you stay here with me. I did
not complete my morning's work in record time in
order to spend the rest of the day alone.' His mouth
twisted. 'Everyone was most co-operative when I
explained I was on honeymoon.'

'But you aren't—we're not.' She took a deep breath.
'You seem to have forgotten—last night.'

'Not at all,' he said calmly. 'As you see, this time I
have ensured we will not be interrupted.'

But that wasn't what she'd meant at all, she thought
swallowing. She said breathlessly, 'I—I think I'll go
for a swim.'

'You have been for one.' He reached out, and coiled
a tendril of damp blonde hair round an exploring
finger. His other hand slid down over her shoulder.
'Now, you should sunbathe a little. With me.'

As if she was in a dream, Samma watched him
remove the long, padded cushions from the loungers,
and arrange them deftly on the tiled floor.

Then he held out a hand to her. *'Alors, ma belle.'* He
was still smiling, but there was a purpose in his face
which would not be denied.

Still in that dream, Samma felt her hand taken,

herself drawn down beside him on to the softness of
the cushions, while a voice in her head whispered, this
can't be happening—it can't . . .

Yet it was. She lay in the circle of his arms, her body
taut, the long sweep of her lashes veiling her eyes in
what, it seemed, would soon be the only defence left
to her. And felt, with a shock that pierced her inmost
being, the first slow brush of his lips on her skin.

He was gentle, almost tender, his mouth making
few demands as he explored the planes and contours
of her face and throat with a slow, lingering pleasure
he made no attempt to disguise.

Gradually, almost in spite of herself, Samma began
to relax. The heat of the sun pouring down on them
was nothing compared with the sweet, insidious
warmth inside her which his caresses were
engendering, as his lean, supple fingers soothed her,
stroking lazily over her shoulders and back.

He drew her closer still, taking her hands and
placing them on his bare chest, letting her feel
through her fingertips the hard, steady beat of his
heart.

He said softly, 'You think our marriage is not real,
mignonne. Well, I am real. And—so is this . . .'

His mouth took hers with breathtaking emphasis.
Samma's lips parted, half in surprise, half in
involuntary response to the frank sensuality of this
new invasion. Her hands stole shyly round his neck to
tangle in his dark hair and hold him closer, while his
own arms tightened round her in fierce reply.

That first time on *Allegra*, she thought, she'd had a
hint of what passion could be. But she hadn't known
even a fraction if it . . .

Roche kissed the line of her jaw, the soft pink recess
of her ear, gently nibbling its lobe. His mouth

travelled downwards, tracing the column of her throat, skimming lightly over the hollows and lines of shoulder and collarbone to where the first soft curves of her breasts had escaped the chaste restraint of the *maillot*.

He lifted his head, a faint smile curving his mouth as he studied the swimsuit's austere lines. His fingers slid under the straps, propelling them off her shoulders and down, and Samma gasped, snatching at the slipping fabric.

'No—please.'

'Yes.' In spite of his amusement, he was inexorable. 'You are too lovely, *ma belle*, to spend our private hours together hiding under unnecessary covering.' He bent and touched his mouth to the sunwarmed curve of her shoulder. 'You are like honey,' he murmured. 'Does all of you taste as sweet, I wonder?'

'You—you mustn't . . .' She barely recognised her own voice.

He shook his head, slowly. 'You are wrong.' His tongue flickered sensuously across the swollen contour of her lower lip. 'Because I must . . .'

His mouth fastened on hers in deep, insistent demand as his hands slid down her body, sweeping away the despised *maillot* with total determination.

Samma cried out in protest, and tried to cover herself with her hands, but his fingers closed round her slender wrists with almost insulting ease.

He said huskily, 'I have dreamed of seeing you like this once more, Samantha, *ma belle*. You will not deny me now.' He stroked her face with his free hand, then let his forefinger glide lightly down her throat to the valley between her bare breasts.

She had almost stopped breathing. The thud of her pulses seemed to fill the universe as Roche began to caress her breasts, his fingers moulding and shaping her startled flesh into delight. She felt the moist warmth of his tongue against her hardening nipples, and a little stifled cry of bewildered pleasure was torn out of her. His mouth moved on her almost fiercely in response, indulging himself in shameless pleasure, while the exploring hands feathered over her ribcage and abdomen to her hips, then down to her thighs, already involuntarily parting to receive his homage.

All her life, she thought, from some dazed and whirling corner of her mind . . . All her life, she'd been waiting for this. For the touch of those subtle, expert fingers, discovering, delighting every secret inch of her.

The last vestiges of apprehension about the sensual mystery into which she was being initiated were dissolving away, along with the remnants of her self-control.

Her body was twisting restlessly against the tormenting, arousing pressure of his fingers. She was making demands of her own now, arching towards him as she offered her breasts to his heated kisses, her total womanhood for his possession.

'*Doucement, mignonne, doucement,*' he muttered hoarsely. She could sense the hunger in him, like a leashed tiger, and in some strange way it added to her own excitement, her own urgency. 'I want to make it good for you.'

It was good already. Her entire body was melting, coming alive in a special way totally outside her experience or imagination, each new intimacy adding to the ferment within her.

Her need, exquisite and all-encompassing, matched his. She knew that now, in some strange way had known it from that first moment on the quay at

Cristoforo.

There were no doubts left. Even without Hugo Baxter's intervention, she would have gone with Roche, she knew. She would have been with him here and now, on any terms he offered, her senses frantic, starving for the fulfilment he was offering.

He lifted himself away from her slightly to strip off his trunks. He was trembling now, his own restraint at breaking point.

Last night—a lifetime ago—Samma would have been too shy to look at him. Now she stared without guile, filling her eyes with the sheer magnificence of his body.

But as he came down to her, drawing her back into his arms, she tensed suddenly, an odd frisson lifting the hair on the back of her neck.

'Qu'est-ce que tu as?' Immediately he sensed the change in her, the withdrawal.

She said breathlessly, 'Someone's watching us.'

'No, ma belle.' His lips soothed hers. 'We are quite alone, I promise. Now come to me . . .'

'No.' She tried to push him away, looking round desperately for something with which to cover herself. 'There is someone. I knew it that night at the hotel when you watched me—and I know it now . . .'

He said tautly, 'Are you trying to punish me for that? Be still, chérie. I need you so much. Let me show you—let me love you . . .'

'I can't!' Samma shook her head in violent negation. 'Not with—someone there. It must be the gardener . . .'

'I gave orders we were not to be disturbed. Neither Hippolyte nor anyone else would dare to intrude. I tell you, there's no one . . .'

'But there is.' She pounded on the cushion with her clenched fist. 'Someone revolting—watching us.'

Roche said something under his breath, then reached for his towel, knotting it round his hips.

Samma watched him stride round the pool, pausing every now and then to examine the tall shrubs which gave the area its privacy. But she knew he wouldn't find anyone. The tension had relaxed suddenly. Whatever presence had been there had now gone.

By the time he returned, Samma had dragged on her *maillot* and covered it with her shift, and was sitting nervously, her arms clasping her knees to her chin.

His anger as he looked down at her was almost tangible.

'No one,' he shot at her. 'As I predicted. Or was it just a ploy to keep me at arm's length yet again, my reluctant bride?'

She shrank. 'You—know it wasn't.'

'Do I?' His voice was harsh with cynicism. 'Perhaps you thought it would be amusing, *ma chère,* to make me suffer a little for a change. To get your own back for having been—forced into this marriage. If so, your plan has been singularly effective. *Dieu,*' he added bitingly, 'I haven't ached like this since adolescence! Next time I attempt to distress you with my attentions, why not simply use your knee? It has much the same effect.'

Samma shook her head, unable to speak because sudden tears were choking her throat, and stinging her eyes.

'Oh, spare me that,' he tossed at her contemptuously. 'I thought I had made it clear I am not impressed by weeping, or hysterics. Or by an overwrought imagination,' he added crushingly.

Samma straightened, her face flushing, 'First you imply I'm lying. Now you insinuate I'm seeing things. Well, I'm not. I don't believe in ghosts—or

Le Diable. And I won't be driven away by these stories—or frightened to death, either.'

He squatted beside her, taking her chin in a bruising grip, making her face him. 'What do you mean?'

She couldn't draw back now, so she said, 'Marie-Christine—why didn't you tell me about—the way she died?'

'Because I hoped it would not be necessary for you to know,' he said grimly. 'Clearly, someone has wasted no time.'

'You can't expect to keep something like that quiet.'

'Perhaps.' He sighed harshly. 'It was a bad time in my life. I did not want it revived, even in the telling.'

'But hadn't I a right to know—to be told—for Solange's sake, if nothing else? It—it must have been a terrible experience for her.'

'Is that really your concern?' Roche's mouth was hard. 'Or are you asking yourself, as so many did, not least *la famille* Augustin, whether my violent ancestry suddenly reasserted itself and I supplied the means to rid myself of Marie-Christine?'

'No.' Samma shook her head violently. 'No, that never occurred to me.'

He released her almost contemptuously. 'I wonder if I believe you.' He shrugged. 'Make no mistake, *ma chère.* I hated Marie-Christine enough to kill her with my own hands. But I hated the bitch she'd been, not the pathetic wreck of a woman who came to Grand Cay.' He paused. 'She was drinking herself to death, Samantha. There was no need for me to hasten the process.'

She shivered. 'That's—horrible.'

'It was a glimpse of hell,' he said. 'Her death—the inquiries which followed—the rumours and suspicion.

I felt dirty. And guilty, too.' His mouth twisted. 'Almost the guilt of a murderer, although my hands were clean. The week before her death, she had been phoning me each day, begging me to let her leave Belmanoir, and move to a hotel in St Laurent. She was irrational, incoherent, and I wouldn't listen to her. She had appeared at the casino a few times during her early months on Grand Cay—made scenes—been ill. I could not face that again. I did not realise her rantings were a cry for help that I could not give.' He sighed. 'She phoned me that last night, but I was busy and I refused to take the call. Somehow, she obtained the keys of Elvire's car and set out—presumably to find me. But she never reached St Laurent.' He gave her a hard look. 'So, now you know.'

'But why did she want to leave Belmanoir so badly?'

He rose to his feet. 'I thought you had already guessed, *chérie.*' His tone flicked at her like a whip. 'She was frightened—scared of the Delacroix curse. What else?'

He turned and walked away, leaving Samma, white-faced and shaking, staring after him.

For a time, Samma stayed where she was, her mind in total turmoil, looking blindly into space; then she got to her feet, and made her way stumblingly back to the house.

She went upstairs, and along the gallery to their suite, where she knocked on Roche's door. There was no answer, but she could hear the distant sound of running water, so she opened the door and walked in. As she'd expected, the room was empty, but the bathroom door was ajar, and it was clear Roche was using the shower.

Samma lifted a hand and pushed her sweat-dampened hair back from her face with a small, weary gesture. She was still trembling, and her awakened body ached for fulfilment. The temptation to strip off what she was wearing and join him under that cool rush of water was almost overwhelming, but she resisted it.

She had to keep her mind clear. She must say what she had to say before her courage deserted her.

It seemed a long time before he came back into the room. He was already half dressed, sliding his arms into the sleeves of a shirt, and he checked abruptly when he saw her, his brows snapping together.

She hurried into speech. 'Roche—we must talk . . .'

'I thought we just had,' he said curtly. 'I regret I do not share your apparent fascination with the supernatural.'

Samma bit her lip. 'I don't believe in that, either,' she said, her voice quivering slightly. 'There was someone watching us. I swear there was.'

He gave her a sceptical look, and began to tuck his shirt into the band of his cream trousers.

'Is that what you came to say?'

'No.' In the folds of her shift, Samma's hands clenched into nervous fists. 'There are some things—about Marie-Christine—which don't make any sense.'

'Now there we are in agreement.' Roche picked up a tie, and began to knot it round his neck. 'Which things in particular?'

Down by the pool—all the way back to the house, she'd been thinking over what she'd been told, adding up the facts and reaching some disturbing totals.

Dry-mouthed, she said slowly, 'Elvire was supposed to be looking after her, wasn't she? Yet Marie-Christine was drunk again—and the keys of the car were—there for her.'

There was a silence, then he said too quietly, 'What are you trying to say? Be very careful, *ma belle*.'

She tried again. 'Was Elvire—a stranger to you when she came here?'

'No.' Still that soft, dangerous voice. 'I had—known her for some time. But she had been away from Grand Cay to train as a nurse. Didn't your—informant tell you that?'

'Yes.' Samma swallowed, aware she was in deep water and out of her depth. 'As a nurse, shouldn't she have kept a closer eye on her patient—guarded against that kind of thing?'

'She was also trying to look after Solange,' he said curtly. 'She had searched Marie-Christine's usual hiding places for bottles, and found nothing, and the car keys were a spare set. She was putting the child to bed when Marie-Christine left the house.' His eyes narrowed. 'What exactly are you implying, *ma chère?*'

She spread her hands desperately, 'Roche, I know you care for her—I'm not a fool—but hasn't it ever occurred to you that your relationship might have made her feel possessive about Belmanoir—resentful of Marie-Christine?'

'You don't know what you are talking about,' he said harshly. 'It is because of our relationship that I would trust Elvire with my life.'

And with Marie-Christine's? she thought, but did not dare utter it aloud. Instead she said, 'If she's a trained nurse, isn't she rather wasted here as a house-keeper? Isn't it time she was getting back to her career?'

'I think that is a decision she must make.' He picked up his jacket. 'Now, if you will excuse me . . .'

She said in a little rush, 'And if I say I'd prefer her to leave—what then?'

Roche's face darkened. He said with icy emphasis, 'Elvire stays here for as long as she wishes. May I remind you, Samantha, this was her home before it was yours. I owe her a roof over her head, and more.'

'Even if it's my roof?' She took a deep breath. 'Roche, I—I don't want her here any more . . .'

He said flatly, 'That is unfortunate,' and walked past her to the door. He glanced back. 'But it is not your choice.'

She said huskily, 'But I can choose, and I do. If Elvire stays here, I—I won't let you touch me again.'

There was a loaded silence, then he shrugged. 'Then that is your decision, *ma femme*. However, I promise your nights will be lonelier than mine,' he added with cynical mockery, ignoring her little wounded gasp. He paused. 'When Elvire returns, you may tell her I shall not be here for dinner this evening. She is still our housekeeper, and the domestic arrangements are her concern, so be civil, if you please.'

Samma looked at him, misery clenching inside her like a fist. Now, it seemed, it had been her turn to gamble—and lose. She realised how Clyde must have felt.

'Very well.' She moistened her lips with the tip of her tongue. 'Will—will you be back later?'

'At bedtime, you mean?' he asked derisively. 'Perhaps, *madame*. But, under the circumstances, why should you care?' He gave her a mirthless smile and pointed to the communicating door. 'Your room is there,' he added curtly, and left her.

CHAPTER EIGHT

By the time Samma got downstairs, Roche was already leaving, his car disappearing down the drive in a faint cloud of dust.

She didn't even know why she'd followed him—what she could have said even if she'd managed to detain him. But she was too late, anyway.

She wanted, she found, quite desperately to cry, and turned back into the silent house, seeking the refuge of the *salon*.

Lying across one of its sofas, she gave way to all the emotional confusion and uncertainty of the past few days, letting it wash out of her in a storm of weeping which left her drained but calm, once its force had been spent.

She had not, she realised at last, been crying wholly for herself, but for the look of bleak and lonely bitterness she had seen on Roche's face as he'd turned away from her.

Just for a moment, she'd seen a crack in the tough, self-assured, dominating façade he presented to the world. For an instant, he'd been vulnerable, and if she'd pulled herself together in time there might have been something she could have done to draw them together, not just physically, but in some deeper, more important way.

But who was she trying to fool? she thought, as she sat up, pushing the hair back from her tear-wet face. Elvire was there ahead of her, so deeply entrenched in his heart and life, it seemed, that there was no room

113

for anyone else.

She'd been a fool to attack Elvire directly, she castigated herself with bitterness. She should have realised that Roche would defend his mistress and believe no wrong of her, no matter what the evidence might be against her. Yet there was no real evidence—except that Marie-Christine had clearly had access to alcohol, and a set of car keys which should not be lying around—and certainly no proof.

She remembered Liliane Duvalle's half-embarrassed remarks about scandal and rumour. Was it any wonder? she asked herself with a sigh.

But if there had been any real case against Elvire, even if it was only negligence, wouldn't the authorities have taken some action? Or would they have hesitated to cause even greater offence to the wealthy and powerful Delacroix name, and settled thankfully for a verdict of accidental death?

Samma thought about Elvire, and her serene beauty. Was she really capable of fuelling Marie-Christine's drinking problem, then encouraging her to drive to St Laurent?

Or was she just inventing a case against Elvire, because they were rivals?

Except that it was no contest, she reminded herself painfully. Roche had shown her plainly where his loyalties, and whatever love he was capable of, truly lay.

That afternoon, he'd decided to satisfy the transient desire that he could have felt for any nubile girl who'd crossed his path, and Samma knew she ought to hate and despise herself for surrendering so readily to his passion, when she knew he didn't really care about her.

And if she *had* given herself to him, what kind of

life could she have expected afterwards? Would she
have had to share him with Elvire—establish some
kind of *ménage à trois?* Roche with his harem, she
thought, shuddering. Even the thought of it made her
feel physically sick.

Yet she couldn't escape the fact that she loved him,
and wanted him more than she'd ever wanted
anything in her life.

But, if she was to keep her sanity and her self-
respect, she had to remain aloof, she thought drearily.

As she got to her feet, she caught a glimpse of
herself in the big mirror above the empty fireplace,
and grimaced. With her tear-stained face and swollen
eyes, she looked barely older than Solange herself.

She would have to wash this evidence of her
wretchedness away, she thought. They would be back
soon, and she didn't want Elvire to have the
satisfaction of seeing she'd been crying.

She went upstairs, letting the silence of Belmanoir
enfold her. For a place with such a chequered history,
it had an extraordinarily peaceful atmosphere, she
thought, as she went along to her room, and across it
to the bathroom beyond. She pushed open the bathroom door, then stopped with a little cry.

Scrawled crudely in lipstick—her lipstick—across
the mirror above the vanity unit was the message,
'You are cursed. Go now.'

Oh, really? Samma thought wrathfully, picking up
the ruins of her lipstick and examining it. I think it's
time I did some cursing on my own account.

The fact that only the bottom section of the mirror
had been used, and that there was a certain awkwardness about some of the lettering, pointed the finger, as
she'd already suspected, directly at Solange.

Her previous companions must have been a pretty

poor lot if they'd let themselves be chased away by
something as rudimentary and obvious as this, she
thought, looking at the mess with disfavour. But
perhaps this was just for starters. Well, it could end
there, too!

She washed her face and hands, brushed her hair,
and was on her way downstairs again when she heard
the sound of a car drawing up outside. For a moment,
her heart leapt, as she hoped, desperately, that it
might be Roche.

Then she heard Solange's excited voice, and realised
her mistake.

The child flew into the hall as Samma reached the
bottom of the stairs. 'Look at me!' she called out
triumphantly.

'I am,' Samma assured her. She could hardly believe
the difference the new hairstyle had made, and not
just to Solange's physical appearance. She seemed
altogether more confident, almost incandescent with
happiness.

'Where is Papa?' she was demanding imperiously. 'I
want to show him how I look.'

Samma bit her lip. 'Actually, he's not here right
now. He had to go back to St Laurent for an
important meeting,' she improvised hastily, only too
aware of Elvire, a silent audience in the doorway.

'Not here?' The delight faded from Solange's face,
as if a lamp had been switched off inside her. 'But
why has he gone? Why couldn't he wait to see me?'

'He'll be back later,' Samma said, mentally crossing
her fingers. 'You can put on your prettiest dress, and
dazzle him then.'

Solange's scowl was fixed on her with the force of a
laser beam.

'I have no pretty dresses, and I don't believe Papa

has a meeting at all. I think you quarrelled with him, like Maman, and now he has gone away again.'

Samma felt a hint of betraying colour rise in her face, but she kept her voice level. 'You are being rude, Solange.'

'Then send me to my room. Isn't that what usually happens?'

'I suppose so,' Samma acknowledged drily. 'But this time I'm going to send you to *my* room. My bathroom to be exact.' She turned to Elvire. 'Please would you ask one of the maids to take Solange some cleaning stuff. She's had an accident with my lipstick, and I think she should be the one to clear it up.'

There was a long silence, and Solange stared down at the tiled floor, her face crimson. 'I don't know what you mean,' she said sullenly, at last.

'I think you do,' Samma said quietly. 'And please don't play any more tricks like that, because they won't work. I'm here, and I mean to stay.'

And Elvire, who was listening to the interchange with obvious astonishment, could take that last remark to heart as well, she thought.

Solange, reduced to a guilty silence, trailed reluctantly upstairs. When she had gone, Elvire said quietly, 'You must excuse her, *madame*. She gets so little of Roche's attention, and yet it means the whole world to her.'

And to me, Samma thought desolately. And to you.

Aloud, she said, 'You really don't have to tell me that.'

'No.' Elvire's tone was curiously dry. She paused. 'Will Roche, in fact, be home for dinner?'

Samma shook her head with an effort. Even that much of an admission was torture, she thought, making herself meet Elvire's gaze. But there was none

of the thinly veiled triumph she'd expected. Instead
Samma saw bewilderment, and something which
could almost have been compassion, before Elvire
shrugged and turned away. 'Then I will warn
Roxanne.'

Samma wanted to ask, Did you leave Solange at the
hairdressers' and come back here? Were you hiding
down at the pool, watching us?

But her own common sense told her it just wasn't
possible. Perhaps Roche was right, she thought, with
a sigh. Perhaps all this talk of pirates and curses was
making her imagination run away with her.

The bathroom mirror was restored to its usual
pristine state, but Solange refused point-blank to
come down to dinner, so Samma ate a solitary meal in
the big dining-room, forcing the food down her taut
throat.

She was sorely tempted to sacrifice her pride, and
follow Roche to St Laurent, but what if he wasn't at
the casino at all? And, anyway, what could she
possibly say or do to bridge the gulf yawning between
them?

I could try the truth, she thought, biting her lip. I
could tell him I love him.

But he might not believe her. Or, even worse, he
might be embarrassed or irritated by such a declar-
ation from her. And she couldn't risk that.

At the same time, she wasn't prepared to sit
passively by, and concede victory to Elvire.

So she would offer him what she knew he
wanted—her body.

She spent a long and restless evening, trying to
figure out how to approach him. She could try
flinging herself into his arms, she thought, but they

might not be open to receive her, after the way she and Roche had parted earlier. Or she could be matter-of-fact, and tell him she hadn't meant what she had said, and wait for him to make the next move. Except that he might thank her politely, and walk away again.

Eventually, just after midnight, she decided what she would do.

She went up to her room, bathed and scented herself, and brushed her hair over her shoulders until it shone. Then she went on bare and silent feet across her room, into his, and stood for a long moment, looking at the empty, moonlit bed.

Trembling a little, she slipped off her nightgown and dropped it beside the bed, where he would be bound to see it.

Then she slid under the covers, and lay there waiting.

It was a long time later, and she was almost asleep when the sound of the car jolted her back to awareness.

She tensed, imagining him entering the house, making his way up the stairs, and along the gallery to his door. By the time the door actually opened, she was as taut as a bowstring. She closed her eyes, willing herself to relax, her every sense conscious of his tall figure standing there in the shadows, watching her. Unmoving.

Perhaps she should sit up, she thought confusedly. Hold out her arms to him. Say his name.

And then she heard it. The slight click of the door as it closed again—behind him.

Propped up on one elbow, Samma stared incredulously into the darkness, and realised she was alone.

It was what she had dreaded. She had offered herself. And Roche had rejected her.

*　　*　　*

Samma replaced the cap on her suntan oil and
screwed it meticulously into place before putting the
bottle back on the table. She was strongly tempted to
throw it as far as the horizon, swearing loudly as she
did so, but she resisted the impulse. After all, the
suntan oil was blameless.

I've got to find something to do, she told herself.
Something to stop myself from thinking.

Three endless days had limped past since the night
of her humiliation in Roche's room. Days which she'd
spent in more or less solitary splendour beside the
pool. And her nights had been spent alone too. She
had fled back to her own room after Roche had left
her, too stunned even to weep, and lain awake in the
darkness, asking herself over and over again what else
she could have expected.

The following day, a surprised Hippolyte had
arrived at the suite to fix to the communicating door
the lock she had once demanded.

And that, Samma thought wretchedly, had been
that.

Solange had returned to school, and came back in
the early afternoon. She'd been obviously nonplussed
by Samma's cool reception of the warning message,
and there'd been no signs or portents since, Samma
thought drily. But there hadn't been much contact
between them either, and this she regretted. Solange
had retreated into a silent hostility which Samma
found difficult to breach.

About the only time she made a voluntary remark of
any kind was at dinner, when her father was present,
Samma realised, sighing. But, as Roche did not come
home every evening, mealtimes were generally quiet
affairs.

And Roche himself? She swallowed painfully. He

treated her with a cool politeness which somehow hurt more than if he'd followed his daughter's example, and totally ignored her.

The only time he'd looked at her as if she was a human being had been the previous evening, she thought miserably, and then only because they'd almost had a row.

Samma had sought him out as he was preparing to drive back into St Laurent to the casino.

'Could I speak to you, please?' Her voice was awkward. She felt as if she was being interviewed by some head teacher, or potential boss. But then, of course, that was what Roche really was—her employer, as she should have made herself remember, instead of indulging herself with crazy fantasies about love and passion. Impossible now to think this cold-eyed stranger had held her naked in his arms and woken her senses to vibrant life.

'Can it wait?' Roche glanced at his watch. 'I am in a hurry . . .'

'I just wanted to ask if there was anything I could do—any kind of job at the casino.' She saw his brows snap together, and hastened on. 'I—I do seem to have rather a lot of time on my hands, and I wondered . . .'

'Are you planning to recreate your role as hostess, perhaps?' he asked derisively. He shook his head. 'I think not.'

Samma flushed hotly. 'I wasn't thinking of that. But if there's nothing at the casino, perhaps I could use my drawing in some way . . .'

'Your career as a pavement artist is also at an end,' Roche said grimly. 'May I remind you that you were warned the house was isolated, and that you are here to befriend Solange.'

'Oh, sure,' Samma said bitterly. 'And you can see

what an enormous success that is! I'm wasting my time here. She doesn't want me. In fact, she doesn't want anyone but you. If I went away, she wouldn't even notice.' She bit her lip. 'Really, that could be the best solution all round. If I just left . . .'

'You will do nothing of the kind,' he said icily. 'I said a year, and I meant it. Attempt to break our agreement, and you will be sorry, Samantha. I promise you that.'

She said in a low voice, 'I'm already sorry,' but he'd left, and didn't hear.

Now, the following day, Samma found herself wincing away from the memory of it. There was no need for him to be so dismissive, she thought sadly. She'd no intention of peddling her portrait sketches in public again. From what she'd been able to gather, it seemed art teaching was minimal at Solange's school, and she'd considered volunteering her services, as a temporary tutor.

I can't spend the whole year swimming, sunbathing and being ignored, she told herself. She could feel a kind of sympathy for Marie-Christine, and wondered, not for the first time, what could have happened to make the marriage go so disastrously wrong.

Roche had claimed, she remembered, to have spent his first wedding night alone, so it seemed their relationship had been in crisis from the first. And yet there was Solange . . .

Perhaps he'd been in love with Elvire all along, and had only married Marie-Christine on the rebound. In that case, why hadn't he proposed to Elvire the second time around?

Perhaps because he knew such a marriage would stir up again all the gossip and speculation about

Marie-Christine's accident, and give the Augustins an
additional weapon in the battle over Solange.

She shivered. Well, that battle was over at least, but
she was the one left wounded.

Oh, come on, she adjured herself impatiently. Stop
pitying yourself! Roche brought you here to do a job,
not become emotionally involved with him. You have
no one to blame but yourself.

She walked to the edge of the pool and dived into
the water, covering two lengths in a swift, racing
crawl.

As she hauled herself on to the edge, she saw to her
surprise that Solange had arrived. It was the first time
the child had been down to the pool area since Samma
had sketched her. And, although she was looking
thoughtful, she wasn't actually scowling for once.

Easy, Samma warned herself wryly, as she smiled at
her. *'Bonjour,* Solange. *Comment ça va?'*

The thin shoulders moved in a slight shrug. She
looked past Samma to the sunlit dance of the water. 'Is
it hard—to swim?'

Samma swallowed her surprise. 'Why—no! I
thought you weren't interested in learning. Would—
would you like me to teach you?'

There was a pause, and Samma felt that the child
was nerving herself to answer. But why? she
wondered. Most children of her age, with a private
swimming pool of this size, would be able to swim like
fishes already.

'Yes, *madame.* I would like to learn.'

She's actually asked me for something, Samma
thought in amazement. Is this some kind of breakthrough?

She said with deliberate casualness. 'Well, fine.
Shall we make a·date for the same time tomorrow—

when you come back from school?'

'Could it not be now?'

'Of course, if you want.' Samma hid her jubilation. 'What about a costume?'

'I have one.' Solange's voice sounded oddly strained, as she tugged a dark green swimsuit out of her school bag. Clearly, she'd come prepared and meant business.

When she had changed, Samma took her to the edge of the pool, and sat beside her, encouraging her to dangle her legs in the water. Solange sat and listened obediently, but her skin had a distinct pallor, and she looked more uneasy by the minute.

Samma went into the water, and demonstrated some leg movements.

'That's all you have to do,' she said. 'I'll hold you up by your arms and shoulders. You don't even have to get your face wet, if you don't want to.' Some people she knew had what amounted to a phobia about such things, and maybe Solange was one of them.

She held out her hand to the child. 'Come on,' she said. 'Trust me.'

For a moment she thought Solange was going to back away, then slowly, gingerly, the child allowed herself to be tugged gently into the water, her hands clinging to Samma's. She looked very small, and very sallow, as if the action was taking every ounce of courage she possessed.

Yet this is the shallow end, Samma thought, puzzled, and I've promised I won't let go of her. What is it, I wonder? At the hotel, after all, quite tiny tots had hurled themselves gleefully into the pool.

Perhaps I should have waited, Samma thought. Bought her some of those armbands, or a ring.

She gave Solange a warm smile. 'That's fine. That's great. Now, I'll support you—like this, and you lie on top of the water, and kick like I showed you.'

Solange closed her eyes, gritted her teeth, and kicked out in entirely the opposite direction. Her foot landed squarely and painfully in Samma's midriff, and she doubled up instinctively, gasping. Solange kicked out again, this time at her legs, catching Samma off balance, and they both went down under the water in a welter of arms and legs and spray.

Choking, Samma struggled up, in spite of Solange, who was clinging like a limpet, still kicking her, and punching and scratching at her arms and shoulders, all the time screaming in a thin, reedy voice.

Shocked though she was, Samma thought, 'This isn't just panic. This is something else . . .'

She hoisted the struggling child out of the water with an immense effort, and crawled after her.

Trying to catch her breath, she began, 'Now what in the world . . .?'

Then she heard Solange scream, 'Papa—Papa! She made me go in the water. She tried to drown me! Oh, Papa!'

'Qu'est-ce qui se passe?'

Eyes stinging, and still spluttering from her unexpected ducking, Samma saw Roche striding towards the pool edge, his face dark with fury.

Solange ran to him, still crying out pitifully. 'Papa, she dragged me under the water. I nearly drowned! I told her I did not want to swim—ever, but she made me. She hates me—she hates me.'

Roche turned on Samma. 'Is this true? Did you make her go in the water?'

'She pulled me in,' Solange put in tearfully. 'I did not want to. I told her that when she came here. I told her she could not make me.'

Samma scooped her hair back from her face, thinking furiously. She said, trying to keep her voice level, 'Yes, that's right—but today I had the impression that she'd changed her mind.'

'She seized hold of my hands. She would not let go of me. She pulled me off the edge,' Solange chimed in again. She lifted her fists and scrubbed at her wet eyes, but not before Samma had glimpsed an unmistakable gleam of triumph.

'You treated a nervous child like that?' Roche asked incredulously. He stroked his daughter's wet hair. *'Tais toi, chérie.* It is all over now.'

Elvire came flying down the path. 'What is it?' she demanded. 'I thought I heard screaming.'

'You did,' Roche confirmed grimly. 'My wife decided to give Solange an unwanted swimming lesson.'

'Ah, *mon Dieu!'* Elvire put her hands to her mouth in unsimulated horror.

Samma said huskily, 'Now, wait a minute. I don't know what's going on here, but there is another side to all this. Solange asked me to take her in the pool.'

Roche shook his head. 'You misunderstood,' he said curtly. 'She would never do such a thing.' He turned to the still weeping Solange, now muffled in a towel. 'Go to the house with Elvire, *ma petite.* You are safe now.'

Samma was gasping as Solange was led away. 'Safe?' she echoed angrily. 'What's that supposed to mean? You think I would have let her come to any real harm?'

'You have already done her immense psychological damage,' Roche returned furiously. 'You admit she told you she did not want to swim, and yet you forced her.'

'I did nothing of the kind.' Samma paused, remembering. 'Well, she did seem a bit reluctant when it came to it, but there was nothing—nothing to prompt all this fuss. I got her into the water, and suddenly she went mad.'

'I am not surprised,' Roche said, his mouth tightening. 'It must have been another nightmare for her.'

'But swimming's a perfectly normal, healthy activity,' Samma protested. 'I was delighted when she seemed to show an interest. I thought I might be getting somewhere at last.'

'And so you allowed that to outweigh your judgement when you saw her fear?' His brows drew together. 'I thought better of you than that, Samantha.'

She said wearily, 'I seem to have been found guilty of a crime I didn't know existed. Will you please explain why it's so impossible that I should be telling the truth? Why shouldn't Solange have changed her mind about learning to swim?'

He said quietly, 'Because you, *ma chère,* are not the first person to try to teach her. Marie-Christine also made an attempt. She threw Solange in—at the deep end—and followed her. But—she was drunk, as usual, and did not realise that Solange had sunk like a stone. If Elvire had not arrived just in time, there would have been a terrible tragedy. Now do you see why there must have been a misunderstanding today? Since her ordeal, Solange has never willingly gone near the water again. For months, even a simple bath at the end of the day terrified her.'

'Oh, God!' Samma's mouth was dry. 'Oh, God—why didn't you tell me about this—warn me?'

'Because it should not have been necessary,' he said shortly. 'Solange has kept her distance from the water's edge ever since. It never occurred to me you would be cruel enough to ignore her obvious fears. I had forgotten, of course, how insensitive and impetuous the young can be.'

'Is that what you think?' Samma shivered, feeling suddenly sick. Solange had set her up, of course. That whole scene had been deliberately staged because the child knew Roche had returned home unexpectedly, and would be coming down to the pool. This was Solange's revenge, she thought, for the humiliation of having to clean the lipstick off the mirror—for having been found out. And it was a potent one indeed!

She felt anger rising inside her, and said, 'You dare to call me insensitive, Roche Delacroix? Well, you invented the word. You bring me here—you push Solange and me together, even though it's obvious she can't stand the sight of me—and you tell me nothing—nothing!' She took an unsteady breath. 'I had to hear about Marie-Christine from a stranger—and now there's this. Your first wife nearly drowned your child —and you didn't tell me.'

'Samantha, listen to me . . .'

'No, I won't listen.' Her voice shook. 'You're the one who's cruel. You want me to be Solange's stepmother, and yet you hide all the facts that might lead to any understanding between us. I'm supposed to be your wife, but you never talk to me. In fact, you avoid me. I'm surrounded all the time by secrets that I don't understand, and when I make mistakes that could have been avoided, or jump to the wrong conclusions, I get the blame. Well, I've had enough. I can't take any more. I'm leaving Grand Cay and you can't stop me.'

Suddenly, all the misery and wretchedness of the past

days came boiling up inside her, and she lifted her hand and slapped him as hard as she could across the face. She felt his anger answer her own, as his fingers closed bruisingly round her wrist. There was retaliation in every line of his body as he jerked her towards him. With a strength she hadn't realised she possessed, she wrenched herself free and fled from him.

As if, she thought, with a sob, the devil was after her.

CHAPTER NINE

IT SEEMED an endless afternoon. Even with the shutters closed against the full blaze of the sun, Samma's room was like an oven, the heat draining her, while her mind rode an eternal weary treadmill.

She had told Roche she was leaving him, yet in practical terms how could she? He had her passport, and the amount of hard cash she possessed would buy her a ticket to nowhere.

In reality, she was no better off than she had been on Cristoforo, she thought wretchedly, but at least she'd had nothing to concern her there, except Clyde's vagaries. She had been spared the agony of heartache which was now wrenching her apart.

She was still stunned by Solange's behaviour. How could a child as young as that be capable of such duplicity? she asked herself desperately. She had not even guessed at the extent of Solange's resentment of her, and her determination to be rid of any companion foisted on her by her father.

Why hadn't she been more wary of Solange's apparent overtures? And why hadn't some instinct warned her that the child would go to any lengths necessary to force her out of Belmanoir?

Because I had this romantic notion that I would succeed where everyone else had failed, she told herself derisively. I could see us all living together, like a normal, happy family. I really thought it could happen.

But she'd underestimated all the factors against her

—Roche's passion for Elvire, Solange's malice, and above all, her own youth and inexperience.

That was all she'd ever had to offer Roche, she thought bitterly. What a fool she'd been to think it could ever be enough!

As the light began to fade from the sky, she sank into a shallow, dreamless sleep, to be awoken eventually by a touch on her shoulder. She sat up with a start to find the lamp beside the bed had been lit, and that Elvire was standing over her.

Samma sat up, pushing her hair back from her face with a gesture that was almost defiant. 'What do you want?' she asked flatly.

Elvire's brows rose slightly. 'I came to tell you that dinner is served.'

'I'm not hungry.'

Elvire studied her for a moment. 'Starving yourself, *madame*, will achieve nothing.'

'And when I want your advice I'll ask for it,' Samma returned angrily. 'Now, leave me alone, please.'

Elvire's lips tightened. 'As you wish.' She turned as if to go, then swung back again. She said with surprising energy, 'I am wrong about you, it seems, Madame Delacroix. When you came here, I thought, "That little one, she is a fighter. She will not give way." Now you talk as if you are defeated.'

Samma's lips parted in sheer astonishment as she stared up at the other girl. She said in a low voice, 'Is it really any wonder?'

Elvire sighed. 'Perhaps not. There are many obstacles in your way, of course.' She gave Samma a grave look. 'And I think perhaps that you see me as one of them.' She hesitated. 'Someone has told you, I think, of my relationship with Roche?'

Samma swallowed, wondering whether she was

dreaming. 'It wasn't really necessary,' she said awkwardly. 'I—I guessed.'

'*Vraiment?*' Elvire smiled wearily. 'We had hoped, Roche and I, that it would remain a secret. But I suppose that was too much to expect.' She shrugged. 'But I can see why you resent my presence here, although I am sorry for it. I had hoped you would be able to understand.'

Samma thought hysterically that this had to be one of the most bizarre conversations of all time.

'But you will not have to suffer me for much longer,' Elvire went on. 'I have been at Belmanoir long enough. It is time I returned to my own life.'

Samma felt as if she'd been pole-axed. She said with difficulty, 'Have you spoken to—to Roche about your plans?'

Elvire shook her head. 'Not yet. But he has always known my stay here was only temporary. He will not stand in my way.'

Samma stared at her. 'Are you quite sure of that?' She bit her lip. 'I had a different impression.'

'Ah.' Elvire's smile was tender. 'He is loyal, Roche, and very protective. When he has learned to trust again, he will be all the man any woman could want.' She sent Samma a clear-eyed look. 'And you, I think, will be able to chase the remaining shadows from his life.'

'With Solange hating me—doing anything she can to get rid of me? Like that little drama she staged earlier today?'

Elvire frowned. 'What are you saying?'

'That I was set up quite deliberately, 'Samma said stonily. 'Solange asked me to teach her to swim— almost insisted on it, then performed her panic-stricken act for her father.' She shook her head.

'Ghost messages on the mirror are one thing. This kind of malice is something else.'

Elvire's frown deepened. 'If it was true, I would agree. But a child like Solange is not capable of such conduct.'

'Oh, no?' Samma asked drily. 'And how did she put my predecessors to flight, may I ask? Conjure up *Le Diable*, or simply hit them with a hatchet?'

There was a silence, then Elvire began to laugh. 'At least you begin to sound more like yourself,' she said crisply. 'Now, come and eat, before Roxanne works herself into a frenzy.'

Samma swung herself reluctantly off the bed. She wasn't sure how it had happened, but it seemed that Elvire and she had become allies in some weird way.

'Is Solange downstairs?' she asked, as she ran a comb through her dishevelled hair.

'No. She has some sedative tablets prescribed for when the nightmares occur, so I gave her one.' Elvire paused. 'The panic was genuine, I would swear.'

'I know,' Samma said wryly. 'It just proves how far she's prepared to go to get rid of me.'

Elvire's brow was creased. 'But for someone of her age to think of such a thing . . . *Ce n'est pas possible, ça.* It makes no sense.'

Very little that's happened here does, Samma thought bitterly, as she sat in solitary splendour in the dining-room, Roxanne's splendid cooking turning to ashes in her mouth.

Not long ago, she'd been envisaging a scenario where Elvire had helped Marie-Christine to a premature death, in order to take her place. Now, suddenly, she saw the other girl as someone she might, under other circumstances, have liked—have even wanted as a friend.

Or perhaps I'm just having an identity crisis brought on by the events of the past few days, she thought, her mouth twisting.

What she could not understand was why Elvire was choosing to leave now, just when her influence over Roche had apparently never been stronger. Or had the other girl simply resigned herself to the fact that Roche would never marry her, and decided she no longer wanted a subsidiary role in his life?

And, even if she did leave, what guarantee was there that Roche would ever want Samma to take her place on any permanent basis?

Perhaps I should have been honest with her, too, Samma thought ruefully. Told her that my stay here is purely temporary as well. If I allow it to be, she amended hastily.

Perhaps Elvire was right, and she was being unnecessarily defeatist. Solange might have won the first real confrontation between them hands down, but she would never get away with that again, and Samma intended to let her know it. And as soon as possible, she decided, pushing away her coffee-cup.

There was a light burning in Solange's room. Presumably the effect of the sedative had worn off, Samma thought, as she pushed the door open and went in.

Solange, propped up by pillows, was reading a large book. She directed a sulkily suspicious glance towards her visitor. 'What do you want?'

'A few words with you,' Samma said affably, sitting down on the edge of the bed.

'I am reading.'

'So I can see. Stories about wicked stepmothers, no doubt. Well, I won't keep you from them a moment longer than necessary.' Samma paused, then said flatly, 'I just want you to know that this afternoon's performance was the final one. I was prepared to be your friend, but you've proved to me that isn't what you want.' She shrugged. '*Ça ne fait rien.* But I'm staying here, whether you want it or not, and there'll be no more phony swimming lessons, or threats from *Le Diable.*' She paused. 'Do I make myself clear?'

Solange said on a triumphant note, 'Papa was angry with you. I know he was. I heard the servants talking.'

Samma shrugged again. 'He had good reason,' she said briefly. 'After what you made him think. But there's a saying, Solange—forewarned is forearmed.'

There was uncertainty in the small face. 'What does that mean?'

'That I won't be caught again,' Samma said bluntly. 'So—forget whatever else you may be planning. Unless, of course, you want Papa to know about the tricks you have been playing.'

The book slid from Solange's hands, and she made no effort to retrieve it. She said slowly, 'You—have not told him already?'

'Of course not.' Samma stared at her. 'What do you take me for? But that little scene you played this afternoon could have had very serious consequences and . . .'

'But you did not tell him that I tricked you?' Solange persisted. 'Why not?'

'Because it's between the two of us,' Samma said crisply. 'Isn't it enough to make Papa angry with me? You don't want him cross with you as well.'

'But you want that,' Solange burst out. 'You hate me. You want me to be sent away from here—away from Papa. Do you think I am a fool—that I do not know this? You will always be jealous of me, because Papa loves me more than you, so you want to see me sent far away from Belmanoir.'

Samma felt a pang twist inside her. Roche had clearly not discussed his plans for her future schooling with his only child.

She said gently, 'Solange, I promise you that nothing could be further from the truth. Where on earth did you get the idea I wanted you sent away?'

'I have always known it. First those others—and now you. They wanted to come here—oh, you all want to come—but to be with Papa, not with me. And, now that Papa has married you, you will arrange for me to go away, so that you can have Papa all to yourself.'

Samma took the small, shaking hands in hers. She said quietly, 'Solange, who's been telling you this nonsense? Neither Papa nor I have any intention of sending you away. I came here to look after you. I've told you that.'

'Until you can persuade Papa to get rid of me.' Solange snatched her hands away.

Samma gave her an even look. 'Well, you've certainly given me sufficient cause,' she commented. 'But doesn't the fact that I haven't complained to Papa about you prove that you're wrong, and that I'm not simply looking for chances to send you away?'

The uncertainty deepened. 'I—do not know.'

'Then set that devious little mind of yours to thinking about it,' Samma advised. She got to her feet. 'And no more tricks.' She smiled briefly, and walked to the door, aware that the gaze which followed her held more bewilderment than hostility.

But this time I'm taking nothing for granted, Samma thought, as she went to her own room. Especially when I still have Roche to face.

She had no real idea what she could say to him, or

what he would even want to hear from her. After her outburst that afternoon, she'd half expected him to follow her, but she'd been left severely alone, and not long after she'd heard his car leave, presumably to take him to the casino.

And her hope that he might be home for dinner had proved a forlorn one, too.

But, if nothing else, she had to convince Roche that he couldn't send Solange away to school—show him how dependent the child was on him. And if he cynically saw her arguments as a ploy to be allowed to remain at Belmanoir herself after the agreed term, well, that was a risk she would have to take, she thought achingly.

Elvire had said she was a fighter. Well, she would battle for whatever tiny percentage of his life he was prepared to share with her.

But when dawn streaked the sky, and the room next to hers remained silent and empty, Samma realised with a sinking heart that Roche might no longer be prepared to grant her even that little. And there were tears on her face when she finally fell asleep.

Her head ached as she eventually made her way downstairs the following morning. As she reached the foot of the stairs, she heard the sound of voices coming from the dining-room.

Solange was sitting at the table, eating grapefruit, and Liliane Duvalle occupied the seat opposite, pouring coffee.

'Ah, Madame Delacroix.' She got to her feet, smiling broadly as Samma entered. 'You will forgive this informality, I know. Mademoiselle Casson gave me the impression you would not be joining us.'

Her eyes, Samma saw with distaste, were sharp with

curiosity. Clearly, it didn't take long for servants'
gossip to reach Les Arbres, she thought with
resignation.

She said coolly, 'I can't imagine what made her
think that. *Bonjour*, Solange.'

She received in response a wary look, and a
murmured greeting.

Liliane Duvalle lowered her voice confidentially. 'I
came as soon as I heard of yesterday's little
contretemps. I blame myself. I should have told you
about Solange's phobia about swimming and its cause.
It would have saved *la petite* a terrible ordeal.' She
shook her head. 'I have been telling her that clearly
you meant well, even though the outcome was
unfortunate.'

'Thank you,' Samma said drily. She glanced at her
stepdaughter. 'What do you say to that, Solange?'

There was a pause, then Solange said sullenly, 'It
was a misunderstanding. It was not Madame's fault.
She was not to blame.'

Liliane Duvalle looked frankly taken aback. 'But I
understood . . .' She stopped, then shrugged briefly.
'However, one should never listen to foolish rumour.
I am pleased to find you both so much in accord.'

Samma poured herself some coffee, and sat down.
'How is your research going?' she asked politely.

Liliane Duvalle threw up her hands. 'Slowly, I
regret. I think my book will be a life's work—a true
labour of love. Every detail I find out about *Le Diable*
is so fascinating, I tend to linger over it.' She gave a
musical laugh. 'A fine thing for a historian to be in
love with her subject, *hein?*' She paused. 'But I forget
the purpose of my visit. I wondered whether *la petite*
would care to spend the day with me at Les Arbres.'
She smiled at Samma. 'After all, *madame,* you are still

on your honeymoon. No doubt you would welcome a chance to be relieved of your responsibilities as a stepmother, and be able to devote an entire day to your husband.'

Samma said calmly, 'It's a kind thought, Madame Duvalle, but Solange and I have plans of our own for today, haven't we, *chérie?*'

She expected to be contradicted, and was resigned to it.

There was a silence, then Solange said slowly, 'Yes, we have plans. I am—sorry, Tante Liliane.'

Liliane Duvalle shrugged, her smile undiminished. *'Ça ne fait rien.* I have been occupying myself by making some new clothes for your beautiful doll, *mon enfant.* I thought we might have had a fashion parade. But there will be other times.' She got to her feet, putting a hand lightly on Solange's hair as she passed the child's chair. 'Your new *belle-mère* takes her duties towards you very seriously, *petite.* I hope you are grateful.'

Solange muttered something ungracious and returned her attention to her grapefruit.

The dining-room door swung open to admit Elvire, carrying a large flat box tied up with ribbons.

She said, 'A messenger has just delivered this for you, *madame.*'

'For me?' Samma's brows rose. 'But I wasn't expecting anything.'

'It is a wedding present,' Solange put in. 'Open it quickly, *madame.*'

Samma complied, stripping away the ribbon ties, and lifting the lid to reveal a mass of tissue. 'What in the world . . .' She delved among the folds, and gasped. 'Oh, my goodness . . .'

It was a dress, a ripple of silk chiffon in creamy

white, its halter bodice frankly minimal, the full skirt misted with a subtle drift of silver flowers.

Her wardrobe upstairs was full of beautiful things, but this was different. It was flagrantly, dreamily romantic, the shimmering slide of the material overtly sensuous as she touched it.

'It is a bridal gown, *non?*' Solange piped, putting out a reverent hand. 'Are you and Papa not really married after all, *madame?*'

Samma swallowed. 'Yes,' she said quietly. 'We are—really married, Solange.' There was a tiny envelope in the box, and her hand shook slightly as she reached for it, and extracted the card it contained.

It said simply, *'Forgive me—Roche.'*

'Where did it come from?' Solange asked. 'Is it a present from Papa?'

'Yes.' Samma's mouth was dry suddenly, her heart thudding violently.

Solange gave a rapturous sigh. 'It is so beautiful. When will you wear it? Will it be tonight?'

Tonight. The word seemed to sing in Samma's head with all kinds of evocative promise.

She said softly. 'Yes—oh, yes.' And thought with a pang—If he is here to wear it for . . . As she folded the dress back into its protective coverings, the card slipped from her hand, and fluttered to the floor. Samma bent to retrieve it, but Liliane Duvalle got there first.

'Oh, la la!' She darted a smiling glance at the message and then at Samma. 'It must have been quite a sin to require such redemption.'

Samma felt a wave of colour sweep into her face. She was suddenly all too aware of Elvire standing there, a silent witness.

She said swiftly, 'Not really. A—a tiff.' She held out

her hand for the card. 'I'll take the dress upstairs.'

'Permit me, *madame*.' Elvire took the box from her, her expression impassive.

'You see, Tante Liliane,' Solange put in, 'we had our fashion parade, after all!'

'So we did, although I am afraid you will find my poor efforts bear no comparison to a *haute-couture* label.' Madame Duvalle gave Samma a knowing look. 'To be mistress of Belmanoir has many advantages, *madame*, as I am sure you are discovering.' She patted Solange's cheek. '*A bientôt, petite.*'

Solange returned, '*Au revoir,*' but it was clear her attention was still focused on the new dress. There was a slight wistfulness in her expression, which was not lost on Samma.

When they were alone, she said, 'Why don't we go and look at your clothes, Solange? And you can show me the ones you particularly like.'

Solange frowned. 'Many of them do not fit me any more,' she said.

Samma examined a fleck on her nail. 'Then perhaps we should get you some new ones,' she said. 'Where do you usually go for your things?'

'Madame Trevaux has a shop in St Laurent. Papa tells her my size, and she sends what is suitable.'

Samma digested this with an inward grimace. For a busy man, she supposed, such an arrangement might be a boon, but for a little girl . . .?

She said cheerfully, 'Well, I think it would be more fun to go into St Laurent and look round the shops for ourselves—try things on.'

Solange could not disguise the swift, excited breath she drew. 'Can we go now?'

'Why not?' Samma glanced at her watch. 'If there's a car I can drive.'

'There is,' Solange assured her. 'It is the one Elvire uses.' She gave a joyous wriggle, then sobered, sending her stepmother a speculative look. 'This is another bribe, *hein?*'

Samma met her gaze. 'No,' she said. 'No more bribes. This is just the way things are going to be from now on. You, *mademoiselle,* are stuck with me, so you may as well make the best of it.'

A curious expression crossed Solange's face, half wary, half frightened, as if something basically unwelcome had occurred to her, but before Samma could ask what was wrong she was smiling again, and the moment was lost.

The shopping trip, Samma thought cautiously, a couple of hours later, had been a modest success. When encouraged to choose for herself, Solange turned out to have an innate sense of colour, and there had been few clashes as the number of carrier bags and boxes in the car mounted. The little girl had looked wistfully at some ornately frilled dresses, but Samma and the saleswoman between them had managed to convince her that an uncluttered line was far more becoming to her.

There was relative harmony between them as they drove back to Belmanoir.

As she braked in front of the house, Samma noticed with a catch of her breath that Roche's car was parked there, too. So, he'd returned at last.

Solange flew into the house, calling to Hippolyte to come and unpack the car, and Samma followed more sedately, trying to control the sudden hammer of her pulses.

Roche emerged from the *salon,* and stood watching her. He was unsmiling, his dark gaze cool and rather questioning.

'Where have you been?'

'I was going to ask you precisely the same thing.' Her voice was faintly breathless, she realised with vexation.

He said, 'I spent the night at the casino. I needed to think.' He motioned her ahead of him into the *salon*. 'I telephoned the house an hour ago, and Elvire said you had taken Solange shopping to St Laurent.' He gave her an incredulous look. 'Is it true?'

'Quite true. I—I told them to send the bills to you. I hope that's all right.'

'Of course.' He frowned. 'But I should have made arrangements—opened an account for you to draw on.'

'There's no need. You've already been far too generous.' She sounded as stilted as a schoolgirl. She paused, taking a breath. 'The—the dress is wonderful, but there was no need . . .'

'I thought there was every need,' he said quietly. 'I have been unfair to you, *ma chère*. You made me see that, and I wished to make amends.' He paused. 'Samantha, will you have dinner with me tonight?'

She swallowed. 'Of course. Will—will you be home at the usual time?'

Roche shook his head. 'I did not mean here. There are still things I must say to you—explanations which I would prefer to make away from this house. Do you understand?' He made an impatient gesture. 'No, that is foolish. How could you?' He smiled at her gravely. 'I need to be alone with you, *mignonne*. Will you come with me?'

Swift, incredulous joy was opening inside her like a sunburst. 'If—if that's what you want,' she managed.

'It's what I want.' He walked over to her, and stood

for a moment looking down at her, at the shyness in her eyes, the betraying bloom of colour in her cheeks. He said softly, 'But not all I want, *ma belle*. From tonight there will be no more secrets—nothing to keep us apart.' He lifted a hand, and tucked a strand of hair back behind her ear. *'D'accord?'*

Samma nodded mutely, suddenly incapable of speech.

Roche bent his head and kissed her on the mouth, lightly, but with a dizzying sensuousness, his hands holding her shoulders to draw her swiftly and intimately close against him. Through the barrier of their clothes, Samma could feel the warmth of his body, the sweet yielding of her own flesh in response.

She seemed to breathe him, absorb him, wanting him as sharply and frankly as he wanted her. She knew that if he was to draw her, in that moment, down on to one of the sofas or even the floor, she would surrender to him. When he straightened, putting her away from him, her disappointment was almost painful.

He said huskily, 'Until tonight,' and left her with the echo of that promise.

CHAPTER TEN

SAMMA put the final dress on its hanger, and stood back. 'That's finished,' she said with satisfaction.

There was no reply, and she flicked a sideways glance at Solange. The child had responded with enthusiasm to Samma's initial suggestion that they should put her new things away in her room, but she'd grown more and more silent, and the familiar sulky look was now firmly in place.

Samma suppressed a sigh. 'What's the matter?' she asked directly. 'Don't you like your new clothes, after all?'

'They are beautiful,' came the grudging reply, after a pause.

'What is it, then?'

There was another silence, then Solange burst out, 'You mean to stay here at Belmanoir, don't you, *madame,* in spite of the curse?'

This time Samma sighed aloud. 'Oh, Solange, you know as well as I do that there is no curse. You invented it so you could play tricks on your companions and get rid of them.'

'A little—maybe,' Solange admitted. 'But the curse is real, and it will fall on you if you stay. It would be safer if you went now.'

In that, Samma thought wryly, she was probably quite right.

She shook her head. 'Sorry, *chérie. Le Diable* himself would have to appear and order me to walk the plank before I'd take any notice. And even then I'd probably challenge him to a duel.'

'You must not joke about such things.' Samma
sudenly realised that Solange was trembling. 'You are
in danger.'

'We live in a dangerous world.' Samma dropped on
to her haunches beside her stepdaughter. 'Solange,'
she said gently, 'you mustn't let these silly old stories
get to you.'

'They are not stories,' Solange denied. 'The hating
is real, and it is all around you. You must believe me.'

Samma smiled at her. 'Well, I'll believe that you
believe it, and that will have to do. And now I'm going
down for a swim. Care to join me by the pool?'

Solange visibly shrank, shaking her head
vehemently, and Samma did not press the point.
There was time, she thought. All the time in the
world.

She was sorry the Delacroix curse had raised its
ugly head again, she reflected as she changed in her
room, but at least this time Solange had been warning
her about it, instead of threatening her, which had to
be a step in the right direction.

On her way downstairs, she remembered that she
hadn't yet told Elvire that she and Roche would be
dining out. She recalled, too, that she'd seen Elvire
going towards her room in the other wing a little
earlier.

She was just about to knock on the door, when she
heard the unmistakable sound of deep and passionate
sobbing coming from within. She stood very still for a
moment, feeling slightly sick. Elvire might have
declared her intention of leaving Belmanoir, but that
didn't inevitably mean her love for Roche was dead.

It must hurt her, Samma decided wretchedly, to
know that he's started paying attention to me. His

sending me that dress must have confirmed all her worst fears. And what kind of happiness can I build with him on the foundation of someone else's misery?

She shivered. Would Elvire be always there—between them, even in absence?

One thing was certain. She couldn't disturb Elvire now that her serene mask had slipped, and she was giving way to her unhappiness and bitterness.

I'm the last person in the world she'll want to see, Samma thought, turning away. I'll speak to Roxanne instead.

But the incident cast a shadow over the afternoon, which not even swimming and sunning herself could dispel.

And, later, as she walked back to the house to begin getting ready for her dinner date with Roche, she felt that same odd conviction that someone was watching her. She halted abruptly, peering through the tall hibiscus hedges.

She said directly, 'Is someone there? Hippolyte—is that you?' But only silence answered her.

She tried to tell herself that she'd imagined it because she was on edge, but she couldn't convince herself. That awareness of prying eyes had been too strong, too definite.

As she entered the house, she could hear from the *salon* Solange's voice raised in angry, tearful protest, mingling with Roche's deeper tones, and groaned inwardly.

'What's the matter?' she asked, as she went into the room.

'You are going out tonight, and leaving me alone here. I do not wish that.' There were bright spots of colour burning in the child's cheeks.

'You grow above yourself, *mon enfant*,' Roche said

coldly. 'Understand that you do not dictate to me now or at any time.'

'But I am frightened to be alone,' Solange said, her face crumpling desolately.

'This nonsense again!' Roche raised clenched fists towards the ceiling in a gesture of total exasperation. He swung towards Samma. 'Will you please explain to this child that the possession of new clothes does not automatically grant her the right to accompany us wherever we go?'

Samma tried to pour oil on troubled waters. 'Papa and I are only having dinner together, *chérie*. Everyone in the restaurant will be grown up. You would be very bored.'

'I want to go with you,' Solange said defiantly. 'I am always being left here alone.'

Samma turned to Roche, 'Couldn't we . . .?

'No,' he said icily. 'We could not, *ma belle*. I refuse to submit to this kind of emotional blackmail from a child. Solange must learn that we need some time to ourselves, you and I.'

'But if she's frightened of being alone . . .' Samma persisted in a low voice.

Roche gestured impatiently. *'Qu'est-ce que tu as?* A houseful of servants, including Elvire, hardly implies total solitude.' He directed a minatory glance at his angry daughter. 'You are becoming spoiled, *ma petite*. I also have a claim to Samantha's time and company. She does not belong to you alone.'

'And she does not belong here, either,' Solange burst out. *'Le Diable* is going to make her sorry that she came here!' she added with a little wail, and ran out of the room.

Samma made to follow her, but Roche's hand closed on her arm.

'Leave her,' he directed curtly. 'Nothing will be
gained by pandering to these tantrums of hers.'

'I suppose not.' Samma bit her lip. 'But I hate to see
her so unhappy.'

Roche's lips twisted slightly. 'I see she has found
the way to that soft heart of yours, *ma chère*. But you
must not let her impose on you.'

Samma looked down at the floor. 'Maybe, if you
gave her more of your time—behaved more warmly
towards her, she wouldn't constantly seek attention
like this,' she suggested in a low voice.

She expected some angry come-back but, after a
pause, Roche said quietly, 'Perhaps you are right,
Samantha, but it is not easy for me for all kinds of
reasons. There is still so much you do not
understand.'

'Then tell me,' she begged.

He lifted a hand and ran it gently down the curve of
her cheek. 'Later, *mignonne*. When we are truly
alone.'

And with that, she supposed, she had to be content.

Upstairs, she ran a deep, hot bath, and luxuriated in
its scented water, letting the odd tensions which the
day had produced drain out of her. She massaged
body lotion into her glowing skin, before slipping on
lacy briefs, and a matching underskirt. The design of
the white dress wouldn't permit her to wear a bra.

Sitting at her dressing-table, she experimented with
various ways of doing her hair, before deciding rather
ruefully to allow it to swing soft and shining on her
shoulders in the usual way. She took extra care with
her make-up, shadowing her eyes so that they looked
wide and mysterious, accentuating the warm bloom of
her cheeks.

I look like a woman dressing for her lover, she

thought, and felt her entire body clench in warm, pleasurable yearning at the thought.

Barefoot, she rose, and went across to the closet to get the dress. Elvire, she thought frowningly, had not put it away with her usual care, demonstrating her emotional agitation. In fact, it was sticking out from the surrounding garments, and half off its hanger.

She thought, 'I hope it's not creased,' then stopped, a little choking cry of disbelief escaping her lips, as she saw the gaping tears and slashes all down the front which had destroyed it. The lovely filmy skirt was in rags, and the bodice had been ripped apart in total wanton devastation.

The dress fell from her shaking hands on to the carpet as nausea rose within her.

Oh, Solange—no! Please don't let it be Solange, she thought with a kind of agony.

Could this really be what the little girl's tearful, angry exit had led to? And what would Roche say when he found out?

If he found out, Samma thought, feverishly bundling the pathetic heap of fabric to the back of the wardrobe. Relations between Roche and Solange seemed strained enough. If he discovered his gift had been deliberately ruined, then his anger would be formidable, and Solange was already far too nervous and highly strung.

If that was all, Samma thought, shivering. The rips in the dress had obviously been made with a knife, or a sharp pair of scissors in a blind fury of hatred and jealousy which went beyond mere temper tantrums. Could a small girl really possess so sick and violent a mind? It didn't bear thinking about.

There was a tap on the door, and Roche said, 'Are you ready, *ma belle?*'

She clutched at the towel she was wearing draped over her bare shoulders. 'I'll be five minutes,' she called back shakily.

There was laughter in his voice, 'You are making me impatient, Samantha. Are you sure you need no assistance—with a zip, perhaps?'

'No.' She got the words out somehow. 'I can manage.'

'*Quel dommage,*' he said still laughing, and she heard his footsteps retreating.

Samma pulled out another dress at random, black, square-necked and long-sleeved. It was chic, and its stark lines added an air of fragility to her blonde looks, but it was not the dress she had dreamed all day of wearing for him, of entrancing him in so that he would forget Elvire for ever—the dress she'd imagined him removing with passionate tenderness.

When she was ready, she surveyed herself. The happy colour in her face, the light in her eyes had faded, she thought sadly. She looked strained, wary again. What was it he'd once called her? 'A little cat that has never known kindness.'

A little cat, she thought, that's been kicked too many times.

She let herself out on to the balcony and went along to Solange's room. The little girl, propped up by pillows, was reading, her face still tearstained. She glanced up with a mutinous thrust of her lower lip, as Samma walked towards her, then her face sharpened with surprise and disappointment.

'Where is your lovely dress?'

'I think you know' Samma kept her voice level. In the big bed, Solange looked so small, so fragile to have inflicted such damage.

Solange frowned. 'I do not understand.'

'Then that makes two of us.' Samma sat down
wearily on the edge of the bed. She said, 'Solange,
things can't go on like this. I thought we had agreed
no more tricks—although what you did to my dress is
worse than any trick.' She glanced round her. 'What
did you use—one of the knives from the kitchen?
You'd better give it back to me and . . .'

'What did I use for what?' Solange's face was small
and pinched suddenly. 'The dress—something has
happened to it?'

'It's cut to ribbons—totally ruined, as you very well
know.' Samma swallowed. 'And this is something we
can't keep between the two of us. Papa is bound to
find out eventually . . .'

'You think I cut your dress? But I did not. I could
not! It was so beautiful. I wanted to see you in it
looking like a fairy princess. I wanted to be with you
when you wore it.' The anguish in the child's voice
was genuine. 'Samma, you must believe me. I would
not do such a thing, even if I was angry—oh, beyond
words.'

'Nevertheless, it has happened, and someone must
be responsible.' Samma kept her voice level. 'Have
you any idea who it could be?'

There was a perceptible hesitation, then Solange
said in a half-whisper, *'Le Diable* . . .'

'Is dead,' Samma said patiently. 'My dress was
damaged by someone who's very much alive.'

Solange shivered. 'But he—makes things happen, I
think. I said you were in danger.'

Her gaze did not meet her stepmother's. Samma
thought, She's protecting someone—she must be.
Someone who established a right to her loyalty before
I ever got here. But whom? Almost against her will,
she remembered the sound of that desolate, bitter

weeping from Elvire's room earlier. Had that lonely grief erupted into malice, and a final despairing blow against the girl who was supplanting her with Roche? It was almost as unpalatable an idea as her original fear that it might have been Solange. She got up wearily.

'We'll talk tomorrow,' she said quietly. 'Don't worry, I'll sort something out.'

Solange gave a small, reluctant nod. 'But take care,' she said in that same scared whisper.

Roche was waiting for Samma at the foot of the stairs. His brows rose in autocratic enquiry when he saw her. 'Why that dress, *ma belle,* and not the other?'

'The—the white dress needs some alteration,' Samma improvised hastily. It wasn't altogether a lie, she thought sadly.

'It does?' Roche sounded faintly surprised, then smiled reluctantly. *'Eh bien,* I am well paid for my arrogance in thinking I could gauge your size with total accuracy.' The dark eyes caressed her with disturbing warmth. 'And what does it matter? You, *mignonne,* look beautiful in anything—or nothing,' he added softly.

Swift heat invaded Samma's face, and she couldn't think of a single thing to say in reply. And the silence continued as she sat beside him in the car, as they sped towards St Laurent.

'Why so quiet?' he asked at last. 'Are you regretting your promise to dine with me?'

'Oh, no!' The denial was so immediate and vehement that she embarrassed herself.

'Then what is wrong?'

She swallowed. 'Oh—things.'

'Solange?'

Samma moved her shoulders evasively. 'Perhaps.'

He sent her a swift smile. 'I said she was not to accompany us, *ma belle,* and I meant it. I want no one in your thoughts tonight but myself.' His mouth twisted in self-deprecation. 'Desire for you makes me selfish, *chérie.*'

Her heart was beating like a drum. It was so difficult to remember she wasn't the first one he'd beguiled with that seductive tenderness in his voice. the first one to be taken to heaven or hell in his arms.

Although the hell would come later, she thought, biting her lip, when he no longer desired her.

She found a voice from somewhere. 'Where are we going?'

'To the casino. I remember you once expressed an interest in it, and I have an excellent chef there.' He shot her a glance. 'I hope you are not disappointed?'

'Not at all.' If he'd suggested a visit to the local electricity plant she would probably have been equally beguiled, she thought ruefully.

Her first sight of the casino made her gasp out loud. A great central tower, flanked by ramparts and gun emplacements, it loomed over the edge of the harbour like some predatory grey stone beast.

'What do you think?' Roche asked, as he swerved the car expertly under its gate.

'It looks more like an armed fortress than a place of entertainment,' Samma said rather dazedly, and he laughed.

'You are right, *ma belle.* It was, of course, *Le Diable's* stronghold. But these days the victims come willingly to be pirated of their loot.'

The forbidding exterior gave no clue to the luxury to be found within, Samma soon discovered. While the character of the building had been retained, no expense had been spared on the décor, and other details. It was romantically and unashamedly opulent, Samma thought, gazing upwards at crystal chandeliers, while her high heels sank into deep piled carpet.

'The gaming-rooms and the restaurant are all on the first floor,' Roche told her. 'And the administrative offices and my suite are on the next floor. We will see them later.'

There was a table awaiting them in the bar, and an attentive waiter hovering to serve drinks.

'A champagne cocktail.' Roche's smile was wicked as he handed Samma her glass. 'I thought you should know what they really taste like. Perhaps it will stop you from hurling it at me.' He ran a slow finger down the curve of her cheek. 'I am still waiting to exact my revenge for that little incident,' he murmured, and Samma's first sampling of her drink was a gulp which nearly made her choke.

When she had recovered her breath, and her equilibrium, she began to look around her, partly out of genuine curiosity, but mostly to avoid the disturbing intensity of Roche's gaze.

The restaurant lay beyond an elegantly draped archway, and Samma could see that nearly all the tables were already occupied by sleek, bejewelled women and their dinner-jacket-clad escorts. From somewhere she could hear dance music being played by a small but sophisticated combo. The whole atmosphere breathed money, and something more. There was a buzz, a genuine excitement in the air that she supposed gambling for high stakes engendered. She shrugged mentally. She herself had never been able to see the attraction, but then she'd had Clyde as an awful warning.

'What are you thinking?' Roche asked, his face quizzical.

She smiled faintly. 'Just wondering where all the rich people come from.'

'I think they flock like migrating birds from one fashionable place to another,' he said drily. 'At the moment, Grand Cay is a fashionable place.'

'And if they suddenly change their minds?'

He laughed. 'Afraid I will let you starve, *migonne?*' he mocked. 'I won't. The casino is only one of my business interests—and the least interesting. Like my black-hearted ancestor, I prefer boats.'

Samma felt a little shiver run through her. She said tautly, 'Could we leave *Le Diable* out of the conversation for once, please? I've had enough of him.'

'My own sentiments entirely. And we have other topics to discuss.' He paused. 'Samantha, do you remember my telling you early in our acquaintance that I had a mistress? It is time I explained to you exactly what I meant.'

Her mouth went dry. 'There's no need. I—I know already. You—you must know that I do.'

'What do I know?' His mouth twisted wryly. 'We are just beginning to learn about each other, *ma chère.* I did not realise you found me so transparent.'

'That's hardly the word I'd have used,' Samma said in a low voice, her gaze fixed on her barely touched drink. She took a deep breath. 'Roche—I can't—share you.'

'You will not have to,' he said softly. 'That period in my life is over. At the time it filled a need—a loneliness, or I thought it did.'

She thought, wincing, of Elvire's need, of Elvire's loneliness. Had she spoken to Roche, told him she was leaving? No more secrets, he had said, but there were still questions she dared not ask. Perhaps there always would be. Perhaps this would be the price she would pay for loving a man like Roche Delacroix.

She said huskily, 'Please can we talk about something else?'

'Later,' he said gently. 'First, we have a small matter of business to transact.' He looked past her, lifting his hand in smiling acknowledgement. As Samma glanced round, she saw Maître Giraud coming towards them.

'Madame Delacroix.' He bowed over her hand, his eyes dancing with admiration. 'You look radiant—*ravissante*. I need not ask if marriage is agreeable to you.'

Samma flushed, murmuring something in reply, while Jean-Paul turned to Roche.

'I have the papers here,' he announced, tapping the document case he was carrying. 'Have you explained your intentions to your bride?'

'Not yet.' Roche took her hand. 'I am making certain settlements on your behalf, *chérie*. It is time your finances were placed on a regular basis.'

'Is that really necessary?' she asked, unevenly.

'It is, believe me,' Jean-Paul put in. 'One must be prudent, after all, and if anything were to happen to Roche . . .'

Samma shook her head violently. 'I don't even want to think about that,' she said. 'Please—can't we leave things as they are?'

'That is impossible,' Roche told her gently. 'You are my wife, *ma belle*, and your status requires safeguards. I wish to do this for you.'

Samma looked down at the table. 'It—it wasn't in our—original agreement,' she reminded him, low-voiced.

His fingers clasped hers more strongly. 'That, I think is something we shall have to re-negotiate.'

There was a faint note of laughter in his voice. 'When the papers are signed, and we are alone.' He got to his feet. 'I suggest we waste no more time.'

Samma felt as if she was being swept away on some slow, inexorable tide.

She was trapped, she thought, between the force of her own desire, and the enigma Roche still represented. Caught, as she'd always been, between the devil and the deep sea which waited to engulf her.

I ought to run, she thought. Escape while I still have the strength—before, like Elvire, I have no pride left.

They rode up to his office suite in a streamlined lift. Roche's room was vast, dominated by a battery of television screens which provided a panoramic view of the gaming-rooms below.

'Don't you trust your staff?' Samma stared at the screens, intrigued in spite of herself at the hectic activity they displayed.

'Implicitly,' Roche returned. 'But sometimes it is possible to see trouble coming, and fend it off before it gets out of hand.' He smiled faintly. 'Hugo Baxter is only one of a breed.'

She grimaced. 'I suppose so.'

Maître Giraud was spreading papers across the big desk. Obediently she signed where she was told, a little alarmed by the sums of money she saw mentioned. Roche added his own signature almost negligently, then opened the bottle of champagne which had been waiting in its cooler.

'To marriage,' he said lifting his glass.

Jean-Paul laughed. 'That is one toast I never expected to hear you make, *mon vieux*.'

A buzzer sounded, and Roche walked round his desk to flick an intercom switch.

He said brusquely, 'I thought I had made it clear I did not wish to be disturbed . . .' He listened frowningly, then sighed. 'Very well, I will come down.'

'Problems?' Jean-Paul asked.

'A request for credit which my house manager does not feel equal to refusing,' Roche said, with a touch of grimness. 'Entertain Samantha until I return, *mon ami.*'

'With the utmost pleasure,' Jean-Paul said promptly, refilling Samma's glass with champagne.

She sipped slowly, assimilating more of her surroundings. Long windows had been opened to the warm night, and a table set with snowy linen and silver cutlery had been placed in front of them. Roche intended them to dine up here, it seemed. And on the other side of the room was a door, half-opened, and affording an unmistakable glimpse of a bed, with its covers invitingly turned down.

'A true home from home,' Jean-Paul commented laconically, following the direction of her gaze.

She swallowed some more wine. 'I—suppose so. And Roche did live here, didn't he?'

'At one time,' Jean-Paul agreed. 'In the bad days which are now, I hope, gone forever.' He paused. 'I will be frank. I was—alarmed by this hasty marriage of yours. Roche and I have been friends for years, and I could not bear it if he made another mistake, but seeing you together has allayed my fears completely.' He sighed slightly. 'In fact, I am almost tempted to try my own luck again.'

'You're not married?' Samma was frankly surprised. Jean-Paul was clearly affluent, ambitious and with more than his fair share of attraction.

There was a silence, then he said slowly, 'At one time I hoped to be, but the woman I loved would not have me. There was, she considered, an impediment which her pride would not allow her to ignore. I was young and intolerant, and we—parted.'

'I'm sorry,' Samma said with sincerity.

'I was a fool,' he said, with a shrug. 'I should have overruled her, swept her off her feet. I see her now from time to time, and I know that for me it is still the same, but for her—who can say?'

He smiled at Samma. 'Perhaps I should engage you, Madame Delacroix, to plead my cause—to convince her that love is real, and marriage can still bring joy.'

She flushed. 'I think I should have to be married for much longer to sound really convincing.' Wanting to change the subject, she went on, 'Those awful people—the Augustins—did they leave?'

'*Mais oui,* and if God is good they will never return,' Jean-Paul said with a sigh. 'All you have to do, *madame,* is stay married to Roche. If you decided to leave him, it might be a different story.'

Samma set her glass down slowly on the desk, aware of an odd sinking sensation deep inside her. 'You mean—if Roche and I separated, they would try again for custody of Solange?'

'*Certainement.*' He smiled at her. 'But I have it on the best authority that your husband has not the slightest intention of letting you go, so be warned.'

'He told you so?' Her heart was thudding unsteadily, and the palms of her hands felt damp.

'Only yesterday,' he said casually. 'He admitted to me, as a friend, you understand, that he would do anything to keep you at his side.' He sighed again. 'That is love, *n'est-ce pas?*' He paused. 'Some more champagne?'

'No—thank you,' Samma managed. She felt sick suddenly—sick and bitterly humiliated. Everything Roche had said, everything he'd done, was revealed in a new and shaming light.

And she'd fallen for it, she thought despairingly. She'd allowed herself to believe that he was beginning to care for her—let herself be seduced with the promise of love—without seeing the harshly cynical motivation which had prompted his advances to her.

I saw only what I wanted to see, she thought, as pain lashed at her.

Jean-Paul was staring at her. 'Are you well, *madame?* You are very pale.'

Out of a constricted throat, she managed, 'It's a little warm in here, and I'm not used to champagne.'

Jean-Paul moved purposefully towards the intercom. 'I will call Roche.'

'No—please. I—I don't want to worry him. I think I'd better go back—to Belmanoir.' She moistened dry lips with the tip of her tongue. She started for the door, then stopped as it opened, and Roche came in.

'*Mon Dieu,* what a scene!' he said ruefully. '*Mignonne,* I'm sorry. I have been neglecting you again, in spite of my guarantee earlier.' He gave her a close look. 'Is something wrong?'

'She seems to be a little faint,' Jean-Paul said concernedly. 'Shall I fetch someone?'

Roche shook his head. 'I will look after her.' He turned to Samma. 'You are probably just hungry, *ma belle.* I will tell them to serve dinner at once.'

It would be so easy to tell herself that the gentleness in his voice was genuine—so easy, and so totally, fatally stupid. She'd been on the verge of making a complete and pathetic fool of herself, yet again. She should be thankful she'd been spared that humiliation at least.

She heard Jean-Paul say something tactful about leaving them together, and then, at long last and all too late, they were alone.

CHAPTER ELEVEN

'WHAT is it, *ma belle?*' His voice and face tender, Roche drew Samma into his arms, tensing when he felt her instinctive recoil. '*Mon Dieu,* you cannot be frightened of me! There is no need, I swear. I will be gentle . . .'

'No,' Samma said hoarsely. 'You're not going to touch me. You're not going to come near me.'

'*Chérie,* what is this? *Qu'est-ce que tu as?*' He stared at her. 'Are you really ill? Shall I send for a doctor?'

She said, 'I'm not ill. I may have been blind for a time, but that's over now.'

Roche flung his head back. 'And what does that mean?' he asked evenly.

She walked over to the desk, where the settlement papers were still lying, as she said, 'You've been very generous today, Roche, but there was no need.' She picked up the papers and tore them across, again and again. She went on, 'I've no doubt you'd have been equally generous in bed. That was the new deal, I take it—the re-negotiation you mentioned. Cash, and——' her voice faltered slightly '—and sex to keep me sweet —to keep me on Grand Cay—because if I left you, the Augustins would make another claim for Solange—and with two failed marriages behind you, Judge Lefèvre might take a different view next time.' She took a deep breath. 'Isn't that how it was?'

He said harshly, 'You seem to have it all worked out, *ma belle.* You tell me.'

It was an effort to meet the blaze of anger in his face

162

without quailing, but Samma bravely continued, 'But you had no need to go to those lengths. As I told you on *Allegra*, I'm here because I feel so sorry for your little girl. Your—money—a relationship—they never mattered. I never wanted either.' The words were like knives, twisting in her. 'I—I know I threatened to leave, but that was in the heat of the moment. I would have changed my mind—for Solange's sake. There was no necessity for a full-scale seduction, with financial inducements. I'll stay anyway—but without the money.' In spite of herself, her voice shook. 'And without you.'

The anger in him was almost tangible. He said too quietly, 'You are so sure the choice is yours to make?'

His hands reached for her, took her before she could back away. Her protesting cry was smothered by the heated violence of his mouth. Her hands rained blows on his chest, until he dragged her so close that her clenched fists were trapped against the hardness of his body, making further resistance an impossibility.

A lifetime ago, he'd teased her—excited her with the possibility of exacting some sensual vengeance from her. Now this had become an angry, terrifying reality. There was no more laughter, no more tenderness —just a stark and ruthless passion intent on enforcing submission, however reluctant.

When at last he lifted his head, she was weak and trembling in his arms, panic turning her limbs to water.

He said with dangerous softness, 'I brought you here to make love to you, my lovely wife, and I shall do so, with or without your permission. You will understand, I am sure, that I cannot promise under the circumstances to show you the understanding and forbearance that I once intended.' He shrugged. 'But as you do not want me anyway, what difference can it make?'

He swung her up into his arms, and carried her into the other room, tossing her contemptuously across the bed. He shrugged off his jacket, dropping it to the floor, and tugged at his black tie.

He said icily, 'If you wish to have a dress fit to go home in, *madame*, I suggest you remove it now.'

Her voice was shaking uncontrollably now, as she saw the abyss which had opened in front of her. 'Roche—please. You don't really want me—you know that . . .'

'How can I know?' His lip curled as he unbuttoned his shirt and stripped it off. 'You have been so sparing with your favours, *mignonne*. You have made me—curious, if nothing else. Now strip, before I do it for you.'

He meant it. She could see it in the smouldering light in his eyes, the harsh set of his jaw.

She gave a little sob, and fumbled for her zip.

In the other room, a telephone began to ring suddenly with loud, jarring insistence. Roche paused in his undressing, and a small, silent sigh of relief rose within her, but after a brief, furious glance in the direction of the desk, he evidently decided to ignore the interruption.

He said coldly, 'You are keeping me waiting.'

She said, 'The phone . . .'

'Can go to hell.' He smiled at her without amusement. 'I gave orders for my—night of love—to be without interruption.'

'But it could be important . . .' The pleading in her voice was unmistakable.

'Nothing, *ma belle*, could match the importance of having you—at last.' His tone jeered at her, made light of the sacrifice of her innocence.

He sat down on the bed beside her, his fingers wrenching at her zip. The dress fell away, and she felt his mouth caressing the nape of her neck, his fingers tracing the long, naked length of her back. Felt the unbidden quickening of her own flesh in response to his touch. Felt all the agony of a need she could not deny.

Very slowly, she turned to him, aware of the flame of his eyes touching her bare breasts. His hands took her shoulders, pushing her back against the pillow, and she made no resistance, her lips parting achingly as he bent over her. She knew the warmth of his breath on her face, the brush of his naked flesh against her own as he came down to her, and a little sigh, half yearning, half capitulation escaped her.

For a long moment, he looked into her widening eyes, then he said with cold mockery, 'And yet you tell me you don't want me.'

He lifted himself away from her, and walked into the other room to the desk, and the clamouring telephone. As if from a great distance, Samma watched him lift the receiver, heard him say curtly, '*Oui?*'

She saw the fierceness fade from his face, to be replaced with concern, as he said swiftly, 'Elvire—*c'est toi?* At this hour? What is wrong?'

But of course, thought Samma, who else could it possibly be? I suppose I should be—grateful . . .

She pulled her dress back into place, fastened it, found her shoes, and was past him and at the door of the office almost before he seemed aware of her presence.

She heard him say her name sharply, but she didn't even pause, running down the corridor towards the lift.

She had a breathing space. Apart from his conversation with his mistress, Roche would hardly be likely to pursue her through the casino next door to naked.

As the lift reached the ground floor, she forced herself to walk without hurrying to the main entrance.

The uniformed commissionaire touched his cap respectfully.

'*Bonsoir, m'dame.* Can I help you?'

'I would like a cab,' she said. 'Is that possible?'

'But of course.' He put his fingers to his lips and whistled, and one of the local taxis appeared as if from nowhere.

'On Mist' Roche's account, boy,' the commissionaire instructed as he opened the door and helped Samma into the car. He paused. 'Where are you going, *m'dame?*'

There was nowhere. No sanctuary—no safe refuge. No escape.

She said wearily, 'Take me to Belmanoir.'

All the lights seemed to be pouring out of the house as the cab drew up outside.

Samma hurried up the steps. She'd hoped to make her return under the cover and privacy of darkness, but even that was being denied her, she thought bitterly.

As she walked in through the door, Elvire came to meet her, her face strained.

'So you have come—thank God!' She stared past Samma. 'But where is Roche?'

Samma shrugged. 'At the casino, I suppose. You spoke to him last.'

'You mean, he has not come with you to search?' Elvire looked shaken—almost appalled.

'Search for what?'

'He did not tell you? *Mon Dieu,* it is beyond belief.' Elvire ran distracted fingers through her hair. 'Solange is not in her room. She has vanished—God alone knows where.'

'Vanished?' Samma echoed dazedly. 'But that's impossible. She's playing one of her tricks—hiding somewhere to wind us all up.'

'We have searched the house, all of us, and Hippolyte has been through the grounds three times.'

Samma felt sick suddenly. 'The pool?'

Elvire put a hand on her arm. 'He looked there first.'

'Could she have gone to Les Arbres to see Madame Duvalle?'

'I have been telephoning the house, but there is no answer.' There was a silence, then Elvire said with a little wail, 'Oh, why should she do such a thing?'

Samma felt heat burn into her face. 'She may be feeling guilty. My new dress was cut to pieces earlier, and I let her know I thought she was to blame. She swore she wasn't responsible, but perhaps . . .'

Elvire gave her an astonished look. 'Your dress? But that is impossible! She has no reason . . .'

'Except that she hates me—that she wants me gone from here.'

'Are you so sure? I had thought things were better between you.' Elvire paused. 'Show me this dress.'

In Samma's room, she stood staring at the deep slashes which mutilated the fabric from neckline to hem. At last, she said positively, 'Solange did not do that. Physically, it is not possible. The rail is high, and she could not have reached to make cuts as long as these.'

'Yet someone did.' Samma's voice shook. 'Someone

else who hates me. Was it you, Elvire?' She saw a look
of blank amazement enter the other girl's eyes, and
hurried on, 'I wouldn't blame you, if it was. You
think I'm a rival, don't you? But I'm not. Roche
doesn't really want me. I threatened to leave him, you
see, and he thought if he was—nice to me, I could be
persuaded to stay.' She bit her lip. 'But that's
all—sorted now. So there's no reason for you to leave.
I'm just staying here to—look after Solange. Roche
and I—there's nothing,' she added on a pitiful little
rush of words.

There was a long, tense silence. Elvire stood,
staring at Samma, as taut as a bowstring, a small
muscle moving in her throat.

Finally, she said, her voice breaking, 'Ah,
Dieu—you little fool! You think then that Roche and
I . . .?' She groaned. 'But it is impossible. You said
you knew—that you understood. I thought that when
Solange spoke about the portraits of the Delacroix
women you must have guessed—seen the resemblance, somehow. I told Roche that you knew the
truth—and all the time you thought that we . . .' She
gave a strained laugh. 'Blame my pride, Samantha.
The devilish Delacroix pride. I sometimes think that
is the real curse *Le Diable* bestowed on our family.'

Samma said shakily, 'Delacroix—you're a
Delacroix?'

Elvire nodded. 'Roche's—half-sister. His father was
mine, too—something I have always hated—resented.
Something I have always tried to conceal.'

'But why?' Samma's head was reeling. 'There's no
real stigma these days . . .'

'You think not? Well, *peut-être* in a more open
society—but this is a small island. My mother came to
Belmanoir as a nurse to care for Madame Delacroix

after her accident. Antoine Delacroix was lonely—desperate. He loved his wife, and had been warned that because of her injuries they might never again enjoy a normal relationship. My mother was beautiful, and they were much in each other's company. It was inevitable, I suppose, that they should become lovers. At the very time my mother became pregnant, Mathilde Delacroix began to recover, and Maman was sent away. Antoine provided money, of course, but he never saw Maman again. He never acknowledged me, although before he died he told Roche of my existence. Roche sought me out, and befriended me. He wanted to claim me openly as his sister, but I would not allow it. I told him I wanted no part of the Delacroix name—that no one must ever know, unless I gave permission.' She gave Samma a rueful look. 'Not even you, *madame, ma belle-soeur.*'

'Did you never tell anyone?' Samma shook her head in disbelief.

'Only one—the man who wished to marry me. He comes from an old and distinguished family—and had an important career in front of him. He needed a wife with advantages, not from a background as questionable as mine, so I refused him, and left Grand Cay. I threw myself into my own work—did too much, and suffered a mental crisis. Roche brought me back here to recuperate and rest. As I recovered, Marie-Christine arrived, and I agreed to stay and nurse her back to some kind of sanity and sobriety.' She paused, with a sigh. 'As you know, I failed.'

Samma stared at her. 'It was Jean-Paul Giraud, wasn't it—the man you loved?'

Elvire gave a constricted smile. 'This time you have guessed correctly. Bravo.'

'It was no guess. It was something he said himself.'

Samma swallowed. 'He—he's still in love with you. Do you know that?'

Elvire was very still for a moment. Then she said, very quietly, 'But nothing has changed. I am still Antoine Delacroix's bastard daughter—and of mixed race, besides. He would be mad to take me. I would be cruel to allow it.'

Samma said with a catch in her voice, 'That's something open to debate, I suspect. But what we have to do now is find Solange.' She looked at the slashes in the dress, and dropped the garment to the floor with an open shudder. 'And quickly.'

They searched the house again, calling the child's name, coaxing and cajoling her to come out of hiding, but there was no reply. Then they went out into the gardens with torches, and hunted again.

'Where's Mist' Roche?' Hippolyte asked Samma, as they made yet another fruitless circuit of the pool. 'Why's he not here, *m'dame?*'

Samma stifled a sigh. 'I wish I knew, Hippolyte.' She had rarely felt so frightened and so helpless. Solange seemed to have vanished into thin air, and she didn't know where to look next. Could Solange have set off on foot for St Laurent to find them, in defiance of her father's ban?

Surely not, Samma thought. Yet—she was frightened. She said she didn't want to be left here.

She stood staring into the darkness, realising with a start just what had attracted her attention.

'Hippolyte—I can see lights in the distance. What are they?'

'Oh, that's Les Arbres, *m'dame.*'

Samma said slowly, 'Is it so close? I didn't realise.' But if there were lights at Les Arbres it meant that Liliane Duvalle had returned. She and Solange were close. Maybe she would have some idea what had happened to the child . . . She stopped suddenly as a thought, totally unwelcome in its novelty, occurred to her.

She said, 'How do I get to Les Arbres, Hippolyte? Isn't there a short-cut through the gardens?'

'Oui, m'dame.' He pointed. 'Along the edge of the old plantation, where the slave cabins used to be.' He gave her a doubtful glance. 'Shall I come too?'

'No,' she said steadily. 'I'll find it. You concentrate on looking closer to home, Hippolyte. This is a long shot.'

Her torch was powerful, and lit the way well enough. Samma ran at a steady jog-trot, her brain teeming as it examined a new and frightening possibility.

Liliane Duvalle, she thought, the close neighbour, and family friend, whose obsession with *Le Diable* equalled Solange's. Who came and went at Belmanoir pretty much as she pleased. Whose presence would probably not even be remarked upon, if noticed. Who had been, on her own admission, a constant visitor to Marie-Christine, and knew of her predilection for vodka.

Oh God, she thought. Tell me I'm wrong. I *must* be wrong!

But, the more she thought about it, the more hideously possible it seemed. She had allowed herself to become so obsessed with Elvire that it had not occurred to her there was another young, attractive woman nearby with whom Roche might have been involved. A woman who might feel injured when supplanted by a younger rival.

She was breathless by the time she reached the house. The light she'd noticed was coming from one of the ground-floor rooms. She made herself slow down, and move quietly.

There was no point, after all, in barging in, making wild accusations which she could not substantiate.

Hearing the murmur of voices, Samma flattened herself against the wall before allowing herself a cautious peep through the open window.

The first person she saw was Solange, crouching, in a big chair. Her eyes were like saucers, her small face pinched and sallow.

She could not see Liliane Duvalle, but she could hear her voice, soft and terrifyingly normal. 'But we are friends, *mon enfant*. That girl is not your friend. She is your enemy.'

Solange swallowed. 'She talks like my friend. She is kind to me. She says she will not send me away.'

'That is what she tells you now, but I know. Tante Liliane has always been right about the women your papa has brought to Belmanoir. They want him—they want his money, but they do not want you, *petite* Solange. Trust me, *chérie*. We will get rid of this woman, as we have the others. She has been clever. She has defied us, but we will win in the end.'

Solange shook her head. 'I do not want to win,' she said defiantly. 'I do not want Samma to go. I like her.'

Liliane Duvalle chuckled quietly. 'So much the worse for both of you,' she said. 'If she stays, she will be sorry. Her dress is only the beginning.'

As Madame Duvalle moved into sight, Samma bit back a cry. The older woman was holding Solange's doll in one hand, and a pair of sharp, long-bladed scissors in the other.

As Samma watched in horror, the scissors slashed at the doll until the long blonde hair fell to the floor in ragged chunks.

'How beautiful will you be then, Madame Delacroix?' Liliane Duvalle said, and laughed.

From somewhere, Samma found the energy to move. She was through the half-open front door, and into the room before she'd even had a chance to consider what strategy she could employ. All she could think of was Solange's safety.

Solange screamed her name, and Liliane Duvalle swung round, her murderous scissors poised above the doll's face.

She smiled gaily. 'All the better,' she said. 'The pretty doll in reality.' And came towards Samma, the blades upraised.

Samma felt frozen. She put out her hands to block the other woman's advance. My face, she thought, I must protect my face! And she was aware, as if in a dream, of hands gripping her waist, lifting her out of harm's way.

Roche said grimly. 'Put the scissors down, Liliane.'

She stopped, staring at him, her face relaxing into warmth and charm.

She said with a little sigh, 'Roche—*mon amour*. You have come to me at last, as I knew you would. I've wanted you for so long—offered myself so many times.' Her voice dropped confidentially. 'But I always knew that one day you would realise that we were meant for each other—why I could not allow any other woman to have you.'

She laughed suddenly, stridently. 'That drunken fool who called herself your wife was easy. I used to visit her—bring her little gifts—in bottles—tell her stories about the past. How alarmed she used to get— and the more disturbed she was, the more she drank.' She tutted. *'Quel dommage!'*

Roche said quietly, 'And the day she died——'

'I had visited her—talked with her.' She giggled.
'*Pauvre* Marie-Christine—she really believed the
curse was about to fall on her. I made sure she had the
car keys, then later I came back. I even drove with her
for part of the way, until we reached a suitable place,
then I let her take the wheel, and I—watched.'

She looked past him to Samma. 'And this child you
have brought to Belmanoir.' She touched the
mutilated doll with her foot. 'Will you want her, I
wonder, when I have finished with her?'

He said steadily. 'I want her, and I want my
daughter, Liliane. I will not allow you to hurt either
of them.'

Her smile vanished. Her voice high-pitched, she
said, 'Daughter? You have no daughter. Marie-
Christine told me so—told me all kinds of things.
How she'd made a fool of you—made you think you
were marrying an innocent virgin, when all the time
she was carrying another man's child.' She sent
Solange a venomous look. 'Why do you keep her with
you? You know you don't love her—that you can
hardly bear to look at her.'

Roche said quietly, 'Marie-Christine lied to you,
Liliane. She was my wife, and Solange is my child.'
He put out his hand. 'Come to me, *petite*.'

'No—send her away. There can only be the two of
us.' Madame Duvalle's scissors fell from her hand, as
she dropped to her knees in front of him. She flung
her arms round his legs, burying her face against his
thighs. 'Send them all away. Love me—only me!'

The harsh, grating sound of her sobbing filled the
room. In a way, it was worse than any of the threats
and revelations which had gone before, Samma
thought, nausea rising in her throat. As Solange ran to
her, she seized the child and held her tight, aware that

Elvire and Hippolyte were in the doorway.

She whispered, 'Get a doctor,' and saw Hippolyte fade away.

Elvire walked forwards and picked up the scissors, sliding them into her pocket. She said gently and calmly, 'Get up, *madame*. You need to rest.'

Liliane Duvalle looked up at her, her face blotched with weeping. 'But I have a rendezvous,' she said with total reason. 'A rendezvous with *Le Diable*. I have been waiting for him all my life, and now he is here with me.'

'He is waiting in your room,' Elvire said. 'Come with me now, and you will find him.'

Slowly, Liliane Duvalle got to her feet, and Elvire led her away.

Roche's face was grey as he watched them go. *'Dieu!'* he said unsteadily. 'When I think what could have happened . . .' He turned on Samma. 'I searched the casino for you, *madame,*' he told her grimly. 'It was fortunate I was able to reach you in time to save you from the consequences of your own folly, once I discovered where you had gone.'

'Tante Liliane came into my room, Papa,' Solange said in a small voice. 'She made me go with her. I did not want to, but she told me *Le Diable* would take me away if I stayed.'

'Le Diable is a story, *petite,'* Roche said gently. 'And stories cannot hurt you any more.'

'But he seemed real,' Solange said. 'He wanted me to do things to send Samma away—like pretending to drown so that you would be angry, and blame Samma. But I did not spoil the dress.'

Roche's brows snapped together. 'What is this?'

Samma bit her lip. 'The white dress you gave me. I found it cut to pieces in my room.'

Roche drew a deep breath. 'And did not tell me?'

'Samma thought I had done it, Papa. She did not want you to be cross with me. She did not tell you about the other things, either.' Solange's face was piteous suddenly. 'Papa, why did Tante Liliane say I was not your daughter?'

Roche's face softened. 'She made a mistake, *chérie*. You are my own, all my own.' He held out his arms, and she ran to him, her face transfigured as he swung her up, cradling her against his chest. Samma felt swift tears prick at her eyes. 'Now you must go home to bed.'

'I will go with Samma,' Solange said graciously. 'Will you come too, Papa?'

He shook his head, as he set the child on her feet. 'I must wait here for the doctor.'

'Is Tante Liliane sick?' Solange asked doubtfully.

Roche touched her cheek. 'Yes, *chérie*. More sick than any of us realised, but she will be better soon. Go now.'

Solange trotted obediently out of the room, but Samma lingered, her eyes searching her husband's averted face.

She said unhappily, 'Roche—I owe you an apology. I've jumped to many conclusions—made so many mistakes . . .'

'So I learn from Elvire.' His voice was a stranger's. 'I too am sorry, *madame,* for the grave mistake I made in bringing you here.' He shrugged. 'But fortunately, it can be corrected.'

She stared at him. 'I don't understand. I'm trying to put things right between us . . .'

His eyes swept over her in icy appraisal. 'And I am telling you, *madame,* that you are free to go—to leave Grand Cay. And the sooner the better,' he added, and walked out of the room.

CHAPTER TWELVE

SAMMA lay on the pool lounger, gazing sightlessly at the endless blue of the sky. She felt half-dead, but was it any wonder? she thought restlessly. Few of them had got much sleep the previous night.

There had been a hasty conference in the *salon* at Belmanoir, attended by the doctor, a startled Jean-Paul Giraud, and a quietly spoken, middle-aged man, who turned out to be Grand Cay's top policeman.

Liliane Duvalle had been removed by ambulance to a clinic in St Laurent, and placed under sedation. Efforts would be made to find her remaining relatives in France, and arrange repatriation as soon as she was well enough to travel. No charges of any kind would be preferred against her.

'At the moment she is inhabiting a fantasy world,' Dr Barras told them gravely. 'Her admission of involvement in the death of the late Marie-Christine Delacroix may be true, or simply part of that fantasy. At the moment, it is impossible to say.' He hesitated. 'And to supply an alcoholic woman with vodka is only a moral crime.'

'I blame myself,' Roche declared bitterly, dull colour staining his face. 'I should have realised that she was becoming obsessed with *Le Diable*—with me —and taken some avoiding action. But to me, she was nothing more than a neighbour who was sometimes a nuisance.' His flush deepened. 'Whose—attentions could sometimes be embarrassing.'

'*Mon pauvre.*' Elvire patted him on the shoulder.

177

'She did throw herself at you, then?'

His mouth tightened. 'Yes, even before Marie-Christine's return.'

Samma found her voice. 'How did she get into the house, and into my room in particular, without being seen?'

Roche did not answer or even look at her, and it was left to Elvire to explain, 'There is an old fire escape at the corner of the balcony. It is half hidden by the vine, and one tends to forget it is there. It seems she used that, especially when she used to visit Solange at night to give her *Le Diable's* latest instructions.'

Samma shuddered. 'That would explain the nightmares. And the fact that sometimes I felt I was being watched.'

The quiet man said, 'You are fortunate, Madame Delacroix, that she did nothing but look until this evening, and that your husband arrived in time to protect you.'

I almost wish he hadn't, Samma thought. If Liliane had plunged those scissors into me, I couldn't hurt more than I do now.

Elvire got to her feet. 'Poor creature,' she said soberly. 'In spite of what she has done, I pity her.' She paused. 'Now, shall we all have some coffee?'

As she'd left the room to fetch it, Samma saw Jean-Paul slip out after her. Perhaps some good will come out of all this after all, she thought.

She had gone to her room shortly afterwards, and lain awake, straining her ears for any sound of Roche coming to bed. But yet again, the adjoining room had not been used.

Samma sighed. Well, at least she knew that the nights when he'd been absent had not been spent with Elvire, she thought, her mouth twisting. But she was no wiser about where he'd actually been, and perhaps she never would be.

She bit her lip. She felt like someone under sentence of death, with no idea when the axe might fall. Roche had already left for the day when she'd arrived downstairs.

But, on the positive side, Solange seemed to have had no trouble in recovering her spirits this morning, and was inclined to make a heroine of herself—a leaning which Samma and Elvire, in concert, had dealt with firmly and succinctly. Hippolyte had then driven her to St Laurent to spend the day with a friend.

'Will you mind being alone?' Solange had asked Samma almost anxiously before she left. 'I will come back this afternoon.' There was a long pause. 'Perhaps, this time, I may learn to swim.'

Samma smiled, smoothing the child's hair back from her face. 'There's no rush,' she said gently.

How could there be, she thought bitterly, when she might not even be there when Solange got back?

She heard a footfall on the path, and sat up hastily, hoping against hope . . . Instead, she saw Jean-Paul Giraud walking towards her, his usual smile markedly absent.

Her heart sank. 'Good—good afternoon,' she managed.

'*Bonjour, madame.* I hope you have recovered from your ordeal.' His tone was as formal as his face.

'I—I think so.'

'Excellent,' he said too heartily, and there was a silence. Eventually he said awkwardly, 'Madame Delacroix—Samantha—you must know why I am here. Roche has instructed me to arrange your departure from Grand Cay. I have been able to obtain you a flight to the United Kingdom tomorrow.' He delved in his briefcase, and brought out a bulging envelope. 'I have your ticket here, also your passport, and some money in cash to deal with—immediate needs, although Roche has asked me to assure you that your original agreement with him still stands.' He paused. 'He told me you would understand what he meant.'

'Yes,' she said, dry-mouthed. 'Couldn't he have given me these things himself?'

Jean-Paul's awkwardness increased. 'He—he feels it is better if you do not meet again. He intends to occupy his suite at the casino in the meantime.' There was another silence, then he burst out, 'Madame—Samantha—none of this makes any sense. Last night you were two people passionately in love. Today—it is over.'

Samma bent her head. She said quietly, 'Roche thought he was buying me, but I wasn't for sale. There was—no love in it. Roche has always been involved with someone else.'

'Roche has?' Jean Paul stared at her, open-mouthed. 'But that is impossible.' He gave a very Gallic shrug. 'Oh—there have been—encounters over the years. He is a man, after all—but an *affaire* of the kind you mention—by no means.'

Samma bit her lip. 'He told me himself he had a mistress.'

Jean-Paul began to laugh. 'He said that—*oh, la la!* It is a joke of ours—about the casino and his other businesses. I reproached him once years ago because there was no woman in his life, and he said, "My work is my mistress, *mon vieux*, and a jealous one. I have no time for any other." ' He stared at her. 'And it is for this you have quarrelled?'

'No.' Samma shook her head wearily. 'That's the

least of it.'

'Ah,' he said. 'Then I am truly sorry.' He glanced around casually. 'Is Elvire in the house?'

'Almost certainly.' She forced a smile. 'Why don't you go and find her?'

When she was alone, she sat staring at the envelope, fighting back her tears. So that was it. She was being flung out of his life as suddenly as she'd been dragged into it. And with no chance of a reprieve.

She threw her head back defiantly. Well, she was damned if she'd be—dismissed like this! There were still too many things left unsaid between them, and Roche clearly intended they should stay that way.

But maybe this time it was *his* turn not to have a choice.

She picked up the envelope, and went up to the house. Jean-Paul's car was standing in the drive, the keys in the ignition. She glanced down at herself. Her pale lemon sundress was respectable enough for a trip to St Laurent, and Jean-Paul would hopefully be too occupied with Elvire to notice his car was missing for quite some time. Therefore . . .

She opened the driver's door and slid behind the wheel. The car started at the first attempt, and she set off down the drive.

The casino was once again a hive of activity when she arrived, but this time only the cleaners and staff were involved. She received a few curious glances, but it was clear she was recognised because no one challenged her as she walked to the lift, and rode up to the administrative floor.

She went straight to Roche's office, and walked in without knocking. He was sitting behind that massive desk, staring down at some papers, an open whisky bottle and a half-filled glass in front of him.

Without looking up, he said harshly, 'Hélène, I told you I would buzz if I needed you. Now leave me alone.'

She said, 'But I'm not Hélène.'

His head lifted sharply, and his expression hardened, but not before she'd glimpsed the bleakness, the vulnerability in his face.

He said glacially, 'What are you doing here? Did you not get my message?'

'Every detail of it.' She put the envelope down on the desk. 'And your little package deal. But aren't you forgetting something?'

'I don't think so. But no doubt you are going to tell me.'

'The reason I came here,' she said brightly. 'Solange, even though she isn't really your daughter at all, is she?'

'No.' His voice was stark. 'Liliane's story was true in every respect. Marie-Christine was a whore who needed a husband. She had a beautiful face and a good body, which I was not permitted to enjoy until after our wedding. That night, having had too much to drink, she gigglingly confided to me that she had already had a lover who was married, and was three months pregnant by him. She seemed to think I was so consumed by passion for her that I would overlook so small a detail. She soon discovered her mistake.'

'And the Augustins didn't know?'

'It seems not, or they would have used the information.' He gave her a long look. 'But make no mistake, Samantha. The lack of a blood tie makes no difference. Solange needs me, and I have given her my name.'

'Then having gone to all this trouble to stake your claim, I'm surprised you want to jeopardise everything now by sending me away. If the Augustins try again, you could lose her.'

'Then that is a risk I will take.' He paused. 'It does not weigh on me as heavily as the knowledge that if you remain on Grand Cay, I shall almost certainly rape you, and end up loathing myself for ever.' He gave her a blazing look. 'There, you have heard me admit it.' He pointed. 'The door is behind you. Use it.'

Her heart had begun to beat slowly and loudly. She said, 'I'll leave when I'm ready. You made me come here—deceived me in all kinds of ways—disrupted my life. I think I'm entitled to some compensation.'

'There is cash enclosed with your ticket.'

'But hardly enough to make up for some of the things I've been made to suffer since I came here.'

His mouth curled. 'Last night, *madame,* you threw my money in my face, with the accusation that I was buying you in some way. Naturally, I hesitated to insult you again.'

'I wouldn't be insulted—as I'm leaving, anyway.'

'Very well,' Roche said after a pause. He pushed back his chair, and walked to the wall behind his desk, touching a concealed switch. A section of panelling slid back to reveal a wall safe. 'How much do you want from me?'

She said huskily, 'A very great deal—but I think I'd prefer to be paid in kind, rather than cash.' She turned and walked across the room to his bedroom. 'You may leave your clothes on that chair,' she added over her shoulder.

She stood, her back turned, staring down at the bed, her stomach churning in mingled excitement and trepidation. She had no idea how he would react to her challenge. He might have her thrown out, he might laugh—or he might . . . The silence from the other room was almost deafening at first, then she thought she heard sounds of movement, but she did not dare look round to check.

When his hands descended on her shoulders, she almost cried out in shock because he had approached so noiselessly.

But the arms which slid round her to hold her were bare.

He said with a ghost of laughter in his voice, *'Et maintenant, madame?'*

Colour flooded into her face. She said in a muffled voice, 'I—I don't know. I thought—you . . .' She stopped with a little gasp. 'I must have been crazy to come here like this!'

His mouth touched the side of her neck, and trailed small kisses down to the curve of her shoulder. 'Not crazy.' His voice wasn't totally even. 'Just very sweet, *ma belle,* and very brave.' He paused. 'And what happens next—is this,' he whispered, sliding down the zip of the sundress, and pushing its straps off her shoulders, so that the garment pooled round her feet. 'And this.' Her briefs joined her dress on the floor.

Roche lifted her on to the bed, and lay beside her, his hands cupping her face. He said huskily, 'I want you so much I am almost frightened to touch you.'

Samma wound her arms round his neck. 'I won't break,' she whispered.

'I think I will.' He began to kiss her, his lips brushing hers in a myriad of tiny caresses, each as light as a butterfly's wing. 'Into a million tiny pieces.'

He wooed her slowly and sweetly, his hands exploring with subtle delicacy every line, contour and curve of her body, making each pulse, each nerve-ending sing with joy. His mouth adored her breasts, teasing each rosy peak into throbbing excitement until she moaned at the wonder of it.

And against her skin he whispered the kind of things she had never dreamed she would hear him say—endearments, small, broken phrases of need and longing, words that spoke only of love.

The world had shrunk to the compass of his arms. Nothing existed outside the slow, delicious torment of yearning he was arousing in her.

She was making explorations of her own, shy at first, learning the texture of his skin, and the shape of bone and play of muscle beneath it. As her hands grew more daring, she felt him tense, his dark face suddenly strained.

'Don't you like that?' she whispered.

'Too much.' He kissed her deeply, parting her lips so that his tongue could probe the full sweetness of her mouth.

She smiled at him, aware of a power she had not known she possessed. 'Shall I stop?'

'No.' He returned her smile.

For slow, languorous minutes, he let her have her way, his pleasure in her caresses sighing from his throat, but when she bent to touch him with her mouth, he stopped her, his hand tangling in her hair.

'Ah, no,' he told her huskily. 'My control is not infinite, and I want this first time to be for you, *ma belle.*'

He kissed the thudding pulse in her throat, and let his mouth drift downwards over her shoulders and breasts with a tantalising lack of haste. Samma felt as if she was being drawn into some inescapable spiral of sensation, the breath catching in her throat, as Roche's lips followed the stroke of his fingers down her pliant body.

She was locked into the spiral now, the ascent to its apex, swift and sharp and quite inevitable. She no longer belonged to herself. She was out of control, her whole being mastered by this torturous ecstasy he was inflicting on her.

Then he lifted himself, moved, and entered her with one fluid thrust. And, as the first scalding wave of pleasure and release welled inside her, she sobbed out his name, and her love for him.

When it was over, they lay for a long time locked in each other's arms, without speaking, kissing a little, touching each other almost with reverence.

At last Samma said, her voice breaking, 'I—I never dreamed it could be like that.'

'Nor I.' Roche wound her hair round his hand and carried it to his lips. 'The first time I saw you,' he said softly, 'you were on the quayside at Cristoforo. You were laughing and your hair was like sunlight. I looked at you and thought—with her, I could begin to live again.' He kissed her mouth. 'After Marie-Christine, I swore that I would use women as she'd used me.' He grimaced. 'But that soon palled. Work, making money, became all in all. I told myself there was no room in my life for love—no need for it.' His hand cupped her breast, stroking it gently. 'How wrong, how stupid could I be?'

Samma nestled her cheek again his shoulder. 'But you were going to send me away.'

'You would never have got on that plane, *ma chère.*' The dark face was serious. 'I would have brought you back—taught you to trust me, somehow.' He kissed the tip of her nose. 'How could you not know I loved you, *ma bien-aimée?*'

'There was Elvire,' she reminded him wryly. 'We were totally at cross purposes there.'

He nodded. 'She is too sensitive about her birth—about the way my father failed to acknowledge her during his lifetime. She begged me to say nothing, to allow you to think she was just the housekeeper. But both of us believed you had guessed or been told the truth about her, and did not approve.'

'Who could have told me?'

'Liliane Duvalle, perhaps. God knows, she spent enough time on my family's private affairs to have discovered that Elvire was my sister. Or Marie-Christine might have hinted something to her.'

'So many secrets.' Samma touched her lips to his skin. 'Learning to trust is a two-way process, *mon amour*.'

'I know,' he said remorsefully. 'But I was so afraid of losing you, Samantha. After all, you made it clear you had agreed to my proposal for Solange's sake only. How could I confess she was not really my daughter, or even hint at the other problems you might encounter? You might never have married me, and I could not risk that.'

'And if I had turned you down?'

'Then I would probably have taken a leaf out of *Le Diable's* book, and carried you off anyway.' He brushed her mouth with his. 'As I'd have done at the airport tomorrow. But fortunately you needed me, *mon coeur*, although not, *hélas*, in the way I wanted you.'

She sighed. 'I thought you wanted to sleep me with me because I was—there. A—a temporary diversion.'

'If you'd examined the papers you signed last night, *ma belle*, you would have realised my plans for us were totally permanent.' He brushed a strand of sweat-dampened hair back from her forehead very tenderly. 'Why did you suddenly turn on me like that?'

She bit her lip. 'The same thing, I suppose. A—fear of being used—without love.'

'Ah, *mignonne*, why do you think, in the end, I walked

away from you last night? Because I could not take
you with anger between us.'

She said, 'You walked away once before, when I
went to your room and waited for you in bed.'

His mouth twisted. 'I had been at the casino, *ma
belle,* trying to drown my sorrows, and the memory of
our quarrel in alcohol. When I got to my room, I
thought at first I was seeing things. Then, when I
realised you were really there, I had to come to terms
with the fact that I was in no fit state to make love to
you.'

'And all those other nights, when you didn't come
to bed?'

'I drove around—sometimes to the beach, or slept
on the couch in my study. I always took care the
servants never saw me. Or Solange.'

Samma traced a pattern on his chest with one
finger. 'About Solange—it's not enough, Roche, to
take responsibility for her. She needs more than that
from you.' She looked at him soberly. 'Whatever her
mother was, she needs warmth and affection, openly
expressed.'

'That is something you will have to teach me, *mon
ange.* I have become used to—hiding my feelings, or
pretending they do not exist.'

'Really?' Samma stretched lithely against him,
delighting in the responsive stir of his flesh. 'I would
never have guessed.'

'Beware, *madame.*' He gave her a ferocious frown.
'You provoke me at your peril!'

Samma pouted in mock-alarm. 'What are you
threatening me with, *monsieur?* The Delacroix curse?'

Roche laughed out loud. 'My own personal
version,' he whispered, and began to kiss her again.

KING OF SWORDS

KING OF SWORDS

BY
SARA CRAVEN

MILLS & BOON LIMITED
Eton House, 18-24 Paradise Road
Richmond, Surrey TW9 1SR

First published in Great Britain in 1988
by Mills & Boon Limited

© Sara Craven 1988

Australian copyright 1988
Philippine copyright 1988
Reprinted 1988
This edition 1993

ISBN 0 263 78411 8

Set in Palacio 10 on 11 $1/2$ pt.
19-9308-58754

Made and printed in Great Britain

CHAPTER ONE

IN THE glowing light of a June afternoon, Ambermere had never looked more beautiful.

Julia brought her car to a halt at the side of the road and slid out from behind the wheel. The faint breeze lifted a few tendrils of waving copper hair and she pushed them back impatiently as she leaned on the wall and stared across the lush green of the lower paddock to the house.

It all looked amazingly peaceful, even deserted, but she knew that apparent tranquillity was only a façade. Inside, there would be a frantic buzz of activity as her mother and the staff applied the finishing touches to the décor for tonight's Midsummer party.

And I should be there, helping, Julia thought, half guiltily, half in amusement. The Ambermere party was one of the most anticipated local events in the year—a pleasant tradition established over generations.

She felt a small sigh of satisfaction rise within her at the thought. That was what houses like Ambermere were all about—custom and continuity. And that was what she would continue to provide, even if she was the only daughter, instead of the once longed-for son.

A month, she decided with sudden restlessness,

was far too long to be away, even though she had enjoyed herself. Aunt Miriam was a wonderful diplomat's wife and there had been parties and dinners nearly every night. In addition there had been tennis, and swimming and polo matches, as well as visits to concerts and theatres with a succession of attractive and attentive young men.

'But no one worthy of Ambermere,' Julia would tell her father presently, with mock regret. It was a joke which had begun in the days of a much younger Julia who had been very much affronted to learn that the family name would die out when she married.

'Then I won't get married,' she had declared to her amused parents. 'Unless I can find a man with the same name as ours.'

'But you might fall in love with someone called Smith,' Lydia Kendrick had pointed out, stroking the small, determined face.

'Then he'll have to change his name to Kendrick,' Julia had retorted. 'If he won't do that, then he's not worthy of Ambermere.'

They had all three laughed about it since, but Julia had come to recognise that she'd been more than half in earnest. She wanted to go on living at Ambermere, and see her children brought up there, bearing her own loved family name. But the man who would fit docilely in with these plans, and father those children, remained a shadowy and amorphous figure. None of the boyfriends who wined and dined her so assiduously, and tried, without any luck, to get her into bed, seemed even remotely to be suitable candidates.

Perhaps I won't get married at all, she thought.

Maybe I'll just run the estate and become known as an eccentric spinster. She grimaced slightly, straightening as she prepared to get back in the car, and it was then she saw him.

A man, a perfect stranger, walking across the lower paddock, where he had no right to be.

Julia's lips tightened as she watched him. He was tall, with glossy black hair, and a swarthy skin, and she didn't have to guess where he'd come from. Her easy-going father had always permitted gipsies to camp beyond the copse, on the understanding that they kept the site tidy, and didn't encroach in any way on the rest of the estate.

And now here was one of them strolling about as if he owned the place. Well, he would soon know differently! Julia decided grimly.

She swung herself up on to the wall, put two fingers to her lips and whistled.

The man's head came round sharply, and he looked at her, but he made no effort to approach. Usually the same travelling people came back year after year, but Julia had never set eyes on this one before. He was darker even then Loy Pascoe, who was the head of the family, and had conducted the negotiations with her father. Julia was aware of unsmiling dark eyes beneath level brows, a beak of a nose, and a firmly emphasised mouth and chin. Not good-looking exactly, she found herself thinking to her own surprise, but with a definite air—seignorial and irritatingly arrogant—about him. Maybe he was some distant relation of the Pascoe clan and just passing through, but that was no reason why he shouldn't obey the same rules as everyone else.

She said clearly and coldly, 'Do you know you're trespassing?'

He stood surveying her silently, hands resting on his hips, but he made no reply. He was wearing well-cut cream denim pants and an elegant knitted shirt, open at the neck to reveal the strong column of his throat, and a shadowing of body hair on his chest. His clothes had obviously cost a great deal of money.

The scrap metal business must be booming, Julia thought cynically. No poor relation, this one.

Her tone glacial, she said, 'I suppose you do speak English?'

There was a slight pause, then he nodded, his face expressionless.

'Well that's something.' Julia's eyes narrowed. 'Then you understand what I mean by trespass?'

Another nod. They were actually making progress.

'My father permits your people to camp on his land on certain conditions. I suggest you go back where you came from and find out what they are. And don't let me find you wandering about here again.'

She climbed lithely down from the wall and got into her car, angrily aware that he hadn't budged an inch. The nerve of him! she thought. She risked a glance in her mirror as she drove off, and realised furiously that he was smiling—laughing at her.

I'll call at the camp and give Loy a piece of my mind, she raged inwardly. Give these tinkers an inch, and they take a mile!

She took a careful grip on her temper, realising she was over-revving her engine. After all, it was only a minor incident, and it was utterly ridiculous to feel, as she did, that it had spoiled her homecoming.

Because nothing could do that. Not now, not ever. Ambermere was going to be hers one day, and she was going to care for it, and cherish it in a way her charming, happy-go-lucky father had never done. He called it openly the Albatross, and laughed at Julia's fury. Her month with Aunt Miriam had been a brief interval of rest and relaxation before she began the serious business of going into the Ambermere office with Mr Greenwood and learning how to run the estate. It was what she had always wanted, although Philip Kendrick had always insisted she would have changed her mind by the time she was old enough for such responsibility.

'We'll see how you feel when you're twenty-one,' he had told her briskly. And he'd been frankly astonished when her birthday had come and gone, and she was still of the same mind about what she wanted to do with her life.

And she would begin as she meant to go on by dealing with this tinker problem, swiftly and personally. If Loy thought she was going to be a pushover to deal with because she was a girl, he would soon discover his mistake!

She parked her car and walked through the copse. The shining trailers were parked neatly enough, but there seemed to be no one around except, for a tethered dog who barked aggressively at her as she passed.

She said, 'Shut up, Ben you idiot,' and knocked on the door of the largest and glossiest trailer.

It opened immediately, revealing a small, white-haired woman in a stridently floral overall. Blackberry-dark eyes surveyed the visitor gravely.

'Well, Miss Julia,' she said. 'It came to me that you'd be here today.'

Julia gave her a level look. Grandma Pascoe was reputed to have the second sight, and made a good income from telling fortunes at local fêtes and fairgrounds, but Julia had never believed the old woman had any special powers, just a good nose for gossip, and a phenomenal memory. And everyone in the county would know that no matter how long she'd been away, she would be back for tonight's party. No ESP required for that! she thought with a trace of cynicism.

She said, 'Hello, Grandma. Is Loy about?'

The white head moved in negation. 'He's seeing a man on business. Come in, Miss Julia. The kettle's boiled, and I've been spreading the cards for you.'

Julia hesitated. The tea would be welcome, but the last thing she wanted was Grandma brooding over the tarot cards on her behalf.

She began, 'I really don't think . . . ' but Grandma stopped her with an imperative gesture.

'You may not believe, missy, but there's a message for you just the same. I've been sitting waiting for you to come and hear it.'

And no doubt cross her palm with silver, the old crook, Julia thought, torn between amusement and annoyance, as she followed Grandma into the trailer and sat down opposite her at the table. The tea was scalding and almost black, and she sipped carefully, as Grandma began to turn over the cards in front of her.

''Tes all change for you, maiden, and a journey across water.'

'I've just done that,' Julia said wearily. Usually Grandma made at least a pretence of seeing the future.

'This is 'nother one.' Grandma gave her a gimlet look.

'I don't think so.' Julia shook her head. 'This time I'm here to stay.'

'See what covers you?' Grandma turned over another card, and gasped. 'The King of Swords! He's come to cut you off from all you know. He's terrible powerful, the King of Swords. You can't fight him, though you may try.'

'You can count on that,' Julia said drily. 'Can you tell me what he looks like, so I can be sure to avoid him?'

'He's close enough to touch.' Grandma's voice lowered to a whisper, and in spite of herself Julia felt a faint frisson of uneasiness chill her spine. 'And you can't avoid your fate, maiden.' She turned over the final card, and gasped again. 'See—the Tower struck by lightning. Your world turned upside down, and no mistake.'

Julia stared down at the card, her brows drawing together. She found herself wishing, ridiculously, that she'd bypassed the camp and let her father deal with the interloper. Then she pulled herself together. She had never been taken in by Grandma's nonsense before, and she certainly wasn't going to start now.

She drank the rest of her tea in one wincing gulp, and stood up. 'Well, the weather forecast says nothing about storms,' she remarked briskly. 'I'll take my chance.' She reached for her bag, but Grandma Pascoe shook her head.

'There's no need for money beween us, Miss Julia. I've given you the warning. I can do no more.' She paused. 'You're a proud girl, and no mistake, with a mind of your own. But that pride of yours will be brought low. It's all here.' She tapped the cards with a bony forefinger. 'Now run away home, and dance at your party while you can.'

Julia almost stumbled down the steps of the trailer, and paused, her heart thumping. There should be a law, she thought angrily, against Grandma Pascoe and her kind spreading forecasts of doom. It was all very different from the handsome husbands and football pools wins that the old lady generally predicted.

She sat in the car, letting her pulses slow to a more normal rate, castigating herself for being an idiot. And she hadn't even left a message for Loy about the trespasser, she realised vexedly, as she started her engine. Well, that would have to wait, because she certainly wasn't going back.

The yard at the back of the house which housed the former stables and the garages was crowded with vehicles, florists' and caterers' vans among them. There was the usual atmosphere of bustle and subdued panic that Julia always associated with the Midsummer party. Although heaven knows why, she told herself wryly, as she slid her car into its usual corner. Everything's always perfect, and this year even the weather's going to oblige us.

She found her mother in the large drawing-room, surrounded by lists. Lady Kendrick looked up as Julia walked towards her, her face breaking into a strained smile. 'Darling—at last!' She embraced her warmly.

'But you're very late. I was beginning to get anxious.'

'I took a slight detour,' Julia said with deliberate lightness. 'And I really wish I hadn't. She gave her mother a searching look. Had those worry lines round her mouth and eyes, the tension along her cheekbones, been there unnoticed before Julia went away? If so, perhaps these few weeks of separation had been a good thing if they'd taught her to be more perceptive. Lydia Kendrick had always been a highly strung, nervous woman, and the vagaries of life with her charming, feckless but much-loved husband had done little to ease the wear and tear on her nervous system.

'Is everything all right?' asked Julia anxiously.

'Everything's fine—and wonderful now that you're here. I can't wait to hear all the news about Miriam—and everyone. But there's so much to do.' Lydria Kendrick gestured helplessly about her, and Julia kissed her cheek.

'I'll go and unpack, then I'll pitch in and lend a hand with it all,' she promised reassuringly. 'Where's Daddy?'

'He's rather busy. Mr Poulton came down first thing this morning. They've been shut up in the study for most of the day.'

Julia's brows lifted. 'Rather inconsiderate of Polly,' she remarked, using her father's joking name for their staid family solicitor. 'He doesn't usually bother Daddy with business meetings on Midsummer Day.' She paused. 'Are you sure there's nothing wrong?'

'Of course not.' Her mother was smiling, but her glance slid away evasively. 'It's just—routine. Probably Polly underestimated the time it would take.'

There *is* something the matter, Julia thought as she unlocked her cases in her sunny bedroom and began to restore the contents to drawers and wardrobe. It wasn't just the uproar of preparing for the party either. It was like some dark and disturbing undercurrent beneath Ambermere's familiar and tranquil surface. From the moment she'd seen that man—that intruder in the lower paddock, her day had seemed disjointed, her homecoming oddly clouded.

'Jools, you're going crazy,' she adjured herself, as she unwrapped the dress she planned to wear that evening from its protective folds of tissue. Aunt Miriam had helped her choose it, and it relied for its chic on its stark and simple cut. She rarely wore that shade of midnight blue, but she had to admit Aunt Miriam was right when she said it darkened her eyes to sapphire. In the past, she'd chosen floating fabrics and pastels—débutante dresses, she thought with a slight grimace. This elegant, sophisticated model was going to open a few eyes—make it clear that Julia Kendrick was no longer a girl, but a woman ready and prepared to embark on her chosen course in life.

She sat down on her dressing stool and lifted her hair on top of her head in a casual swirl, studying herself, experimenting. The brief knock on her door made her start, and she looked up guiltily to see her mother had joined her.

'Are you waiting for me?' Julia jumped up. 'I'll only be a few minutes.'

'No—no. Everything's running like clockwork really—as it should after all these years.' Lydia Kendrick's voice was pitched higher than usual, and she dabbed at her mouth with a lace-edged handkerchief. 'Jools darling, I shouldn't be here talking to you like this. Your father told me to wait until after the party—not to spoil things for you on your first night—but I can't . . .'

Julia put a protective arm round the slender shoulders, helping her to the window seat and sitting beside her.

'What is it, love? Has Daddy been backing losers again? Is that why Polly's here, to give him the usual rap over the knuckles?'

Lydia gave a strangled sob. 'It's worse than that,' she said hoarsely. 'So much worse. I don't know how to tell you . . .' There was a pause while she obviously fought for control. Then she said brokenly, 'Jools—your father is having to sell this house.'

Julia had the oddest sensation that everything in the room had receded to a great distance. Her voice sounded very clear, however, and very cold.

'Is this some awful joke? Because I'm afraid I don't find it very funny . . .'

'Would I—could I joke about something like this?' Her mother's tone was piteous. 'Ambermere has to go. That's why Mr Poulton's here. He's been here every day almost for the past two weeks. Your—your father's had a lot of financial setbacks. The Mullion Corporation takeover—there was talk of insider trading—he had to resign from the board, although he swears he had nothing to do with it. And that's not all. Some time ago, Daddy changed a lot of our investments, because he felt we needed more return from our money. Some of the new investments were—high-risk, but he thought it was worth the gamble.' She swallowed nervously. 'We lost a great deal—too much. It's been a disaster. We have to sell Ambermere, Jools, because we can't afford to go on living here. The party tonight will be the last we'll ever give.' She began to cry, her throat wrenched by small gusty sobs.

Julia sat holding her, feeling frozen.

Worth the gamble, she thought. Those words had a hollow ring. All her life, her father had been a gambler, preferring to live his life on a knife-edge of insecurity. There were years when his betting and baccarat losses had been phenomenal. Julia could remember tearful scenes, and an atmosphere of gloomy repentance which she had only partly understood at the time.

Later, it had been explained to her that their income was adequate as long as they lived quietly and without undue extravagance. But that wasn't Philip Kendrick's way. Country life bored him, except in small doses. He was always looking out for some scheme which would restore the family fortunes to some fabled pre-war level. He'd been like some small boy, looking for adventure, she thought. But now the adventure had gone hideously wrong.

She said, 'Why—did Polly let him?'

'He didn't tell him anything about it until it was too late. You see, Daddy had been taking advice from some American he'd met in Monte Carlo—some financial wizard.' Lydia's lips tightened. 'Apparently this man's just been indicted for fraud in New York.'

Julia felt sick, 'Oh, God—Daddy's not involved in that?'

'Oh, no.' Lydia's fingers tore nervously at her

handkerchief, but her voice was decisively reassuring. 'Darling, I know how you must feel—but Daddy did this for the best. The costs of running a house like this, an estate like Ambermere, are punitively high. He wanted you to have—a proper inheritance, not to have to scrimp and save all your life.'

Julia felt immensely weary. 'Why didn't you tell me—call me back from Aunt Miriam's?'

'We wanted you to have a good time. And there was nothing you could have done.'

'There must be something. I'm not going to let Ambermere go like this.' Julia tried to smile. 'Perhaps no one will want to buy the Albatross. No one we know has that kind of money.'

There was a long silence, then Lydia said quietly, 'These days, darling, estates like this tend to look for buyers from abroad. And Mr Poulton has found one for us.'

'Abroad?' Julia echoed dazedly. She shook her head. 'Not some Arab prince? I don't believe it . . .'

'Not quite. In fact——' there were bright spots of colour burning in her mother's cheeks '—I would almost prefer it. This man is Greek—a so-called tycoon. His name is Alexandros Constantis.'

'Constantis?' Julia's brows snapped together. 'That's familiar. Does he have a relative called Paul?'

'I wouldn't know,' Lady Kendrick said with distaste. 'What I've heard of his antecedents is bad enough. I have no wish to enquire into his immediate family. Not that they have very much to do with him,' she added with unaccustomed waspishness.

'Then it must be the same man,' Julia said slowly,

thinking, remembering. 'I had dinner with Paul Constantis a few times—he was charming. He had a post at the Greek Embassy—something fairly junior, I gathered, but he used to joke about nature having intended him to be a millionaire until fate, in the shape of his cousin Alex, had prevented it.'

'Poor boy,' Lydia Kendrick said, almost fiercely. 'I imagine that's only too true. You're too young to remember the scandal, of course, but George Constantis was an immensely wealthy man, with a fortune in banking and property all over the Mediterranean. He was a widower, and childless, and his estate was expected to go to his sister and her children. Then lo and behold, on his deathbed, he suddenly revealed that he had an illegitimate son and had left his entire business empire to this child.' She shook her head. 'The family wouldn't have objected to some kind of provision, naturally, but to have this person no one had ever known existed foisted on to them—over them—was appalling. He wasn't a child, of course. He was already a grown man—but it was said he'd been dragged up in total poverty in some slum, and could barely read or write. There was some mystery about the mother, apparently. It seems she was some little peasant girl Constantis had seduced.

'They fought, of course. They tried to prove he wasn't Constantis's son at all, insisted on blood tests, but they were inconclusive, so then they tried to overturn the will in the courts, saying this Alex had exerted undue influence on the old man while he was ill. It was quite a *cause célèbre*. But they lost—and he took everything.'

And now, Julia thought, rage rising inside her, now

he's trying to take Ambermere from me. But he won't. Not someone like that.

'An uncouth barbarian,' Paul Constantis had called him, she remembered. Well he wasn't going to lay his vandal's hands on her home, if she could prevent it!

She got to her feet, 'I'm going down to talk to Daddy,' she said, trying to keep her voice level. 'There must be something we can do. And surely this Constantis creature can't be the only prospective buyer we can find?'

'Apparently he's made an excellent offer,' her mother returned. 'He does a great deal of business over here, and wants a permanent residence where he can entertain.'

'Bouzouki nights with plate smashing, no doubt,' Julia said grimly, moving to the door. 'We'll see about that!' She ran along the gallery and down the wide curve of the big staircase, letting her hand slide down the highly polished balustrade as she had always done. As she always would do, she told herself. Ambermere had to be saved somehow.

As she reached the foot of the stairs, the study door opened and her father emerged with Gordon Poulton at his side. He looked tired and haggard, and in spite of her bitterness Julia felt a wrench of her heart at his obvious distress.

He looked up and saw her, and tried to smile. 'Jools, sweetheart, no one told me you were home. 'How marvellous!'

She ran to him. 'Daddy, tell me it's not true. Promise me you haven't sold Ambermere to this appalling Greek peasant!'

She heard Gordon Poulton make a shocked noise, and saw her father's brows snap together in sudden quelling anger. From the shadowy doorway behind them, a third figure detached itself and stepped forward.

Julia felt as if a hand had closed round her throat. She knew him at once, of course. It was the man she'd seen in the lower paddock and taken for a tinker.

No wonder he'd laughed at her! she thought dazedly.

Only this time he wasn't laughing at all. As the hooded dark gaze swept her from head to foot, she felt as if the flesh had been scorched from her bones by some swift and terrifying flame.

It was all she could do not to fling up her hands to defend herself.

The Tower struck by lightning, she thought, from some whirling corner of her mind, and the King of Swords, coming to cut down her pride and separate her from everything she loved.

CHAPTER TWO

THE SAPPHIRE dress looked superb. Julia regarded herself critically in the full-length mirror, making a minute adjustment to the seams of her stockings, and tucking an errant strand of hair into place in her carefully casual topknot.

She looked elegant, poised and sophisticated—just as the daughter of the house should, she thought bitterly. But she was only attending the party under protest, and after the most thunderous row she'd ever had with her father. Even the thought of it now could still make her shudder.

'How dare you, Julia!' Sir Philip's voice had been glacial, when they were finally alone together. 'I'd hoped your time with Miriam might have cured you of your tendency to impulsive and inopportune reactions. You realise nothing is signed yet between Constantis and myself, and you could have jeopardised the negotiations by your insolence?'

'Then I'm glad,' she had answered defiantly. 'Daddy, you can't sell Ambermere to a man like that! There must be some other way.'

'If there was, then I'd have found it.' His tone sharpened. 'You're a child, Julia—a spoiled child. I've done you no favours by sheltering you from life's realities.'

'Is that how you categorise Alex Constantis?'

21

Julia's laugh broke in the middle. 'Then I'm glad you did—shelter me. He can't have Ambermere—he can't!'

'He can—and I desperately hope he will.' She had never seen her father look so stern. 'And you, madam, will do and say nothing else to put the sale at risk.'

'Well, you have no need to worry about that.' Julia glared back at him. 'I'll make very sure our paths don't cross again!'

'In fact you'll meet him again this evening,' Sir Philip told her grimly. 'He's dining with us, and staying on for the party.'

Julia's lips parted in a despairing gasp. 'You can't have invited him!' she wailed. 'Not someone like that. Our friends will think we approve of him—that we're endorsing him in some way.'

'And why shouldn't we?' Sir Philip slammed his desk with a clenched fist. 'My God, Julia. Where did you learn to be such an appalling little snob? Alex Constantis may have inherited money initially, but he's made another fortune on his own account since he became head of the Constantis empire. And in today's world, it's money that counts, my dear, as I'm afraid you're going to find out. So far, he's been reasonably accommodating. I just pray you haven't ruined everything with your muddle-headed stupidity. He has a reputation for being a tough operator.'

'For being a bastard!' Julia flung back at him. 'Which is, of course, exactly what he is.'

'And what have we, precisely, to be so stately and moral about?' Sir Philip demanded. 'If the first Julia Kendrick hadn't caught the Prince Regent's eye, then we would never have owned Ambermere in the first place. Perhaps you should remember that.' He paused, surveying her defiant, tight-lipped face. 'And remember this too, Jools. Tonight I expect you to be civil to Alex Constantis—beginning, perhaps, with an apology.'

'Will a plain "sorry I spoke" do, or would you like me to grovel—lick his shoes even?'

And so it had gone on, covering the same wretched ground, the same recriminations, until finally they had reached a kind of armed truce. Julia did not have to apologise in so many words, but she wouldn't be allowed to feign a headache and miss the party either. And she would be polite to Alex Constantis.

'I know it's a terrible situation for you, darling,' her father had said more gently, just before she went up, reluctantly, to change. 'But we're still a family, and that's what matters in the end. Bricks and mortar, however historic, aren't that important.'

The trouble was, Julia thought dispiritedly, her father had right on his side. She had been abysmally rude about Alex Constantis. But how could she have known he was lurking about in the study doorway like the Demon King, ready to pop up at just the wrong moment? And if she had known would she honestly have behaved differently? Somehow, she doubted it.

And where rudeness was concerned, honours were about even, she thought. He had snubbed her totally and succinctly, after her father had awkwardly attempted to introduce them, reminding Sir Philip coolly that they were due to visit the Home Farm, and walking off with him without deigning Julia a second look.

But that was all to the good, Julia thought, her mouth suddenly dry. Because if the second look lived up to the first, she might end up permanently singed.

There was little doubt that the evening ahead was going to be an ordeal. Her father had made it clear that he intended to introduce Alex Constantis to their neighbours and friends as the future owner of Ambermere, and Julia wasn't at all sure she could bear it.

She had almost decided against wearing the new dress, telling herself that it didn't matter what she looked like—that the oldest rag in the wardrobe would do for a—awake like this evening promised to be.

But her pride had reasserted itself. Her ship might be sinking, but she would nail her full colours to the mast—and she would let no one, but no one know how much she despised and resented Alex Constantis. Her innate realism told her that too many avid eyes would be watching for any sign of grief or distress. Their friends would understand and sympathise, she thought with a sigh, but there were others in the neighbourhood, less well disposed towards the Kendricks, who had been prophesying doom and disaster for years.

And now the doom had come upon them in the unwelcome shape of this—Greek upstart, she thought wretchedly.

Paul Constantis had been philosophical about the enforced change in his circumstances, but Julia had sensed an underlying bitterness. She'd sympathised with him, without feeling too involved, but she was concerned now all right. Because by some incredible, nauseating coincidence, Alex Constantis was going to take Ambermere from her, just as he'd preyed on the Constantis family fortune. He was going to steal her home.

'Bricks and mortar aren't important,' Sir Philip had said.

Not to you, Daddy, Julia thought in aching silence. Never to you—but to me.

She was aware that her love for Ambermere was a local byword, could imagine the shock waves when people realised this would be the last Midsummer party. But no one would pity her tonight—or laugh at her either, she told herself almost savagely, as she lifted her scent spray and misted herself with fragrance before turning resolutely to the door and making her way downstairs.

It was still quite early, and the special guests who had been invited to dinner before the party proper began had not begun to arrive yet, so Julia expected to have the drawing-room to herself for a while.

But to her horror, Alex Constantis was there before her, standing on the hearthrug, staring up at the enormous portrait of the Regency Julia Kendrick which hung above the fireplace. Twentieth-century Julia had never cared for this constant reminder of how her family had acquired Ambermere. She had always been vaguely embarrassed by the pride of place given to a woman who had shamelessly betrayed her husband, and behaved like a tart with Prinny. And she loathed the lighthearted family tradition of drinking a toast to the first Julia as a climax to the Midsummer party. But perhaps, in the circumstances, that particular ritual could be forgone this year.

She hesitated in the doorway, wondering whether she could steal away before he saw her, but the wretched man must have had eyes in the back of his head, because without turning, he said, 'Come in, *thespinis*, and tell me about your ancestress.'

Julia came forward with deep unwillingness, strongly tempted to repudiate all knowledge of the flame-haired beauty in her shockingly fashionable transparent draperies.

But before she could speak, he added drily, 'And do not try to deny the relationship. The family resemblance is there—and the colour of the hair.' He turned and looked at her fully, the glittering dark gaze sliding with unabashed interest over the untrammelled cling of the midnight dress. 'And the fact that you both wear so little,' he ended silkily.

In spite of herself, Julia felt dull colour rise in her face. The cut of the dress demanded a minimum of underwear, but it infuriated her that this stranger—this interloper, should be so immediately aware of the fact—and be graceless enough to refer to it.

At the same time she was forced to acknowledge that his voice was attractive—low-pitched and resonant, with barely a trace of an accent. Not, she thought, what she would have expected from someone of his background.

She said coolly, 'As you're a stranger to Britain, Mr Constantis, perhaps I should warn you that sexist remarks are no longer welcomed here.'

'Sexist?' Alex Constantis repeated the word as if it were utterly new to him, then shrugged. 'Yet we are still born male and female, *thespinis*. The human race does not yet allow for neuters. Nor will it continue for much longer unless a man is able to tell a woman that he finds her desirable.'

To her fury, Julia felt her flush deepen. Did this person actually mean . . . No, of course he didn't. He was simply getting his own back by deliberately setting out to embarrass her.

She said crisply, 'You were asking about the portrait, I believe. She was the wife of the first baronet, and her name was Julia.'

'You were named for her?'

'Yes.' Julia forbore to add 'unfortunately', knowing it would involve her in explanations which she didn't wish to give. Alex Constantis's grin was far too insolent already.

He glanced back at the portrait. 'She is very beautiful. To possess such loveliness would be a rare acquisition.'

Again Julia had the uneasy feeling that his remark was a loaded one, intended to needle her. At this rate, she thought crossly, I'll be spending the entire evening blushing like a schoolgirl!

She forced her voice to remain level. 'I'm afraid the portrait isn't for sale, Mr Constantis. You're buying a house, not a family history.'

He said softly, 'The past does not concern me, *thespinis*—only the present—and the future. And it is not altogether certain that I shall buy Ambermere.'

Julia groaned inwardly. Aloud, she said stiffly, 'If you're having second thoughts because of anything I've said or done, then I'm sorry.'

'Are you?' He spoke in the same reflective tone, but

Julia felt an inexplicable shiver run down her spine—as if he'd threatened her in some way.

Oh, I'm being ridiculous, she thought with exasperation.

She tried to speak lightly. 'Perhaps we'd better declare a truce. May I offer you a drink?'

'Thank you. Do you have Bourbon?'

'Of course. It's what my father drinks.' Julia moved to the side table where the decanters stood, and poured a measure into a glass, angrily aware that her hands were shaking.

'Come on, Jools,' she whispered to herself. 'Get it together.'

To add to her self-consciousness, she felt certain Alex Constantis had spotted her nervousness, and was amused by it, although his expression when she handed him the glass was enigmatic.

'You are not joining me?' he asked, and Julia shook her head.

'It's going to be a long evening,' she excused herself, with a bright smile which only touched her lips.

'Then—*yiassou.*' He raised his glass to her, then drank.

Julia began to wish she had in fact poured herself a drink as well. It would have given her something to fidget with—to concentrate on—anything rather than just having to stand here, the object of his undivided attention.

'So, tell me more about your namesake,' he said, after a pause. 'She was the mistress of the Prince of Wales—isn't that right?'

Julia's lips tightened. 'You seem perfectly well

informed already.'

'There is a small bookshop opposite my hotel in the village. I bought a local guide book, and such a story was mentioned.'

She shrugged. 'Then what more is there to tell?'

'Her husband—this first baronet. What kind of a man was he?'

'He was one of the Prince's circle,' Julia said reluctantly. 'Though not a close friend. He was a gambler.'

'So that is where the tendency comes from,' Alex Constantis said meditatively. 'Was he also as unlucky as your father?'

Julia shot him a look of indignant surprise, annoyed at the implied criticism in his words. 'I don't think I want to discuss that with you.'

'Yet it has a certain relevance.' The dark eyes were hooded. 'If your father had been luckier in his wagers—in his speculation, then your family home would not be for sale to the highest bidder—and we would not be here together now.'

She said tautly, 'Please don't remind me.'

He laughed. 'The truce did not last long, *thespinis*. But no matter. My instinct tells me that to war with you might be more interesting than to make peace.'

'And your instinct, of course, is never wrong.' Julia was heavily sarcastic.

'Where women are concerned—rarely.' He was still smiling. 'Another sexist remark!'

Julia bit her lip. 'Could we change the subject, please?'

'Certainly.' He drank some more Bourbon. 'Shall we talk about the weather, or shall I tell you how beautiful you look in that dress, and how much I would give to see you without it?'

Shame and anger welled up inside her, as if she had indeed been stripped naked in front of him. If she had had a drink in her hand, she would have thrown it straight into his mocking, arrogant face, she thought savagely. She wanted to hit out, to beat at him with her fists, but she knew, somehow, that such a gesture would only amuse him.

My God, she thought. He's demanding a full pound of flesh in return for my having called him a peasant!

From somewhere she managed to conjure up a light laugh. 'Would you give me Ambermere, Mr Constantis?'

His brows lifted slightly, as if her reaction had surprised him, and he said, 'No.'

Julia shrugged again. 'Then the deal's off.' She made herself meet his gaze. 'You'll just have to—eat your heart out.'

His smile widened, and he shook his head slowly. 'Don't count on it—Miss Kendrick.'

For an endless moment his eyes held hers. Julia was suddenly, terrifyingly conscious that she could neither move nor speak—and that every pulse point in her body seemed to be beating with an alarming independence.

She wanted to say 'No.' To assert her separateness from him, her rejection of him, and his degrading jibes, but the muscles of her throat refused to obey her.

It was the external sound of other voices, and footsteps approaching down the hall, which broke the spell at last. And if she'd burned before, Julia now realised she felt icily, deathly cold.

As Alex Constantis turned to greet her parents, she crossed to the empty fireplace and stood staring down at it, as if there were flames there which could warm her, and stop the wild, inner shivering which threatened to tear her apart.

Lydia Kendrick was polite to her unwanted guest, but there was none of her usual warmth in her manner, and Julia surmised that she too was under orders.

Her father seemed his usual ebullient self, laughing and talking as if Alex Constantis was an old and valued friend, but Julia could see the lines of strain round his mouth, and thought how they would deepen if the offer for the house was withdrawn.

She felt as if she was living through some kind of nightmare.

She had hoped the situation would be eased when the other dinner guests arrived, but among the first-comers were the Bosworths, and Vivvy Bosworth lost no time in drawing Julia into the morning-room.

'Jools, there are the most amazing rumours all over the place. People are saying your father's sold the estate to some Greek millionaire. Surely it can't be true?'

Julia pinned on a smile. 'We're certainly hoping the deal goes through.'

'Oh, don't con me, Julia Kendrick!' Vivvy gave her a minatory look. 'I've known you far too long—we swapped rattles in our prams, remember? You'd rather lose your right arm than this house.'

Julia's smile wavered and collapsed. She said

wretchedly, 'Oh Vivvy, the house is going to be sold whatever happens, but I honestly don't know whether Alex Constantis is going to buy Ambermere or not.' She swallowed. 'What I do know is I'd sooner see it burn to the ground than belong to him. He's the most hateful man I've ever met!'

Vivvy gave her a limpid look. 'Darling Jools, no man with all that money could possibly be hateful!' She sobered, giving Julia a quick hug. 'There's nothing I can say to make you feel better about this, but I felt I had to warn you. Stepmother's on the warpath. She was smirking to herself all the way here, and that's always bad news for someone.'

Julia received the news with a grimace of dismay. Gerald Bosworth's first wife had been a warm and smiling woman, popular with everyone, and genuinely mourned when she died after a long illness. It was generally agreed locally that Gerald, who had nursed her with total devotion, should marry again in due time, but no one, least of all Vivvy and her brother Alastair, had expected it to happen so soon, or to find themselves with a young and glamorous former actress as a stepmother. Tricia Bosworth at first bewildered her new neighbours, who tried to make her welcome for Gerald's sake, and later aroused their resentment with the deliberately poisonous sweetness of some of her remarks. Because she was Gerald's wife, and everyone liked Gerald, it was impossible to exclude her from social gatherings, but there was always an edge when she was around.

'An actress!' Julia had once said bitterly, smarting from Tricia's smiling comments about adolescent gaucherie. 'What's she ever been in, for heaven's sake?'

'She claims to have been in an RSC production of *Antony and Cleopatra*,' Vivvy had returned dejectedly. 'Probably playing the asp.'

Tricia had always gushed about Ambermere, its beauty and its history, but she wouldn't be shedding any tears over the Kendricks' loss, and the thought of her openly probing their wounds over dinner was unbearable.

What else can go wrong? Julia asked herself unhappily. How could the passage of a few hours change one's entire life so fundamentally?

'Cheer up.' Vivvy linked an arm through hers. 'She may choke on a fishbone and die before she can start.'

Julia smiled reluctantly. 'Can't we arrange for two fishbones?'

'Never kill off a millionaire unless you're mentioned in his will,' Vivvy warned solemnly. 'What's he like—old, fat and repulsive?'

'No,' Julia said colourlessly. 'I suppose he's attractive—if you like that sort of thing.'

'I'm sure I could learn to,' giggled Vivvy. 'Lead me to him!'

As Julia took her into the drawing-room, she gave vent to a soundless whistle. 'Attractive? My God, Jools, are you crazy? He's gorgeous!'

Unwillingly, Julia had to concede that Vivvy spoke with a certain justice. In the casual clothes he had been wearing when she first encountered him, he'd looked a force to be reckoned with. Now, in the dark formality of dinner jacket and black tie, Alex

Constantis possessed a disturbing, charismatic presence which was drawing every female eye in the room.

Well, they said wealth and power were aphrodisiacs, Julia thought savagely, then bit her lip. She was being unfair, and she knew it. Even if he were penniless, any woman with blood in her veins would look at him, and look again. Except me, she reminded herself grimly.

But that was not as easy as it seemed. To her chagrin, Julia found she was placed opposite him at the long oak table in the dining-room, and no matter how rigorously she limited her attention to the companions on either side of her, she was still uneasily aware that he was watching her across the heaped bowls of early roses, and the flickering candle flames.

Tricia Bosworth leaned forward. 'So you're going to be the new master of Ambermere,' she said in her husky drawl. 'Do tell us—has Julia persuaded you to change your name to Kendrick yet?'

Julia put her knife and fork down, her mouth suddenly dry.

Alex Constantis's brows lifted. 'I do not quite understand.'

Mrs Bosworth laughed. 'Oh, it's been a standing joke locally for years. Julia has always sworn that the family name should continue here—either by finding another Kendrick from somewhere to marry her, or forcing some other unsuspecting soul to change his name. I wondered if she'd started her campaign with you yet. She's always claimed to be prepared to go to any lengths to keep Ambermere hers.'

'So I have already gathered.' The faint irony in his voice, and the flickering glance he sent the deeply slashed bodice of the midnight blue satin dress, were not lost on Julia.

'I'm sure you have,' purred Tricia then she paused, smiling. 'Are you married, Mr Constantis?'

The dark face was shuttered. 'No.'

In the hideously embarrassed silence which followed, Julia prayed for the floor beneath her chair to open, and swallow her for ever. She heard Gerald Bosworth mutter, 'Tricia, for God's sake!' and saw Vivvy's appalled and sympathetic grimace.

Into the silence, Sir Philip said pleasantly, 'As you say, Mrs Bosworth—a standing joke. But I don't think Julia, as a woman, should have a silly childhood boast held against her. Now, may I offer you some more duck?'

Conversation around the table resumed again in an atmosphere of relief, which Julia could not share. If Tricia Bosworth had openly gloated that Ambermere had to be sold, it would have been bad enough, but the other woman had deliberately set out to humiliate her in front of Alex Constantis. If she'd received a blow-by-blow account of the day's events she couldn't have planted her barbs more effectively, Julia thought, wincing.

And only he would not be aware that Tricia Bosworth made a speciality of such malice.

And somehow she had to smile and go on, pretending it didn't matter. She took a surreptitious glance at her small gold watch, wondering how long it would be before she could make some excuse and seek the refuge of her room.

Tonight, as never before, she found herself welcoming the duties as hostess with her mother which kept her perpetually on the move from group to group as the house filled with guests.

She had half expected, half dreaded that Alex Constantis would seek her out with some taunting reference to Tricia's words. But perhaps he too had been embarrassed by the exchange, for he never came near her.

Her father was almost always at his side, guiding him through the crowded rooms explaining, making introductions, while their friends loyally strove to mask their surprise and dismay at the news.

And even now it could all be for nothing, Julia thought with misgivings. Wouldn't it be hysterical if Tricia proves to be the final straw, and the whole deal falls through? But she didn't feel much like laughing. Even if Alex Constantis withdrew from contention, another buyer would come along. Ambermere could not be saved, and she had to come to terms with that.

As midnight approached Julia realised that the toast to the first Lady Kendrick was going to be drunk as usual.

'Oh, God, I can't face that,' she muttered to herself, slipping through the partially open french windows on to the terrace.

There was no breeze, but the night air felt refreshingly cool against her uncovered shoulders and arms. A scent of flowers hung in the air, making her starkly, poignantly aware that this was the last Midsummer night she would ever spend in this house.

She leaned on the balustrade, gazing sightlessly

over the starlit gardens, wondering painfully what changes Alex Constantis would make if he bought the house. He would probably plough up the south lawn and replace it with a swimming pool, and a helicopter pad, she thought scornfully, and she should be glad she wasn't going to be around to see such desecration.

She could hear the laughter and the cheering from the drawing room, and the cries of 'To Julia', which followed her father's traditional, humorous speech, and wondered how many of the particpants realised they were drinking the toast for the last time. Julia Kendrick—scandalous wife, daring mistress, Toast of the Town—had reached the end of her reign.

She felt sudden absurd tears sting at her eyelids, and thought, 'To Julia'. And heard, with sudden shock, the same words echoed aloud from only a feet away.

She whirled round, her hands flying to her mouth to cover the little startled cry forced from her. 'You!'

'Yes,'

Somehow, in the shadows of the night, he looked taller—more powerful than ever, the dark face an unreadable mask as he stood between her and the sanctuary of the lighted window.

He said, 'I came to wish you goodnight, *thespinis.*'

'You're—leaving?' The words seemed to twist out of her suddenly dry throat.

He smiled. 'That is what you're hoping for, *ne?*' He shook his head. 'I am sorry to disappoint you. I shall be back—later today.'

'You're going to buy the house?'

'I think so. You have rekindled my interest in it.'

'I—have?'

'Certainly. Ambermere must be a unique property, if it can rouse such passionate commitment in you.' He paused. 'I wonder, in different circumstances, if you would ever have found the husband you are looking for, Julia Kendrick—a man so little a man he would deny his name and his birthright in subjection to your whim.'

'It wasn't a whim,' she denied huskily. 'How could you possibly understand?'

'You think perhaps that I have no right to the name I bear?' The dark eyes glittered at her. 'Well, you are not the first to say so—even though there have been few who would dare utter the words to my face.'

'Because they're all so terrified of you?' Her voice sounded high and rather breathless. 'When you take Ambermere, you'll have done the worst you can. You have no power over me after that.'

'You don't think so?' Slowly he advanced on her, making her retreat until her back was pressed against the balustrade with no further physical withdrawal possible. 'But you are wrong, Julia Kendrick. Because if I take Ambermere, I shall also take you.'

His hands descended on her shoulders. He used no particular force, but with the first shock of his touch on her bare skin, Julia knew her flesh would bear the imprint of his fingers as if he had bruised her.

She tried to say 'No!' but he was bending towards her, shutting out safety, blocking the starlight, and the word was stifled on her lips by the stark, demanding pressure of his mouth. She tried to resist, to keep her own mouth closed against his insistence, but it was a battle she could not win. A battle he was determined, with total sensuality, that she should lose.

In some distant corner of her mind, she admitted this. Recognised that this confrontation had been inevitable since she had entered the drawing-room that night.

A sigh trembled through her, and she capitulated, allowing him to invade her mouth and deepen the kiss in any way he wanted. But even that was not enough. His lips, his tongue demanded a response she had never before been required to give—a response she wasn't even sure she capable of. She couldn't breathe, and her legs seemed to be turning to water, as his hands pushed the straps of her dress from her shoulders, then drew her against him so that her bared breasts were brought into aching, erotic contract with the hard wall of his chest.

And from somewhere in her innermost being, she felt the first slow uncurling of heated, treacherous, unbearable excitement.

Her hands went up to clasp the lapels of his jacket as an insidious weakness began to spread through her. When he took his mouth from hers, she gasped, her head falling back helplessly as his mouth traced a path down the column of her throat.

But as his hand lifted to close intimately on one small naked breast, she cried out in outraged modesty, summoning all the strength of will which still remained to her in order to drag herself out of his arms. She was shaking so much she thought she might fall, her hands fumbling as she tried to drag her dress back into place, to hide her body from that dark, devouring gaze.

For one shuddering moment she thought he might reach for her again, and shrank back against the support of the balustrade.

She heard him catch his breath, and saw the savage, single-minded hunger die from his face, to be replaced by an odd wryness.

He said, to himself, 'A virgin. And that, of course, changes everything.'

Then, before Julia could move or speak, he turned, and walked away from her into the darkness.

CHAPTER THREE

JULIA stayed in her room until late the following morning. Downstairs she could hear the whine of vacuum cleaners, and a subdued hum of voices and movement, as the small army of cleaners from the village restored order after the party. Normally, she would have got up and pitched in with them.

But this time she didn't seem capable of doing anything but lying staring at the ceiling, letting the events of the previous day, and more particularly, the previous night, re-run in her mind like some slow-moving action replay.

It was still impossible for her to believe that she had behaved like that—responded like that, especially with a man she resented and despised. She even wondered whether she had dreamed the whole thing.

It had been, after all, Midsummer Night. But Alex Constantis's kisses were far from being 'the stuff that dreams are made on', Julia thought wryly.

And she couldn't blame alcohol either, for she'd hardly drunk anything all night.

Oh, damn him, she thought savagely, burying her face in the pillow. Damn him to hell!

Her behaviour had been totally out of context with the rest of her life. She had never been the type to walk willingly into any man's arms. 'Passionately

41

aloof' had been the rueful description from one of her admirers, and she had liked that. She'd had a life planned out for herself in security and harmony at Ambermere, and nothing was going to interfere with that, especially the kind of casual sexual diversion so many of her friends seemed to take for granted. True, the threat of serious disease had changed their thinking in recent months, but Julia had had to make no such adaptation.

I was fashionable without even knowing it, she told herself half derisively.

Now she was being forced to consider whether the strong-mindedness she had always prided herself on might not simply have been lack of serious temptation.

No, she thought, thumping the mattress with her fist. I won't believe that. Yesterday I was knocked sideways by the news about Ambermere, that's all, and I went a little mad. But today I'm sane again.

Sane enough, certainly, to think about plans for her drastically altered future.

Soberly, she considered her strengths in book-keeping and word-processing which she had intended to use in the administration of the estate, working alongside her father. Surely they were sufficient to find her some kind of secretarial work. And a number of her former school friends were now living and working in London, and always looking for an extra flatmate to help out with the rent.

I'll survive, she told herself. I'll have to.

She got up, took a quick bath, then dressed in jeans and a shirt before going downstairs.

Mrs Parsons the housekeeper was coming along

the hall with a tray of coffee for Sir Philip's study, and Julia followed her.

'Morning, Jools.' Her father's greeting was a shade over-hearty. 'You slipped away rather early last night, didn't you?'

'I wasn't really in a party mood,' Julia returned levelly, and Sir Philip nodded, shuffling the papers on his desk.

'It's a hell of a thing,' he said sombrely. 'Jools, if there was any other way, you know—don't you . . .'

'Yes,' Julia acknowledged with a sigh, 'I know.' She poured out the coffee and handed her father his cup. 'Although I suppose nothing's settled yet.'

'As a matter of fact it is.' Her father gave her an awkward glance. 'Alex Constantis telephoned after breakfast to confirm his offer. Polly and I are meeting his lawyers this afternoon to work out the final details. It's all going to happen rather fast, I suspect.'

'I'm sure it will,' Julia agreed drily. Even when he was standing still, Alex Constantis gave an impression of being consumed by restless dynamic energy. Once he had made up his mind he wanted something, he would allow no grass to grow under his feet until he possessed it, she thought, a frisson of unease prickling between her shoulderblades.

'He's coming over later,' her father went on. 'We spent rather a long time at the Home Farm yesterday, and he wants to see the rest of the estate.' He paused. 'I told him you'd be happy to be his guide.'

'You said what?' Julia sent him a horrified glance. 'Oh, Daddy, you couldn't have done! I never want to set eyes on that man again as long as I live!'

'Then that's unfortunate.' Sir Philip frowned.

'What I said yesterday, Jools, still applies. I expect you to be civil, and keep any personal antipathy you may feel under control. Nothing's actually signed yet, after all. And you're the best person anyway for a job like that. Constantis was asking me last night about the damnfool remarks that silly woman poor Gerald lumbered himself with was making at dinner, and I explained to him how much the estate meant to you. He was very understanding.'

'I'm sure he was,' Julia said bitterly. She sighed. 'All right then, Daddy, I'll do what you want, on condition it's the last time I have to meet Mr Constantis. Tomorrow I'm going to London to start job-hunting.'

Sir Philip stared at her. 'But there's no need for that. Once the estate is sold, we won't be penniless. I thought we might move to the Riviera, or somewhere in the sun. These English winters are no good for Mummy's chest, you know, and . . .'

'No darling,' Julia said gently. 'You two go ahead and make whatever plans you want. I have to start organising a life for myself.' She lifted her chin. 'I'm not a child any more.'

'No,' Sir Philip said rather sadly, 'I suppose not.'

An hour later Julia waved her parents a smiling goodbye. Lydia Kendrick had decided to accompany her husband to London to do some shopping, a decision which Julia suspected sprang from the news that Alex Constantis was due at Ambermere shortly.

Lucky Mother, she thought with a sigh. I wish I could cut and run!

As she went back into the house, the telephone rang, and she reached for it with a feeling of foreboding. But it was only Vivvy.

'Where did you disappear to last night?' her friend asked plaintively.

'I began to feel like the skeleton at the feast and went to bed,' Julia excused herself.

'Not swept off your feet by the dishy Mr Constantis, I hope,' giggled Vivvy, then she lowered her voice conspiratorially. 'By the way, Jools, Dad and Stepmother had a mega-row last night over her remarks at dinner. Alastair and I could hear them in their bedroom shouting at each other. I think Dad's rose-coloured glasses have cracked at last.'

'I'm sorry,' said Julia, and meant it.

'I'm not,' Vivvy returned with equal sincerity. 'She's an utter bitch, and everyone could see it but him. But she'll have to be more careful in future, which can only be a step in the right direction.' She paused. 'Actually, I thought Alex Constantis handled the situation pretty well. He's incredibly glamorous and sexy, Jools. Pity he's not looking for a wife, really.'

'Well, he'll be here at any minute for a tour of the estate,' Julia said coolly. 'I'll put in a good word for you.'

'For me?' Vivvy shrieked. 'Don't be an idiot! I was thinking of you. Tricia may have been out to make trouble, but she had a point, actually. If you married Alex Constantis, you'd still have Ambermere.'

'Thank you,' Julia said drily. 'But there's a limit to the sacrifices I'm prepared to make, even for Ambermere.'

Vivvy giggled again. 'Some sacrifice,' she said caustically. 'Quite apart from his money, I bet he's fantastic in bed.'

For one frightened moment Julia found herself re-living the reality of being in Alex Constantis's arms. The remembered scent of his skin, the warmth of his body seemed to fill her senses, as if he had been standing there beside her. A shiver ran through her. She gave a shaky laugh.

'You're the limit. Viv! What would Reverend Mother say if she could hear you?'

'She'd sigh, and offer to pray for me again,' Vivvy said ebulliently. 'Poor soul, I bet she's never off her knees.'

Julia's hand was trembling as she replaced the receiver on the rest after Vivvy had rung off. Her friend had only been joking, she knew, but her starlit encounter with Alex Constantis had taught her swiftly that any involvement with him was no laughing matter.

'If I take Ambermere, I shall also take you.' The words seemed to sting in her brain.

The only reassurance she could draw from the incident was the change of heart he'd undergone once he'd concluded she was a virgin. Although heaven alone knew how he'd guessed that, she thought with embarrassment. But clearly her total lack of sexual experience was a drawback as far as he was concerned.

And a lifesaver to me, she thought, squaring her shoulders, as she heard the sound of a car on the drive outside. She wiped suddenly damp hands on her denim-clad thighs. And now it was daylight, and the sexy party gear was shut away, along with the madness which had afflicted her last night. She was her practical workaday self once again.

There's nothing to fear, she told herself. Nothing.

She went out of the front door and stood looking down at him as he got out of the car. A new Aston Martin, she noticed in passing.

Alex Constantis walked to the foot of the steps and paused, a faint smile playing round his mouth as he surveyed her.

'*Kalimera,*' he said softly. 'Did you sleep well?'

I won't blush, Julia vowed silently and grimly. I bloody well won't!

She said coolly and untruthfully, 'Perfectly, thank you.'

'You are fortunate, Julia *mou*. Each time I closed my eyes, I dreamed you were beside me, and reached for you.' His smile widened. 'It was frustrating, believe me!'

Thrust deep into the pockets of her jeans, Julia's hands clenched into tense fists, then relaxed.

She said crisply. 'You may find such remarks amusing, Mr Constantis. I find them embarrassing and degrading.'

'Do you always find the truth disturbing? Or am I the first man brave enough to admit that he wants you in his bed?'

'Well, I don't want you,' Julia said sharply, aware of the deep, uneven throb of her pulses. 'I think you'd better go.'

'When I've seen the rest of the estate. Your father assured me you'd be delighted to be my guide.'

'That's his first mistake today. As he has to deal with your lawyers, I hope it's the last.' She glanced at her watch. 'Perhaps we could make it a quick tour.

I'm afraid I can't offer you lunch . . .'

'I do not expect you to,' he said silkily. 'I have brought a picnic for us to share. And the tour will take as long as necessary. You are, after all, the expert.' He paused. 'And I do not want statistics about yield per acre, either, *thespinis*. I want to see this land, this house through your eyes. You understand?' At her unwilling nod, he walked to his car and opened the passenger door. 'Shall we begin?'

At first Julia was as taut as a bowstring, wary of his proximity in the confines of the car, but as the tour proceeded, she began half unconsciously to relax, reassured by the fact that he seemed to need both hands for driving, and showed no disposition to lunge at her.

She had half expected to have to explain the workings of the estate in words of one syllable, but soon discovered her mistake. His questions were sharp and searching, revealing a keen and demanding intelligence. Julia had her work cut out to keep up with him, she discovered with no great pleasure.

Under his interrogation, in spite of herself, she began to talk about Ambermere, the way it had been in the past, the plans she had had for the future, her voice softening as she identified favourite landmarks, the places dear to her since childhood. Every hedge, every clump of trees seemed to have some deep and personal meaning, she realised with anguish, the eager spill of words choking in her throat.

He said, 'I think it is time we had something to eat. Can you suggest a place?'

Julia swallowed, grabbing at her composure. 'If

you take the left fork, it will bring you down to the lake. But you can drop me here. I should really be getting back to the house . . .'

'After we have eaten.' The words were quietly spoken, but the underlying note was implacable.

In the sunlight, the lake's waters gleamed like gold.

'It's something to do with the sediment,' Julia explained. 'And quite harmless. Fish thrive in it. And of course, it's how the house got its name.'

'Of course.' He handed her a rug. 'Spread this out, if you please, while I get the food.'

Nervously, Julia complied. She wished now that she had organised lunch for them at the house after all. A rug by the undoubted seclusion of the lake had all the connotations she most wanted to avoid. The dining-room at home would have been far less intimate, she thought, biting her lip.

The picnic hamper was a revelation. There was smoked salmon, and thick wedges of a creamy chicken pie, as well as salads, and crisp rolls. To follow there were nectarines, grapes, and thick, luscious strawberries, sprinkled with kirsch.

Julia's eyes widened, as she watched Alex Constantis deal effortlessly with the opening of a bottle of champagne.

'Isn't this all rather lavish for a simple day in the country?' she asked with a touch of sarcasm.

'You mean—rather vulgar?' He slanted a glance at her, as he handed her a glass. 'But what else could you expect from a peasant? Anyway, you forget I have a decision to celebrate.'

Julia's throat tightened. 'You're mistaken, Mr Constantis. I haven't forgotten a thing.'

'You are very formal.' He filled his own glass. 'Could you not bring yourself to call me Alex?'

'I think formality is preferable, under the circumstances.'

'As you wish.' He lifted his glass. 'Then let us drink together—to Ambermere, and its future.' He paused, seeing her hesitate. 'It does have one, I assure you, *thespinis.*'

Julia flushed slightly, then raised her glass in turn.

Silently he handed her a plate, cutlery, and a linen napkin, and they began to eat. In spite of her reservations, Julia found herself enjoying the food, and eating her full share of it. Being in the open air always sharpened her appetite, she thought ruefully, as Alex offered her a second helping of strawberries.

She shook her head and leaned back on her elbow, relishing the warmth of the sun, and the scent of the grass. If she'd been with anyone else, she thought ruefully, she would have been relaxed completely, having the time of her life. But Alex Constantis, even when playing the courteous host, as she could not deny he had done, was a menace to her peace of mind.

Aware that he was watching her, she hurried into speech. 'You speak very good English. Where did you learn it?'

His brows lifted slightly. 'I had an adequate education.' He paused, then added drily, 'Despite what you may have been told.'

'Told?'

Why, yes. Your father mentioned last night the vacation you had just enjoyed—the Embassy to which your uncle is attached. My cousin Paul has a posting to the same capital. I am sure you must have encountered him at some point. You are too beautiful for him to overlook.' His mouth twisted slightly. 'Nor could he have resisted telling you, as he tells everyone, how I robbed him of his supposed heritage. His mother and sister are equally voluble on the same subject.'

'You can hardly blame them,' Julia said bluntly. 'Usurpers are rarely popular.'

He laughed. 'So that is how you regard me,' he said, and there was a brief silence. At last he said, 'Hearing you talk about your home earlier was a revelation, Julia *mou*. You speak of it as a woman speaks of her lover.'

She looked down at her glass. 'Ambermere's been my life. I thought it always would be.'

He said laconically. 'And so it can.' He paused. 'If you marry me.'

Julia sat up with a jerk, spilling champagne on her shirt. She said unevenly, 'If that's a joke, it's in very poor taste.'

'Yet I am perfectly serious.' Alex reached across and removed the glass from her hand, setting it down at a safe distance. 'A house like Ambermere needs a woman, and my mother tells me it is time I was married.' The powerful shoulders lifted in a slight shrug. 'Maybe she is right.'

'So you propose to a woman you hardly know just because your mother thinks it's a good idea?' Julia managed a scornful laugh. 'Incredible!'

'Totally, if your premise were correct,' he agreed, unmoved. 'But we are not exactly strangers to each other, Julia *mou*.' He paused. 'Last night you asked

me if I would give you Ambermere. Today I tell
you—yes. But on my terms, not yours.'

'It's unthinkable!' Her voice sounded like a
stranger's. 'I suppose you actually believe what that
ghastly woman said. That I'd lend myself to such a
disgusting—degrading arrangement—that I'd sell
myself.' She scrambled up on to her knees, her small
breasts heaving stormily. 'And to you, of all people!'

'Now why do you say that?' His voice was still
mild, but there was a disturbing glitter in the dark
eyes as they rested on her. 'Is my blood somehow
unfit to mingle with yours?'

'It's nothing to do with that,' Julia returned
defiantly. She took a deep breath. 'To be frank, Mr
Constantis, you're not my type. In fact, you leave me
cold.' She sent him a brittle smile. 'Not the way, I'm
sure, you'd want your wife to feel.'

He picked a long blade of grass, brushing it
meditatively across his chin as he surveyed her. 'It
would cause difficulties, certainly. But is it, in fact,
the case?'

He was taunting her, Julia realised furiously,
needling her with a reminder of their shared
memories of the previous night.

She said tautly, 'We're all guilty of uncharacteristic
behaviour at times, Mr Constantis.' She shrugged,
with an attempt at insouciance. 'Put mine down to
too much alcohol—plus the fact that you took me by
surprise.'

For a moment there was silence then Alex
Constantis shrugged too, a graceful, half-humorous
lift of the shoulders. He said softly, 'Then, if that is
the only way, so be it.'

As he moved, Julia realised his intention and recoiled, sprawling backwards on to the rug as she did so.

As she tried to recover herself, Alex was there beside her, his body pinning hers to the ground, one hand capturing both her wrists and holding them above her head, rendering her helpless.

She said hoarsely, 'Let go of me, damn you!'

'Why?' The smile on his lips did not reach his eyes. 'What possible effect on you can this have?' He bent his head, brushing her lips almost negligently with his. 'Or even—this.' His free hand began to unbutton her shirt.

She said on a little moan of despair, 'No—oh God, no!' her body twisting and writhing as she sought to free herself.

He lifted himself slightly away from her, but only to thrust one lean, muscular thigh between hers.

He said, with a ghost of a laugh. 'Go on fighting me, *agapi mou*. I like it.'

The intimate pressure of his body against hers left her in no doubt as to what he meant, and embarrassment heightened the angry colour in her face.

'You swine!' she choked. 'You—you . . .'

'Bastard?' he jeered. 'Why don't you say it?' His fingers moved downwards, unhurriedly completing their task, and tugging the edges of her shirt aside.

She was wearing a bra today, but the fragile lace provided only a token covering, and Alex smiled in sensuous anticipation as he looked down at her. His hand found the small clasp in the valley of her breasts, and dealt with it expertly.

The breath caught agonisingly in her throat. The

sun dazzled her half-closed eyes, and in its centre he was total darkness as he bent towards her.

His fingers stroked one soft, pink-tipped mound, shaped it, held it for the caress of his lips. A whimper, half rejection, half need, rose in her throat as for the first time she felt his mouth against her naked flesh. A shaft of hot, shamed excitement pierced her body as his lips surrounded the engorged, rosy peak. His tongue circled her nipple languorously, playing with it, softly strumming the heated tip until the mingled pain and pleasure of it made her cry out, her body twisting again, but this time in the tumultuous unfamiliarity of abandonment.

He turned his head and began to kiss her other breast, and the warm, secret centre of her womanhood clenched in sharp delight, as she felt its aching reponse.

His hand moved down slowly, exploring her ribcage and the flat plane of her stomach, to the waistband of her jeans, and stopped. As if she was outside her own body, no longer in control, Julia felt her slender hips lift slightly, arching her, thrusting her against his imprisoning thigh.

Alex raised his head and looked down at her, his own breathing suddenly harsh and ragged, then with disconcerting swiftness he rolled away from her, and she was free.

For a long moment Julia lay still, her whole body throbbing as her paralysed mind tried to come to terms with what had happened to her.

From a thousand miles away, Alex's voice reached her softly, mockingly. 'If I leave you cold, Julia *mou*, then the man who can warm you is to be envied indeed.'

With a little choking gasp, Julia turned on her side away from him, trying to deal with recalcitrant clips and buttons with shaking, clumsy hands.

She couldn't believe what had just happened. How she had lain there and let him do that to her—and even wanted more. She wanted to leap to her feet and run away—to somewhere he would never find her—where she would never have to face him again.

A swift, humiliated glance over her shoulder revealed that he was repacking the hamper, his movements economical. It was clear that what had transpired had no means affected him in the same way, she realised wretchedly.

She had provoked him, and he had countered, and now she had to live with the knowledge that she had been his for the taking, she, the cool, the un-approachable.

Oh, God, she thought. It can't be true. It can't.

She looked up to find him standing over her, hands on hips. Dry-mouthed, she stared up at him, her hand shielding her eyes from the sun.

He said, 'Do you wish to go home?'

'I can find my own way.' Her voice sounded husky and unfamiliar.

She was sure he would argue, insist, but to her surprise he shrugged, carried the picnic things to the car, then climbed in and drove away.

She stayed where she was for a long time, staring unseeingly at the amber waters of the lake. Then eventually she got shakily to her feet and began to make her way towards the copse, where the gipsy trailers were parked. She had to see Grandma Pascoe again. There were things she wanted to ask her—things she had to know.

Ambermere, she thought, her nails scoring the soft palms of her hands—the Tower struck by lightning. And Alex Constantis—the King of Swords, coming to humble her. It was all mumbo-jumbo and coincidence, of course, but it was horribly, uncannily accurate at the same time.

And she wanted no more of it. She wanted the familiar comfort of handsome strangers, and unexpected windfalls.

But when she reached the copse she was aware of a strange stillness. She ran into the clearing and stopped, looking around her incredulously. It was empty. The trailers had gone, leaving the usual bare places on the grass, and the blackened patches where fires had been lit.

Julia cried out to the unheeding trees, 'But you can't leave me like this—you can't! You've got to take it all back—make things better.'

But only the silence answered. The Pascoes had gone, and heaven only knew when—or if—they would be back.

She walked home slowly, head down.

Safely in her room, she stripped and showered, letting the warm water teem down over the body she'd always taken so much for granted, and which had so totally betrayed her. She wanted to wash away the memories of Alex's hands—his mouth. To belong to herself again.

She dressed in old, familiar clothes—a wraparound skirt in a swirl of jade green, and a white blouse, square-necked and loose-sleeved. She brushed her damp copper hair until her scalp tingled, then tied it at the nape of her neck with a length of chiffon to match her skirt.

Julia Kendrick looked back at herself in the mirror with her usual composure, but the slow, subtle grind of frustration deep within her body told her it was a façade—a lie.

If he had stripped her naked—taken her—she would have made no move to stop him. She knew that, and it terrified her as nothing else—not even the loss of Ambermere—had ever done.

She'd been his—and he had been the one to draw back, to call a halt. That was what she now had to try to live with.

She stepped out on to the landing, nearly colliding with Mrs Parsons.

'I'm sorry, Madge.' She made herself smile, speak calmly. 'Were you looking for me?'

'You have a visitor, Miss Julia.' Mrs Parsons gave her an arch smile. 'I thought it was Sir Philip he'd come to see, but he asked for you instead.'

Hidden by her skirts, Julia's hands balled into tense fists, then relaxed. She maintained her cool, even though every instinct was warning her to run back into her bedroom and bar and bolt the door.

She didn't ask who it was. She knew already. Knew too why he was there. She went downstairs and across the wide hall to the drawing-room. Alex Constantis was standing near the fireplace. He had changed too, to the dark formality of a suit, and silk shirt and tie.

For an endless moment they stared at each other

across the room.

Then he said, with harsh abruptness, 'Will you marry me?'

Words of negation, of rejection filled Julia's brain, jostled each other for utterance.

From somewhere a long way outside herself, she heard her voice say, 'Yes.'

Alex nodded, a faint dull flush along his hard cheekbones. He said, 'I will speak to your father tomorrow.'

Then he walked past her to the door and was gone.

Julia fumbled her way to a sofa and sank down on to the cushions, trembling violently.

She thought, What have I done? Oh, God, what have I done?

CHAPTER FOUR

THEY WERE married three weeks later in a brief register office ceremony which spoke louder than words of her parents' total disapproval of her headlong decision.

Julia had never before faced such outright and prolonged condemnation of any of her actions, and she found the days preceding the wedding wretched and emotionally draining.

'You can't do this thing!' Lydia Kendrick had declared tearfully over and over again. 'You can't marry a man simply because you want to go on living in this house. It—it's obscene!'

And Julia replied wearily as she had done so many times, 'It isn't just the house . . .'

Lady Kendrick snorted. 'Then what else is it, pray? You can't pretend you're in love with that man—that upstart!'

No, Julia couldn't pretend that. She had no real idea what her feelings were towards Alex Constantis. And the devastating sensual impact that he'd made on her untried emotions was hardly something she could discuss with her mother, she thought ruefully.

By tacit consent, no public announcement had been made about their enagagement, although Alex had presented her with a ring—an exquisite star sapphire. He had handed it to her with a challenging lift of the

brows, as if daring her to find it too large or too
ostentatious, and she had thanked him with a quiet,
'It's beautiful.'

But he hadn't offered to place it on her finger, and
most of the time Julia left the ring in its satin-lined
box. The gift was a token to satisfy a convention, she
thought, but it had no more significance than that,
and certainly Alex, as she'd learned haltingly to call
him, never demanded to know where it was.

And if her own feelings about this marriage were
ambivalent, she had no idea at all about his. On the
surface, he played the role of the attentive fiancé so
skilfully that even Sir Philip and Lady Kendrick had
no real criticism to level. He was civil, even charming,
in the face of her mother's almost overt hostility. And
he raised no objection at all to the wedding being
little more than a hole-and-corner affair.

Julia herself was aware of a nagging disappointment. She had always envisaged herself standing at
the altar in the small parish church, a vision in white
silk chiffon, with family, friends and well-wishers
crowding the pews.

She had imagined Alex himself wanting a full-dress
ceremony too, to drive home to the locality and the
world at large that although his own antecedents
might be questionable, he was marrying into an old
and respected family.

Yet he seemed totally uninterested in the details of
how Julia was to become his wife. And the next shock
had been to learn that not one member of his family
would be attending the wedding.

'No one?' Julia had stared at him. 'But surely . . .'
'So who am I supposed to invite?' He had given

that characteristic shrug. 'My cousin Paul, who at the moment regards himself as my heir? His sister Zoe? My aunt Sophia?'

Julia had hesitated. 'But there's your mother.' She tried a smile. 'I haven't even met her yet and . . .'

'There is plenty of time for that.' He paused. 'My mother's health has not been good lately—she's had a virus—and a journey to England might tire her—apart from any other considerations,' he added with faint irony.

Julia had flushed. Alex was clearly concerned about the reception his mother might meet, and in all honesty she could not blame him. A simple Greek peasant woman could be destroyed by Lydia Kendrick's icy politeness.

But Alex's lack of supporters at the wedding was not the only surprise of the engagement.

Julia had assumed that once she had promised to be Alex's wife he would lose no time in pursuing his seduction of her to the ultimate conclusion. But, in fact, nothing could have been further from the truth.

He visited or telephoned her each day, of course, and on the two occasions when he had had to go abroad for a few days, he'd arranged for flowers to be sent.

His wooing of her, if that was what it was, had been conducted on strictly formal lines. He sought no opportunities to be alone with her, and when they were together he kept his distance. And his kisses were confined to the merest brushing of his mouth across her lips or cheek at arrival or leavetaking.

Julia had begun by being puzzled at his lack of

demonstrativeness, become angry, and then reverted
to bewilderment again. She didn't want him to make
love to her—that went without saying, she told herself defiantly—but at the same time his ability to remain aloof was a little disturbing, reminding her yet
again how little she knew of the man she was going
to marry.

Even more disturbing was her own reaction, each
time she saw him or heard his voice on the telephone.
She could neither deny nor defend the slow-burning
excitement uncoiling inside her, but she could hide it,
matching, on the surface at least, his coolness with
her own. Although how far he was deceived it was
impossible to say, she admitted ruefully. And no
doubt he was supremely confident of his ability to
sweep away all barriers between them on their
wedding night, reducing her once more to the state of
mindless passion she had experienced that day by the
lake.

Well, that was the life he'd offered, and which
she'd accepted, she thought with a little sigh.
Mistress of his house by day, mistress of his body by
night. She could hardly complain now of the
starkness of the bargain between them.

But the thought of what it might mean to surrender
completely to a man like Alex Constantis had come to
dominate her thinking as the hours and minutes to
her wedding ticked away.

Grandma Pascoe's warning that the King of
Swords would humble her pride had returned to
haunt her over and over again, much as she tried to
dismiss it.

The night before her wedding day, she was prey to

swift, troublous dreams in which Ambermere became a house of empty, echoing rooms, through which she ran in an endless search—for what?

And as Philip Kendrick drove her, tight-lipped, to the register office in the nearby market town, Julia found herself wondering, with sudden chill, if Alex would even be there. That had been another of the previous night's dreams—finding herself, surrounded by curious eyes, waiting for a bridegroom who never arrived. Was that why he had invited no guests of his own to the ceremony—because he knew it would never take place?

Stop being ridiculous, she adjured herself almost frantically. Of course he'll be there. You're letting Grandma Pascoe's wild predictions get out of all proportion.

Alex was marrying her to provide himself with someone to run the house and estate he had acquired—and because he desired her, she reminded herself with a faint shiver. He had no reason to humiliate her publicly. She was letting her imagination run away with her.

Nevertheless, it was almost a relief to find him waiting there, with a tall, fair-haired man whom he introduced as Andrew Carstairs, his personal assistant in the UK.

Andrew Carstairs shook hands with Julia and her parents, and made appropriately genial comments, but it was clear he was no more impressed with this hasty, almost perfunctory marriage than the Kendricks themselves.

Within minutes, it seemed, it was all over, and Julia was driving back to Ambermere with her new husband. The wedding ring felt strange and heavy on her hand, she thought, twisting it round and round. She rarely wore jewellery, but this particular piece she would have to accustom herself to. She stole a sideways glance at Alex, but his shuttered expression gave no clue as to what he was thinking.

Apart from telling her that her simple white silk dress with its covering flower-embroidered jacket looked charming, and making his vows, he had said little, and the silence now between them in the car was beginning to prey on Julia, and make her nervous.

She said, 'A few of the neighbours are coming to have a drink, and wish us luck. I hope you don't mind.'

'Not at all, as long as their good wishes are not too prolonged. We have a plane to catch.'

They were flying to Athens, and joining Alex's yacht *Clio* at Piraeus, she knew, but their destination after that, he had told her, was a surprise.

Julia was not too concerned to solve the mystery. A cruise in the Aegean was no bad way to begin one's married life, after all, even if the marriage itself had not been made in heaven.

And when they returned, Sir Philip and Lady Kendrick would have moved to the temporary refuge of the Dower House, while negotiations were completed for the villa they were buying in the hills above Nice.

And Ambermere will be mine, Julia thought.

She was thankful, in the event, that the wedding reception had not been more formal or elaborate. Some of the congratulations were a little too hearty, as if the speakers were trying to convince themselves of their own sincerity. And she was aware of speculative looks behind the smiles.

Even Vivvy seemed slightly stunned that the one-time joke was a joke no more, and Julia was, in fact, Mrs Alexandros Constantis.

As soon as she could decently excuse herself, Julia went up to her room to put the few last items in her dressing case.

She was just checking the contents of her handbag when a sound from the doorway made her look round, and Tricia Bosworth strolled into the room.

'All alone?' She glanced around. 'I thought you might be closeted with Mummy, receiving some last-minute maternal advice on how to control men's baser animal instincts. Not that it'll do you much good,' she added with a faint shrug. 'No doubt you think you've been very clever—keeping Ambermere in the family, so to speak—but Alex Constantis will make you pay for the privilege, my dear, tonight, and every night. I only hope you don't find the price too high.' She giggled. 'Or is no sacrifice too great to make for Ambermere?'

Julia fastened the locks on her dressing case. 'None whatsoever,' she agreed serenely, aware that her colour had risen and longing to slap Tricia Bosworth across her sneering smile.

'Well, you've got guts, I'll grant you that.' Tricia sat down uninvited on the edge of the bed. 'So, do you plan to civilise your wild Hellene—turn him into an English country gentlemen? Or just smooth off the rougher corners a little?'

'I haven't decided yet,' Julia returned, maintaining

her composure with an effort.

'Of course,' Tricia went on, 'If you play your cards right, you don't need to see much of him at all. He can go off round the world, making money, and you can stay here, playing the gracious châtelaine, and spending it for him.'

'It sounds an ideal arrangement.' Julia found herself wondering almost dispassionately whether any other bride on her wedding day had been tempted to pick up the heavy silver-backed hand mirror from her dressing-table and smash it over a guest's head.

The important thing was not to show the least trace of irritation, and give Tricia Bosworth the petty victory she sought.

'Well, you seem to have it all worked out.' To Julia's relief, Mrs Bosworth rose, smoothing a none-existent crease out of her hyacinth-blue dress. She walked to the door, then turned, smiling. 'They say these Greek peasants are the most amazing studs. We must have a girls' get-together when you return from your honeymoon, and you can tell me if it's true.' She gave Julia a wink that managed to be both lascivious and conspiratorial, and departed.

Bitch, Julia thought, skaking with temper. Dirty-minded, evil-tongued bitch!

She sat down on her dressing stool, making herself breathe deeply, trying to relax. She couldn't go downstairs looking as she did, her eyes glowing with fury, and bright spots of colour burning on both cheeks.

The next rap on the door admitted Mrs Parsons. 'Mr Constantis asks if you're ready, Miss Julia—I mean Madam.'

'Quite ready.' It wasn't true. A host of butterflies were waging war somewhere in her midriff as she realised she was committed now—that there was no turning back.

And at the same time she was wondering why Alex had sent Mrs Parsons, instead of coming to tell her himself that it was time they left. Tricia Bosworth's lewd comments, although poisonous, had no foundation in fact, she though wryly. Alex had made no attempt even to kiss her so far, and the only time he had touched her was when he'd taken her hand during the ceremony itself. She supposed that as a nervous bride she should find his restraint reassuring—a sign of his consideration, but instead it made her uneasy. Was it reassurance—or simple indifference?

He knew he could make her want him when the time came, she thought, as she walked along the landing to the stairs in Mrs Parsons' bustling wake. Perhaps he'd decided that romancing his wife, making her feel special, was an unnecessary refinement to their relationship.

If so, it was a bleak prospect.

He was standing, obviously impatient, at the foot of the stairs, and Julia paused halfway down the broad flight, watching as he shot a glance at his watch, clearly not for the first time. Look at me, she heard herself begging silently. Smile at me. Hold out your arms, and I'll run to you.

When he did look up, she smiled down at him, tentatively, shyly, willing the dark face to soften, the hooded eyes to gleam with desire for her.

But he said abruptly, 'Say goodbye to your parents quickly, Julia. We are already running late.' And turned away, leaving her feeling, foolishly, as if she'd been slapped.

Julia leaned on the rail, watching the lights of Piraeus fade as *Clio* slid smoothly into the Saronic Gulf. Athens had been drily, enervatingly hot, and she had been grateful for the air-conditioning in the limousine which had taken them through the city and down, eventually, to the great bustling harbour.

She would have liked to linger, to extend her first look at the reality of Greece, but Alex had swept her inexorably on to the launch which was waiting to take them out to *Clio*.

Clio herself was a revelation. The stateroom to which Julia had been shown by an attentive white-coated steward was only marginally smaller than her bedroom at Ambermere, and completely dominated by a king-sized double bed. Julia had spent a couple of hilarious holidays sailing on the Solent with some boat-crazy friends, but the accommodation she'd enjoyed then was light years from this, she thought, blinking at the bathroom with its exquisite porcelain furniture and gold fittings.

But then being on board *Clio* was not like sailing at all. Julia was hardly aware of the yacht's motion, although the swarthy Captain Restaris, who had greeted them when they came on board, had warned that there might be a slight evening swell when they reached the open sea.

Julia lifted her face gratefully to the breeze. She still had no idea where they were going, she thought. Alex had been no more communicative on the plane than formerly. In fact, he'd immersed himself in papers produced from the briefcase which had accompanied him on to the plane. He'd apologised briefly for the necessity, it was true, but Julia had received the daunting impression that even if she'd protested, it would have made no difference. Not even the fact that it was his wedding day could deter Alex from overseeing the smooth running of the Constantis empire, she thought with a faint sigh.

But there was no doubt that he had her comfort in mind. She had been surprised to find waiting in her stateroom a slender, olive-skinned girl in a neat uniform who told her that she was Androula, come to wait on the *Kyria*. Julia had never had the services of a personal maid before, but it was pleasant to have her unpacking done for her, her bath run, and her clothes for dinner laid out ready.

And Androula's presence also had the effect of keeping Alex at bay, Julia realised rather ruefully. All the time she was dressing, and doing her hair and make-up, she had been on edge, expecting the door to open and admit him. But, once again, he had left her privacy undisturbed.

Nor were there any of his clothes or toiletries in her cabin, indicating that he had his own quarters elsewhere, although the satin sheets and twin lace-trimmed pillows reposing invitingly on the big bed seemed to demonstrate that he intended to sleep with her; but Julia was beginning to realise that with Alex it was unwise to take anything for granted.

In the meantime, there was dinner to get through. The steward Basilis had served her a cocktail in the big saloon, but she had felt conspicuous and out of place, being there alone, with no sign of Alex, and had made an excuse to take her drink up on deck.

Where she had remained ever since, she thought, with a slight grimace. *The Neglected Wife*—Act Two.

Surely Alex didn't intend to simply ignore her until—until bedtime? He couldn't be so unthinking—so cruel. Or could he? Had she already made too many assumptions about what being married to him would be like?

She heard a soft footstep behind her and tensed, but it was only Basilis come to tell her that dinner was served.

When she reached the saloon, Alex was waiting there, and she knew an absurd feeling of relief.

She said rather shyly, 'I've been up on deck. It's a beautiful evening.' She paused. 'Didn't Basilis tell you where I was?'

'Yes, but I had some work to finish.'

'And is it—finished, I mean?' Julia took her seat opposite him at the table and spread her napkin on her lap.

'Almost, I think. Why do you ask?' Alex filled her glass with wine.

Julia swallowed. 'Well, you seem to have been so occupied—I've seen so little of you . . .' Her voice trailed away into an embarrassed silence.

There was a silence, then he said drily, 'You flatter me, *agapi mou*. I had no idea you were so eager to be alone with me—to be the object of my—undivided attention.' He paused, the dark eyes running over her face and down to her shoulders and silk-veiled breasts in a caress as explicit as if he had reached out and touched her with his hand. 'But it will happen soon enough, I promise you.'

Julia bit her lip, feeling colour storm into her face. What was happening to her? That must have sounded as if she was begging for him to make love to her. And really, all she had wanted was some acknowledgement that she existed—that she mattered to him, even marginally.

Well, now she knew her exact standing in the scheme of things. When he had finished his paperwork, he would take her to bed. But while her mind, and her pride, recoiled in outrage from such cavalier treatment, she knew, to her shame, that her body was already responding with greedy anticipation to the prospect of his lovemaking.

Alex didn't have to humble her pride, she thought in self-derision. Where he was concerned, she had none.

The meal that Basilis served was delicious, but Julia tasted little of it, although she made an effort to eat.

Alex talked lightly on various topics, none of them personal, and Julia tried to follow his lead. There were a million questions she wanted to ask, but with Basilis always solicitously hovering, it was impossible. So perhaps it was better to chat about the Greek National Theatre, and the problems which the tourist boom had brought in its wake.

Besides, what could she say? 'Why did you marry me?' She bit her lip. That might be dangerous ground to cover—might bring an answer she did not want to hear.

But what would be the right answer—the answer she wanted him to give? That seemed equally dangerous to comtemplate.

When Basilis had served them small cups of thick, sweet coffee, he finally vanished.

Julia's mouth felt dry. She said haltingly, 'Your boat is fantastic. Like a floating palace.'

'It was built for my father. Since I came into my inheritance, I've used it a great deal. It has been my only real home.' He shrugged. 'There have been apartments—hotel suites, but they mean nothing.'

'And now you have Ambermere.'

'Yes, I have it.' He pushed his chair back and came round the table to her, pulling her out of her seat. 'And also, my beautiful one, I have you.'

For a long moment he looked at her, letting her see without evasion the open hunger in his eyes. Then he touched his fingers to his lips and put them gently, fleetingly on her mouth, before letting them slide down over her chin to the long line of her throat, and further down to the valley between her breasts, already aching for his touch, and still down over the clinging silk of her dress to the warm, moist joining of her thighs.

Julia gasped, her head falling back under the shock of his touch, as she realised the extent of her own need for him—and the power it gave him over her.

She said his name in a little cracked, imploring voice, her dazed eyes fixed on the firm line of his mouth. She wanted his lips on hers, longed for them, thirsted for them.

She heard him give a soft triumphant little laugh. 'Soon,' he said. 'Soon, *matia mou*, we will be together, alone, just as you want.' His hands moved to her hips, pulled her against him, so that for one agonising, dazzling moment their bodies ground together. Then he released her. 'Go now,' he told her quietly. 'Go to the cabin, and wait for me. I will come to you there.' As she turned half blindly towards the door, he added, 'And don't undress, Julia *mou*. I want that privilege for myself.'

The cabin had been prepared, she saw. The curtains had been drawn, and a lamp lit beside the bed, casting a softly intimate light. The covers had been turned down, and her white lace nightgown arranged across the bed in readiness. A basket of peaches had been placed on the bedside table, next to a bottle of champagne on ice. And there was fruit juice too in a tall frosted jug.

She was trembling and her mouth felt dry as she looked around her. The perfect setting, she thought, for a night of love. All that was lacking was her lover. 'Soon', he had promised, but every minute seemed an eternity.

She poured herself some of the fruit juice, and wandered round the cabin as she drank it, restless, unable to settle, her eyes fixed almost painfully on the door, as she waited for it to open.

What in the world could be keeping him away now? she asked herself, half in amusement, half in despair. He wanted her, so why wasn't he here with her now?

She poured some more juice and drank it, although she wasn't sure she cared for it overmuch. She didn't recognise the flavour, and there was an odd kind of aftertaste which lingered on her tongue. There was a quilted armchair beside one of the portholes, and she sat down in it, leaning back against the cushions, as the minutes ticked by.

She let her mind run back over the events of the day, remembering with a pang her mother's rigid face, and Tricia Bosworth's drawling malice. But she mustn't think of things like that now. She would prove to her parents and the world that she could make a success of her strange marriage.

She realised her eyelids were beginning to droop, and sat up with a jerk. If Alex didn't hurry, she would be asleep. She glanced at her watch and saw that she'd been waiting over half an hour.

He had told her not to undress, but she had to fight this drowsiness somehow. She got up from the chair, and swayed a little, putting a hand to her head. The stress of the wedding, the subsequent plane trip must have drained her more than she'd thought. Her head felt muzzy, and her eyelids seemed to have lead weights attached. She made her way, stumbling a little, to the bed, and sat down. The mattress felt as soft as a cloud, welcoming the weight of her body, and, sighing a little, she succumbed to the pleasure of complete relaxation.

She wanted to stay awake for Alex, but she was so sleepy—so desperately, inexplicably sleepy. She had to close her eyes—she just had to, and when Alex came, he would kiss her until she woke.

She was smiling as she drifted away into unconsciousness.

CHAPTER FIVE

SHE AWOKE to a fierce dazzling light. She opened her eyes slowly and wincingly, aware that her head was throbbing, and lay still for a moment, assimilating her surroundings with a sense of growing bewilderment.

She was no longer in her cabin on board the *Clio*. The bright light was sunshine, pouring in through an unglazed window, and reflected off the whitewashed walls of a small room.

She was lying on a hard, narrow bed, covered by a thin threadbare blanket, and as she moved, the springs protested clamorously.

Slowly and gingerly, Julia sat up. Under the blanket, she discovered with a sense of shock, she was naked. She looked round the room. Apart from the bed, there was little furniture, just a rickety chair, and a small chest with a domed lid. Nothing that she recognised, or which belonged to her. No personal possessions, and certainly no clothes.

Julia put her hands to her head, trying to remember, to make sense of this new situation. She had been waiting for Alex, she recalled, and she had dozed off. But that had been well before midnight, she thought, and judging by the position of the sun, it was now noon. Had she really slept all this time? And how in the world was she here, in little more than a hovel, when the previous night she had been wrapped in luxury on board the *Clio?*

Suddenly Julia began to be very frightened. She remembered an article she had once read about modern-day piracy. Had the *Clio* been boarded in the night, and had she been kidnapped—taken prisoner while she slept? If so, what had happened to Captain Restaris and the rest of the crew? And most important of all—where was Alex?

In one corner of the room was an open trapdoor, with a wooden staircase little better than a ladder leading down.

Julia sat up with determination, winding the blanket round her body like a sarong, before swinging her bare feet down on to the uneven concrete floor. She stood up, then sat down again abruptly, assailed by an oddly familiar dizziness.

And as she waited for her head to clear, she heard the sound of someone climbing the wooden stairs.

She looked wildly round for something with which to defend herself, but there was nothing but the chair, and she couldn't reach it in time. She shrank back towards the wall, the bedsprings providing an inharmonious accompaniment, as a man's dark head appeared through the trapdoor.

As she recognised him, Julia's lips parted in a soundless gasp.

'Alex!' Her voice cracked in relief. 'Oh, thank God! I've been terrified. What's happened? What are we doing here?'

'You have been asleep,' he said. 'And I have been waiting for you to wake up.' He took the chair and swung it round, sitting astride its seat, his arms resting on its back.

She looked at him remorsefully. It seemed she had denied them both their wedding night. 'Oh, Alex, I'm sorry.'

'Don't be,' he said. 'I intended that you should sleep.'

'You—intended?' Julia propped herself up on the single pillow and stared at him. Once again she remembered that awful debilitating drowsiness. She said slowly, 'The fruit juice—there was—something—in it?' Alex nodded, and she burst out, 'But why?'

He said laconically, 'Because I felt my plans for our honeymoon might not meet with your approval, and I wished to avoid an unnecessary scene.'

'I don't understand any of this.' Julia pushed her hair back from her face. 'Where's the *Clio*? And what's this awful place?'

'The *Clio* has gone,' he said. 'And this "awful place" '—he pronounced the words with open distaste—'happens to be the house where I was born.'

Julia bit her lip. 'I—I'm sorry,' she said awkwardly. 'I didn't realise. It was just such a shock to wake up and find myself—here.'

He nodded, the dark eyes watching her almost dispassionately. 'I meant it to be so.'

'You meant . . .?' Julia drew a deep breath. 'Alex, what's this all about? Why are we here, like this?'

'It is quite simple. You married a peasant, *kyria*. Now you are going to find out what life is like as a peasant's woman. It should prove—instructive, wouldn't you say?'

There was a silence. Julia put a hand to her head.

'Is this some kind of joke?'

'No.'

'You expect me to spend my honeymoon here—in this house?'

'I expect more than that.' He began to tick off on his fingers. 'You will clean for me, and you will cook, and wash my clothes, and tend the garden. You will feed the chickens, and also milk the goat.'

'I'll do nothing of the sort!' Julia sat up energetically, grabbing at her blanket as it began to slip. 'Have you gone mad? I'm your wife, not some kind of domestic slave, and . . .'

'No,' he said, 'you are not my wife. Not yet. You are the woman with whom I went through a ceremony of marriage. But you belong neither in my bed nor in my heart.'

Her throat felt suddenly constricted. 'What do you mean?'

'I was so easy to dazzle, *ne*? Or so you thought. The vulgar Greek peasant—the usurper of the family fortune. All names that you called me—showing your contempt for me. But when you found I wanted your house, that was different. You decided to sacrifice yourself—the well-born English rose and the rough Greek.' He smiled without humour. 'There is a story, is there not, of Beauty and the Beast? Is that how you saw me, Julia *mou*? As a beast you could tame? You despised me, but you thought you could manipulate me and my money to provide the life you wanted.'

'No!' Julia shook her head, her eyes widening with shock. 'No, that's not true . . .'

'You married me for a house,' he interrupted inexorably. 'Well, *matia mou*, I make you a gift of this one. It is not as—stately—as Ambermere, but it will serve, until you learn your place.' His mouth curled as he looked at her. 'And as I do not want you as a wife, then a "domestic slave", to use your own quaint phrase, you must be.'

'Alex, you don't—you can't mean this! It's our honeymoon. I know I shouldn't have said those things to you, and I'm sorry, but it was a long time ago, and in the heat of the moment. I was upset about losing Ambermere—surely you see that? But everything's changed now—we're married.' She swallowed. 'And—I—I need you.'

'Do you?' He laughed softly, but there was an underlying note which chilled her. 'Then, as you once said to me, *agapi mou*—eat your heart out.' He swung himself lithely up from the chair and pointed to the domed chest. 'You will find some clothes in there. Dress yourself, and come down, and I will explain your duties.'

'Alex!' As he began to turn away, Julia knelt up on the bed, deliberately letting the blanket slip down below her breasts. 'Alex, you can't mean this.' She swallowed. 'Don't you want me—just a little?'

The dark eyes flicked over her without emotion. 'Of course,' he said. 'You are very lovely, as I discovered last night when I took the clothes from your body with my own hands. But there is no respect between us, Julia, and without respect there can be no marriage.' He threw his head back, the dark eyes glittering coldly at her. 'You are spoiled and proud, and there is no beauty in that. If you are ashamed of me—of what I was—then that is your problem. While you are here, you will learn to solve it.'

'And if I don't?' She still couldn't believe this was
really happening.

'Then the marriage will be annulled. I will not take a
women who despises me, or who thinks she can use
me for her own selfish purposes. So cover yourself or
not as you wish. It makes no difference.'

He stepped down on to the top rung of the stair, and
vanished.

Julia collapsed back on the bed, huddling the blanket
around her. In spite of the heat, she felt deathly cold,
and a slow, scalding tear ran down the curve of her
cheek.

This couldn't be real. It couldn't! It was another of
those awful dreams, and presently she would wake on
board the *Clio* wtih Alex's arms around her.

But no nightmare, however potent, could have
invented this awful squeaky bed with its hard, lumpy
mattress, or the blanket scratching at her naked skin.
There was a terrible reality about all these things—and
about the way Alex had looked at her—the things he'd
said.

Wincing, she remembered some of the words she had
used to him, and about him. If she was honest, he had
every right to be angry, and her parents' attitude to him
over the past weeks had simply compounded the
injury.

But that didn't mean she was going to tamely submit
to being treated like this.

I'll talk to him, Julia thought. Reason with him. Make
him see that he's wrong about me. Make him know
that I want him, that I'm proud to be his wife.

She got off the bed and trod cautiously over to the
chest, wondering what clothes he had brought for her

to wear. Unless he had allowed Androula to do the packing, he had probably chosen all the wrong things. She hoped he had included some of those pastel cotton jeans and tops.

When she lifted the lid, she stayed very still for a moment, staring down at the chest's contents. These weren't her things—any of them. There were a couple of dresses, one dark red, the other a muddy shade of green, both clean but desperately shabby. There was a headscarf, and a pair of cheap plastic sandals. And that was it.

Julia turned the pathetic pile of garments over, her hands shaking. Nothing from her trousseau—none of the pretty leisure clothes and romantic evening silks and chiffons. Not even a pair of her own shoes—or a bra and brief set.

'Aren't you ready yet?' This time she hadn't heard his approach up the ladder, and she spun round with a little cry.

'I'm not ready, nor am I likely to be.' She pointed into the chest. 'These are not my clothes.'

'Consider them a loan.'

'I wouldn't consider them for a jumble sale,' Julia said coldly. 'I'd like my own things, please.'

'Still so imperious,' Alex said calmly. 'But you will learn.'

'I doubt that. Where are my clothes?'

'On board the *Clio.*' He paused. 'And many miles from here.'

Julia assimilated this. 'You really mean she's sailed without us? I don't believe you.'

'Go and look for yourself.'

She gave him a mutinous look. 'Without clothes?

How can I?'

'There are clothes there for you. 'Not, admittedly, what you have been accustomed to, Julia *mou*, or what you hoped I would provide for my wife, but adequate.'

'Apart from one major omission. You forgot to include any underwear.'

He shrugged. 'The weather is warm, and the dresses will cover you well enough.'

Julia stared at him. 'You actually think that I'm going to walk about in front of people wearing nothing but a dress and a pair of sandals? Well, I'm damned if I . . .'

'Calm yourself.' He did not raise his voice, but she heard the warning note plainly enough. 'There is no one to see you but myself.'

'No one . . .' Julia stopped, and drew a breath. 'Why not? What is this place?'

'It is an island called Argoli,' he said. 'No one lives here any more. We are totally, completely alone, *agapi mou.*' He paused, then added mockingly,' Just as you wished us to be.'

'Did I say that?' Julia flung back at him. 'I must have been out of my mind! And I still don't believe any of this.'

Stumbling a little over the trailing blanket, she went over to the window and leaned out. 'There's a street,' she said. 'And houses. And I can see a church . . .'

'All empty. The villagers moved to the mainland five years ago. One day I hope to provide some kind of industry to tempt them back, but until that time, their absence makes this place ideal for my purpose.'

Julia craned her neck in the opposite direction, catching a glimpse of azure sea. Slowly she drew herself back into the room. She didn't have to go and check on the *Clio*; she knew that it would not be there. She was here, it seemed, for the duration, with a man intent on his own unique revenge for the slights he had suffered at her hands.

Alex said, 'Put this on,' and tossed the red dress at her feet. He paused. 'Unless you want me to dress you.'

Julia faced him, lifting her chin challengingly. 'Yes,' she said, 'I do.'

Alex shrugged, then bent and retrieved the dress from the floor. As impersonally as if he was changing a dummy in a department store window, he stripped the blanket from her and threw it on to the bed, before tugging the dress, not altogether gently, over her head, turning her so that he could pull the zip up. Even when fastened, the dress hung on her like a tent. Glancing down at herself, Juila didn't know whether to laugh or cry.

'Do you wish me also to put on your shoes, or can you manage those yourself?' Alex jibed.

He couldn't have demonstrated his indifference to her, naked or clothed, more plainly, Julia thought wearily. She bent her head. 'I can manage.'

'Good,' he said. 'Then come downstairs. You have a meal to prepare.'

'I can't cook,' she protested. It wasn't strictly true. She could manage omelettes, beans on toast and other snacks, but living at home with Madge Parsons reigning as queen of the Ambermere kitchen, there had been no incentive to improve her culinary skills.

'Then you will learn. Or you will be very hungry.'

Unwillingly Julia put on the sandals and followed him

through the trapdoor. 'And if I fall off these stairs and break my neck, I suppose there's no hospital here either?'

'If you break you neck, Julia *mou*, I doubt whether a hospital can help you. I advise you to take care.'

And he didn't just mean on the stairs either, Julia realised wretchedly.

She stood and looked round the downstairs room with a sinking heart. It was just as unsophisticated as the bedroom, if not more so.

There was an ancient blackened stove, still filled with ashes which looked as if they'd been there since Homer was a lad. There was a square table in the middle of the room, covered with chipped Formica, and flanked by two folding plastic chairs. There was a strictly functional camp bed in the corner where Alex, presumably, had spent the night. And there was a sink bowl resting starkly in a sturdy wooden frame, its downpipe leading out through the wall below the window being its sole concession to modernity.

Julia swallowed. 'There aren't any taps,' she heard herself say.

'There is no running water,' came the equable reply.

'Then how on earth . . .?'

'There is, however, a bucket,' Alex went on briskly, as if she hadn't spoken at all. 'In which *yineka mou*, you may fetch water from the well in the street. For drinking purposes, there is also a spring at the back of the house.'

'And that's it?' Julia looked at him in frank disbelief.

'As you say,' he agreed laconically.

'Oh, this is impossible—a joke!' Julia sat down on one of the plastic chairs.

'I hope you will still be laughing at the end of the day.' He paused. 'I sugggest you begin by lighting the stove.'

'That thing? Does it still work?'

'I hope so. The Japanese enjoy raw fish in their diet. You, I think, would not.'

'And nor would you,' Julia returned defiantly. 'So, if the stove won't light, we'll have to declare a truce, and return to civilisation.'

'Oh, no, *matia mou.*' As he shook his head, Alex's smile did not reach his eyes. 'Because the stove will light perfectly well, with sufficient kindling. So do not try to play games, or you will be sorry.'

Their glances met and clashed, and it was Julia, to her shame, who looked away first.

He was completely mad, she told herself, but the madness would pass. He might have been brought up in this discomfort and squalor, but that didn't mean he had to like it. Everything about Alex Constantis spoke of him enjoying the good things in life, so this sojourn on Argoli had to be as much a penance for him, as for her.

Making me miserable is one thing, she thought. Punishing himself at the same time is another. I give this—horror—two days at the outside. And in the meantime I'll have to humour him.

She got to her feet and walked through the open door into the sunshine beyond, pausing for a moment, her hand shading her eyes, to get her bearings.

Away to her left, the village street sloped downwards between the sparse and empty houses,

and behind them neglected olive groves shimmered
in the heat, their leaves like silken, silver canopies.
Beyond that, there seemed to be little but bare rock,
stretching upwards towards the stark, unsullied blue
of the sky.

Utter desolation, Julia thought with a shiver, just
like the emotional morass inside her. She found her
hands had clenched into shaking fists, relaxed with
an effort, and walked round to the rear of the house.

There had once been a fair-sized garden scratched
here in the red and dusty earth, but it was now
overgrown with weeds, although the chickens Alex
had mentioned were pecking fervently in the
undergrowth. In the distance, the promised goat
grazed in the shade of a gnarled olive tree.

Julia bit her lip, as she turned away and surveyed
her immediate surroundings. There was nothing to
lift the heart here either. Some rusting oil drums, a
mangle with wooden rollers which looked as if it
belonged in an industrial museum, and a few new-
looking bags of sand and cement. There was also a
small hut. Julia glanced inside, and recoiled. These
were clearly the usual offices, so beloved of English
estate agents, although there was little usual about a
hole in the ground with a crumbling concrete
surround, she thought, shuddering.

She took another long look around her, then
turned back to the house, stopping with a little cry as
she realised Alex had followed her, and was standing
a few yards away, hands on hips, surveying her
enigmatically.

'So, how do you like your new estate, Julia *mou*?'
The underlying sneer was quite palpable. Probably

he expected her to throw herself on her knees at his feet, babbling for mercy.

She lifted her chin. 'It's—basic,' she acknowledged coolly. 'I'm still looking for the woodpile.'

'Then you will look for a long time. On Argoli, if you want wood, you collect twigs and fallen branches where you find them.' He waved a hand towards the sheltering olive trees. 'Good hunting.'

'Now just a minute!' Julia exploded. 'You actually expect me to go scavenging for wood in this heat . . .?'

The dark brows snapped together menacingly. 'I have already told you what I expect. Do not make me repeat myself.'

'Oh, forgive me,' she bit back. 'And while I'm—hewing wood, and drawing water in the old tradition, what will you be doing, exactly? After all, there's no taverna here for you to sit in and—gossip, and gamble with the other men. Isn't that how the division of labour goes round here?'

Alex shrugged. 'If that is what you choose to think,' he returned coolly. 'But don't worry *matia mou*, I shall be well occupied. I have our food to provide, for one thing. I hope you like fish,' he added with a trace of mockery.

'I suppose I have no choice,' Julia said stonily.

'Now you begin to understand at last.'

Sudden inspiration came to her. 'But if we're really the only people here, where did the chickens come from—and that bloody goat? They don't look as if they've been starving here since everyone left.'

'The goat's name is Penelope,' he told her softly. 'And I suggest you make a friend of her, Julia, if you wish to have milk while you are here. But you are right, of course. They are as new to Argoli as yourself. I had them imported specially.'

'You must have been planning this for a long time.' Julia's voice was husky.

'Oh, yes.' Alex gave a meditative nod. 'Since the moment I decided to marry you, Julia *mou*, instead of taking you as my mistress.'

The sheer arrogance of him had her reeling. She said thickly, 'You think—you actually think I would have done such a thing?' She threw back her head, and laughed. 'You should have stuck to your original scheme, *kyrie*. I could simply have slapped your face and walked out of your life, sparing myself—this ridiculous farce.'

His mouth curled. 'How you cling to your illusions, *agapi mou!* From the time we met, I could have taken you at any time, and you know it, if you have a breath of honesty anywhere in that delectable body. All during our engagement you were wondering why I didn't kiss you—touch you as you wanted me to. Every smile, every look, every word told me you couldn't wait to sleep in my bed. And I was tempted, believe me,' he added with faint self-derision. 'But other considerations prevailed.'

'Your even more burning desire to humiliate me.' Her voice shook.

'When you agreed to be my wife, you chose to share my life,' he said with a shrug. 'At the moment my life is here, and you will learn what it means to live it.' He gave her a level look. 'Learn quickly, Julia *mou*, and the lesson will soon be over.' He paused. 'Now go and find your wood—but wear your headscarf,' he added warningly. 'You are not used to the fierceness of the sun here.'

She said between her teeth, 'Heatstroke would be a welcome alternative to your plans for me, believe me.'

'Another illusion,' he said lightly, but his eyes never left hers. 'Accept the first part of your schooling, Julia. Learn to obey me.' He added starkly, 'If you fight me, you will lose, and you will find the consequences truly humiliating, I promise.'

'Meaning that you'll beat me, I suppose!' Julia said with contempt. 'How truly macho! Unfortunately for you, there are laws now against behaviour like that, even towards your wife.'

'But unfortunately for you, *agapi mou*, no laws operate here but my own,' he said almost silkily. 'And there are other ways of punishing a recalcitrant woman than taking a stick to her.' He paused, his brows lifting. 'You wish, perhaps, to discover some of them?'

Tension seemed to envelop them. Julia could feel it crouching in the air like a distant storm. She wanted to call his bluff, but for a piercing, terrifying inner conviction that he wasn't bluffing at all.

She bit back the hot, defiant words crowding to her lips. She had a war to win. She couldn't afford to lose a first, and possibly decisive battle.

'No.' She swallowed. 'I—I'll do as you say.'

'Very wise.' Alex glanced at his watch. 'I will be back in just over an hour. I shall expect to find at least coffee keeping hot on the stove when I return. You will find any supplies you need in the store cupboard beside the sink.' He gave her a faint smile. 'And do not waste time trying to think of ways to escape, *agapi mou*. Except for a few lizards, we are alone here.' His smile widened. 'An idyll, *ne*—if not the kind you once expected to share with me.'

He walked away, and disappeared round the side of the house. By the time Julia could force her shaking legs to follow, there was no sign of him.

She stood alone in the deserted street and listened to the silence. In spite of herself, she wanted crazily, desperately to call his name, bring him back to her side if only for a moment.

'Oh, God,' she said aloud, her voice bitter. 'You fool! You stupid, pathetic, weak-kneed—idiot!'

She couldn't still want him—not a man who could treat her with the kind of callous contempt Alex had displayed. A man who didn't care for her—who didn't even desire her enough to mitigate his need to revenge himself on her. And even if he did—relent eventually—what hope, what future could there be in such a relationship?

Julia lifted her face to the burning, alien sky and felt the first heavy, scalding tears emptying down her face.

CHAPTER SIX

THE HOUR that followed seemed to Julia to encompass several lifetimes.

Cleaning out the stove had been a major operation, the flying dust and ash stinging her eyes and nose, and clinging to her hair and perspiring skin.

And she couldn't delude herself that the armfuls of wood that she'd collected and carried awkwardly back to the house were going to last even the rest of the day. The stove seemed to have a voracious appetite, or maybe she just hadn't discovered the knack of regulating it yet.

Oh, let it be that! she thought longingly.

Nor could she have dreamed how back-breaking the simple task of hauling up a bucket of water on a rope could be. She seemed to have spilled half the precious load over her feet, as she struggled back up the street, her arm muscles protesting at the unexpected weight they were supporting.

But she had managed to heat a pan of water almost to boiling point on the stove, and had found a big jar of instant coffee in the cupboard Alex had indicated, as well as a couple of thick enamel mugs.

He'd spoken as if they would live only on fish, but the cupboard had also contained a plentiful supply of tinned food. Rather too plentiful, Julia decided with a private grimace. It was clear she wasn't going to be let off lightly with just a token segregation here.

In a lean-to building on the other side of the house she had found gardening implements, and tools, as well as a sack of potatoes, and a fair supply of charcoal, to be used, she supposed, for grilling food under the cast-iron grid at one side of the stove.

Now Julia sat limply at the table, staring into space. She had somehow to find a way of getting out of this lunatic situation. She couldn't endure another day like this.

But it was useless to hope that Alex might relent. He was clearly intent on grinding her into the dust, she thought miserably, just as Grandma Pascoe had predicted.

Uncouth barbarian, she thought. His cousin Paul doesn't know the half of it. Yet, shameful though it was, she couldn't deny the physical attraction that still existed between them. That had been there from the first, outraging every cherished belief in her own fastidiousness—her ability to remain aloof, to flirt lightly at a distance. Alex had swept them away the first time he had touched her, she thought bitterly, remembering his taunt about her 'illusions'.

She was certainly deluding herself if she thought she could disguise her unguarded, almost greedy response to his lovemaking. When he'd claimed she had been his for the taking, he'd spoken no more than the truth, reluctant though she might be to admit it.

The only comfort she could cling to, she thought wearily, was that Alex had made it clear he was no longer interested in her body, But the realisation that his contempt for her outweighed any desire he'd ever felt for her was somehow the greatest humiliation of all.

She should be glad he didn't want her, she told herself fiercely. This way, it was easier to hate him for what he was doing to her.

She swallowed. While he kept her at arms' length, she was safe. The problem would be if and when Alex decided to make their marriage a real one. Could she yield her body to him without surrendering her emotions as well? Or wouldn't it be better to cut her losses from the start—ask him for the annulment he had already mentioned as a possibility?

'Why are you sitting there? Why haven't you cleaned up the house yet?' Alex's voice cut harshly across her reverie, and she jumped.

'I lit the stove.' It was an effort to reply normally. 'And the coffee's ready.'

'So I should hope,' he said grimly. 'I see you have managed to cover most of the room with ash as well as yourself. Before you sit and rest, you clear up the mess you have made.' He went outside for a moment, returning with a sweeping brush which he tossed to her. 'Here.'

Helplessly Julia watched him put a heaped spoonful of coffee in a mug, and add boiling water, before taking the drink and one of the chairs out under the sagging porch roof which fronted the house.

She discovered she wanted to burst into tears, and gritted her teeth instead.

'Beast!' she muttered through them. 'Brute!' And, as she began awkwardly and inefficiently to sweep the dirty floor, 'Bully!'

It seemed to take for ever, and she couldn't believe

it looked much better when she'd finished, she thought, sighing.

When she had finished, her throat felt as if it was coated in grit. Her thirst for coffee had disppeared completely. All she wanted now was some cool water, she thought, dipping the other mug into the bucket.

She raised it to her lips, but before she could drink it was snatched away.

Alex said, his voice molten with anger, 'You do not drink water from the well unless it has been boiled, you fool of a girl! Did I not tell you? Water for drinking comes only from the spring.'

'I forgot,' Julia said defiantly. 'And surely it wouldn't matter just once?'

'It might matter very much,' he said impatiently. 'Now come with me.'

His hand gripped her arm as he walked her up through the grove of olive trees, past the tethered goat with her mild curious face to the place where water gushed out of the bare rock, cold and crystal clear.

'I didn't bring the mug!' Julia wailed.

'Use your hands—like this,' Alex demonstrated, cupping his palms beneath the small torrent. He would have allowed the water to run away again, but Julia gripped his wrists.

She said huskily, 'Please . . .' and bent her head to drink from his hands.

For a brief second he was motionless, then he muttered something harsh and violent in his own language, freeing himself without gentleness, letting the water spill. His fingers twisted into her hair, pulling her up to face him. There was anger in his eyes and a heated flush along his cheekbones as he said, 'Make your own cup, girl.'

He turned and strode away from her, back towards the house. Julia remained where she was, staring after him. Just for a moment, she thought slowly, she had seen him affected by the intimacy of her action. She had seen him vulnerable. It was hardly a breakthrough, but it proved she still had a weapon she could use against him.

She cupped her hands and drank, cupped and drank, until the burning in her throat had subsided, then she let the icy water trickle over her wrists and hands, before splashing handfuls on to her grateful face. Murder on the complexion, she thought, but who cares?

When she got back to the house there were two fish lying on the table, with a knife beside them, Alex was lighting some charcoal beneath the grill.

'Supper?' Julia averted her gaze from the two pairs of dead eyes which seemed to be staring at her. 'Poor things!'

'You would prefer to go hungry?' His voice was cool.

'No, but there's plenty of tinned stuff.'

'That is for emergencies—when the fish do not bite,' he told her with a touch of grimness. 'Now, clean and prepare them. And be careful—the knife is sharp.'

It looked positively lethal, Julia thought, swallowing. 'You said—clean them?'

He glanced round at her. 'Is there some problem?'

She tried to speak lightly. 'A small one. I've never

—actually dealt with a fish—before its arrival in the dining-room, that is.'

Alex got to his feet, dusting his hands on the faded jeans which, she had already noticed, fitted him like a second skin.

'Your domestic gifts are pitifully few, *yineka mou*,' he remarked with faint grimness. 'I suppose I should be grateful you can boil water.' He came to the table, and picked up the knife. 'Now watch.'

Julia obeyed, her face twisted into a grimace as she observed the swift expert movement of the knife, then saw with horror that he was presenting its handle to her.

'Now it is your turn,' he told her.

'Mine?' She bit her lip. 'I don't think I can.'

'And I say you must.' His voice was implacable. 'Do you wish to spend the rest of your life as a useless ornament, *pedhi mou?*'

'This has probably been the least ornamental day I've ever spent,' Julia said wearily, taking the knife from him.

Five minutes later she looked down at the mangled result of her efforts.

'That will be yours,' was Alex's only comment.

She supposed she'd asked for that. Under his tight-lipped guidance, she put the fish carefully on the grille above the glowing charcoal, and sprinkled them with seasoning, herbs and olive oil.

While the fish were cooking, Alex showed her how to make a salad, Greek style, with chopped cucumbers and enormous tomatoes, black olives and slices of *feta* cheese, the whole thing dressed with more of the thick, tangy green olive oil, and a squeeze of juice from a lemon she was sent to pick from the tree in the next garden.

'That looks wonderful.' In spite of her struggle with the fish, the smell of them cooking was making her mouth water, reminding her how long it was since her last meal.

She couldn't help remembering the saloon on *Clio*, the immaculately laid table with its shining silver and spotless linen, and contrasting it with her present surroundings.

'Well, make the most of it,' warned Alex. 'The fresh food will not last for ever.'

Julia's eyes widened when he produced a bottle of golden wine, and opened it.

'Retsina,' he told her. 'Have you tasted it?'

She shook her head. 'I've had ouzo, of course.'

He poured some of the wine into a tumbler and handed it to her. 'Try it.'

Julia sipped, and choked. 'My God, what's that taste?'

'Resin from the casks it's stored in.' Alex looked amused. 'Is it too strong for you? It is an acquired taste.'

'I thought it was part of the punishment—that you were trying to poison me.' She put the glass down on the table.

'Why, no, *agapi mou*,' There was a grin in his voice. 'My vengeance will not be accomplished so quickly—or so finally.'

'Thank you,' said Julia with irony.

The appearance of her fish hadn't improved while it was cooking, but its freshness and flavour were superlative, and she finished every morsel.

For dessert, to her surprise, Alex produced some grapes, explaining that there was a vine grown wild elsewhere in the village. The grapes were large, slightly sharp, and utterly delicious, and Julia felt replete when she had finished her bunch.

She said, 'That was a marvellous meal.' She leaned back in her chair, yawning. In spite of her enforced sleep the previous night, she was genuinely tired again. All the unaccustomed exertion, she told herself wryly.

'Tomorrow it will be your responsibility.' During the meal, the atmosphere had relaxed slightly, but now Alex's voice was brusque again. 'And you cannot sleep yet, Julia *mou.*'

She looked across the table at him, smiling, lashes lowered demurely. So she hadn't been mistaken, she thought exultantly. He did want her, after all. 'No?' Her voice sounded suddenly husky.

'You have to wash up, and tidy the room.'

If he'd picked up the bucket and tipped the remaining cold water over her head, she couldn't have felt more—quenched.

She said, 'Of course. I'd better heat some more water.'

The sun was setting as she finished, but the air was still warm, without a breeze. Julia pushed her hair out of her eyes, and thought longingly of her turquoise-tiled bathroom at Ambermere.

When Alex came in for the coffee she'd made, she said, 'I wish there was a shower.'

'There is a bath,' he said. 'Shall I fetch it for you?'

She guessed what it would be like, and she was

right. It was galvanised, and practical in the extreme, permitting the bather to sit, knees to chin, or stand. But it was better than nothing.

There was a domed chest beside his bed, similar to the one upstairs, and Alex delved in this to produce a rough towel and a new bar of soap.

'Luxury,' she said, with irony.

He put the soap and towel down on the table, and turned to the door. He said harshly, 'Do not take too long.'

In a voice she barely recognised as her own, she said, 'Won't you stay—and wash my back?'

Alex swung round, and looked at her. 'Is that—truly what you want, *agapi mou?*'

'Yes,' she said unsteadily, knowing with a pang of self-disgust that it was no more than the truth. 'Oh, Alex, yes. . .'

He shrugged. 'Alas,' he said, 'it has been a day of disappointments for you, has it not?' He walked out of the door, leaving her alone.

The water was barely tepid, but Julia revelled in the feel of it on her skin, in spite of the ache of frustration deep inside her. She soaped and rinsed every inch of her body, feeling some of her weariness ease as she did so. She washed her hair too as best she could. When she had finished, she wrapped herself in the towel and dragged the bath with some difficulty to the door to empty it. Once again Alex seemed to have vanished off the face of the earth.

Not a very large earth, Julia thought, as she put the bath away. Only a few miles long, and even fewer wide. He couldn't be that far away.

She had twisted her hair up on to the top of her head,

and now she shook it free, sighing soundlessly. It was
all very well telling herself he'd gone for a long walk
because he was aching himself, but the fact was she had
been rejected again.

I'm going to have to stop leading with my chin, she
told herself ruefully.

In the meantime, the bath had relaxed her enough to
make her ready for what passed for a bed upstairs.
Carrying her dress and sandals, she climbed slowly up
the wooden steps.

A thin moon had risen and was framed in her
window. It was unlucky to see a new moon that way,
she thought hazily, but how much worse could
everything get anyway?

She put the dress down on the chest, with her
sandals beside it, then climbed on to the bed, pulling
the sheet over her, grimacing as the mattress groaned at
her.

She was almost asleep when she heard his footstep
on the stair. She sat up immediately, propping herself
on her elbow, staring across the shadowed room at
him, her mouth suddenly dry.

Alex said softly, 'So you are awake.' As she watched,
he peeled off the shirt he was wearing and let it drop to
the ground. It was the first time she had seen him even
partially stripped, and her widening eyes flicked
achingly, yearningly over the broad, muscular
shoulders and strong hair-roughened chest, The dark
hair grew in a vee down over his stomach, and
disappeared into the waistband of his jeans.

Stunned, Julia watched him unzip the jeans and push
them down over his hips. He dropped them on to
his shirt, and followed them with the dark

briefs that were his last remaining covering.

She had never seen a man naked before, except in pictures and sculpture, and Alex could have modelled for any of them, she realised. He was—beautiful, his body lean, magnificent and totally virile.

She stared at him without shame, filling her eyes with him, wanting him with sharp completeness.

He reached out a bare foot and touched the pile of clothes.

'Laundry,' he said quite gently. 'For the morning. Goodnight, my beautiful wife. Sleep well.'

He went down the stairs into the silence, leaving her alone in the moonlight.

Julia opened reluctant eyes the following morning to the sound of hammering. At first she thought it must be some special kind of migraine, brought on by wretchedness and lack of sleep, then she realised it was coming from outside the house.

She got slowly out of bed, looking with loathing at the dress she had worn the day before. There was no way she was putting it on again before it had been laundered.

The word made her wince as she saw the pile of clothes Alex had so cynically discarded the night before.

She averted her gaze and went over to the chest, extracting the other dress. It fitted no better than the first one had done, but she supposed she should be thankful that Alex allowed her the privilege of a change of clothing at all.

She put on her sandals and went carefully down

the wooden stairway and out into the open, following the sound of the hammering. Alex was there, fitting what seemed to be a new window-frame to the aperture at the front of the house.

Julia swallowed. *'Kalimera.'*

He flung her a caustic glance. 'Half the morning is over. I'll have coffee and eggs for breakfast. And today Penelope will need milking.'

It was like waking from a nightmare, Julia thought, as she collected some wood for the stove, then going to sleep again, and finding yourself back in the middle of the same bad dream.

It took some time to find where the hens were nesting, and a couple of them did not take kindly to having their eggs removed. Julia had two nasty pecks on the hand before she was able to beat a retreat back to the house.

Penelope was still grazing peacefully. She looked placid enough, but goats were an unknown quantity to Julia. She'd seen cows being milked, of course, at the Home Farm, but the milking shed there, with its scrupulous hygiene and very latest machinery, was light years away from conditions here.

She toyed with the idea of telling Alex that she'd milked Penelope, but spilled the milk on the way back to the house, but dismissed it wistfully. If the goat wasn't milked she would be in pain, and there was no justification for making the poor creature suffer, no matter how opposed Julia might be to any kind of involvement with her.

She beat the eggs, then chopped up some potato, green peppers, onions and tomato, making a kind of giant tortilla. When it was done, it was fluffy and golden, filling the kitchen with a warm, savoury smell. Julia brought it to the table, while Alex was rinsing his hands at the sink, and served it out on to two plates. The bread left from the day before was a little stale, but still edible, and she added a chunk to each plate.

Alex sat down and picked up his fork. Julia watched under her lashes, expecting an appreciative look or a brief word of praise for her efforts, but her husband ate every scrap in silence.

When he had finished, she said, 'Did you enjoy that?'

'I was too hungry to notice,' Alex told her curtly. 'Tomorrow you will get up when I do. Apart from your duties, you will have bread to make.'

'I'll have *what?*' Julia dropped the empty plates back on the table with a clatter, searching his face for some leavening gleam of humour, and finding none. She said huskily, 'How much more of this treatment do you think I'm prepared to take?'

'As much as I decide is necessary.' He got to his feet. He was shirtless, and the ancient cream shorts he was wearing clung to his lean hips. 'When you know your place, Julia *mou*, when you've learned to be properly submissive, then I may think again.'

She said very quietly, 'I hate you.'

'Do you, *agapi mou?*' His smile mocked her. 'And yet something tells me I would only have to kiss you—touch you as I did that day by the lake, and you would be drinking from my hand again.' His eyes held her in a challenge as old as the rocky hillside above them. 'Well, shall we put it to the test?'

There was a silence, then Julia shook her head, her

copper hair falling defeatedly across her face. Today, it seemed, she was the vulnerable one.

It irked her all the time she was clearing away the breakfast things, and laboriously heating the water to wash the clothes, to realise how disappointed she had been over his failure to praise her cooking. Yet he was quick enough to criticise when things went wrong, she thought rebelliously.

It took her an hour to wash the clothes. She had never realised before how completely she had taken for granted the automatic washing machine and tumble-dryer at Ambermere. Not that she'd used them very often, she reminded herself ruefully. Mrs Parsons emptied the linen baskets and did the laundry, and a woman from the village came in to do the ironing. And a lot of the sweaters and blouses that she and her mother wore required careful hand washing, she recalled, grimacing, as she laboriously tried to wring the excess water out of Alex's jeans.

She put the wet garments in a plastic bowl and carried them outside.

'Is there a washing line?' she asked.

'No.' He had almost finished the window, she noticed. 'Spread the clothes in the sun. They will soon dry.'

Now why didn't I think of that? Julia asked herself wryly. She went to the back of the house and spread the garments carefully over some convenient bushes, watched with disapproval by the hens, and with her usual curiosity by Penelope.

'I suppose I should milk you,' Julia told her conspiratorially. 'But I can't face it yet. What was it the Vicar used to say? Sufficient unto the day is the evil thereof.'

She wandered back to the house, and stood watching Alex as he deftly applied putty to the remaining cracks round the frame.

'Where did you learn to do that?' she asked.

'Here, and in other places.'

'Was that your work before . . .'

'Before I hijacked the Constantis millions?' he supplied drily. 'No, *pedhi mou*. I learned to do it because it needed to be done, and I was the man of the house.'

And Argoli wasn't a society where there were useful workmen at the other end of a phone, or even money to pay them, Julia thought, abashed.

She said, 'Why are you doing it?'

'Because the other frames have rotted. I removed them on a previous visit.'

'No, I didn't mean that. If no one lives here, and there's no chance of them returning for some time, isn't it rather a wasted effort?'

'I do not think so. After all, Julia *mou*, we live here.'

'Yes, but only temporarily.'

He turned, the dark brows lifting sardonically. 'What makes you think so?'

Julia stared at him. 'Well, it's obvious. You're the head of heaven knows how many companies, worldwide. Sooner or later you'll have to go back to the real world.'

'But for me *this* was once the real world,' he said softly. 'Suppose I have decided this is what I prefer? That I am tired of jets and anonymous capital cities that all look the same. Tired of the endless deals and the boardroom wrangles. That I want back the simple life I once knew.' His smile taunted her. 'Maybe even that I want my son to be born here as I was.' He saw the shock in her eyes, and his smile widened. 'That startles you, *ne?* You thought that in spite of everything I would still allow you to have your proud dream—to bear a child for Ambermere, perhaps even give it your name.' He shook his head. 'No, my lovely wife.'

Her lips parted to tell him the thought of Ambermere had not, incredibly, crossed her mind. That it was the prospect, however distant, of carrying his child inside her which had sent her suddenly and dizzily rocking back on her heels.

But that was something she could never admit to him.

She lifted her head, smiling coolly in response. 'So, what's your proud dream, Kyrios Alexandros? To keep me here, barefoot and pregnant?'

He said slowly, 'And if so, what will you do? Plead for mercy?'

Julia shook her head. 'It won't be necessary.' The dark eyes narrowed in challenge, but she carried bravely on. 'You're your father's son, and you can't just—turn your back on your responsibilities. Besides, you've tasted power now and you like it. Bringing me here, making me jump through all these hoops, is just an example. You've done it, because you can. You couldn't revert to being Alex Nobody again, even if you wanted to. And I don't believe you really want to.'

'How confidently you speak,' he said silkily. 'Yet how little you really know me. Must I remind you, *agapi mou*, that you are still a stranger to my heart, and to my bed?'

Julia shrugged. 'For the moment,' she said, keeping her tone almost nonchalant. 'But that won't last for ever—not if you want the son you've been talking about.'

'I want a child.' The last lingering trace of amusement had disappeared from his face. 'What I have yet to decide, Julia *mou*, is if I wish you to be his mother.'

Pain slashed at her as if he had lifted his hand and struck her down. She gave a small inarticulate cry and ran from him, her sandals slipping on the rough stones, down the street between the empty houses, towards the sea.

CHAPTER SEVEN

JULIA sat on the edge of the crumbling breakwater, her back against the remains of a concrete post, gazing unseeingly at the point where sea and sky merged in a haze of exquisite blue.

It didn't seem possible that she could hurt so much, and still go on living.

She could have borne anything rather than the knowledge that Alex did not consider her fit to have his baby. It was after all the ultimate degradation, especially when, barely minutes before, her body had reacted joyously and spontaneously, filling with trembling warmth, at the mere idea of conceiving his child and carrying it under her heart.

I should have known, she thought, her throat constricting in agony. I should have known.

She had asked herself how they could ever have a real relationship after the way their marriage had begun. Well, now she knew. Alex had no intention of keeping her as his wife.

She closed her eyes, damming back the tears that threatened to overwhelm her. What good would crying do?, She had to look ahead, try and make some kind of plan for when he tired of his cruel game he was playing with her, and let her go. And soon she would, but not now. All her tired brain could come up with now was images of Alex—the dismissal in his eyes, the sneer in his voice.

She pulled herself to her feet, brushing the dust
from her crumpled dress, and began to wander along
the breakwater, trying to imagine the tiny harbour as
it must have been in its heyday with dark-sailed
caiques tied up along the quay, and groups of
fishermen mending their chats, and talking with that
peculiar Mediterranean intensity which suggests that
World War Three may be declared at any minute.

She tried to smile at her own picture, but it blurred,
and she stood for a while, head bent, fighting to
regain her composure.

When at last she lifted her head again, the boat was
there, crossing the mouth of the harbour—a sharp-
lined sailing dinghy, with a single occupant, its blue
sails making the most of the afternoon breeze.

For a moment Julia stared at it as if she'd seen an
apparition. There might be no one else on Argoli, she
thought dazedly, but there could well be other
inhabited islands close by. Islands with airports, or
even ferry services back to Piraeus. She hadn't
looked, she hadn't explored. She'd barely moved
outside a fifty-yard radius of the house since she had
arrived.

The boat was travelling briskly towards the rocky
promontory which formed the other side of the
harbour.

Julia began to run frantically along the breakwater,
waving her arms in the air.

'Ahoy there!' she shouted. 'Oh, stop—come back,
please!'

For one heart-stopping moment she thought the
solitary sailor had seen her, that his head had turned

towards her where she stood at the very end of the breakwater, dancing in frustration. It was all the encouragement she needed. She kicked off her sandals and dived into the sea.

It was colder than she'd bargained for, and she came up gasping, only to see the dinghy passing swiftly and unheedingly beyond the promontory, and out of sight.

'Oh, no!' Julia managed through chattering teeth, before she began to swim swiftly and desperately after it. She had covered a couple of hundred yards before she realised that she was being utterly ridiculous. That she hadn't a hope in hell of catching up with the dinghy, even if the man in it really had seen her—of which there wasn't the slightest guarantee.

She was nearer the rocks of the promontory now than she was the breakwater, so she began to swim slowly and despondently towards them, letting the buoyancy of the water lift her, barely moving her arms and legs.

The splash she heard barely registered until, with startling suddenness, Alex was beside her in the water, his hands reaching for her with a strength that would not be denied.

Alarmed, Julia kicked out. 'Let go of me!' she choked through a mouthful of salt water.

'Relax.' His voice was a snarl. 'Stop struggling, you little fool!'

He turned her on to her back, still fighting and gasping, and began to tow her towards the promontory. At its edge was an enormous rock, weathered flat to form a platform rising out of the

sea, and it was this Julia found herself being hauled
on to, not gently.

She lay there for a minute, coughing up the water
she'd swallowed, wiping her streaming eyes. Alex
was kneeling a couple of feet away from her, his
bronzed chest heaving as he sought to recover his
breath.

'*Christos*, Julia,' he said at last, his voice uneven.
'Never do—never contemplate such a thing again!'

He must have seen the boat, she thought, horrified,
and guessed her intention to swim to it.

She lifted herself into a sitting position, pushing
back her sopping hair with a defiant hand.

'I felt like a swim. I didn't realise it was forbidden.'

'A swim?' he echoed in scornful disbelief. 'In your
dress?'

Julia shrugged. 'Why not? The choice of beachwear
in this hellhole is strictly limited.'

He said hoarsely, 'Don't lie. When I got down to
the beach, you were making no attempt to swim. You
were already sinking when I reached you . . .' He
closed his eyes with a visible shudder.

Realisation dawned on Julia. 'You thought I was
drowning?' she asked. 'You thought I'd thrown
myself in—deliberately?' She threw back her head
and laughed harshly. 'Overcome by your sadistic
treatment of me, no doubt.' She invested her voice
with as much scorn as his own. 'Well, you flatter
yourself, *kyrie*. Nothing you can say or do would
drive me to those lengths, so I'm afraid you had your
ducking all for nothing. As I said, I wanted a swim,
and I took one. I'm sure the slaves' trade union
would allow it.'

She got to her feet, climbed from the platform, and made her way across the narrow stretch of coarse sand to the place where she had left her sandals.

Let him think she'd thrown herself in, she thought almost feverishly as she pushed her damp feet into the unyielding plastic. Let him think anything, as long as he didn't guess about the boat—realise that help could be at hand. She would come down here every day from now on, on the pretext of going for a swim. If one boat had come along, there would have to be others.

Her wet dress felt revoltingly cold and clammy, and she pulled the clinging fabric away from her body with a grimace, wondering if the one she had washed earlier would be dry by now.

Alex was waiting for her. As they walked back up the village street side by side, she was aware of his sideways measuring glance.

He said, 'Julia, you must understand I was concerned when you ran away like that—when you did not come back . . .'

'Oh, I'm sure you were.' She hunched a shoulder. 'What other little menial task did you have lined up for me, I wonder?'

'It wasn't like that.' There was an odd urgency in his voice. 'What I said to you . . .'

'Was no worse than anything else you've said and done since our so-called marriage,' Julia cut in crisply. 'Perhaps I was down at the harbour a long time, but I needed to think—and I have.' She took a breath. 'This—everything about our relationship—has been a grotesque mistake. You don't want me as a wife, and I don't want to go on with this—

farce any longer than I have to. Until you decide to let me go, I'll work for you—not as your wife, but as a servant. The wages I require are my clothes back, and a one-way ticket back to England, and those aren't negotiable.'

'And how precisely do you intend to enforce your demands?'

'I shall go on strike,' she informed him, head high. 'And a hunger strike too. I think you'd have some explaining to do, Kyrios Alexandros, if you allowed your bride to starve to death in front of you!'

There was a silence. Julia waited, wondering frantically what she would do if Alex called her bluff, but at last he shrugged.

'So be it,' he said, without particular emotion. 'My servant, and on those terms.'

She waited for relief to flood through her, but all she felt was a peculiar stultifying numbness.

They arrived back at the house in silence. Alex walked to the chest beside his bed, withdrew a pair of cotton slacks and a towel, then without sparing Julia even a glance, stripped off his wet shorts.

He began to towel himself briskly. Julia stood as if transfixed, her body suffused by that old treacherous heated yearning as she watched him.

He said almost casually, still not looking at her, 'A servant should not be in the room when her master is naked. Go and occupy yourself elsewhere.'

Pressing her hands to her burning face, Julia fled back into the sunshine.

Stumbling a little, she made her way round to the back of the house, and stopped with a cry of horrified incredulity. Penelope turned and gave her a look of mild enquiry, the remains of the red dress hanging from the corner of her mouth.

'Oh, God!' Julia wailed. She grabbed the dangling fabric and pulled at it frantically. For a moment the goat resisted, her jaws still working rhythmically, then she released the material, and Julia sat down heavily, what was left of her dress clamped to her breast. 'You bloody animal,' she yelled. 'Just because I wouldn't milk you!'

'What's the matter?' Alex spoke from just behind her.

'This.' Breast heaving, eyes sparking, Julia scrambled to her feet, holding out the well-chewed remnants.

Alex surveyed them with raised brows, as he fastened the waistband of his pants. 'Goats will eat anything. Didn't you know that.'

'No, I didn't!' she raged. 'I notice she didn't eat any of your bloody things. I suppose you trained her specially!'

A muscle twitched beside Alex's mouth. 'She did not eat my clothes, *pedhi mou,* because she could not reach them. Her tether would not permit it. If you'd put the dress in a different place . . .'

'Oh, of course it's my fault!' Julia felt hysteria rising within her. 'I was supposed to know the rotten little beast has a stomach like a dustbin . . .' As Alex doubled up suddenly, his shoulders shaking, her voice rose. 'Don't you laugh at me you bastard! Don't—you—dare laugh . . .' She launched herself at him, her clenched fists pummelling his chest and shoulders, her nails raking at him.

Even off guard as he undoubtedly was, Alex was

too quick for her, his fingers pinioning her furious hands at the wrist, his other arm circling her, drawing her forward against the cool dampness of his skin.

'That is enough,' he ground out, as she tried to kick his shins. 'Calm yourself.' He shook her slightly.

'Let go of me, damn you!' Almost crying with temper, Julia glared up at him, and caught her breath at the sudden intensity in his dark gaze.

He said huskily, 'Do not give me orders, Julia *mou*, not now, or at any time.'

He bent his head and his mouth came down on hers, parting her lips, invading her mouth with a kind of controlled savagery.

She moaned in her throat and tried to pull free, but his hand tangled in her mass of wet copper hair, enforcing her submission, holding her still while his mouth and tongue tasted her, drank from her, drained her until she trembled in his arms.

The scent of his skin, with its faint lingering tang of salt, seemed all she could breathe. Her hands lifted not to claw but to cling, as the sun dazzled on her closing eyelids, and her soft mouth answered the hunger of his kiss with her own.

His hands swept down her body through the wet cling of the dress, seeking, moulding every line and curve of her slender figure, lingering on her breasts, the gentle swell of her hips, her graceful thighs. She gasped, pressing herself against him, as his caress became suddenly, dizzyingly more intimate. His tongue thrust against hers more fiercely as his hand touched her, stroked, explored and tantalised.

A wordless cry broke from Julia, smothered against

his mouth, but it was enough to shatter the fragile sexual thrall that held them.

Alex tore his mouth from hers with a groan, a dark flush heightening the slash of his cheekbones.

He said something in his own language that was almost a snarl, and pushed her away from him. Julia's legs were like water, and she collapsed down on to the stubble of grass, conscious of nothing but the sensuous, yearning throb of her body which only he could satisfy.

She tried to say his name, hold out her hand to him, but his eyes looked down at her almost blindly, the swift, unsteady rise and fall of his chest revealing his own chaotic emotions.

He said hoarsely, half to himself, 'I did not—intend that.'

He turned and walked away, leaving her there, huddled on the grass, staring after him, her eyes wide with bewilderment, and new hurt.

Julia removed the milk pail to a safe distance and got up, giving Penelope a consoling slap on the flank. 'There you are, you monster,' she whispered.

The first time she had tried milking the goat, Penelope had reacted to her initial struggles by kicking the milk over. The second time, she had kicked Julia quite painfully on the knee. They had now reached a stage of cautious neutrality.

Odd, Julia thought, as she carried the milk back to the house, how you got used to all kinds of things which had once seemed totally impossible. She sniffed the smell of baking bread as she stepped into the dimness of the house, and set the pail down, wiping some beads of sweat from her forehead. The first loaf she had made had been an unmitigated disaster, its shape and texture like a housebrick.

But she had improved since then, out of sheer necessity, and although she would have won no prizes, her bread was at least eatable.

Practice makes perfect, she thought wryly. She had collected some water from the spring earlier, and now she filled a glass and stood in the doorway sipping it gratefully, and looking up at the shimmer of the sun on the high rocks.

A week had passed, but she still hadn't been able to put those shattering moments in Alex's arms out of her mind, try as she might.

Alex had not returned to the house until late that evening, his face shuttered and forbidding, and Julia had not dared asked where he'd been. Nor had she found the courage to refer to what had transpired in those stolen, sun-drenched minutes, and Alex had never indicated by either word or gesture that he even remembered the incident had taken place. Julia supposed she should be grateful for that.

She told herself so often. But her body, aroused for a fulfilment it had been so harshly denied, was unconvinced.

She drove herself hard, getting up while the sun was still low in the sky, and doing the chores, which had once seemed so difficult, and were now a matter of routine. It was good to get the bulk of the work over before the real heat of the day, she'd discovered. And it also meant she had more time to herself.

She used it to explore every inch of the island. The interior was rocky and barren, but its very starkness had a beauty all its own, she found. And on the other side of the island there were a couple of small but spectacular beaches with firm golden sand shelving gently into the warm and lazy sea.

Julia had wondered to begin with why the village hadn't sprung up around them, the island's most obvious amenity, then castigated herself for thinking like a tourist. A fishing community needed a harbour with sufficient draught for its boats, not a beach to sun itself on.

She had also found where the dinghy had come from, or thought she had. There was another island lying to the west, and much bigger than Argoli, a humped shape, with mountains on the horizon.

But although she had kept her eyes skinned, she had seen no more blue sails, or any other colour, for that matter.

Her explorations also gave her an excellent excuse for avoiding Alex. Since that day in the garden he had treated her, as she had requested, like a servant. There were no more taunting jibes to skin her raw, but those, she thought, she would almost prefer to the icy formality with which he now treated her. The only time she was in his company for any length of time was during meals, and she was aware all the time they were together of a sharp tension between them, dangerous as an electric current.

During the day he was as busy as she was, working on the repairs to the house, which was beginning to look quite prosperous, especially as it had received another coat of whitewash. It was in the evening, when the light faded and the moon rose, that the walls seemed to close in on them, reminding them that they were alone together.

Julia had formed the habit of slipping away to her room as soon as the velvet darkness began to encroach. It was impossible to sit in a room with someone and not speak or even look at him.

But looking held danger. When she was sure he was unaware, she would study him under her lashes almost obsessively, committing him, face and body, to memory against the day when she would never see him again.

It was madness, and she knew it. The sensible thing would be to start erasing him from her mind, so that she could ultimately pretend these burning, tormenting days had never happened.

Each night she lay awake, watching the moon until it faded, and she could fall at last into an uneasy sleep. But even there she wasn't safe. Her dreams were torture, where he held her, caressing her, murmuring love words to her, yet always without the ultimate possession, so that she woke, perspiring and feverish, her body clamouring for satisfaction, her arms reaching for him.

Most days Alex went fishing, and Julia seized the opportunity to wash the hated green dress, wrapping herself sarong-style in a towel while she did so. Then she would go down to the harbour, and the stone platform by the sea, or one of the beaches, spread the dress out, and swim or sunbathe in the nude until it was dry.

She had to reluctantly admit that she had probably never looked better, apart from the shadows under her eyes induced by her disturbed nights. But whereas most brides had good reason to look like that, she thought unhappily, she had none. She had always been slim, but now she was lithe, her muscles taut with the unaccustomed exercise she had been taking. Her skin was golden too, without a strap mark or a bikini line to spoil the perfection of her tan.

What a waste! she thought wryly.

She glanced down at herself and pulled a face. The green dress had never been vibrant, but its constant immersions and bleachings had faded it badly. And she was aware she had been in contact with Penelope too.

Laundry time again, she thought with a sigh. Sometime later, the dress in a wet bundle under her arm, she made her way unhurriedly to her favourite beach, about half a mile from the village. Here two leaning rocks had formed a slight hollow filled with pale gold sand, and an olive tree at the edge of the beach provided some welcome shade in the hottest midday hours.

She spread the dress on a rock, dropped the towel on the sand, and ran to the sea.

It was at times like this that she could almost be happy, she thought, as she turned and twisted like a mermaid in the water. She could forget that her marriage was a disaster, a failure as soon as it had begun. She could nearly, but not quite, forget the man who had awoken her to passion's possibilities, without teaching her its consummation. She wondered whether there would ever be sufficient time or circumstance to wipe Alex from her mind and emotions, or whether she would be left scarred for ever.

Sighing, she stood up and began to wade back

towards the shore, wringing the water out of her hair as she did so, lifting her face to the warmth of the sun.

As she stepped through the shallows on to the sand, she saw him. He was standing like a statue beside the rock where her dress hung. His face was unsmiling, almost ravaged as he watched her walking towards him.

Julia stopped. She had nothing to cover herself with. Alex was standing between her and the towel. She could always, she supposed in some distant corner of her mind, hide herself with her hands.

Although he was so still, she could see a muscle working in his throat—could see the flagrant starvation in his eyes as he looked at her.

He said, wearily, as if he had returned from a long journey, *'Ti orea pou ise.* How beautiful you are!'

She lifted her hands almost languidly and swept the mass of damp curling hair back from her shoulders. She was Eve. She was all woman, and she smiled at him. Then, without haste, she began once more to walk towards him.

By the time she reached him he was naked too, his clothes almost wrenched from him. His arms closed round her, and their mouths and bodies met. He stormed her with kisses, her lips exploring her face and throat with frantic need. They sank together to the warm sand behind the wall of rock, their clothes making a bed for them.

Julia had dreamed Alex would kiss her like this, caressing the hollows in her throat, finding her pulse points and setting them throbbing like jungle drums. She had longed to feel the tenderness of his hands on her breasts, fondling the soft curves, stroking the rosy nipples with his fingers and tongue until they stood proudly erect. The reality was a delight that was almost pain.

His lips moved downwards on an erotic journey over each sun-gilded contour, whispering his pleasure, his desire against her skin. Half afraid, Julia began to touch him in turn, her hands shaping his shoulders, and the long strength of his back, down to the taut buttocks.

She hesitated, and Alex kissed her mouth and carried her hands to his body, showing her without words what he wanted. She was shy at first, wary of his sheer male power, but he murmured husky-throated encouragement as her fingers became more assured, and then more wanton, making him groan softly.

Alex bent his head and laid a trail of light, teasing kisses across her flat stomach, and down to the joining of her thighs. She was melting, longing for his touch, but the first intimate, sensuous brush of his lips shocked her into sudden tension. Her hands tugged at his hair.

'No—please . . .'

Alex lifted his head, his dark eyes intent as he laid a silencing finger on her trembling lips.

'Trust me,' he whispered. 'There are many paths to pleasure, my innocent. This is only one of them.'

He bent to her again, and with a little sob Julia abandoned herself to his dictate. Urgency was unfurling deep within her like the petals of some strong, wild flower, running like fire through her veins. Her body began to twist restlessly, her hands clenching and unclenching, her voice whimpering something that might have been his name.

Just as she felt she could bear no more, the need inside her threatening to shatter her into a thousand tiny pieces, Alex moved, suddenly and swiftly, his body covering hers, his hands sliding under her slim hips to lift her towards him.

For one burning moment she felt his warmth and hardness against her, then slowly, and with infinite care, he entered her. For a moment there was pain, and she flinched. Then, feeling him hesitate, terrified that he might draw back, she arched against him, acting out of pure instinct, her hands clinging to his sun-warmed shoulders, her slender legs locking round his waist, knowing triumphantly that the last fragile barrier had been swept aside, and that, at last, he was totally sheathed inside her.

For a brief while they remained still, Alex's face almost tortured as he looked at her.

He said unsteadily, 'I have wanted this—so much, you cannot know . . .'

'Can't I?' Her voice broke as, slowly and sweetly, he began to move on her, inside her, with her. 'Oh, Alex—*Alex* . . .'

She felt the rhythm he had initiated, joined it, let it possess her, marvelling, as she did so, at its tenderness, its simplicity. They kissed, gently at first, lips and tongues searching out each other's secrets with a growing wonderment, then with a fierce sensual passion which reflected the deepening thrusts of their seeking bodies.

The first slow convulsion of sensation inside her took Julia almost unware. The next made her cry out in mingled joy and pain, as the pleasure took her, carried her mindlessly to some other dimension of time and space, held there suspended in a sweet agony which threatened to tear her apart. She felt Alex shudder wildly in her arms, his voice groaning something in his own language as he reached his climax in turn.

Slowly, still wrapped, enfolded in each other, they drifted back to reality. Julia felt languid, boneless with voluptuous contentment. As Alex began to move away from her, she halted him, twining her arms round his neck, sliding her hands over his sweat-slicked shoulders.

'Don't leave me,' she whispered, huskily, her eyes shining with invitation and promise. 'Not yet . . .'

But there was no answering smile in the dark gaze that surveyed her. Almost casually, he reached up and detached her clinging hands, freeing himself totally from her embrace. He rolled away from her and lay, trying to control his unsteady breathing, an arm flung across his face.

Julia propped herself up on one elbow, uncertainty settling like a stone inside her, as she watched him.

'Alex?' She put out a hand and touched his face timidly. 'Is something wrong?'

'What could be wrong?' Alex sat up and reached for his jeans. 'You were as warm and willing as any man could wish. I hope you were equally satisfied?'

Colour rushed into Julia's face. 'It was—wonderful.' She tried to speak evenly. 'So—why—why don't you . . .?'

'Have you again?' he cut across her faltering words, with brutal directness, as he fastened his zip.

'Yes.' She made herself meet his gaze.

He laughed harshly, his eyes flicking insolently over her nakedness. 'So eager, *agapi mou?*' he asked. 'So greedy for me? Or do you just wish to boast to that woman in England about your—Greek stud?' He smiled without amusement at the expression of dawning horror in her face. 'I see you understand me at last. So you must also understand why I must disappoint you.'

He rose to his feet. 'Enjoy your memories, my beautiful wife. They are all that you will have,' he added with icy quietness, and walked away from her.

CHAPTER EIGHT

JULIA stumbled back to the village, looking neither to right nor left, oblivious to everything but the pain of this final blow.

She could remember in searing detail every taunt, every snide innuendo that Tricia Bosworth had uttered, and the total recall made her blood run cold.

But she had put the whole distasteful incident out of her mind, she thought desperately. She hadn't mentioned Mrs Bosworth's visit to her room to a soul. So how—how had Alex known? Had Mrs Bosworth sought him out—made some kind of insinuation? It didn't seem possible, even for her.

By the time she had struggled back into her dress and sandals, and gone after him to try and explain, Alex had been out of sight, and although she had run to the top of the track which led down to the beach, calling his name, there had been no reply.

But when she did catch up with him, would he believe the truth—that she had been shocked and digusted by Tricia Bosworth's remarks, but had written them off as another example of her malice? It did not seem altogether likely.

Her stance might have had more credibility if she hadn't called him a peasant—and said all those other things to his face, she thought wretchedly.

In her distress, she missed the path she usually took, and finally emerged at the side of the harbour scrambling, uncaring of bruised toes and grazed arms and legs, over the rocks of the promontory

The sailing dinghy, its blue sail neatly furled, was moored beside the breakwater.

Julia stood motionless, staring across at it, her heart thudding.

There was no one around. All she had to do was climb aboard and sail away. She had handled boats like it a dozen times. And it wasn't like stealing, she appeased her conscience feverishly. When she reached the big island she would make some explanation to the authorities—ensure the lone mariner was rescued.

She had to get away from Argoli—away from Alex who hated her, who only wanted to punish her, who had even made love to her out of some kind of perverted revenge.

Well, she couldn't take any more. She'd had enough of his cruelty—his neglect. He had shown her paradise, then condemned her to a lonely hell. Let him stay in it alone, she thought, swallowing the painful lump in her throat.

Keeping a wary eye open for the returning owner, Julia trod round to the breakwater. The dinghy was quite new, and clearly very expensive. She cast a practised eye over the equipment. It was ideally designed for single-handed use.

So what was she waiting for? All she had to do was climb down into the thing. She could feel the faint breeze stealing across the water, beckoning her to freedom . . .

She shivered suddenly, wrapping her arms round her body. Freedom, she thought bitterly. What freedom was there without Alex? Separation from him would be a prison, with eternal solitary confinement.

She went on staring down almost compulsively at the boat, aware of a deep and terrible trembling spreading through her body.

The means of her release had come far too late, she thought dazedly. Standing there, more alone than she had ever been in her life, she realised suddenly and completely that she loved Alex—that she had probably been in love with him almost from the first. That was why she had agreed to that whirlwind marriage, she thought, her nails digging into the palms of her hands. Not for Ambermere, but because she wanted to be with him always. She had fooled herself with reasons, with rational arguments, but in truth, it was as simple as that.

It's taken all this time for me to understand, she thought wonderingly. If we'd had a normal marriage—the usual honeymoon, I'd probably have admitted it long ago, but Argoli—this whole mess got in the way. And Ambermere, beloved though it is, has been just another obstacle, preventing me from seeing how I really felt—what I really wanted.

And if our marriage had been a conventional one, perhaps I still wouldn't have faced up to the truth. Maybe I'd still be telling myself that I'd sacrificed myself for Ambermere. Alex brought me to Argoli to teach me a lesson—and I've learned to know myself at last, but too late.

The sad finality of the words in her head made her shiver.

But I can't leave him, she told herself desperately. I'll never leave while there's even a remote chance I can win him over, make him change his mind about me. He wanted me today, and that's a beginning. I can make him want me again, somehow, she thought with a pang of nostalgia for all the lovely seductive clothes, the cosmetics and the scent, aboard the *Clio* and long gone, looking down with a grimace at the tatty green dress, her broken fingernails and callused hands.

And if desire is all there is, if I can never make him care for me in the way I need—then I'll live with that somehow.

This is what he's brought me to—yearning for a smile from him, a kind word. And, God help me, I wouldn't have it any other way.

She turned slowly, away from the boat, and walked up the street to the house.

A man was emerging from the front door, hands thrust into the pockets of immaculate white shorts. His blue and white shirt was open to the waist, and his swarthy face wore a brooding frown.

The lone sailor had been exploring, Julia thought—then stopped with a faint gasp as she realised who he was.

She wanted to turn and run into one of the empty houses, and hide, but it was too late. He had seen her, and lengthened his stride.

Julia stood her ground, moistening dry lips with the tip of her tongue as she saw the total incredulity in his face.

'Julia?' he asked uncertainly. 'Julia Kendrick? But this is not possible!'

Julia gave him a neutral smile. 'Hello, Paul. How are you?'

Paul Constantis went on staring at her, his brows drawn together in a frown of disbelief. 'I think I am going out of my mind! Argoli has been deserted for years, No one ever comes here.'

Julia shrugged. 'Yet here I am, she countered, trying to speak lightly, as her mind ran in circles trying to think what to say—what to do.

He said slowly, 'Then it was you I saw that day.' He gave a strained laugh. 'I thought it was a hallucination. A girl with red hair waving at me from an empty place—a desolation.' He spoke the words with distaste, his eyes narrowing as he looked at her, really seeing her for the first time. 'But what are you doing here—what has happened to you, in the name of God? Were you shipwrecked—has there been some disaster?'

He was comparing her present appearance with that of the chic and soignée girl he had taken to dinner some lifetime ago, she realised.

She said, carefully, 'Not exactly. It—it's difficult to explain . . .'

'No,' Alex said, coldly and quietly, 'it is perfectly simple.'

Neither of them had heard him approach, yet there he was, standing only a few yards from them. Julia jumped, and Paul Constantis swung round as if he had been electrocuted.

'Alexandros?' The word emerged as a croak.

'*You?*'

Alex shrugged. 'Why not?' He stared at Julia, his face icily cynical. 'Well, *pedhi mou*—tell my cousin Paul how you came here, and why. He is waiting to hear, and I am sure he will find the story quite—fascinating.'

Paul Constantis's eyes went from one to the other, his face sharpening into sudden avidity. He attempted a laugh. 'Is there some mystery? I—I did not know you two were even acquainted. I am clearly intruding . . .'

Julia lifted her chin. 'Yes, you are, rather,' she said, smiling to rob the words of offence. 'You see, Alex and I are here on our honeymoon.'

There was a moment of intense silence, then Paul Constantis began to laugh.

'This is a joke, *ne?* It is only a few weeks since we parted, Julia *mou*, and you claim in that time to have met my cousin Alexandros—to have married him? It is impossible!'

'But it's also the truth.' Julia wasn't sure her legs would obey her, but she forced them into action to cross the distance that separated her from Alex, so that she could stand beside him. He made no welcoming gesture, but he didn't turn away either. 'Alex and I have been married for—nearly ten days, haven't we, darling?'

His face was guarded. 'Yes.'

'But it cannot have happened! There would have been some news—some announcement—the papers would have picked up such a marriage.' Paul Constantis wasn't laughing any more. He dragged a handkerchief out of his pocket and wiped his forehead. 'Why wasn't the family told?'

'I told my mother,' Alex said drily. 'I imagined she would have—broken the news. As you are here now, I presume you are staying with her.'

'Yes, all of us,' Paul said thickly. 'She invited us—said it was time for a reconciliation, that she had a surprise for us. We thought'—he stopped suddenly —'that is, we did not imagine . . .'

'I understand,' Alex's voice deepened ironically. 'And now you know.'

'Yes,' said Paul, almost biting out the words. 'Now I know.' He looked them both over, frowning. 'But what are you doing here? A honeymoon in this place, *po po po*. No man would do such a thing to his bride. No woman could accept it . . .'

'Haven't you ever heard of a working honeymoon?' Julia broke in calmly, her heart thumping. 'All the usual places seemed so—boring and conventional. When Alex mentioned that he was thinking of restoring this house on a deserted island, it sounded quite incredibly romantic.' She slid her hand into Alex's unresponsive clasp. 'And it's been wonderful, hasn't it, darling? We've done such a lot of work on the house. It will make a marvellous retreat when it's finished—somewhere quiet to bring our children . . .'

'Ah, yes,' Paul said meditatively. His glance touched the unbecoming folds of the green dress at Julia's waist, slid down and away. 'Now perhaps I understand—this hasty marriage.'

There was another silence, and Julia felt a wave of heat sweep over her as she realised what Paul was getting at. Her lips parted in angry protest,

then closed as Alex pressed her fingers warningly.

'But you are right that it is quiet here. In fact it is
almost—primitive.' Paul's good-looking face wore an
overt sneer, and Julia remembered, with an inward
wince, that she had caught him emerging from the
house. 'You are very brave, Julia *mou*, and very loyal
to endure such conditions.'

'There's not much endurance called for,' Julia
returned crisply. 'Alex is my husband, and wherever
he goes, that's where I want to be.'

'What a charming sentiment!' Paul turned to Alex.
'No wonder you kept your marriage so secret, my
cousin! Any man would wish to enjoy such
love—such devotion in uninterrupted bliss.' He
shook his head in mock regret. 'And then I had to
blunder in! But when I saw Julia in the distance at the
harbour some days ago, I had the strangest
impression that she was in distress—that she needed
help. Isn't that absurd?'

'Quite absurd.' Julia rested her head against Alex's
rigid shoulder. 'Especially when you only caught a
glimpse—and even then you thought I was a
hallucination.'

'And instead you are Alex's bride, and only too
real,' Paul Constantis said, his smile humourless.
'So—when do you plan to leave this—idyllic
seclusion?'

'Now that our secret has been discovered, there is
small point in remaining,' Alex replied brusquely.
'When you return to Lymnos, please ask my mother
to send Yannis for us at once.'

'With the greatest of pleasure.' The charming

mask was back in place. 'Does she know you are here?'

'No. She understands that a honeymoon is a private affair.'

'Of course,' Paul agreed. 'And she is—so good at respecting secrets, is she not? It will be a wonderful surprise for her—and also for my family.' His eyes flicked towards Julia. 'They will enjoy meeting your new wife, my mother—and my sister Zoe.'

He nodded affably, then walked away towards the harbour, not looking back. As soon as he was out of sight, Julia felt Alex move abruptly away from her.

She said, 'Are we really—leaving here?'

'You heard me say so.' His voice was forbidding.

She swallowed. 'And do I have to meet your mother—the rest of your family—looking like this?' She bit her lip. 'Or is it part of the ongoing humbling process?'

He said roughly, 'Of course not. *Christos,* what do you take me for? There are clothes for you here, and have been since the beginning.'

'Then if I might have them, please.' Julia took a step towards the dark doorway, but Alex halted her, his hand on her arm.

He said, 'Why did you do that? Why did you pretend? You could have told him the truth—repaid me a hundredfold for everything I've made you suffer here.' He laughed harshly. 'He would have loved to hear how I've kept you here against your will—humiliated you in every possible way. He could have rescued you—carried you off to tell the story of your wrongs to the world's press. They would have found it a—sensation.' He paused, the dark eyes boring into her face. 'So—why didn't you tell him the truth?'

Because I love you, her heart cried silently. Because my instinct is to protect you, in spite of everything.

She gave him a steady look. 'Perhaps I feel that whatever's happened here is our own private business.' She freed herself gently from his clasp. 'And maybe my thirst for revenge isn't the equal of yours,' she added quietly, and walked into the house, leaving him staring after her.

The loaf of bread she'd made that morning was still in the middle of the kitchen table. She touched its crisp crust with the tip of her finger. Well, that was one accomplishment she would not need again, she thought without any particular pleasure.

She had heard that long-term prisoners sometimes grew to love their jails, and she could believe it, although her stay on Argoli had not been a lengthy one. She seemed to have lost track of time, as one day succeeded the next. But the day that matters—the one I shall remember—is this one, she thought. The day when, however briefly, I belonged to Alex at last.

Her body shivered in delight at the memory of it, then tensed at he walked into the house carrying a suitcase which she recognised as part of the luggage which had accompanied her on to *Clio*.

'You had better change,' he told her brusquely. 'Once Paul delivers my message, the boat will be sent for us at once.'

Julia stared down at the table. 'Won't your mother think this is all rather—strange?'

'Perhaps,' he said, shrugging. 'But she will say little. Her own life has not been lived on particularly conventional lines.'

Julia bit her lip. 'I suppose not,' she said colourlessly. 'Does—does she speak English?'

He gave her a cynical look. 'Afraid of finding yourself in the company of yet another ignorant peasant, Julia *mou*?'

'No.' She shook her head. 'Alex, for God's sake, can't we forget all that nonsense—please? I've paid for the things I said—for the things I thought. Please don't blame me for all that Tricia Bosworth said. I've no idea why she talked in the way she did. She made me feel sick . . .'

'And me too,' he said reflectively. 'That day of our wedding, I was prepared to forget the past. You looked so lovely, so innocent as you came to me, that any thought of punishing you, of salving my pride at your expense, seemed disgusting—grotesque. So I decided to abandon my plan to bring you here. Instead, I thought I would woo you gently to accept me, and the life we would make together. I even wondered if I could make you fall in love with me a little.'

'But Alex . . .'

He held up his hand, silencing her. 'No, listen to me. All that time at the house, surrounded by other people, I was in torture. I wanted so much to be alone with you—to have you to myself. When you went to your room, it seemed to me that you had been gone for ever, so eventually I followed. The door was open—and I—heard everything.'

A smile twisted his lips. 'Oh, I knew why you were marrying me, Julia *mou*. I should have been under no illusion—but, foolishly, I had hoped that you might have begun to regard me differently. And because I knew I'd been a fool, I became angry all over again. so we came here.'

'But you don't think I agreed with all those revolting things she said—those ghastly, twisted lies?' Julia jumped to her feet. 'You can't think that!'

He said harshly, 'I know what I heard, my beautiful wife. And there was not one word of contradiction, of denial from you. You—went along with everything she said.'

'It may have seemed like that,' Julia said desperately. 'But it wasn't. Oh, Alex, you have to believe me! I didn't argue with her because I didn't think she was worth it—didn't want to give her the satisfaction of a scene, or letting her see that she could upset me. I—just wanted her to go. She's a liar—a malicious troublemaker. Anyone would tell you that.'

He said unsmilingly, 'And yet at our first encounter, when she talked of you marrying for Ambermere, she spoke no more than the truth.'

'No,' Julia denied, almost wringing her hands. 'Oh, Alex, you're so wrong . . .'

'Yes,' he said quietly. 'Wrong from the beginning. Wrong about everything.' He shrugged. 'But what does that matter, after all? In these days, a mistake, however grave, does not have to become a lifelong

tragedy. We do not have to punish each other any
longer. You shall have Ambermere, Julia *mou*, as part
of our divorce settlement.'

'You're going to divorce me?' She felt stifled, as if
the walls were closing in on her.

'It will be a mutual arrangement, and I hope a
civilised one.' His mouth twisted. 'Perhaps our
marriage can end in dignity, if nothing else.'

'But it's hardly begun . . .' Julia moistened dry
lips with the tip of her tongue. She asked flatly,
'Don't you—want me any more? You—you seemed
to . . .'

'My self-control was undermined, *agapi mou*,
by the vision of you emerging from the sea like some
exquisite Aphrodite.' His smile did not reach his
eyes. 'However, I do not—compound my follies.'

'So how do you intend to present me to your
mother, to the rest of your family—as your housekeeper?'

'In public you will be my wife, naturally. In
private—my guest.' Alex paused. 'We will keep our
visit as short as possible, I think.'

'Yes.' Julia's nails were buried painfully in the
palms of her hands. 'That would be best.' She
paused, trying to force a smile. 'Your mother will be
disappointed. I remember you telling me that she—
wanted you to be married.'

Alex shrugged. 'Then I will have to ensure her
disappointment is kept to a minimum. Fortunately, I
do not have to look far for another bride. A year ago,
my Aunt Sophia began dropping hints that I should
make reparation to the family for the financial loss my
existence has caused them by marrying my cousin

Zoe.'

'How very—convenient, for both of you.' Her stiff mouth would barely frame the words. Jealousy wounded her like a savage claw. It took every atom of will-power she possessed not to go on her knees to him, beg him to give their marriage another chance. 'And how does the bride-to-be feel about it?'

His grin was frankly cynical. 'Amenable—what else? In fact, now that she has seen my money slip away from her once, she may even be gratifyingly eager.'

'Then there's nothing more to be said.' Julia picked up the suitcase. 'Thank you for this, at least.'

'I hope there is everything you need,' Alex said courteously. 'Androula packed it, not myself.'

'Then I'm sure it will be fine.' Oh God, how could she mouth these platitudes when her heart was breaking—her entire world falling apart?

He held out his hand. 'Let me take it upstairs for you.'

'No, thank you. I can manage by myself.'

That was something she would have to get used to, she thought, as she walked, head held high, to the wooden stair. Being—by herself. Alone at Ambermere. Once that had been the summit of her ambitions. But the Julia Kendrick who had planned her life in such splendidly selfish isolation had changed—had gone for ever. And in her place was a girl, heartsore and vulnerable, who had come to know what she wanted from life, now and for ever, only to find it was too late. And that her chance of happiness with the man she loved had been cruelly snatched away.

CHAPTER NINE

YANNIS was a small man, broad-shouldered, grizzled of hair, and blue of chin. He greeted Alex like an old friend, pounding him on the back, and pouring out a flood of exuberant Greek.

The smile he turned on Julia revealed crooked teeth, and also a warmth that almost melted the ice round her heart. He took her hands in both of his, growling something in his own language which she could not understand, but the look of intense admiration which accompanied it needed no translation.

He helped her down into the powerful launch which awaited them with exaggerated care.

As they moved out of the harbour, Julia was careful not to look back. Her control was on a knife-edge, she knew, and she could not break down in front of Alex. He might not desire her any more, she thought fiercely, but she would make damned sure he didn't pity her either, because that would be more than she could bear.

The first thing she had seen when she'd opened the suitcase in the privacy of her room had been her wedding dress, and this was what she was now wearing. She had come downstairs almost fearfully, when Alex had called up to say the boat was coming, wondering what his reaction would be. For a breathless moment he had stared at her, his whole attention arrested, then his mouth had tautened cynically, and he'd turned away.

It was the last bid for his attention she would make, Julia told herself drearily, as the launch, with Alex at the wheel, sped towards Lymnos.

The trip took barely half an hour. Time had stood still on Argoli. Now it was rushing past her like the breeze from the sea, as ephemeral as the wake creaming behind them. Reminding her as if she needed such a reminder, how soon her life with Alex would be over.

As they got near the island Julia could see a cluster of white houses, and other buildings, topped by a church, spilling down to the water's edge round a small harbour, but Alex bypassed this, continuing along the coast.

It was very different from Argoli, Julia realised. Apart from its size, Lymnos was greener, with far more trees. The coastline was rimmed by silvery horsehoes of sand, and the interior was almost mountainous. She wondered whether her stay would be long enough to enable her to see something of the island, then dismissed the idea impatiently. That was, after all, the least of her troubles.

The first and most immediate ordeal would be meeting Alex's mother. She tried to form a mental picture of her, but failed completely. Alex had said so little about her, after all, but from the few hints he had dropped, Julia had gathered that his mother was a woman of character.

I wonder what she'll expect me to call her, she thought nervously. I wish I knew more Greek. I'll

have to take lessons . . . And stopped, with a pang, as
she realised they would never be needed.

It was nearly evening, and the sun was going down
over the sea, spilling a path like flame across the
restless surface of the water. She found herself
wishing, ludicrously, that she could snatch the
wheel, send the launch speeding along that glittering
path to the edge of the world, to somewhere she
could be alone with Alex—where the rest of the
human race would never find them.

But there was no chance of that. Already he was
turning the wheel, aiming the launch smoothly
towards the shore and the small private landing stage
which was begnning to take shape in the distance.

There was someone waiting there for them—a
woman, clad in elegant violet silk trousers, and a
tunic top in a deep pinky-red, like some exotic
fuchsia. Shoulder-length tawny hair, discreetly
streaked, framed a face that was vibrantly attractive
without being in any way classically beautiful, and
her irrepressible smile revealed very white teeth as
she advanced to meet them, arms outstretched.

Zoe? Julia asked herself, wincing, then breathed
again as she realised the newcomer, at close quarters,
was considerably older than first impressions
suggested. Her face was also unmistakably familiar,
she thought with bewilderment.

'Alexandros *mou!*' The woman's voice was deep
and throaty, as she threw her arms round Alex's neck
and kissed him warmly. 'Wicked one—deceiving me
like this, pretending that you were cruising on *Clio*
when all the time you were just across the water!'
She hugged him again. 'But I do not blame you. A

yacht, even when the crew is as well trained as yours, is too public for a honeymoon.' She turned to Julia, almond-shaped eyes sweeping her candidly. 'So you are my new daughter. Welcome to Lymnos, dear child.'

Julia was aware she was gaping, and closed her mouth hurriedly. *This* was Alex's mother? she asked herself dazedly. This was the supposed peasant girl George Constantis was said to have seduced?

Because now she had heard her voice, she could also put a name to that smiling, distinctive face too.

She found her own voice from somewhere. 'You—you are Maria Xanthe.'

'Why, yes,' the older woman said with amusement. 'You seem surprised.'

'I am,' Julia managed. Her heart was thumping, and her throat was dry.

Maria Xanthe, she thought, her mind reeling. The actress who had taken Hollywood by storm years before—flared across its skies like a meteor, then retired at the height of her fame. The actress whose films still enjoyed a cult following all over the world. Maria Xanthe, incredibly, was Alex's mother.

'You mean Alexandros did not tell you?' Maria Xanthe's brows drew together slightly. She turned to him. 'But why not?'

Alex slid an arm round her waist. 'I wanted you to be a surprise for her, *kougla mou.*' He directed an ironic glance at Julia. 'Also, I wished to save my wife from any—further preconceptions.'

'Well, you have succeeded in the first of your aims,' his mother said with faint tartness, giving him a repressive look. 'The poor little one looks as if she has been poleaxed! Perhaps it is not so much a surprise for her as a terrible shock, hmm?'

'Not in the least.' Julia dragged together the rags of her composure. 'Anyway, I should be used to Alex's—surprises by now. This is a great honour, Madame Xanthe. I've seen all your films.'

The actress laughed. 'No, it is not possible—you are too young. Ah, but there is English television, of course.' She gave Julia a bland look. 'And which of my films did you most enjoy, child?'

Julia realised she was being gently tested. She said, 'Well, *Darkness at Dawn* is the one they show most often, but I prefer *North of the City.*'

Maria Xanthe gave her an approving look. 'It is a favourite of mine too.' She slid her arm through Julia's and began to lead her along the landing stage towards the small beach, and the gardens beyond. 'I am going to like this beautiful girl you have married,' she tossed laughingly over her shoulder to Alex. 'I forgive you for hiding her away from us all on Argoli.' She turned back to Julia. 'It is sad to see the island deserted, *ne?* It was once so busy, so happy—so important to me. Now, I can hardly bear to go there.'

'It will be happy again, Mama,' Alex said quietly. 'When the people return.'

Maria Xanthe laughed. 'When he first said that to me, I thought it was just a dream. But I know now that what my Alexandros says, he does, no matter what the cost to himself or his resources.' She squeezed Julia's arm. 'So be warned, little one.'

'I think I've already discovered that for myself,' Julia said quietly.

'So soon? *Po po po.* But then you have been quite alone, with nothing to do with your days and nights but—find out about each other and about love. That is good, I think.'

Julia smiled weakly in response. Nothing to do, she thought wryly. How little Madame Xanthe knew! Clearly she imagined they had been sharing some sun-baked idyll together.

She wondered how her mother-in-law would react if she told her, 'My days were filled with the hardest manual labour I ever dreamed of, with no time off for good behaviour, and my nights were spent tossing and turning on the grottiest mattress in western civilisation, longing for a lover who never came to me.' Perhaps it would be Maria Xanthe's turn to be poleaxed.

The villa was beautiful, a gracious, rambling structure, hung with bougainvillaea, and all white except for the doors and louvred window shutters, which had been màde from some rich, dark wood.

Madame Xanthe nodded when she saw Julia's entranced expression. 'You like my home? It is yours too now.'

Julia began to say something deprecatory and grateful, encountered Alex's harshly cynical glance, and subsided into wretched silence.

Inside, it was exquisitely cool, with large old-fashioned fans whirling on the ceiling.

'They are for show,' said Maria Xanthe, kicking off her high-heeled sandals and walking barefoot across the marble tiles of the wide hall. She gave Julia a conspiratorial grin. 'We have air-conditioning too—something I grew to rely on during my time in

America.' She threw open a massive pair of double doors. 'Now, come and meet the others.'

Julia knew a cowardly impulse to turn and run, then, steeling herself, she followed Maria Xanthe into the room beyond.

It was an awkward little tableau which confronted her. The first person she saw was Paul, clearly on edge, and standing behind a sofa on which two women were seated.

One of them was no longer young, her face lined and haughty. She was wearing the traditional black of a widow, but her dress was made from silk and complemented lavishly with diamonds at wrist and throat.

'Julia, may I present to you Madame Sophia Constantis, who is my guest here. Paul, her son, I believe you already know. And this is Madame's daughter Zoe.'

Zoe Constantis was a beautiful girl, sloe-eyed and olive-skinned, with a sleekly voluptuous body discreetly displayed in an expensive orchid pink dress. Her good looks were currently marred by the sullen expression she made no effort to dissemble. She shook hands with Julia, as did her mother, but their greetings were perfunctory in the extreme, and the looks which accompanied them were positively inimical.

If Alex hadn't already told her Madame Constantis's plans for Zoe and himself, she would have little trouble guessing, Julia thought with irony.

She watched Alex step forward, kiss his aunt's hand and cheek, then turn to Zoe, and looked away abruptly. I—cannot—watch him kiss her, she thought

savagely, feigning an interest in a large portrait of
Maria Xanthe which hung above the empty fireplace.

'Bah, don't look at that! It is a terrible likeness. The
painter was very young, and a little in love with me,
and his hand shook.' Madame Xanthe gurgled with
laughter as she handed Julia a glass. 'Here, *pedhi mou*.
A dry martini—another American legacy.'

Julia swallowed. 'I don't think . . .'

'Ah, yes, you need it,' her mother-in-law said
firmly. 'You are a little pale suddenly. Maybe you are
tired.' She lowered her voice, giving Julia a
mischievous look. 'Would you prefer to have dinner
alone, in your bedroom perhaps with Alex?' She
sighed. 'If I had known you would visit me, I would
not have filled the house with these other guests. But
I meant it for the best. George would have wished me
to be kind to his family, and we cannot always be
enemies.'

'I'm sure Alex agrees with you.' Julia took a sip of
her martini, and gasped. 'Wow!'

'Strong, eh?' Julia was treated to that outrageous
grin again. 'It is what you need, little one. You are
tense, I think. One moment you are alone with my
Alex, making love, the next you are surrounded by
these people who look at you as if you are a bad
smell.' She nudged Julia gently. 'But you are not
alone. How do you think they looked at me when we
first met? They must have asked themselves a
thousand times what kind of woman I would be.' She
giggled softly. 'The truth sent them almost into a
frenzy!'

'But surely they already knew,' Julia protested.
'You're so famous, they must have heard of you.'

'Of Maria Xanthe, yes, but that is my acting name. I
am really called Maria Cristoforou, and that was the
name that appeared on Alex's birth documents. That
was why I was able to preserve my anonymity, until I
chose to abandon it.' She rolled her eyes comically.
'Can you imagine, *pedhi mou*, the scandal they could
have caused if they had known who I really was
during that absurd court case? That I could not
endure. But now that they depend on Alex to support
them, to maintain their lifestyle, they do not dare say
a word.' She shrugged a shoulder. 'And who would
care now, anyway?' Sudden tears sparkled in the
vivid eyes, and were brushed away. 'My poor
George has been dead so many years.' She whirled
round, clapping her hands for attention as a
uniformed maid appeared in the doorway and stood
waiting deferentially. 'It is time for dinner.' She took
Julia's hand. 'You will sit next to me, my child.'

Julia remembered little about the meal. She tried to
eat some of everything that was placed in front of
her, but was never sure whether or not she had
succeeded. Maria Xanthe controlled the tensions
evident round the table with a flow of light,
inconsequential chatter which involved everyone.

But all Julia was really aware of was Alex's eyes,
like dark chips of obsidian, watching her above the
candle flames. She could sense the anger in him, feel
it reaching out to her.

Oh, please, she pleaded silently. It's not my fault if
your mother likes me—if she's trying to make me feel
at home here.

The meal seemed to last for hours, and then there
were the tiny cups of thick sweet coffee to be

swallowed, with liqueurs which tasted of tangerine. Eventually it was over, and Julia could ask to be shown her room. Madame Xanthe insisted on escorting her there herself.

It was a large room, plainly but comfortably furnished, the coverlet on the wide bed, and the curtains, handwoven in what Madame Xanthe told her was a local design.

'Everything in the house I chose myself,' she said with simple satisfaction. 'I think now you have everything you need—except for your husband, and I will send him to you soon.' She leaned forward and kissed Julia on the forehead, tracing a swift sign of the cross there as well.

'Bless you, little one,' she said. 'Be happy, love my Alex well, and make me a beautiful grandchild.'

She vanished, and Julia was alone. She felt weary to death, but sleep was beyond her. She wandered restlessly round the room, examining everything. She peeped into the small bathroom, staring at the deep tub, the rows of fluffy towels, and the shelves of lotions and essences with a kind of wondering fascination. She had almost forgotten what it was like, she thought, to wallow up to her neck in scented water. Well, she would give herself a practical reminder here and now.

She picked up the nightgown which had been laid out on the bed in readiness, then filled the bath with steaming water, adding a liberal sprinkling of oil, perfumed with carnations. She shampooed her hair and applied conditioner, then lay back, luxuriating in the comfort of the water.

But though her body was relaxed, her mind was

still trapped on the same unhappy treadmill.

If Tricia Bosworth had not come to her room, how different her life would have been! On his own admission, Alex had been having second thoughts about marooning her on Argoli. He had spoken, too, of wooing her gently, she thought with swift pain, and for a moment she indulged herself with a mental image of what that wooing might have been—of herself seduced with warmth and tenderness into passion and its consummation. Then with a little trembling sigh, she wiped it from her mind. It was too poignant to contemplate, and she could torment herself for ever with all these 'might-have-beens'.

She climbed out of the bath and wrapped herself in one of the largest towels, before using the hair-dryer provided. She chose the body lotion that matched the bath oil, rubbing it into her skin, until it was fragrant and glowing, then slipped her nightgown over her head and went back into the bedroom.

Alex was standing by the windows, looking out into the darkness.

He said expressionlessly, without turning his head. 'My mother said you were asking for me.'

Julia flushed. 'No—that is—your mother has a rather romantic view of our relationship ' She swallowed. 'Alex you've got to tell her the truth. It's not fair to let her believe that this a real marriage, She's made me so welcome, I feel a total fraud.'

'Her attitude has created difficulties, certainly,' he said. 'But so has the presence of Thia Sophia and her children. Especially after you played the part of the loyal and loving bride so thoroughly in front of my cousin Paul this afternoon,' he added with faint grimness. 'He will think it curious to say the least if, only a few hours later, we make it known that our marriage is over.' He paused. 'And he may begin to ask the questions we least wish to answer.'

'Yes, I suppose so—but at the time, I couldn't think of anything else to do.' Julia bent her head unhappily. 'What do you suggest?'

'That any public rift should take place after we leave here,' he said curtly. 'It will be easy enough to arrange. My frequent absences on business will provide an undeniable excuse.'

She said tiredly, 'You really have it all worked out, don't you?' She shrugged. 'Well, play it any way you want. But now perhaps you'd leave me alone. I'm rather sleepy.'

He turned slowly and looked at her, the dark eyes sweeping her thinly veiled body in a mocking assessment that made her tingle.

'Leave you, *agapi mou?*' he drawled. 'Now where do you suggest I go?'

'I really don't know,' she shrugged. 'But there must be plenty of other rooms.' She lifted her chin. 'Your cousin Zoe's, for one.'

'Ah, yes,' he said softly. 'But my cousin Zoe has her virginity to consider. The first time a man will be allowed into her room, or her bed, will be on her wedding night.'

She said raggedly, 'Then you'll just have to wait, won't you?'

'It seems so.' He paused. 'But while I am waiting, I shall abide by the conventions.' He gave her an edged smile. 'I regret, my wife, that while we remain on Lymnos we shall have to share this room.'

Julia said fiercely, 'No!'

'How fickle you are,' he said derisively. 'Only a few short hours ago, you were clinging to me—begging me, with every inch of your delectable body, to take you again.'

She sank her teeth into her bottom lip, trying to suppress the memories that his contemptuous words had aroused.

'That was then,' she said. 'This is now.'

'Yes,' he said slowly, 'this is now . . .'

He walked towards her, and Julia backed away.

She said on a little breathless note, 'Don't come near me!'

'Is that an order?' mocked Alex.

'It's an appeal to your sense of decency. Our marriage is over, so why—torture me like this?'

'Torture?' he repeated, his brows lifting. 'I heard no screams for mercy earlier.' He put out a hand and slid one of the straps of her nightgown off her shoulder, his thumb stroking her skin.

The breath caught in her throat. 'No—please!'

His fingers lifted to her hair, gently parting the strands that curled on to her shoulders, cupping the slender nape of her neck. She shivered almost convulsively, and Alex stared down at the sudden thrust of her breasts against the apricot silk of the nightgown, his dark eyes kindling, his firm mouth suddenly compressed.

He tugged down the other strap, freeing her from the tiny lace-trimmed bodice. He released its sole fastening, and the silk drifted down to her hips, clung for a second, then whispered to the floor.

He said very quietly, 'No?'

Silence surrounded her, crushed her. She tried to speak, but the muscles of her throat betrayed her. She shook her head, letting her hair fall across her face, as she lifted her hands to cover herself in the age-old gesture of modesty.

Alex said something softly, violently in his own language. His hands went round her and he lifted her on to the bed, tossing aside the coverlet but pulling the single sheet over her, hiding her.

Julia lay on her side, her whole body a curve of tension. Alex had gone round to the other side of the bed. Although she could not see him, she heard the faint rustle of his clothes as he removed them. She felt the mattress beside her dip under his weight, and her mind went blank with mingled fear and longing.

But he did not touch her, and when she evenutally dared a swift, furtive glance over her shoulder, it revealed that he was lying on his back as far from her as it was possible to get, his arms crossed behind his head as he stared at the ceiling.

Her throat contracted in sudden pain, and, almost involuntarily, the first scalding tears squeezed from beneath her eyelids and trickled slowly down her face. She caught her breath, then released it on a little trembling sigh.

She felt Alex move, lift himself up on his elbow.

He said, 'Julia?'

His hand took her shoulder, pulling her round to face him. For a long moment he looked at her, then gently he wiped the drops from her cheeks with his finger.

He said quietly, almost painfully, 'In all our time together, you have never wept until this moment.'

His arm went round her, pulling her against him, and her body went rigid, her hands bracing against the firm wall of his chest to push him away.

'Ah, Julia.' His voice was strained. 'Let me comfort you, if nothing else.'

He drew her to him, pillowing her head against his shoulder, his hand stroking the silky sheen of her hair, while she wept until there were no more tears left, then, still cradled against him, lulled by the beat of his heart, eventually she slept.

CHAPTER TEN

JULIA awoke early the next morning, her mind still programmed for Argoli.

Fetch the water, she thought, stretching, with a yawn, feed the hens . . . then paused, aware that her movement had not brought the usual creaking and groaning from the mattress.

Her eyes flew open, and with a gasp she registered her new surroundings, and the undoubted reality of Alex next to her, still asleep.

She turned her head and stared at the long naked curve of his back. Then, remembering her waking thoughts, she leaned across and shook him.

'Alex,' she said urgently. 'Alex!'

He groaned, and rolled to face her. His hair was tousled and he needed a shave, but her whole body clenched in longing at the sight of him.

'What is it?' he muttered. '*Christos*, it is barely dawn!'

'Penelope and the chickens,' she said. 'We left them behind on Argoli.'

'You've woken me to talk about goats and chickens?' He covered his eyes with his hand. 'May God give me patience!'

'But it's important,' Julia protested. 'They can't be left to starve—and Penelope will need milking . . .'

'All of them have been returned to their rightful

156

owners.' He sounded goaded beyond belief. 'Now may I have some peace?'

She said, 'Oh,' in a subdued voice, then, 'I'm sorry.'

'No more sorry than I, believe me.' He turned away again, punching the pillow into shape.

'Please don't be angry with me,' she said. 'I was worried . . .'

Alex threw her a glance of total incredulity over his shoulder.

'After everything that has happened, your only anxiety is a few animals? My God, now I've heard everything!'

'Oh, you're deliberately misunderstanding me!' Julia snapped angrily.

'I hope I am,' he returned grimly, and there was silence.

She put out a hand and touched his shoulder. The sensation of his cool, smooth skin under her fingers made her tremble. 'Alex—forgive me, please?'

He said, with a faint groan, 'Julia, go back to sleep.'

Her voice shook. 'Last night you held me.'

There was another pause. 'That was then,' he said, his words an ironic echo of her own. 'This is now.'

'Yes,' she said. 'This is now . . .'

She laid both palms flat on his shoulderblades, then bent forward, and with a catch of her breath kissed him where the dark hair grew low on the nape of his neck.

She felt the muscles in his back tense beneath her hands, then slowly he turned over and lay, facing her, his face expressionless. He put out a finger and smoothed an errant tress of hair behind her ear, then cupping his hand behind her head, he drew her towards him.

He began to kiss her, brushing his lips gently backwards and forwards across hers. For a while she lay passive, relishing the tenderness of the caress, resisting the urge to respond eagerly and carry it forward into a new dimension. But gradually the growing clamour of her flesh could not be denied, and she kissed him back, her lips parting, her tongue flickering heatedly against his.

He lifted his head at last and studied her for a long moment, holding her a little away from him. Then he tossed the tangled sheet away to the bottom of the bed and knelt, lifting her on to her knees in front of him.

Then he touched her slowly, his hands gliding with delicate sensuality over her breasts, down to her hips, and the swell of her buttocks to her flanks, then, softly and tinglingly, up her arching spine to her shoulders, repeating the movement over and over again, until every inch of skin, every nerve ending was pulsating in response. His fingers swooped to the silky triangle of hair between her thighs, touched her fleetingly, achingly, then left her again, to begin a whole new cycle of caresses.

Julia couldn't breathe. She couldn't even think coherently. She was aware of nothing but the wicked, tantalising sweep of his hands over her naked flesh, and the sweet, melting fire of need building inexorably inside her.

She tried to speak, but the only sound that escaped her taut throat was a little whimper of pure longing.

Alex said harshly, 'Yes, ah yes, *agapi mou.*' He

lifted her back against the pillows and came down against her, pinning her against the length of his hotly aroused body.

All control was gone, and there was no holding back any longer. Their mouths found each other, sucked and tore in frantic delight. Their hands moved in feverish, explicit demand.

She twisted against him, seeking him, and when he entered her she cried out sharply in pleasure. There was no pain this time, just a total completion, his body filling hers, making her one with him.

She clung to him, her nails raking his back and shoulders, her body moving with his in raw abandonment. Sunlight filled the room, and she was part of it, and so was he, and the pulse of her inner being seemed stronger than the universe as it met his. Caught in the heart of the sunburst, they were consumed, then flung out into some vast and dizzying void.

Afterwards there was silence. Reality returned slowly, and became Alex's arms still wrapped around her, Alex's head resting on her breasts. His weight against her was heaven, she thought, and holding him to her, she drifted into a sleep of sheer exhaustion.

The next time Julia awoke the bed beside her was empty. She lay for a moment, staring at the rumpled pillow, and remembering.

She must have been out for the count, she thought, blushing, because she hadn't been aware of Alex leaving, or of the fact that he had drawn the sheet up to cover her again.

She wondered what had woken her, and was alerted by a firm, slightly impatient knock on the bedroom door, which indicated that it might not have been the first.

'Er—come in,' she called, wriggling down in the bed and pulling the sheet to her chin.

The door opened to admit a plump, grey-haired woman, her black dress covered by a vast snowy apron. She was beaming with smiles, and carrying a tray laden with fruit juice, coffee, a selection of warm rolls and preserves, and several slices of honey cake.

She set the tray down beside Julia in the place which Alex had vacated, and burst into a flood of Greek. Julia looked at her in bewilderment, spreading her hands to convey her lack of comprehension, but nothing stemmed the torrent of words.

'Baraskevi.' Maria Xanthe, wearing a caftan in shades of peacock blue and gold, came into the room. She patted the older woman on the shoulder, speaking soothingly in her own language, and ushering her towards the door.

When it was safely closed behind her, she turned back smilingly to Julia. '*Kalimera*, little one. Baraskevi is my housekeeper here. I suppose Alex has told you all about her?'

Julia shook her head, horribly self-conscious about her lack of attire beneath the thin sheet, and also the fact that her nightdress was lying on the floor several feet away from the bed.

'No?' Maria Xanthe frowned. 'But that is astonishing—quite extraordinary! When he was a child, she was a second mother to him. He was born in her house on Argoli, and grew up as part of her family.'

'You mean the house we were living in—that Alex was repairing?'

Madame Xanthe's frown deepened. 'What are you saying? You used Baraskevi's house? Surely not? It has been empty longest, and is in a worse state than any of the others. The priest's house, for instance, is quite habitable, almost comfortable. Why didn't you stay there?'

Julia drank some fruit juice. 'Oh, I expect Alex had his reasons,' she said, trying to speak lightly. 'I—I thought from what he said that the house belonged to you.'

Maria Xanthe shook her head in bewilderment. 'Has he told you nothing then of his early life?' She sighed a little. 'I hoped that he would have spoken openly of it to you, his wife. Then I would know that he had forgiven me for sure.'

Forgiven her for what? Julia wondered, startled.

She said, 'Would you like some coffee? Baraskevi has brought two cups.'

Maria Xanthe shrugged. 'She thought Alex would still be with you, no doubt.'

'Do you know where he is?' Julia began to fill the cups.

'He took the car into Lymnos town a little while ago. Zoe has gone with him.'

Julia spilled some coffee on the tray. She said in a stifled voice, 'I see.'

'The island is quiet now,' Maria Xanthe went on, after a pause. 'But at the weekend things are different. Many people from Athens have villas here, and they come on the ferry. I have a number of friends among them.' She nodded. 'I shall give a party for you, *pedhi mou*. Introduce them all to my beautiful new daughter.'

'Oh, please, there's really no need,' Julia broke in, alarmed.

'But I love parties, and now I have a really good excuse.' Her mother-in-law patted her cheek. 'You cannot be shy, Julia *mou*, or unused to entertaining. I have seen pictures of your wonderful home in England, so you must be accustomed to welcoming guests.'

'Perhaps you should talk it over with Alex first,' Julia said desperately. 'You see, I—don't speak any Greek, which makes things difficult.'

Maria Xanthe laughed. 'Not with my friends. All of them speak English well,' she said. 'With Baraskevi there could be a problem. I shall have to interpret while she tells you about how beautiful Alex was when he was a baby, and how naughty as he grew older. She will also tell you how many candles she used to light for him in the church. She always said God listened specially to her prayers because she was born on Good Friday. That is what her name means—Friday. And now that he is safely married, to a beautiful wife, all her prayers have been answered.'

Julia spread some peach jam on a fragment of roll. 'I hope I don't disappoint her,' she said colourlessly. 'Wouldn't she have preferred him to marry a Greek girl?'

Maria Xanthe shrugged. 'Perhaps, but she knew in the end Alex would do just as he wanted.' She drank some of her coffee, looking preoccupied. 'But I still cannot understand why Alex should have taken you to that house. For me, naturally, it has sentimental associations, but for a bride on her honeymoon, *po po po!*'

Julia forced a smile. 'I wouldn't have thought it was the ideal place to have a baby.'

The other woman laughed. 'Oh, that was not intentional, *pedhi mou.* Let me explain. I was staying here on Lymnos, waiting for my baby to be born. One morning I felt—oh, restless. I wanted air, a breeze in my face. So I persuaded Yannis to take me in his caique to Argoli to visit his sister. He did not want to—he tried to argue, but I would not listen. We had hardly arrived at Baraskevi's house when without warning my pains began. Two hours later Alex was in my arms.' She sighed. 'But I was glad he was born there. It was on Argoli that I had met George Constantis. I was not famous then, you understand. I was with a small Greek company which was making a film using Argoli as location.'

She smiled reminiscently. 'I had a very tiny part in this film, and he was an important man who had put up some of the money for it. An old story, you might think, but it was not so. We fell in love at first sight, and although we were not fated to live our lives together as we wished, we stayed in love.'

She took a slice of the honey cake. 'Was it like that for you and my Alex? Did you know when you first saw him that he would be the man for you?'

Julia said constrictedly, 'Not at once, perhaps, but very soon. We—had a picnic by a lake, and we'd quarrelled. I—I thought I would never see him again. I felt wretched—empty as I walked home, and I

didn't understand why.' She thought silently, Maybe
I didn't want to understand . . .'

'Sometimes it is good to quarrel,' Madame Xanthe
said softly. 'Especially when making up can be so
sweet.'

Julia bent her head. 'I think Alex and I quarrel
rather too much,' she said stiltedly.

Madame laughed. 'Well, that is natural,' she said.
'Two strong personalities, learning to live together.'
She gave Julia's hair an amused tweak. 'And hair this
colour! Your lives together will never be dull.' She
drained her coffee and replaced the cup on the tray.
'You like to swim, Julia *mou*? Well, when you are
ready, join me by the pool.' She pulled a comic face.
'It is a way to escape from Thia Sophia's disapproval.
She does not care for the sun.' She gave Julia another
smile, and departed, tactfully ignoring the discarded
nightgown.

Julia made herself eat some more breakfast, then
went into the bathroom to shower, before putting on
a black and white bikini and a matching hip-length
jacket. She looked at herself in the long mirror and
gave a small sigh.

It had been a blow to waken after that passionate,
rapturous lovemaking and find that Alex was gone. It
was even more shattering to discover that he was
now with Zoe.

He couldn't have chosen a more emphatic way of
showing her how little their coming together had
meant to him, she thought with painful bitterness.
What a fool she'd been to think their physical
attunement could possibly affect the future of their
relationship! To Alex, it had just been sex, a way of

ridding himself of frustration, but unimportant in the long term.

He had married her for all the wrong reasons, she thought miserably, and was now totally intent on freeing himself from the disastrous result of his impulse.

She turned away, biting her lip. Even without Tricia Bosworth's malevolent intervention she would still have found it difficult to convince Alex that her early hostility to him had been fuelled by a complexity of emotions she had been too inexperienced to analyse or express.

And now it was too late.

That silly fantasy about living alone at Ambermere, her own mistress, was all set to come true, just when she had realised it was the last thing in the world that she wanted.

It wasn't the easiest morning Julia had ever spent. Maria Xanthe's warmth and friendliness to which, in other circumstances, Julia would have joyfully responded, was yet another pitfall. There were so many topics of conversation to be avoided, so many no-go areas, she realised ruefully.

Paul Constantis had also decided to spend the morning beside the pool, which created additional difficulties. Julia was aware that he was listening avidly to everything that was said, and found this disturbing. Madame Xanthe might have arranged a reconciliation with the rest of the family, but Julia wasn't convinced this went deeper than the surface. Paul, she was sure, would seize any opportunity to damage Alex if he could, and this meant she had to

be doubly careful when Madame Xanthe referred yet
again to their honeymoon on Argoli.

Alex and Zoe returned shortly before lunch was
served, the other girl hanging possessively to his
arm, wreathed in smiles.

Sick at heart, Julia looked away, wondering what
Alex had been saying to his cousin to light her up like
that. Had he hinted, she wondered, at what the
future might hold? If so, then the sooner she left
Lymnos the better. Every giggle from Zoe, every
flutter of her eyelashes was like a knife turning in her
heart.

Murmuring something about the heat of the sun,
she swung herself off her lounger and started back to
the villa.

Before she had got even half-way, a hand fell on
her shoulder, and Alex's voice said sharply, 'Julia,
wait!'

She turned reluctantly to face him, thankful for the
sunglasses that masked her eyes. 'Yes?'

'We must talk.'

'I thought everything had already been said.' A
small, fragile hope began to burgeon inside her.

His face was taut, his mouth grimly set, as he
looked at her. 'I owe you an apology. I—should not
have imposed my presence on you last night, as I did.
If I'd used another room, then—this morning—could
not have happened. I offer my profound regrets, and
my assurance that it will not occur again.'

The hope withered and died. Julia said with an
effort, 'Thank you, but you don't have to apologise.
It—it was my fault too.' She paused. 'I—I think I
should cut my visit here as short as possible.' She

tried to smile. 'Your mother is talking of giving a party for me.'

Alex mouth tightened. 'I will deal with it,' he said abruptly, and turned away.

Just a minor problem, thought Julia, watching him go. And ridding himself of an unwanted wife would only be another one.

She sighed soundlessly and went back to the house.

Julia stood by the tall windows of the *saloni*, staring listlessly across the gardens. In the ten days since Alex had brought her to Lymnos, this room had become very much her refuge. She usually retreated to it in the afternoons, so that she didn't have to see Alex and Zoe together.

Everywhere she went was where they seemed to be, she thought bitterly. If she was down beside the pool, Zoe would be there displaying her admittedly gorgeous figure in a series of ever more minuscule bikinis. If she went to the bay, Alex would be teaching Zoe to windsurf, or they would be water-skiing. At first Paul had been with them too, but now they made no pretence of needing anyone else's company but their own.

Julia had been offered her turn on the windsurfer, and behind the speedboat, but it was clear that the suggestion had been polite and perfunctory, and once she had refused, it was not made again.

Why doesn't he let me go? she asked herself wearily. Why does he keep me here, enduring this?

One of the worst times had been when it had become obvious that Alex was occupying a separate

bedroom. It was, she had realised helplessly,
impossible to keep such an arrangement private.

Maria Xanthe had been openly distressed about it,
and even Thia Sophia had delivered herself, over
dinner one night, of a majestic and largely
incomprehensible lecture on the duties of a wife to
her husband.

Sheer hypocrisy, Julia thought tiredly. The old
witch must be secretly delighted about it all. She
certainly never failed to beam approving glances at
her daughter when she flirted outrageously with
Alex.

'So here you are,' said a voice, and Julia half turned
to see Paul watching her, his eyes frankly
speculative.

'Well spotted,' she returned drily.

He laughed, and came to stand beside her. 'I've
missed you these past few days,' he remarked. 'My
leave will be over soon, and I have to get back to the
Embassy.' He paused, then said almost idly, 'Why
don't you come with me?'

Julia jumped. She said coolly, 'You seem to forget
I'm married.'

'I forget nothing Julia *mou*. It is my cousin Alex who
seems to have difficulty with his memory.' His hand
began to stroke her arm. 'I cannot bear to see how he
neglects you,' he whispered.

Julia stepped firmly out of range of his caressing
fingers. 'Please don't concern yourself,' she said
crisply. 'Alex and I—understand each other very
well.'

His brows lifted. 'Every wife should be so sympathetic! Or is it perhaps that you just don't care?

You are very beautiful, Julia, but it takes more than beauty to warm a man's bed. Does your bridegroom not please you—or are you frigid, perhaps?' He took a step towards her, smiling. 'That was not the impression I got during our evening together. You should have married me, Julia *mou*, not my cousin Alex's money. I could melt you . . .'

'How dare you!' Julia took another step back, to find herself against the wall. 'I hope you know that you're making an utter fool of yourself.'

'Am I?' he murmured. 'Well, let us see . . .'

He reached for her, his mouth fastening on hers, his tongue trying to force its way between her tightly closed lips. Julia braced her hands against his chest, trying desperately to push him away, and when that didn't work she kicked him as hard as she could on the shin.

Paul let her go, cursing, and she ran behind one of the sofas. 'Get out of here!' she told him breathlessly.

'Little wildcat,' he said, half laughing, half angry. 'I should have taken you while I had the chance!'

'You never had the chance,' Julia said icily. 'Don't come near me again, unless you want me to tell Alex.'

'Do you think he would care?' Paul shook his head. 'His whole attitude tells the world he has made a mistake which he regrets. Cut your losses, Julia *mou*. Come with me.'

'Not if you were the last man alive!'

He shrugged. 'Then you are destined to be very much alone, I think.' He gave her a nonchalant look and walked to the door.

Julia sank down on to the sofa, wiping her mouth

violently with the back of her hand.

She thought, trembling, I can't take any more of this. I've got to get away from here. I've got to . . .

CHAPTER ELEVEN

'YOU ARE leaving?' Maria Xanthe asked in astonishment. 'But Alex has said nothing!'

A myriad excuses and explanations, each more feeble than the last, chased through Julia's mind and were discarded.

She said quietly, 'Alex doesn't know. 'I—I'm going alone, Madame Xanthe.'

There was silence, then Maria Xanthe gave a deep sigh. 'I—see. Well, it was evident that all was not well between you, *pedhi mou*, but is it really necessary to leave—to give up? Whatever Alex has done, could you not find it in your heart to give him a second chance?'

Julia gave her a startled look, 'No, you don't understand. It's Alex who wants to be rid of me.' She bent her head. 'From the moment we met, I behaved badly, you see—said some stupid things. Alex only married me to—punish me for them.'

'What are you saying?' The older woman looked appalled. 'To marry for such a reason! No one would do such a thing. You have misunderstood, my child.'

'I only wish I had.' Julia bit her lip. 'You thought Alex had taken me to Argoli out of sentiment.' She shook her head. 'It was to teach me a lesson. I—I called him a peasant, and he decided to show me what a peasant's life was like, the hard way, by making me work from sunrise to sunset.' She swallowed. 'He also made it clear that he didn't intend the marriage to be a—a real one.'

Maria Xanthe said shrewdly, 'But about that, he changed his mind?'

'Yes—eventually.'

'Oh, my poor children!' Maria made a gesture of appeal to the heavens. 'No wonder you both look so bruised! That there are so many silences between you.' She gave Julia a straight look. 'You love my Alex?'

'Yes,' Julia admitted sadly. 'But he doesn't know that—and he wouldn't believe it either. He thinks I married him just so that I can go on living in my family home.'

'That beautiful English house that he has bought? I wondered about the reason for that. Doesn't it seem to you, *pedhi mou*, that he must care for you a great deal to do this thing for you?'

Julia shook her head. 'He'd decided to buy Ambermere before he'd even met me. Later he discovered—how much the house meant to me, and as he—needed a wife, it seemed a convenient arrangement.'

Maria Xanthe snorted. 'Needed a wife! What nonsense is this? Alex has been fighting to stay single for the past ten years. Then suddenly—so suddenly, he telephones and says that he is going to be married to an English girl with hair like flame. He said nothing of any—arrangement.' She made the word sound like a blasphemy, and in spite of her unhappiness Julia found herself smiling.

'So first this marriage was for punishment. Now it is for convenience,' Maria went on, after a pause. 'Which is the true reason, I wonder? Or is it neither of them?'

'I no longer know what to think,' Julia returned wearily. 'It's all such a hopeless—mess.' She gave a little sigh. 'I can't blame Alex for wanting to cut his losses and be free. In fact, I don't blame him for anything.' She flushed slightly. 'I really was an appalling little snob. I—I needed a lesson.'

'Perhaps,' Maria Xanthe shrugged. 'But my son's methods seem a little drastic. Even so, you are a beautiful girl, Julia *mou*, and a passionate one, I think. Could you have not found some way to convince Alex that he was wrong, that he meant more to you than—this house?'

'I hoped I could,' said Julia, in a low voice. 'But I failed there too.' Briefly, she outlined Tricia Bosworth's intervention and its consequences. 'So you see, Alex had every reason to feel—betrayed.'

'Ah, yes.' Maria Xanthe sighed deeply. 'And not for the first time, *pedhi mou*. I have my own share of guilt in all this.'

'You have? I don't understand . . .'

'When I found I was to have my George's child, I was not ashamed, you understand, because I loved him. But I was frightened. Times were different then. People were not so—understanding. The fact that I had an illegitimate child could have damaged my career.' She paused. 'Alex was only a few weeks old when my agent contacted me to tell me the results of a screen test I'd had for a Hollywood studio. The news was good—they wanted me. But they wanted someone fresh, without encumbrances, without a past.'

She clasped her hands together in her lap. 'Baraskevi was childless, and she had cared devotedly for Alex and myself when he was born. Gradually I convinced myself that the baby would be better off if he stayed with her. If he was brought up on Argoli simply and healthily, rather than being ''a film star's child'', dragged round in my wake from location to location. I told myself I was doing it for him, all for him. Maybe I even believed it,' she added with a grimace.

'But it wasn't true?' Julia stared at her.

'In part, I think so, yes. Nothing about Hollywood ever suggested it was a good environment for bringing up a child. So Alex grew up, miles away, an island child, thinking Baraskevi was his mother.'

'Did you never see him?'

'I saw him often. Sometimes, if George could get away, he came with me. But we were visitors, nothing more, to him. Honoured guests.' She smiled sadly. 'When George decided to make Alex his heir, he had to be told the truth.'

'And how did he take it?'

'He was hurt badly. At first he did not believe it, then he became very angry. He accused me of being ashamed of him, of rejecting him for my own selfish reasons. For a long time he would not look at me or speak to me. And like you, *pedhi mou*, I could not blame him for his bitterness. In those early days I was ambitious. I did not want a scandal. But I had been punished too. There was not a day that I did not think about my son, and long to have him near me.'

'But he did forgive you.'

'Eventually, yes. But it was not easy. I had to break down the hurt—the resentment—prove to Alex over and over again that I loved him, that I would never reject him again. Slowly he began to trust me—to care in return. We developed a relationship, and now things are good between us, although it is still not generally known that I am his mother, even now. The family know, and the lawyers, but few others. And now that I live in retirement my activities are no longer of such great interest to the newspapers.' She patted Julia's cheek. 'But I am still careful. You may have wondered why I did not come to the wedding, for example.

'But—and I blame myself for this—the past has made Alex wary too. He has always taken his pleasure lightly—reluctant to commit himself deeply to a woman. I had begun to think he would never marry.' She paused, then said gently, 'If he had reason to believe you did not love him, Julia *mou*, it could explain why he has been so harsh with you—so unforgiving. For him, perhaps love has come to mean—betrayal.'

She put a hand over Julia's. 'And he did love you, little one. When he spoke to me of you, it sang in his voice, in his words, and I was so happy for him, so thankful that I cried with joy.' She shook her head. 'These last few days—seeing the separation between you, the coldness—have almost broken my heart.'

'And mine,' Julia whispered, and Madame Xanthe put her arms round her and hugged her fiercely.

'So—what is to be done?'

'Alex wants a divorce,' Julia said simply. 'He intends to marry his cousin Zoe.'

Madame Xanthe grimaced. 'That is a joke,' she said grimly. 'Only not funny. She would bore him in a week, that one.'

'But that doesn't alter the fact that he's been paying her a lot of attention.'

'And because of this, you intend to run away. What answer is that?'

'The only one I can think of.' Julia's hands twisted together in her lap. 'I need to think—get things into perspective. Here, I'm too close to it all.' She lifted her chin. 'I'd like to catch the evening ferry to Piraeus.'

'Ah, no.' Madame Xanthe shook her head. 'If you are determined to go, then at least I insist that Yannis takes you in our own boat in comfort.'

'Thank you.' Julia hesitated. 'Actually, I was going to ask if I could—borrow Yannis for a while today. There's something I want to do, something I want to see again before I go.'

'I think I can guess.' Maria Xanthe's eyes were misty. 'Yannis is at your service, little one. Just tell him at what time you wish to leave.' She paused. 'Are you going to say goodbye to Alex?'

'He's taken Zoe sailing for the day.' Julia's teeth sank painfully into her lower lip. 'I've written him a letter.'

'I see,' Maria Xanthe said heavily. 'I wish it could all have been different for you, *pedhi mou*. You are the daughter I always wanted.'

Julia hugged her in turn. 'I shall miss you too,' she whispered.

Argoli was languid in the afternoon heat as Julia walked slowly up the village street. No breeze stirred the silver of the olive trees today, and the only sound was the buzz of the unseen cicadas.

She had arranged with much careful sign language for Yanni to return for her in three hours, and then he would take her straight to Piraeus. Once in Athens she would find a hotel for the night, and hope to get a scheduled flight the following day back to England.

But first she had had to come back here—to the place where the brief drama of her marriage had been played out, half comedy, half tragedy.

When she reached Baraskevi's house she stopped and took a long look at it. Alex's renovations and repairs had made an amazing difference, she thought, running a finger along the edge of one of the new window-frames. And there was plenty of land at the back for the house to extend into, if only . . .

She stopped herself abruptly. There was no future in that kind of thinking, those kind of regrets.

Now she had to rely on the letter she had left for Alex. Such a slender foundation on which to build her hopes, but it was all she had.

In my own way, I'm as much a gambler as my father, she thought. But the stakes are even higher. I've got my happiness, my whole life on the line.

She went into the house. Even after a few days the living-room had a wistful, neglected look, and dust was beginning to gather on the surfaces.

She wondered if Alex's plans for the islanders' return would succeed, and if he would ever use this house again himself. Maria Xanthe had been brutally honest about her motives for leaving him here, but on the other hand, Julia could think of few better places for a young child growing up.

Her remark to Paul about the possibility of using the house as a holiday retreat had been made on the spur of the moment, but it was still a wonderful idea, or would have been under other circumstances. Perhaps Alex would still bring his children here, she thought with a pang, although she couldn't see the sybaritic Zoe warming to conditions here.

But there was no denying that Alex had been safe and loved on Argoli, even though the subsequent discovery that his secure world was built upon deception must have been a terrible blow to him.

She sighed. No wonder Alex was as he was! That vulnerability she had sensed went deeper than she could ever have guessed. Not even Baraskevi's devotion could have shielded him from the fact that his mother had virtually abandoned him, she thought sadly. That knowledge must have made him question the value of his very existence.

And I've just made everything worse, she thought.

Looking back on the short period before they were married, Julia could see that there had been endless opportunities then to tell Alex—to show him incontrovertibly that she loved him. She could have broken down the formal barriers that he had imposed on their courtship and brought warmth and life to it. On their wedding day, they should have been so close that nothing and no one, least of all Tricia Bosworth, could have come between them. Together they could have laughed away her pathetic barbs.

But pride had still been a factor then, and that, and her uncertainty about his feelings for her, had kept her silent and aloof. So, instead of the reassurance he needed from her, Alex had received chilling evidence that she was just as mercenary, just as scathing towards him as he could have feared.

Slowly Julia climbed the wooden stairway to the upper room and stood looking round her. It was just as she had left it, except the green dress was no longer on the floor beside the bed where she had dropped it. Nor was it in the chest. In fact, to her absurd disappointment, it had completely vanished.

And she had wanted it. One of the reasons for coming here had been to get it, to take it back to England with her. It was a link with the past, a signal reminder of that brief time here with Alex—probably the only one she would ever have.

There was no guarantee, after all, that he would even read her letter, let alone believe any of the things she had said in it. He might well feel so relieved about her departure that he would consign her letter to the waste basket, and herself to some kind of mental limbo.

With a little sigh she went downstairs and out into the sunlight, standing irresolutely for a minute. Perhaps it had been a mistake to come here. She would have done better to bypass Argoli altogether, and got Yannis to take her straight to Piraeus without sentimental detours for souvenirs that didn't exist, reviving memories which could only bring her pain.

In the meantime, she had another couple of hours to kill. I'll go and get some water from the spring, she thought, then go to the beach.

She took an empty bottle from one of the cupboards and rinsed it again and again under the cold, sparkling water, before filling it to the brim.

She walked back down the track, between the gnarled trunks of the olive trees, past the spot where Penelope had been tethered, and back into the full glare of the sunlight.

He was standing a few yards away, watching her, and at the sight of him, so unexpected, so sharply, poignantly beloved, Julia cried out, and the bottle of water fell from her hands and smashed on the stony ground at her feet.

He said hoarsely, 'I was on my boat, and I saw Yannis leaving here. I wondered . . .' He swallowed, and Julia saw his hands clench into fists at his sides. 'What are you doing here?'

'I came for one last look. When Yannis comes presently, he's taking me to Piraeus.'

Alex drew a breath. 'You are going?' he demanded. 'Without a word to me?'

'I thought everything had already been said.' Julia moistened her lips with the tip of her tongue. 'And I have—written to you. The letter's in your room at the villa.'

He smiled bitterly. 'Thank you for that, at least.'

The dark eyes swept over her from the top of her head to the soles of her sandalled feet. He said, half to himself, 'So this is how it ends.'

'I thought a clean break was best,' she said. 'Particularly . . .' She stopped.

'What were you going to say?'

'Oh, that everyone knows the situation between us—and it's becoming embarrassing.' She tried to smile. 'Your cousin Paul seems to think I need—consolation.'

'And do you?'

'Not from him.'

'Yet you knew him first.'

'I met him,' she corrected.

'And, from that meeting, got your original impressions of me.' The dark gaze held hers. 'They were important, I think.'

'But it's the last ones I shall remember,' Julia said huskily, and there was a silence. She added, 'Don't let me keep you from your sailing. Zoe will be wondering where you are.'

'She is not with me. She complained, as usual, that the wind was spoiling her hair, and the spray was ruining her clothes. So I restored her safely to dry land, and her doting mother.' Alex laughed harshly. 'I don't think water is her favourite element, but it has been—almost amusing to see what lengths she has been prepared to go to in order to impress me during this week.'

Julia bit her lip. 'That's not very kind of you.'

'But I am not always kind,' he said. 'As who should know better than you, *matia mou?*'

Julia looked down at the ground. 'I—I'd better clear up this broken glass. If you're going to have other animals here . . .'

'There will be nothing,' he said bleakly. 'I shall not come here again.'

'You're going to waste all that hard work on the house?'

'It is already wasted.' He shrugged. 'But why should you care, Julia *mou*, about a peasant's hovel on a remote island? You are going home to your beloved Ambermere. You will soon forget this place, and everything about it.'

'I wish I could believe that. And the letter I wrote you concerns Ambermere.'

Alex frowned. 'I have already told you that I will give it to you when we are divorced. I will not go back on my word.'

'I'm sure you won't.' Julia lifted her chin. 'Actually, what I want is your permission to sell it.'

'You wish to—sell Ambermere—your home?' The dark face was incredulous. 'What are you talking about? Have you gone mad?'

'No,' she said quietly. 'I think I've managed to become sane at last.' She swallowed. 'You talk about Ambermere being my home, but if I have to live there alone, it's nothing but an empty shell. It means nothing—nothing at all. And that's what I wrote to you in my letter.'

'Why should you tell me such a thing?' His voice was rough. His eyes seemed to bore into her face.

For a moment Julia's courage almost failed her, and then she remembered Maria Xanthe's words, 'I had to break down the hurt—the resentment.' Now was her chance. Could she really do less?

She took a step towards him. Her voice quivered. 'Because I thought if Ambermere was no longer there, clouding the issue, you might believe me if I said I loved you.'

Alex was very white under his deep tan. 'Julia, be careful what you are saying. Don't joke with me.'

'I was never more serious,' she told him passionately. 'What more can I do or say to prove it? I love you, Alex, and I want you and I need you. You set out to humble my pride. Well, I've none left where you're concerned.' She gestured round her. 'What do you think I'm doing here now, but thinking—and remembering? I tried to hate you for all that you put me through, but instead I ended up loving you more than ever.'

She gave a little choky laugh. 'I came back to look for that grotty green dress you made me wear, so that I would have something—tangible to remember you by. Only it's gone. I don't even have that any more.'

He said hoarsely, 'I can tell you where it is. It's in my room at the villa, under my pillow. It was all I had of you, *agapi mou*. I kept telling myself that it was all that I deserved to have, after the way I had treated you.'

Julia said shakily, 'I asked for it—every little bit. Oh, Alex—*Alex* . . .'

He took a quick stride towards her and pulled her roughly into his arms. His mouth took hers in a kiss of aching, passionate tenderness, and his hands held her as if he would never let her go.

When they drew apart, they were both trembling.

Alex said huskily, 'I have dreamed so often of you telling me that you loved me, my beautiful one. Now it is true at last.'

'It's been true for a long time.' Julia stroked his cheek, and ran a caressing forefinger across his lips. 'I would have told you that the first night on board the *Clio*, but I didn't get the chance. And you wouldn't have believed me anyway,' she added gently.

'Forgive me.' Alex took her back into the shelter of his arms. 'I accused you of pride, Julia *mou*, yet it was my own pride that was hurt. I wanted to lash back at you, make you suffer as I had done. But when I made you sorry, it gave me no satisfaction. You were so brave about it all.' He put his lips against her forehead.

She gave him a teasing smile. 'When I'd recovered from the first shock, it was quite a challenge!'

'Can you forget it ever happened, my sweet one?' Alex's voice was urgent, pleading. 'Can we wipe out the last miserable weeks, and pretend that our marriage begins now at this moment?'

'Well—we could.' Julia smiled up at him, sliding her arms round his neck. 'But there are certain things that happened here that I'd quite like to remember.'

His brows rose quizzically. 'Indeed?'

'Why, yes,' she said. 'I actually learned to make edible bread. And I managed to milk Penelope. Real achievements, those.'

'They must have been,' he murmured gravely. He bent his head and kissed her slowly, and very thoroughly. 'Is there nothing else you recall, hmm?'

'I seem to have a dim recollection,' Julia said demurely, and gasped as Alex swung her off her feet and up into his arms. 'What are you doing?'

'Jogging your memory, *matia mou.*' He grinned down at her wickedly. 'Which of us has the better mattress, I wonder? I know, we'll try them both.'

They came together in laughter which was all the sweeter for the pain which had preceded it. They undressed each other between kisses, murmuring the words of love so long withheld, their bodies joining with a hunger which would not be denied, both giving without limit, reaching the sharp agonised delight of fulfilment together.

A long time later Julia said drowsily, 'We'll have to get a bigger bed.'

'Will we?' Alex lifted his head from the scented pillow of her breasts and smiled at her. 'There is a bigger bed at the villa.'

'But it isn't here,' she objected. She paused. 'Besides, we'd have to face Thia Sophia, and she won't be pleased to find that you aren't marrying Zoe after all.'

He grinned sardonically. 'But Zoe will be more than relieved I think. I drove her hard, lost my temper with her more than once, *matia mou*, while I was trying to make you jealous. Did I succeed?'

'Only too well,' Julia admitted with a little sigh. 'Poor Zoe!'

'Not to mention her brother,' remarked Alex, between his teeth. 'So he wished to console you. I must remember to thank him for his kindness.'

'I already have,' Julia confessed. 'His shin may well

be scarred for life.'

'And so may my back,' muttered Alex, easing his shoulders. 'Wildcat!'

'I'm sorry,' she said remorsefully.

'I'm not.' He kissed her, biting softly at her lower lip. 'You are the woman of my dreams and more, *eros mou.*'

'Then why did you move to another room at your mother's house?'

'Because I was ashamed of wanting you—of forcing myself on a woman who didn't care for me. Of behaving like—some Greek stud.' He put his finger on her lips, silencing the protest she was about to make. 'Oh, yes, I could make you want me in return, but I needed so much more from you than just a response.' He kissed her again. 'And now I have it.'

She began to touch him, sliding her hands over his body, revelling in her freedom to do so.

'Darling, do we have to go back to Lymnos? Couldn't we arrange for some supplies, and stay here by ourselves?'

'You'd be more comfortable at the villa,' muttered Alex, groaning pleasurably at the caress of her fingers. 'Getting a bigger bed here will take time.'

'But we've got time,' Julia said eagerly. 'And there's lots more work to do on this house. Another room at the back would be nice.' She stroked the dark hair back from his forehead. 'We'll need more space, when the children come.'

'Our children,' Alex said with a short sigh of contentment. 'Conceived here, and born at

Ambermere. How does that sound, *agapi mou?*'

'It sounds wonderful—but Alex, I meant what I said. You can sell the house, if you want.'

He shook his head. 'I don't want. I love the house, and I love you, my beautiful girl, and we are going to live at Ambermere and be happy.'

She said softly, 'It doesn't matter where we live, as long as we're together. Oh, Alex, I love you so much!'

'And I love you, my wife, to my life's end, and beyond.'

'To my life's end and beyond,' she echoed, and drew him down to her once more.

Mills Boon

Proudly present
to you...

BETTY NEELS' 100TH ROMANCE

Betty has been writing for Mills & Boon Romances for over 20 years. She began once she had retired from her job as a Ward Sister. She is married to a Dutchman and spent many years in Holland. Both her experiences as a nurse and her knowledge and love of Holland feature in many of her novels.

Her latest romance *'AT ODDS WITH LOVE'* is available from August 1993, price £1.80.

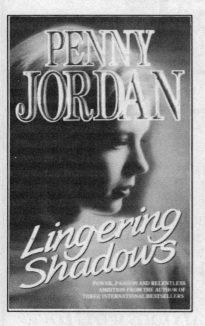

The truth often hurts . . .

Sometimes it heals

Critically injured in a car accident, Liz Danvers insists her family read the secret diaries she has kept for years – revealing a lifetime of courage, sacrifice and a great love. Liz knew the truth would be painful for her daughter Sage to face, as the diaries would finally explain the agonising choices that have so embittered her most cherished child.

Available now priced £4.99

W●RLDWIDE

Next Month's Romances

Each month you can choose from a wide variety of romance with Mills & Boon. Below are the new titles to look out for next month, why not ask either Mills & Boon Reader Service or your Newsagent to reserve you a copy of the titles you want to buy — just tick the titles you would like and either post to Reader Service or take it to any Newsagent and ask them to order your books.

Please save me the following titles:		Please tick	✓
THE WEDDING	Emma Darcy		
LOVE WITHOUT REASON	Alison Fraser		
FIRE IN THE BLOOD	Charlotte Lamb		
GIVE A MAN A BAD NAME	Roberta Leigh		
TRAVELLING LIGHT	Sandra Field		
A HEALING FIRE	Patricia Wilson		
AN OLD ENCHANTMENT	Amanda Browning		
STRANGERS BY DAY	Vanessa Grant		
CONSPIRACY OF LOVE	Stephanie Howard		
FIERY ATTRACTION	Emma Richmond		
RESCUED	Rachel Elliot		
DEFIANT LOVE	Jessica Hart		
BOGUS BRIDE	Elizabeth Duke		
ONE SHINING SUMMER	Quinn Wilder		
TRUST TOO MUCH	Jayne Bauling		
A TRUE MARRIAGE	Lucy Gordon		

If you would like to order these books in addition to your regular subscription from Mills & Boon Reader Service please send £1.80 per title to: Mills & Boon Reader Service, Freepost, P.O. Box 236, Croydon, Surrey, CR9 9EL, quote your Subscriber No:.................................... (If applicable) and complete the name and address details below. Alternatively, these books are available from many local Newsagents including W.H.Smith, J.Menzies, Martins and other paperback stockists from 10 September 1993.

Name:...

Address:...

....Post Code:............................

To Retailer: If you would like to stock M&B books please contact your regular book/magazine wholesaler for details.

You may be mailed with offers from other reputable companies as a result of this application. If you would rather not take advantage of these opportunities please tick box ☐

Forthcoming Titles

DUET
Available in August

The Sara Craven Duet

**DEVIL AND THE DEEP SEA
KING OF SWORDS**

The Anne Mather Duet

**A FEVER IN THE BLOOD
DARK MOSAIC**

BEST SELLER ROMANCE
Available in September

PILGRIM'S PROMISE Emma Goldrick
TO LOVE AGAIN Carole Mortimer

MEDICAL ROMANCE
Available in September

RED SEA REUNION Margaret Barker
HEART ON HOLD Lynne Collins
HEART CALL Lilian Darcy
A DOUBLE DOSE Drusilla Douglas

Available from W.H. Smith, John Menzies, Martins, Forbuoys, most supermarkets and other paperback stockists.

Also available from Mills & Boon Reader Service, Freepost, P.O. Box 236, Thornton Road, Croydon, Surrey CR9 9EL.

Readers in South Africa - write to:
Book Services International Ltd, P.O. Box 41654, Craighall, Transvaal 2024.